Cry Baby

Rebecca Griffiths

Cover design: Steven Allan Griffiths RI
Title of painting: 'Ghost of an Earlier Self'

ISBN: 9798555869869

For Steven. Without you there would be nothing.

ACKNOWLEDGMENTS

Special thanks must go to my friend and trusted reader, Jo Robertson and her fabulous reviewing and blog site: mychestnutreadingtree.wordpress.com

But most of all, my thanks and love must go to my husband, Steven, for his indomitable belief, love and creative inspiration. And an extra special thanks to him for allowing me to use one of his beautiful paintings as the cover for this book.

Cry Baby Bunting
Daddy's gone a-hunting
Gone to fetch a rabbit skin
To wrap poor Baby Bunting in.

Traditional nursery rhyme

EIGHT YEARS BEFORE

I climb the stairs.

Hatred building with each creaking tread.

I'm in the mood for trouble. The bitch has had it coming for years, going about like a tart in her short skirts and make-up, rubbing my nose in it . . . yeah, she's had it coming all right.

I open the door without bothering to knock. See the window's been flung wide to receive the dying day. She's sitting with her back to me, dolling herself up in the mirror. When she twists around, I see her red painted whore of a mouth.

'What d'you want? You're not supposed to be in here.' She doesn't look as bothered to see me as she should.

I watch her take a last leisurely pull on her fag, squash it flat in an ashtray and fumble for the table edge. I can tell she's been drinking, that she needs its support to get to her feet. Good, it'll make what I've got to do easier.

She stands where the last slant of daylight partitions the room and I close the door behind me, shutting us in. There's no one else around. There's no one to see what I'm going to do. We are alone. I wonder if she knows this, knows how much danger she is in?

She gives me the 'Just you try it' look, so I think I might as well, and inch towards her. Close enough to smell the booze on her breath. Sickly sweet like rotting fruit.

Disgusted, I turn my head away for a second or two. Think: she's on the brink of doing this anyway, so there's no need to feel bad, I'm only doing what she's too gutless to do. Yes, of course, this is what she wants, and if not, who cares? I'm a saviour, I should be rewarded for helping her out — rewarded for saving her from the life that's killing her.

'I asked you what you want?' She thinks she's being assertive, her fists on her hips.

Her eyes are dark and feisty, and I know I'm going to have to box clever. Not that I'm overly concerned, I worked it all out before getting here. I won't fail. I can't fail. There's too much at stake.

'Just get out, will you. I don't want you in here. I don't want you anywhere near me.

'Since when have you been fussy about anyone coming near you? You've always been happy to spread your legs for anyone. And that's been the problem, hasn't it? That's why I'm here now.'

Why am I bothering to retaliate when it's all too late for arguing? I must stay focused; I can't be diverted; I've only got one shot at this.

'Get out. I want you to get out,' she shrieks, all indignant. It makes me want to smash her face in.

'I don't think you're in any position to tell me what to do, do you?'

I must communicate something in my expression because she responds by tottering backwards to press her spine to the frame of the open window, in a futile attempt to distance herself.

It gives me another idea. A better idea than the one I came in here with.

'I wouldn't stand there if I were you,' I tell her and feel myself smile. I've never felt so powerful, so in control.

'Get away from me. Go on, get out.'

I'm not going anywhere. I am wise, I take my time.

Outside, the sun is setting over the sea. Salmon-pink and curd-yellow as night folds itself into the darkening blue. We stand for what seems an age, neither saying a word. I can tell that me watching her like this is making her nervous. Her hands keep fidgeting with her hair and tugging down her micro skirt. She wants to tell me to stop looking but knows this is a waste of breath, that nothing she says will help her, that she isn't getting out of here.

'What d'you want?' she asks again.

Then, as if reading my mind, her eyes widen in fear as I take another step closer. It pleases me to see her flinch . . . terror taking shape behind her eyes.

It wouldn't take much to push her.

To make it look like she jumped.

What's left of the daylight is shining pink on her cheeks and I hear her suck back her breath.

'There's no point screaming,' I tell her. 'No one's going to hear you.'

She wipes her mouth on an agitated fist. Lipstick leaving a blood-red smear behind on her hand. She inadvertently tips back her head to the ceiling, exposes the white curve of her throat. Then, sensing her defencelessness, she drops her head.

'Please go away . . . leave me alone,' she pleads.

'Leave you? Yeah, I'll leave you,' I tell her, feeling no pity. 'I'll leave you, but only after I've killed you.'

ONE

Present Day

Melanie struggles to hear what her husband is telling her above the din of the call centre.

'You what, Gareth? I missed that.'

'I said we've got it.'

'What? We've got the pub?'

'Sale went through five minutes ago. It's all ours, Mel.'

'Brilliant.' Her whoops for joy rise above the clamour of buzzing telephones.

'Go and tell your boss today's your last day.'

'I can't just drop them in it? I'll have to give notice.'

'Why? You don't need a reference. You'll be working for yourself from now on.' His voice, as always, is measured and forthright.

Melanie ends their call and intends to do as he suggests, just as soon as she's worked out what to say. Head in hands, her mind drifts. The stiffened sails of her memory pulled wide by her demons, as it so often is when she's sitting here, watching the clock above her manager's door, counting the hours before logging off and going home. On her desk is a framed photograph of her and Gareth on honeymoon. She searches their faces for any sign of what had been marching towards them on life's horizon and is thankful to find nothing of the horror that was to come. Her gaze then shifts to a snapshot of their twin daughters:

Georgie and Sophie, aged four. Her chest tightens, her breathing audible. This is possibly the last picture ever taken of them together.

Her boss doesn't ask Melanie to sit. She doesn't congratulate or wish her luck with her exciting new venture either.

'A gastropub in Wales?' The tone is derisive and critical. 'Who d'you think you are? — someone off *Escape to the Country.*'

'Spiteful cow,' Melanie mumbles on the walk back to her desk to collect her stuff. Which aside from the pair of photographs, a tube of hand cream and a plastic Shaun the Sheep toy from last year's Secret Santa, amounts to little.

'Watch out,' she warns those she is leaving behind. Not that anyone looks up from their monitors. 'Go and do something worthwhile . . . this will be all you have to show for your life, otherwise.' She shakes her half-filled carrier bag and exits the building.

TWO

Ashock. The sea. Melanie, waking stale and stiff in the passenger seat of their Mazda, is stunned by the drama of it. A twist in the road and there it is, filling the horizon, making her gasp. The monotony of motorway has been swapped for a tunnel of wind-whipped hedgerows and when Gareth turns off, it is to swing down on to a track that travels out on a sliver of rock pointing into the sea.

'See that island over there—' his finger guides her gaze beyond the sheep-scattered slopes, to a rocky outcrop girdled by a glittering belt of blue. 'That's an ancient site of Celtic spirituality.'

His voice is proud, as if there marks the very stepping stone to heaven and she stares obediently out through the window at the rain-fenced fields and lean acres of sky.

The route into this small Pembrokeshire town is only just wide enough for the car and shrubbery scrapes against its sides as if meaning to hold them back. Tangled and high, the thorny hedges are thick with sloes and blackberries. Melanie makes a mental note to take Georgie out to gather them in before the birds claim them.

'Are we nearly there?'

'Minutes away.'

'You've made brilliant time. Sorry for nodding off.' She yawns and looks at his profile, at the dark stubble on his jaw she swears has grown in the hours she's been sleeping.

'That's all right. But you should have put your tooth

guard in, you've been grinding your teeth.'

'Oh, hell, was I?'

'You're not anxious? Regretting this move?'

'Don't be daft, I'm excited. It's exciting.' She turns to their seven-year-old daughter in the seat behind. 'You all right, Georgie? Did you manage to get any shut-eye?'

'Yes, Mummy. But Murray's tired.' Her daughter extends an arm and pushes her blue teddy between the front seats for her to see.

'Get some air in here, shall we? Liven us up a bit.'

She drops the window and inhales the sea and something of her childhood. Not the vinegar-laden chip shop smell or the hot, sweet candyfloss sampled on summers in Hunstanton with her grandmother but something of the wild, the essential. Aside from when they came to view the pub, it must be eight years since Gareth first brought her to Wales. The week of his father's funeral. The first time she was introduced to her mother-in-law.

The road dips and, as the Mazda begins its slow pull out on to the main road through the town, Gareth puts his foot down. Takes the half-moon bridge over the river too fast. The car bounces and Melanie clutches her stomach.

'Sorry,' Gareth chuckles. 'I couldn't resist. I used to do that with my sister when I first passed my test.'

'Bet Tegan didn't like it either,' Melanie grimaces while reading the sign giving the name of the town: the bold black letters on white.

'*Pencarraw*,' she says, liking how the syllables fill her mouth.

'Pencarew,' Gareth corrects her lightly and sounding more Welsh than she's ever heard him. 'We're home. Are you happy?'

'I'm happy.' She smiles. For the first time in more than three years, this isn't a lie.

The road dips again, down between a row of tall, pastel-coloured B&Bs advertising en suite rooms and WiFi. Their gardens, luxuriant and sheltered by the hills rising steeply behind, show off blue hydrangeas, large as heads clad in nineteen-forties' swimming caps. They pass bus stops with routes heading north along the coast to St David's and south to Pwllglas. Gift shops and tearooms with tables set out on the pavement in the late-August sunshine. A classy looking homeware store. Jimmy's Fish Bar, its sign like a sail and flapping in the soft Welsh breeze. A delicatessen and the Peppermint Post Espresso Bar where she and Gareth enjoyed a celebratory breakfast after viewing the Monkstone Arms on that dull spring day.

'Buzzing, isn't it?' she says when Gareth is forced to slow for a group of tourists who want to cross the road. 'I wasn't expecting it to be as busy this late in the season.'

'Bank holiday weekend. Sun's out.' He twiddles the dark chest hair that peeps over the collar of his rugby shirt. 'This place is a little gold mine.'

'Oh, look, there's the pub.' Melanie jabs an excited finger to where the Monkstone Arms nestles high above the bay. It commands a striking position, with the plunge of the sea at the bottom of its garden. 'I can't believe it's ours,' she beams. 'Well, partly ours, I know the bank owns most of it. But it's got Mr and Mrs Sayer on the deeds.'

'We were lucky to get it.'

'One good thing to come out of Brexit, it put a load of buyers off.'

'That and the amount of money it needs to bring it into the twenty-first century.'

'Good job we've got the imagination to see its potential.'

'You're the visionary, Mel. I'll just keep bringing in the dosh until you're ready to open for business. The place is for you to turn into whatever you want.'

She slides a hand on to his thigh and continues to pick out interesting landmarks for their daughter who is eager to be liberated from the confines of the car seat she is almost too big for.

'Look! There's your new school.' She swivels to

Georgie again. Sees her gummy smile, the bounce of sunshine on her light brown plaits . . . the glaringly unoccupied space beside her on the back seat. A space that has been empty for more than three whole years.

Melanie's stomach lurches again. But it has nothing to do with the road this time.

THREE

The removals firm has been and gone. The flat above the pub, where they are to live, is surprisingly habitable when compared to the shabby guest rooms up a separate flight of stairs and the rundown public rooms on the ground floor. Melanie, Gareth and Georgie pace the accommodation piled high with plywood crates, sofas and bookcases, familiarising themselves with its layout as they listen to their footfalls reverberate against the exposed floorboards. Melanie goes about flinging windows open, as delighted with the late summer sunshine as she is with the essence of autumn travelling the rooms on the breeze.

'Look, Mummy. The sea.' Georgie reaches up on tiptoes. 'This is going to be my bedroom.'

'Is it now?' Melanie gathers her in a ball of giggles.

'How's about we leave the unpacking till later?' Gareth suggests as he tugs on a crewneck sweater over his rugby shirt. 'Go and explore the beach. I could do with stretching my legs.'

'Yeah, come on. We could fetch fish and chips on the way back.'

They make this arrangement standing opposite each other in the plain-walled room. Holding hands as if caught in a still moment in a dance.

Downstairs, in what they hope will be the bar and restaurant in precisely four months, they swap their smart urban shoes for the rubber boots they bought for this new rural life.

'Can Murray and me go and play outside?' Georgie

asks.

'No, darling. Best wait for us.'

'It's all right, Mel. She can't come to much harm out there.'

'Okay.' She isn't sure, but doesn't want to be a killjoy. 'Not on the climbing frame, though, it's not safe.'

A quick look out on what will be the beer garden when they've exchanged the giant plastic dinosaur and rusty climbing frame for a set of wooden benches and tables. Melanie and Gareth watch Georgie skipping over the grass, chattering to Murray as she gives him a guided tour of their new playground. Then, with a quick exchange of smiles, they refocus on the pub's potential, keen to reaffirm why they've risked selling their three-bed semi on a perfectly pleasant estate in Bromley, for a venture with no guaranteed returns and something their less-encouraging friends have called hare-brained. Shadowy and cool, the pub smells of stale beer as they move around the extensive low-beamed spaces, touching the giant inglenook fireplaces the sales particulars boasted date back to the Middle Ages. Looking around at the abandoned goggles and gloves, the numerous brown-ringed coffee mugs, a lone broom propped against a wall. Evidence the workmen — employed by their brother-in-law, Bryn, and off enjoying a well-earned Bank Holiday weekend — will be back on Tuesday.

Kicking through debris, trying not to inhale plaster dust from the rough floor, they absorb the rambling beauty of this extraordinary setting. Sensing the ghostly presence of generations past, Melanie pats the peeling wallpaper and imagines the souls of their predecessors pressed between the centuries'-old colours and patterns. Thinks the chipped gloss on skirting boards and doors, showing layers of yellow, turquoise then finally brown, mark the passing of years like the rings on a tree.

'Bryn's lot haven't wasted time. They're already an improvement,' she points at the large patio doors.

'Still needs a load of work, but yeah,' Gareth agrees.

'It's all going in the right direction.' He puts an arm around her and kisses the top of her head. Not the most demonstrative of men, she melts whenever he shows this kind of affection.

'Think it's got to look worse before it can start to look better,' she nuzzles close to his ear. His dark, day-old stubble, already maturing into an impressive beard, is rough against her lips. 'And I'll be pitching in when Georgie's back at school.'

Gareth kisses her lips this time, his eyes closing for a moment. 'D'you reckon it'll be ready by Christmas?' he says when he opens them again.

'Going to do my best.' She slips an arm around his thickening waist. 'But I'm going to miss you.' She rests her head on his shoulder, breathes in his aftershave, storing it away for when he's back in London and she and Georgie are on their own.

'I'll be here weekends; the weeks will fly by. I'll try and get home Thursdays when I can, the internet signal's strong enough to work from here.' He checks his mobile to verify his claim. 'And it's an extra short week this week, don't forget. I don't have to go back till Wednesday.'

'Hardly worth going back at all.' She twists away, reluctant to show she's teary.

'I'd better show my face, Mel. You know what they're like.' He rolls his eyes. 'But when this place is up and running, it'll be goodbye job, goodbye London, and we three can be together all the time.'

*

Down on the generous spread of sand, the lowering sun, when it floats free from the clouds, is surprisingly hot. They take off their boots, tuck their socks inside and roll up the bottoms of their jeans. Holding hands, three in a row, they race to the shore and wade in up to their knees. A dog, ownerless and self-governing, stops to sniff their bare ankles making them giggle before it trots off like a little pony to cock its leg against a chunk of driftwood. When Georgie breaks away to splash through the shallows, plaits swinging and gabbling to Murray, Melanie removes her sweater, knots it around her middle and sits down beside Gareth on the sand. They can indulge in a few minutes of this, she thinks, feeling the seawater tightening the skin on her shins as it dries.

She trails the progress of a silver-rimmed cloud and lets her gaze travel over the necklace of cottages that line the curved throat of the bay. The broken spine of Pencarew Castle, romantic and melancholy, with its brutal history, perched on its rocky promontory. She sees a distant sheepdog dart over the bracken-covered slopes gathering sheep behind the town and traces the Pembrokeshire Coastal Path from clifftop to beach, then up to the opposite headland. Its track dotted with walkers in primary colours.

She and Gareth talk for a while. Then, running out of things to say, they fall into a comfortable silence. In the break in their conversation, she sees how he stares off into the middle-distance, watching their child. He is smiling and looks the most content she's seen him for years. Without shifting his gaze, he places his hand on hers; a hand that is brown to the wrist, like a yachtsman's hand. How handsome he is in his cream crewneck, she smiles to herself, falling in love with him all over again.

They sit on. Neither feeling the need to speak, content with the sound of the sea, until a buzzing from above. Closing her eyes, the sun strong on her face, her mind curves back to those days, those dreadful days that spanned into months after Sophie died. When she didn't dare open the curtains, didn't dare feel the sun on her face, refusing the reality. They stretch their necks to watch a white-winged Cessna make its airy flight over the bay and head inland. Melanie knows Gareth will be remembering his father: a local businessman wealthy enough to keep up his private pilot's license and his flying hours right until the end. An end that came just before the twins were born.

'When are we seeing your Mum?' Her question betrays her, he'll know she's been thinking of Rhodri now. A man she never met but if the photographs Gareth's mother, Bronwyn, keeps on her windowsills are to be trusted, was as good-looking as his only son.

'No need to make a special visit, she'll be at the party. Tegan's invited the whole bloody town.'

'Kind of your sister to organise that. You're going to have a great time.'

'Aren't you?'

'You know me and parties,' she pulls a face. 'Are you playing golf with Bryn tomorrow?'

'If you don't mind?' Gareth blinks through the spangled brightness.

'Course I don't, it's your weekend too. I thought me and Georgie could go blackberry picking.'

'Mm, tempting,' he says, sarcastic.

She shoves him sideways and makes him laugh.

'Hungry?' She notices their lengthening shadows.

'Yeah. Fish and chips, is it?'

'Yum,' Melanie smacks her lips together and tastes sea salt.

'Georgie!' Gareth calls. His words, blunted by the wind, are lost to the crashing cacophony of waves and the raucous fanfare of herring gulls circling above. 'Come on, we're going now.'

They regroup in the dip in the dunes to brush damp feet free of sand and put on their socks and wellingtons.

A woman, striking because of her diminutive frame and long black hair, scurries past. She turns her head as she walks, nervously tugging the cuffs of her outsized jumper over her red knuckles. Melanie smiles. A programmed response that is not reciprocated. The woman isn't looking at her, she is too busy staring at Gareth. The eyes beneath their thick straight brows as dark and sour as apple seeds.

FOUR

Night has somehow become dawn and Melanie, cold beneath her dressing gown, rotates in her kitchen chair to receive it. She sees her face, grey as the tide, reflected in the bloodless glass panel of the back door. She did go to bed but as soon as her head hit the pillow, it was exchanged for colour charts and kitchen tiles and fears she will miss some crucial detail that means they won't be able to build a viable business.

Not naturally a morning person, it's the jobs she's done that means she's seen more than her fair share of sunrises. With Gareth and Georgie asleep in upstairs rooms, she steps out on to the dew-soft lawn, thankful the wind has, at last, eased. All night long, the south-westerly squall has been throwing its lopsided weight against the high walls of the pub. It makes her wonder what winter will be like.

Swathed in a purple blush of dawn, she follows the jumble of path to the boundary fence and senses, rather than sees, the sea swaying beyond it. Inhaling the tangy breeze, it pickpockets her memory and blows her back to a time before she ever thought of becoming a chef, a wife, a mother. Until something moves down on the beach. It winks through the mauve miasma. In the slow slide of time, the sun has pushed its fingers eastward over the sky and she stares the shapes of upturned fishing boats into being. Their gutless hulls suck the little light there is and resemble the bellies of washed-up whales. Eyes narrowing, she leans against the fence and peers down to where the tide has been and gone. The sand is hard and rippled and seeing it sweeps her up and deposits her back to the candlewick bedspread of childhood holidays on her grandmother's Norfolk farm. To a room with rambling rose wallpaper, she could call her own for a few short weeks each year. A room that, away from the red-hot throated hearth of downstairs, was as cold as the morgue. But still more welcoming than anything she was to experience after her grandmother died and the farm was sold.

She shivers and scans the shoreline, blows on her hands and rubs them together. Then comes a scrabbling, a whimpering, and the dull clank of chains. There, beyond the fishing net graveyard and creel pots. She tightens the belt of her dressing gown and dives through the guano-encrusted gateway. The crunch of sand beneath her slippers and she rushes down the steep path to the beach. A child? Her first thought, although, she hopes with all her heart she's wrong.

The whimpering, louder now, makes her break into a run that, when she hits the fudge-soft sand, has her whipping off her slippers. Loping up and over the dunes, the marram grass spiking her calves, she sees it just as it sees her. Yelping, cartwheeling, pulled up on to hind legs by a chain, it coils itself into some grotesque and desperate dance. It must be the skinniest dog she's ever seen. Inching forward, more accustomed to cats, Melanie isn't sure what to do. But closer, crouching, palms extended, the dog calms, stops its violent thrashing and acrobatics and pushes its salt-crusted snout into her hand in some form of greeting. Tail drumming the upturned boat it's fastened to; she hopes the animal is more enthusiastic than wrathful.

'Are you a nice doggy?' Melanie lisps her need for assurance, realising she hasn't removed the tooth guard her dentist says she must wear to stop her grinding her molars away. 'Who's tied you up and left you like this, boy? You're not going to go for me, are you?' The dog licks his response: sorrowful, resigned, before slumping down, head on paws.

Nearly light, she sees the beach is deserted. Only a stir of indistinguishable seabirds disturbs the spill of rocks behind. Even the sea has retreated, leaving a clean stretch of beach: no fishermen, no walkers; all is empty under the hush of a burgeoning day. Unhooking the dog, she carries it and her slippers, barefoot up the precipitous sandy track from beach to pub. Once inside the kitchen, she runs the dog a bowl of water and wipes her feet free of sand.

'I won't be long,' she slurs her promise through her gum-shield and attempts to close the door on the dog's sorrowful stare. 'Don't look at me like that, I'm going to try and snatch forty-winks.'

Willing it to understand, she eventually shuts the door on the dog and the soft thrum of the few household appliances the previous owners left for them to use until their new ones arrive. She hovers in the bar for a moment, waiting for the dog to make a noise, which when it doesn't, has her heading upstairs to join her husband.

Less than an hour later, Melanie wakes to sounds of activity from outside. Pushing back the bedcovers she steps into a surprising spill of sunshine that slides between a gap in the curtains and gazes down on the head of someone sent by West Wales Homes to remove the FOR SALE sign.

'Got tons to do today.' There's excitement in her voice as she watches the estate agent being whiplashed by the tail of his jacket in the wind.

'And we've the party at the golf club.' A rustle of sheets and Gareth turns on his side. He looks at her and smiles his sleepy smile. 'Be fun to see the old crowd. Gives me the chance to show you off too. You decided what you're wearing?'

'My red dress.' Melanie, a hand through her shaggy fair hair. 'If I can find it among that lot.' She thinks of the crates still left to unpack and turns from the window.

'Lovely, yeah.' He rubs his eyes and yawns. 'You'll find it, we'll sort what's left before breakfast.'

There is movement from the adjacent room. The creek of floorboards and the closing of the bathroom door.

'Missed your slot.' Gareth flings back the duvet and pats the bed. 'Might as well wait in here with me.'

Melanie speedily removes the tooth guard and pulls her nightclothes over her head. Back between the sheets, she snuggles against his bare body with its legendary red Welsh dragon tattoo, smiling at how this is the best place on earth.

*

A shriek from below. Georgie, first to the kitchen, has found the dog. Melanie jogs downstairs wet from the shower with a Buzz Lightyear towel wrapped around her. She finds her daughter kneeling amid bricks and rubble cuddling the dog.

'I found the poor thing chained to a boat.' Water from her hair drips down between her shoulder blades. 'But we can't keep him, sweetheart.'

'Why not?' Gareth is behind her. His toothpaste breath fresh on her neck. He moves past Melanie to join his daughter. 'God, he's thin.' He bends to stroke the dog's sand-caked ears and knotted black coat, laughing when it licks his hands. 'We'll nip him to the vets; get him checked over.'

'But we don't know the first thing about keeping a dog.'

'How difficult can it be? All he needs is a warm place to kip, some decent food and regular walks.'

'All right, but we don't want some crackpot accusing us of stealing him. He wasn't a stray; he obviously belongs to *someone*.'

'Someone who doesn't deserve him.' Gareth in a

shirt as blue as his eyes.

'Please, Mummy. *Please.*' Georgie brushes the grit from her knees.

'Okay,' Melanie adjusts her towel. 'But it'll have to wait till Tuesday, it's a Bank Holiday Monday, remember. But we'd better feed him something. Try soaking some Shreddies, Georgie, I bet he'd like them.' She points to the now motionless tail, worn out from wagging. 'Looks like he's about to keel over.'

*

'D'you think Aunty Tegan's invited some children for me to play with?' Georgie, sitting up at the kitchen table, scrapes out her cereal bowl.

'I'm sure she has.' Gareth's rummaging through bags of groceries there is nowhere to unpack.

'Murray's excited about it, aren't you, Murray?' The faded blue beany toy Georgie's had since her cradle, is made to dance in her lap.

Melanie pours out tea, passes Gareth his *Dark Side of the Moon* mug. She watches Georgie jump down from her chair to put her bowl in the rusted metal sink. Tries to turn the tap and fails.

'Don't worry, sweetheart,' she reaches from behind. 'This—' she forces the hot tap open and rust comes off on her hand. 'Is all going to be replaced soon.'

Georgie strokes the dog and looks pleased to see he's eaten every scrap of his breakfast just as she's done. 'I've called him Slinky Dog.'

'Have you? That was a quick decision.' Melanie blows on her tea, swaps secret smiles with her husband.

'Did you sleep all right?' Gareth asks. 'I heard you get up hellish early.'

'I didn't disturb you, did I?' she frowns. 'I slept for

20

a bit but I suppose I'm so excited about everything.'

'So long as you're not overdoing it. I don't want you going back on the tablets.'

'Oh, no. I've done with them.'

Melanie watches her family circle one another. Convivial, congenial: a perfect choreographed dance. She then shifts her attention to the end of the pine table — about the only thing in here they are keeping — and finds the ghost of their dead daughter. Smiling, trapped in childhood, she is watching her twin and her father in a way Melanie herself is. It was a concern that Sophie would get left behind in their old home, that she wouldn't know how to follow them to Wales and it was why Melanie, who never felt comfortable living there, persevered with the house in Bromley.

'You decided what you want for breakfast, Gareth?' Snapping back to the now, her hand hovering over the sliced wholemeal. 'I could do you some toast?'

'No, I'll get myself something at the golf club.' He strokes the iconic light-splitting prism on his mug and she can tell the rainbow stripes becomes a crispy rasher of bacon . . . sausage . . . fried egg . . . tomato.

'Sure?' Melanie, eyebrows expectant, grips the teapot by the scruff of its tweed-covered cosy, transports it from the ravaged worksurface to tabletop: a she-cat with a kitten.

A guilty nod as Gareth sips from his tea.

'Bet you'll have a fry-up.' Georgie's read her father's mind. 'Can we trust him, Mummy?' She has found the notches chiselled into the doorframe that, rising higher and higher, probably charted the previous owners' children as they grew up.

Gareth taps his midriff. 'I'm well on track, thanks. Down another four pounds this week.' He gives his daughter a playful cuff around the ear.

'If you say so,' Georgie pokes a fingernail her mother painted a metallic sea-green at his stomach.

'Go on, you don't want to keep Bryn waiting.' Melanie replenishes what's been relegated to a dog's bowl with another serving of pre-soaked Shreddies. 'D'you want us to meet you there?'

'That'd be best.' Gareth drains the last of his tea. 'Where's my jacket?' He taps the pockets of his jeans for the car keys.

Melanie points to the back of a chair and watches him throw his checked blazer over his shoulders, theatrically tugging the sleeves down over the gold-plated cufflinks she bought him last Christmas. Things, if he'd noticed, had worn down to the cheap metal beneath, he'd never wear.

Not once has she seen him rush. Every gesture he makes is considered and, enriched by his striking good looks, means you have no choice but to look at him. Not that Gareth is the kind of bloke you'd want to turn your back on, or so Melanie, eavesdropping on conversations, has heard. His colleagues say how impossible it is to predict his moves, how he never gives anything away. They say he revels in risk-taking, that the bigger the gamble the better, and admit he has a rare gift for reading the financial markets in ways others don't. She supposes it must be true, as unlike many of his contemporaries, her husband has remained relatively unscathed by the recession.

Gareth is kissing her goodbye when his mobile beeps in his pocket. He takes it out, scans the screen.

'Who's that?' Melanie enquires.

Gareth doesn't respond.

'Gareth? That's not work, I hope. It is Sunday, you know.' She waits for him to answer. '*Gareth?*' she tries again.

'What?' He looks up. And does she glimpse a look of fear on his face?

'I hope that's not work pestering you.'

'You what?' Gareth pushes his phone away. 'Oh, um . . .um . . . it's no one. No one you need worry about. Catch you later, yeah?'

And with a quick inspection of his blazer, a hand to his hair in the mirror by the door, he's gone.

FIVE

Melanie and Georgie walk along Castle Row looking for the footpath Tegan told them to take. Passing well-to-do villas that hang well back from the cliff edge and the sheltered shore below, they eventually find the sign beneath its hood of ivy. The narrow path spirals upwards between a high rocky outcrop where wood sage and greater celandine cling to crevices in the huge slabs of blue-grey slate. They pass a pair of whitewashed cottages huddled against the rock. Almost engulfed in bindweed and deadly nightshade, she can tell these modest dwellings have been converted to holiday-lets by their plastic plants and gravelled front gardens.

'Good job I didn't wear my heels, this is steeper than I thought.' Melanie, panting, looks down at the rock-strewn shore below and envisages calamitous shipwrecks and pirates.

The track continues to climb, providing ever more spectacular views of the coastline. They see oaks and sycamores on the headland, stunted and dwarfed by the wind. The only shelter for Pencarew Castle, which in turn grips the grim cliffs above the seashore.

'Want to stop for a minute?' Melanie clasps Georgie's damp little hand in hers. 'Catch our breath?' She suggests this just as a shaft of sunlight spears the dolphin-smooth skin of the sea and turns it silver.

'If you like.' Uncomplicated and steady-eyed, Georgie agrees.

They reach an elevated grassy knoll topped with a

bench; its wood bleached by the weather. They sit listening to each other's breathing through the cold, rippling call of a curlew. To their left, a battered kissing gate with a sign saying: TO THE BEACH. They lean over it and gasp, thrilled by its terrifying steepness.

'There's the golf club.' Georgie points to where the path dips and widens out between a bank of gorse.

'Not so far.' Melanie considers the squat, white building nosing out across the low dunes and generous sands towards Ireland. 'And thankfully all downhill.' She dabs her brow with a tissue found in her clutch bag. 'Hot, isn't it? I'm feeling hot in this get-up.' She tugs the neck of her dress, blows down inside. 'I'd have been better in jeans. I can't imagine others dressing up. I don't look too dressed up, do I?'

'No, Mummy. You look pretty. You always look pretty.' Georgie grins her gap-toothed grin.

'You—' Melanie flings her arms around her child and squeezes her tight. 'Are the loveliest girl in the world to your silly old mum.'

'You're not silly, Mummy. And you're not old.' Georgie: a swish of her plaits, a flash of her father's blue eyes.

'Shall we get this over with? She checks her face in her vanity mirror and applies fresh lipstick.

'Don't you want to go?' Perceptive as always, Georgie purses her mouth and points a finger, indicating she too would like a touch of *firefly*.

'Yes.' Melanie obliges her and dabs on lipstick. 'This is a chance to make new friends.' She snaps shut the mirror and gets to her feet just as a bright bay mare gallops along the fence beside them.

Georgie squeals excitedly at the sight of her.

'D'you want me to see if there's a riding stables nearby?'

Georgie nods she would.

'I might have some lessons myself, I used to love

riding when I was a kid.'

'I didn't know you could ride.'

Melanie smiles into her memories. 'My cousin, Cassie, had a pony. Just as sweet as this little one.' She pats the mare that has stopped to say hello and guides Georgie's hand to stroke her muzzle. 'When I stayed with my gran in Hunstanton, which I did every school holiday until I was nine, Cassie would let me ride him on the beach.'

'I bet that was brilliant.' Georgie giggles, pulling her hand away when the pony snorts. 'I'd love to do that.'

*

'There you go.' Melanie's brother-in-law passes her a glass of white wine. 'I thought you could do with another.'

'Thanks, Bryn.' She takes the long-stemmed glass and brings it to her lips.

'Enjoying yourself?' He drinks from his pint.

'Yeah, it's great.' She swallows, wipes lipstick off the rim. Bryn's caught the sun, the brick-red band across his forehead looks sore.

'Why are you over here on your own then?'

'Oh, just taking a breather.' She watches sunlight through the trees throw a stirring pattern across the ceiling.

'You settling in all right?'

'Yes, fine. Fine. Everything's fine.' She fiddles with the beads on her necklace.

'One *fine*, I'd believe you. But two, then three — something's up.' He winks, boyish, cheeky.

She sips from the glass and laughs at his face pulling.

'Has Bronwyn been having a go? Is that it.'

Melanie takes a fortifying mouthful of wine. Feels it spread through her like sunshine, travelling her veins. 'No, the basilisk stare seems to be sufficient for this evening.'

'The what?'

'The silent treatment.'

'She's not forgiven you for marrying her son, that's her trouble.' Bryn drinks his beer and she watches the bob of his Adam's apple.

'I think it's got more to do with me not being Elizabeth.'

'Ugh, she'll get over it.'

'When? We've been married years.'

'My Mam's the same with Tegan. No one's good enough for her little boy.'

'But Tegan's lovely.'

'And so are you.' Another wink to put her at ease.

They stare out at the impressive sea views through a set of giant sliding doors that open to the smooth fairway of the eighteenth hole. A smart decking area set with benches and parasols gives Melanie ideas for the pub.

'Fab weather.'

'Better make the most of it. When the winter comes you city slickers aren't gonna know what's hit you.'

'I grew up in deepest Norfolk. Can't you tell by my accent?'

'You haven't got an accent.'

'I did have. Living in the south-east must've diluted it.'

'Whereabouts in Norfolk?'

'A small village on the coast.' She shivers into her memories of the flint-sharp easterly wind of her childhood.

'You still got family there?'

'My Mum's in King's Lynn; I never knew my father.'

'Brothers or sisters?'

'No. Only child, thank God. Mum had enough trouble bringing me up.' A tight laugh she knows doesn't reach her eyes.

'D'you get home much?'

'Not if I can help it. Sad times. Bad memories. Best to keep away.'

'That's a shame.'

'I suppose.' A stiff smile. 'But I've got Gareth and Georgie now, they're my family. And you guys.' Emotion quivering means she's unable to share how blessed she feels nowadays. How, as a youngster, when things were only her and her mother (and not always her mother), she'd watch families together, jealous of their closeness, their happiness, believing it was something for others and never for her. 'Did you two enjoy your game of golf?' she steers their conversation to safer waters.

'It was okay.' Bryn rubs a hand over his goatee and Melanie sees a tattooed T and F on the inside of his wrist. 'Better again when I could get him to put his blasted phone away.'

'It's his job,' Melanie says as if this explains everything. 'They never give him a moment's peace.'

Bryn shrugs and takes another pull on his pint.

Warm in here. The air is thick with voices and the spent breath of conversations. Sweat breaks out along her hairline, between her shoulder-blades. She wonders how she might appear in her beautifully tailored dress. Her matching red lipstick and silver dragonfly earrings. *Husband Stealer . . . Home Wrecker . . .* the ugly phrases she imagines people call her are never far away. Do people know how she and Gareth got together? Only if Bronwyn's filled them in. Melanie tries to accept it could be her paranoia misinterpreting the looks and uncertain smiles from these strangers but, believing herself to be at fault and deserving of criticism, it's difficult to take their friendliness at face value.

Her self-recriminations are severed by the sudden appearance of her daughter leading a gaggle of children in a conger through the chattering grown-ups.

'She's got them all licked into shape.' Tegan emerges too, in emerald green, the dribbling Ffion in her arms.

'Tegan!' Melanie, careful not to spill her wine, greets her sister-in-law and baby niece with a hug. 'Wow, you look gorgeous.' And she does, the pink glow of evening is reflected in Tegan's chestnut waves. 'It's so good of you to organise all this.' She flings out an arm to encompass the lounge: a room filled with stout leather club chairs and low glass tables, a hot and cold buffet set out against the far wall. A room dressed with welcome banners and balloons that not so long ago didn't permit women, never mind children. 'It's quite a gathering,' she projects her voice above a sudden surge of laughter. 'I had no idea Gareth had so many friends.'

'Any excuse for a knees-up, this lot.' Tegan, a twinkle in her eye. 'I'm glad to see Bryn's been looking after you—' she pauses to kiss her husband, who in turn kisses the baby. 'That brother of mine's bloody hopeless.' An exaggerated sigh. 'Fancy leaving you on your own.'

'We're not joined at the hip.'

'Even so.'

Tegan's look borders on pitiful and makes Melanie want to scream. 'Leave him alone. He's allowed to enjoy himself; he's not seen some of these people for years.' She flaps a hand in the general direction of her husband: his easy swagger, hands in his pockets.

Tegan makes a noise. 'Not sure I'd be so understanding. Elizabeth certainly wasn't.'

'He knows how much I hate being in the limelight. But look at him, he's a natural. That's why we're going to be such a great team. Him doing front-of-house, me in charge of the kitchen.'

Melanie, Tegan and Bryn watch Gareth work the room, pressing the flesh.

'You'd think he was running for president. Reckons he's a right player.'

'Anyone'd think you didn't like your brother.' Melanie rolls her eyes at Tegan.

'Course I *like* him, I'm just not blind to his ways like you … cos you're in *lurve.*'

'You make it sound like it's something to be ashamed of.'

'Take no notice of her, Mel,' Bryn chips in. 'Your Dad was the same,' he reminds his wife. 'A real schmoozer was Rhodri.'

'Yes, you're right,' Tegan agrees. 'People did seem to gravitate towards him. Mam says it's why he was such a successful man, people trusted him. He lived, ate and breathed that business of his.'

'This lot are probably picking Gareth's brains for advice on where they should invest their hard-earned cash. Or whatever it is he does, it's way over my head.' Bryn admits.

'Mam always thought he'd go into teaching with his geography degree. Who'd have thought my big brother would end up an investment banker. In the city.'

'Gareth, a *teacher?*' Bryn chokes on a mouthful of beer. 'You've got to have patience to be a teacher, and your brother is about the most impatient person I know.'

'I'm glad he's not a teacher,' Melanie says. 'And anyway, Gareth's found his niche.' She asserts, feeling the need to defend him. 'He's achieved so much.'

'That's what concerns me. *Him*, giving it all up once the pub opens?' Tegan, sceptical. 'You really think he can?'

'It's what he says.'

'But what about his whopping salary, the bonuses? He'll miss the money, won't he? Not to mention the high life.'

'He's not making that bigger bucks, not compared to some.' Melanie wants to play it down. 'And we'll be earning a good living from the pub if all goes to plan.'

'If you're sure?'

'We're in this together.'

Tegan and Bryn swap looks.

'Oh, there's Tom and Sian.' Bryn drains the last of

his pint. 'Mind if I leave you ladies to it?'

'You're as bad as Gareth. *Abandoning* us.' Tegan sulks, swaps the baby to her other hip.

'It's about the sink unit we ordered for you,' he says to Melanie. 'I wanna know if he managed to get hold of the supplier.'

'Off you go then.' Tegan jiggles Ffion to stave off grizzling. 'Get Sian to come over and join us.' She then turns her attention to Melanie. 'Bet you've not eaten yet, have you?'

A shake of her head.

'No wonder you stay so lovely and slim.' Her sister-in-law prods her own midriff and frowns. 'My brother's packed on the timber.' Tegan's gaze slides to Gareth again. To his head of dark curls bobbing amid the sea of party guests. 'He's thinning on top, too.'

'A bit, maybe.' Melanie cocks her head to the side, sees the wet patch Ffion's left behind on her mother's shoulder. 'I like it, I call it his little solar panel.'

'He'll never wear a number seven shirt again.' Tegan, happily picking apart her brother's appearance, doesn't appear to have heard.

'He's pretty fit, way fitter than me.' Melanie rushes to Gareth's defence yet again. 'He goes running most nights.'

'Yeah, but you can tell it's a struggle to keep the weight down.'

'Bloody-hell, Tegan, you don't mince your words.'

'Never seen the point of that. Just say it how it is, that's me. Gareth would be the first to admit it, he's stocky, see.'

'But fast. He used to be fast. I heard he was a real star on the rugby field.'

'Yes, he was all that. But the older you get and, well, he's thirty-five now.' Tegan wrinkles her nose. 'It's his height that's against him. What is he? Five-eight?'

She gives a curt nod; Tegan's forthright manner can

sometimes be a little too much.

'Same as Dad. A true Celt. Unlike you—' she steps back to admire Melanie. 'So tall and slim. You're like a model. You make it look easy but I bet you workout all the time.'

'Thing is, I don't. Apart from walking, I don't do anything.'

'Just lucky then?'

'Just lucky.' The words stick in Melanie's throat.

'It's why I'm surprised Gareth doesn't want to show you off.'

'He has, I've met loads of people.'

'Would've been the perfect opportunity.'

'Tegan. Stop it.' Melanie touches her sister-in-law's arm, wanting her to listen. 'Stop making problems where there aren't any. I can survive a few minutes on my own.'

'Good job with him being away in London all week. Hey—' a thought obviously occurring. 'That's why he's not showing you off, he doesn't want to draw attention to the fact his lovely wife's going to be on her own.'

'What's that?' Gareth is beside them and Melanie sees he's caught the sun as Bryn has but, with his olive complexion, he hasn't gone red. 'What don't I want to draw attention to?' He kisses the nape of her neck and triggers an infinitesimal shiver that travels her spine.

'Your sister reckons I'm going to be inundated with unwanted attention as soon as your back's turned.' She squeezes his hand, loving the weight of him against her, the warmth of his body through his clothes. But the pleasure is accompanied by a stab of unhappiness to think that the day after tomorrow, he'll be miles away.

'I didn't say that.' Tegan, finished with her mineral water, gives the empty glass to Melanie to put on a nearby ledge. 'Seriously though, you should get a move on and eat something. This lot are like a pack of locusts. They've a new chef here, he's very good.'

'Competition, eh? Perhaps we could poach him.

What d'you think, Gareth?'

'Can't think he'll be able to match your expertise.' He kisses her neck again, whispers, 'Have I told you how gorgeous you look?'

'Yes, you have.' Melanie, shy under her husband's unusual public display of affection, puts down her wine and spreads her arms. 'Can I hold her?'

Tegan passes her Ffion and Melanie buries her nose in her baby neck, wanting her smell. It makes Ffion giggle. 'What a gorgeous baby-boo you are.' She coos. 'And getting so heavy.' She shows Ffion the beads around her neck and carries her to a window to point at the sea which, beyond the glass, looks as still as a millpond and too good to be true.

'You two are going to be happy here, you know.' A softer Tegan links an arm through her brother's. 'You can put all that trouble behind you. Your life in Bromley would never have let you do that. There must've been memories everywhere, you poor things.'

'That's what my therapist said.' Melanie, looking into the baby's supine stare for answers regarding the universe. 'She said we needed a fresh start and that I needed a project to get my teeth into.'

'The pub's going to give you that in spades.' Gareth gives a broad, white smile.

'Are you still having counselling?' Tegan wants to know.

'Not anymore.'

'And the antidepressants? I know you needed them early on, but you were worried, weren't you, Gareth? Worried Mel was going to become dependent on them.'

There isn't time to respond. A laugh they all recognise, sharp as glass, splinters the general hum. They turn in unison to Bronwyn — Gareth and Tegan's mother — as she cruises into the room accompanied by several of her Women's Institute cronies. A hand is raised in their general direction, but she doesn't come over.

'I'd better go and say hello. She'll only get the

hump.' Gareth ducks away. 'I'll nip to the bar on the way back. Can you have a proper drink if you're breastfeeding?' he asks his sister.

'I shouldn't. Although,' Melanie watches Tegan's grey eyes travel over Ffion, a touch of her baby's chubby knees. 'I don't suppose a small one will do much harm. I'll have a white wine, please.' And she turns to exchange a few words in Welsh with a middle-aged woman.

'Get you another, Mel?'

'Go on then. Thanks.' And she and Ffion watch Gareth stride away, hear the exaggerated shriek Bronwyn gives when she sees him.

'You make him so happy.' Tegan, re-joining her. 'I'm sorry if I was a bit full-on earlier, I'm a bit of a ratbag at the moment.'

'It's called sleep deprivation.'

Tegan laughs. 'Even so, I shouldn't be like it with you.'

'I don't take any notice, it's a brother-sister thing, and what would I know about that?'

'Best thing he did, marrying you.' Tegan gives Melanie an affectionate squeeze.

'Shame your mum doesn't think so. Has she said anything?' She returns Ffion and retrieves what's left of her wine.

'About you?'

Melanie nods and strokes the condensation-wet glass.

'Only to say she's pleased you've persuaded Gareth to come back here.'

'She said that?' Melanie, doubtful.

'Yes. She also asked me to invite you to a Macmillan coffee morning she's hosting.'

A gulp of wine. Then another to finish it. 'Will you be there?'

'Oh, yes.' Tegan sniffs Ffion's nappy. 'Better change her. Won't be a minute. Get me her buggy would you, Mel? It's in the lobby.'

She does this and is pleased to see the bashful beige bunny she and Gareth bought and posted as soon as Ffion was born has been chosen to accompany her this evening.

Tegan wheels the baby away and alone, Melanie watches Gareth saunter to the bar. Handsome bugger, she smiles at how relaxed and happy he looks. But within seconds, exchanging words with the woman who serves him, she sees his cheeriness is swapped for a glower.

Melanie may be too far away to hear their exchange, but she can tell it's more complex than the ordering and paying for drinks. She recognises the woman as the one who walked past them on the beach yesterday. She is tinier than she remembers, bird-like even, but curiously striking, despite her dowdy dress-sense. It's her hair, she decides: a mane of liquorice-black, twitching like a feral animal about her shoulders. Melanie reads the hand gestures, the body language and guesses the woman needs to try hard to make Gareth remember her. And when, at last, the penny drops — displayed in the way Gareth slaps his forehead — the woman scribbles something down on a beer mat and forces it into his reluctant hand.

'Do you know the woman working the bar?'

Back from changing her baby, Tegan leans on her heels to look. 'Yes, that's Delyth. Delyth Powell.'

'I could see her talking to Gareth, so I'm assuming he knows her.'

'They used to be in the same class at school.' A glance at the now sleeping Ffion. 'Delyth had a massive crush on him,' a sharp laugh. 'Well, most of the girls did.'

'Flattering she still remembers him.' Melanie, steadfastly unconcerned; she refuses to be jealous of her husband's popularity in the way she knows his first wife was.

Tegan giggles. 'He doesn't look very happy to see her.'

Melanie laughs too. 'Is Delyth married?'

'No. As far as I know, she's never been in a steady

relationship with anyone.'

'Does she live in Pencarew?' She takes care to pronounce the name of the town the way Gareth taught her.

'Six, seven miles away. On the coast road towards St David's. Fab spot. On her parents' farm. Gweld Y Môr.' Tegan slips easily into Welsh to give the farm its proper name.

'*Gweld-e-what*?'

'Gweld Y Môr,' Tegan repeats, slowly, using her hands to pinch it into shape.

'Sounds pretty. What does it mean?'

'See the sea. Well, that's a rough translation. Place was legendary for its Welsh black cattle until her father died.'

'Oh, dear. When was that?'

Melanie imagines Tegan totting up the years. 'Ooo . . . it was just before Gareth went off to uni, so she'd have been eighteen.'

'That's sad.' Melanie darts another look at the raven-haired woman.

'Yes, it is. Delyth's had a tough time of things, all in all.'

Melanie watches Gareth pay for their drinks and pocket the change. But curiously, before he picks them up to carry them over, he rips the beer mat in half, then half again and, with a furtive look around, drops it on a nearby table.

SIX

'If you drive me to Pwllglas in the morning, you can have the car. I can get a train to London.' Gareth flicks the indicator and takes a sharp right turn. 'They're giving me a company car next week. I don't know what but it's bound to be decent. I'll drive back here in it Friday then.'

'Friday?' Melanie strokes the dog who sits between her knees in the footwell. 'I thought you were coming home Thursday?'

'Hardly worth me going back for one day.' He fetches up a laugh.

'I suppose.' She abandons her appeal before it has the chance to sprout wings and stares out through the car window. Sees the perfect bow of a rainbow spearing the humpbacked bruise of cloud.

They are returning from the vet's in Pwllglas. A man, after taking their details to pass to the police, gave Slinky Dog a thorough going over and quelled their concerns by affirming how, after twenty-eight-days, if no one claimed him, the dog was legally theirs. The dog hasn't been badly treated, the fact he's thin was probably down to the owners needing to choose between feeding him or feeding themselves and it wouldn't take long to bring him up to peak condition.

'*What?* No way.' Gareth yelps when he steers the Mazda between the high stone pillars marking the entrance to the Monkstone Arms. 'What the fuck does she want?'

Melanie is about to tell him not to swear in front of

Georgie, then remembers Georgie isn't with them. Invited to her new friend Nia's house for tea, she won't be back for hours.

'Not her. *Please*, not her.' Gareth parks up beside a muddy blue Defender and cuts the engine. 'I'll deal with this,' he says, his mouth pulled into a hard, straight line. 'You stay here.'

He unclips his seatbelt and pitches from the car, slamming the door behind him. Melanie watches him stomp away under a hood of squabbling seabirds; his operatic hand gestures almost comical. She recognises that thing he does with his neck and knows he's projecting his voice ahead of him but, shut inside the car, she can't hear what he's saying and can't see the person he's shouting at either. Not until she unwraps her long legs from around the dog and squeezes herself over the gear stick into the driving seat.

The person standing on the pub's doorstep is a woman Melanie is coming to recognise. Drowned in a pair of monster boots and a home-spun jumper the colours of Neapolitan ice cream, she looks like a child who's raided the dressing-up box. Nothing matches and everything looks as if it once belonged to a larger person. Her black hair pulled back by the wind coming in off the sea, reveals a pale, pinched face and a pair of huge dark eyes. How dejected she looks, how sad. Melanie, instantly sorry for her, wants to listen to their exchange and turns the ignition so she can drop the window. Leaning out, she sees the woman meekly offer Gareth an envelope and a jar of something that he refuses to take. Whatever he says makes her flinch and Melanie, on the verge of intervening, watches whoever this Delyth character is, place the items on the front step and walk away.

She bites her lip. Cross with Gareth for ordering her to stay in the car, but crosser with herself for doing as she was told. She blushes when the woman returns to her bashed-up Defender — a hulk of a vehicle she looks way too small to drive — passing close enough to the Mazda's open window for Melanie to hear her muttering some misplaced apology.

Keen to offset her husband's hostility, she raises a hand to wave the woman away. But Gareth is beside her, his bulk blocking her view, and the shock when he smacks her arm down makes her gasp.

'Ouch, that hurt.' Melanie brings her hand back inside the car. 'What the hell's got into you? That was really rude. She was only being kind. What have you got against her?'

He refuses to answer and, to communicate her annoyance, she slips free of the car and ignores him. Trailing the dog behind her, she bends to retrieve the jar of jam and envelope with its greasy thumbprint and steps into the gloomy bar without once looking back.

*

In the hollowed-out shell of the kitchen, Melanie sets about making tea. The only sound is of water rising to the boil. She slices open a new packet of biscuits, watches Gareth snatch one, two, then three, munching them in quick succession. Melanie takes one for herself. Feeds half to the dog. The pub, now the workmen have gone home for the day, is eerily quiet. With nowhere to sit, they stand side by side amid dustsheets and scaffolding, the work-in-progress.

Gareth licks his fingers, opens the flap of the envelope and pulls out a crudely-made card. The capital letters spelling: **HAPPY NEW HOME** in glitter and felt-tip pen.

'You should've at least said thank you. She must've made that especially,' Melanie says, in case the thought has escaped him. 'It was kind of her to go to such trouble.' A gentle nudge, wanting to rally him, wanting him to snap out of whatever's got into him. 'The jam looks nice. It's homemade. Strawberry. You love strawberry.' A flash of the woman's pitiful eyes, her restless hands. 'What did you say to her?' she quizzes. 'She looked very upset.'

Gareth, holding the card at arm's length as if afraid it might contaminate him, persists in his silence.

'Talk to me. What did you say to her?'

He jerks his head as if he's only just hearing. '*I said*—' a weighted pause, into which he heaves a heavy sigh, 'that I didn't want her bothering us. *I said* I was going to be away all week and you had your hands full getting this place up and running.' He leans back against the pockmarked work surface, folds his arms. '*I said* I didn't want her pestering you.'

'Well, I certainly think she got the message.' Melanie, sarcastic, weighs up whether to make him his tea, thinking he doesn't deserve it but pours it anyway. 'But I don't see why you had to speak on my behalf.' She passes him his mug, pours one for herself. 'I can make my own decisions. I am a big girl.'

'I know that, but I needed to nip whatever agenda she has in the bud.'

'*Agenda*?' Melanie mocks his choice of word. 'She was only being friendly.'

'I'd forgotten all about her, you know,' Gareth lowers his voice and gives no indication he's listening. In the same way, he makes no apology for his behaviour, it seems as though everything, now the woman has gone, is business-as-usual.

Melanie sips her tea and watches the curl of his lip when he reads whatever's been written inside the card, before screwing it up and dropping it into the bin. He squints at the jam and is about to fling that too when she stops him; a hand on his arm, lifting it from his grasp.

'I never liked her at school.' Lost in private thought, he replenishes the dog's water bowl. 'She was always a pain in the neck.' He adds over sounds of Slinky's lapping.

'I saw her talking to you at the golf club yesterday.

Tegan told me a bit about her. Sounds like she's had a difficult time. I feel sorry for her.'

'Well, don't.' Gareth looks the angriest she's ever seen him. 'She's a malicious, moaning cow.'

'Gareth!' Melanie is startled by his outburst. 'What's got into you, why are you being so horrible?'

He presses his palms to the cracked wall tiles, opens his mouth as if to say something, then seems to change his mind.

'Because, I have to tell you, I was so embarrassed about the way you behaved just now. We should have invited her in, it's the least we could have done. I would have.'

'That's because you're a soft touch,' he snaps, relinquishing the wall.

'Better to be a soft touch than a rude bastard.' She stands her ground. Wonders if this is the ruthless side she's heard others speak of and, if it is, why she hasn't seen it before? 'That was shameful, whatever would your mother say?'

'Leave my mother out of this,' he shouts then takes another biscuit.

Whoever that woman is: a wisp of air, as soft as breath, a fleeting, floating shadow; she's certainly made her presence felt and has undoubtedly altered the dynamics between her and her husband. Yes, Melanie thinks, small and insignificant that Delyth woman may be, she's certainly rattled Gareth's cage.

'What's the matter with us?' she probes through his crunching sounds. 'We never argue.'

'I know, we don't.' He swallows, gives her cheek a brusque kiss. 'This is what she wants. That woman would love nothing more than for us to be at loggerheads.'

'Oh, come on, why would you say that? She seemed harmless enough to me.'

'You wouldn't say that if you knew her,' he says darkly. 'She's so fucking *needy*.'

41

'And we all know how much you hate that.'

'Yes, I do, as a matter-of-fact, and I make no apology for it.' He raises his hands, but this is no surrender. 'That woman's a parasite, Mel. She feeds off the kindness of others. Kind people like you. I've seen the way she operates and I want you to promise me you'll stay away from her.'

'For God's sake, have you heard yourself? And anyway, since when did you get to tell me who I can and cannot see?'

'You're right. I'm sorry.' Contrite, his countenance softening, he drinks his tea. 'But you're too soft by half, you are.'

'So you keep saying.'

'It's why I love you.' His cheek is hot when he presses it to hers for a moment; her soft and gentle husband back again. 'I'm just trying to protect you, that's all,' he says, turning to leave.

'*Protect me?*' she blurts. 'From what? Anyone can tell that woman couldn't hurt a fly.'

But he is gone, and the room turns and settles around her. The minutes pass, then she remembers the homemade card and fishes it from the bin. Finding it and removing an old tea bag it's stuck itself to, she smooths it out and reads the message written inside:

Welcome back, Gareth . . . it says, in a slanting hand with long-stemmed letters . . . I'm sure you and your family will be very happy here. And don't worry, you know how good I am at keeping secrets.

42

SEVEN

Brambled and fruit-stained, Melanie and Georgie, their harvest of blackberries in plastic bags that swing in time with their marching, head home for a cup of tea and an iced bun bought from the Co-op. With Slinky Dog working as a trailblazer, his leash looped over Melanie's arm, their chatter is easy.

'You looking forward to starting school tomorrow?'

Georgie gives an enthusiastic nod. 'Nia's going to show me round.'

'That's nice of her. You've made a real friend there.' Warm from her uphill climb from the coastal path, Melanie unzips her parka.

'Her sister's nice too.'

'What's her name again?'

'Carys.'

'Pretty name.'

'It means *love*, in Welsh. I'm going to be learning Welsh at school.'

'I know you are. You can teach me.'

'I already know a few words. Nia's family all speak it. They live in a lovely house. It used to be the Post Office but it wasn't busy enough, so they got shut down.'

'I suppose we're lucky Pencarew's still got a primary school. So many have been closed in rural locations like this.'

'Daddy went there, didn't he?'

'Yes, he did.'

'Was Daddy born in Pencarew?'

'Yes. Nanna Bronwyn had Daddy and Aunty Tegan at home. Lord knows where the nearest hospital is.'

'There's one in Pwllglas.'

'Get you, Little Miss Information.' Melanie puts an arm around Georgie and they fall into a synchronised step.

The early-September evening, gathering clouds to the west turns from gas-blue to yellow to blood-red.

'Are we going to bake a pie?' Georgie digs her purple-stained fingers into the bag and plucks out a blackberry. Inspects it for the spiders she was warned about before popping it in her mouth.

'Not until Uncle Bryn's fitted the stove. We'll have to freeze them for now.'

'I'm fed up with them microwave dinners.'

'*Those* microwave dinners,' she corrects. 'Me too, sweetheart.'

'Look, Mummy.' Georgie dives to retrieve a large wing feather on the tarmac, passes it to Melanie.

'Oh, wow. That belongs to a big bird. I wonder what? Your Daddy would know. He'd know the Latin name for it too, probably.'

She thinks of Gareth as she tests the sharpness of its point against her palm. Thinks how handsome he'd looked in his burgundy tie and dark suit when she dropped him off at Pwllglas station. A shave and a shower, and he'd transformed himself into the City Boy once more. She thinks of the text she sent him: words of love she'd whispered as they'd kissed goodbye that she'd wanted to reiterate in writing. Not that she's heard anything back. But she mustn't mind, he'll be home soon and it isn't as if she hasn't got her daughter and the dog for company. She won't leave him more messages, hating him to think she was needy. That was a label he stuck on his first wife; a label he stuck on that Delyth woman too.

'People used to write with these,' she tells her only child. 'They'd dip them in ink and do the most beautiful handwriting.'

'But not now?'

'No, we all use biros now.'

'Miss Patel said I've got lovely handwriting,' Georgie gives her a look. 'But I won't be seeing her again, will I?'

'Miss Patel? No, probably not.' She lays the feather on the verge. 'But you're going to have lots of nice teachers at your new school.'

'What are you doing with that feather, Mummy?'

'I'm putting it here in case the bird who lost it wants to come back for it.' They look up to where a red kite floats in a placid arc above them.

'Like you do when you find someone's glove?'

'Yes, I suppose.'

'D'you think it could belong to him?' Georgie, eyes shining, points upwards at the large bird of prey.

'Maybe.' She ruffles her daughter's hair, that for once isn't constrained by plaits. 'And if it does, he can have it back, can't he?'

They are still giggling when a man in shabby clothes limps past them, downhill, towards the church and the sea. He is big and dark like a bear. Not that Melanie's been close to a bear, but it's what he makes her think of with his heavy growth of beard, his thick head of hair. As untidy as the hedgerows they've spent the afternoon foraging, the sight of him strangles the laughter in their throats.

Quickly evaluating his raggedness, his lameness, Melanie decides this is someone who's seen a battle or two. He reminds her of the homeless people who would congregate around Charing Cross station in the years she worked as a pastry chef at the Savoy. The army of dispossessed men, women, sometimes teenagers, she would give the perfectly edible cakes and pastries the hotel would otherwise have slung out.

Georgie, stretching the length of her arm, is focused on the man. Melanie does her best to pull her back but she's oddly persistent. The dog is curious about the stranger too: straining on his lead and wagging, he won't be drawn back either.

'Don't stare, Georgie. I've told you, it's rude to stare.'

'But it's him, he's staring at us, Mummy. Look—' Georgie protests. 'And he looks really, really cross.'

EIGHT

Under the drama of a meringue-whipped sky, Melanie, out with Slinky Dog, is high on the headland. Dodging the sheep turds, she sees tufts of fleece snagged on barbed wire. Chillier than the past few days, there's a definite downwards shift to winter. But it's still milder than the low-lying watery flatness of East Anglia would be at this time of year. Since the glorious weather over the bank holiday weekend, it's been blustery showers and little in the way of sunshine, and the forecast is for rain again later. But for now, conditions are clear enough to enjoy uninterrupted views across the sea to the great, black backs of unknown mountains in the distance. And tracing their sprouting jags, that are as sharp and unnatural as Georgie might outline with felt-tip pens, Melanie's eyes follow a flock of feeding oystercatchers, their striking pied plumage conspicuous along the foaming littoral below.

Hearing the swoop and call of terns and plover, the sudden kee-kee-kee of a kestrel, she looks up in time to see its chestnut spread spinning above. Ankle deep in late sea cabbage, it snags her rubber boots as she paces it out, occasionally pulling herself and the dog over barbed wire and stone-walled boundaries. Ghosts of fences past haunt this section of the coastal path; their ancient, weather-whittled posts bereft of wire and poking through unkempt grasses and thigh-high nettles. Arthritic fingers, she thinks of them as; indicators of long-ago existences eked out between gaps in the weather.

With the thrum of a bumblebee left over from

summer, close to her ear, Melanie thinks how she fell in love with the Monkstone Arms even before she and Gareth stepped over the threshold. On a day when April was blossoming in the town, with crocuses in people's gardens, daffodils in the gaunt hedgerows. A time of budding possibilities. Because once inside the building, with the potential its low-beamed rooms were showing them, it took root in her soul. With a childhood spent in and out of care, followed by years of renting shabby digs in London, then the soulless suburban semi that was Gareth's home with his first wife, and never Melanie's, the pub showed her the possibilities of a home. A vision of stability, peace and comfort; the decision to buy was instantaneous on her part. A place with boundless opportunities is how she relayed it to Georgie when they returned to Bromley: 'It'll be a new beginning for the three of us.'

Continuing up the steep sheep track; a flash from the sea as the sun strikes the water. She turns, believing it to be a signal of some sort, and looks back on how far she's climbed. Makes out the castle walls rising serene and majestic above treetops already rusted with autumn. She thinks of the horrors that went on four-hundred years ago, how prisoners — men, women and children, the guidebooks say — were incarcerated in damp, underground cells until they were strung up on Crow's Hill or burnt as witches. Funny to think that Pencarew Castle, cushioned in its lush belt of green, should be such a popular suggestion made by the tourist office for a fun afternoon out.

She shifts her gaze to the fishing boats bobbing on the horizon and enters the same silent plea she's been doing since she arrived. Praying to the rocks and the wind for nothing else to go wrong in their lives; for them to be allowed to keep this happiness, now they've found it. Turning slightly, she sees the pub garden sloping down to the crumbling shoreline. Up this high, she gets a bird's-eye view. What a fine building it is, she sighs into the plump thermals rolling in off the sea. The largest building for miles, with its steep, stucco-clad sides that bravely brace whatever the Irish Sea throws at it. How proud it makes her. But as quickly as her pride balloons, it is punctured by the familiar stab of fear: that she isn't nearly deserving enough, that she still hasn't been punished enough for the pain she caused a perfectly decent woman.

It starts to spit and Melanie tugs the hood of her parka over her head. Too windy for proper rain, she looks out from under the faux-fur rim to read the clouds like the expert weatherman she's becoming. She's right, the rainclouds part again to provide — as her gran would say — enough blue for a pair of sailor's trousers. She calls for the dog, wanting his company and the distraction he brings; digs through her coat for the saliva-encrusted tennis ball. Her fingers rasp up against the sediment of sand she carries around with her. Always filling her pockets with shells from the beach, she pulls one out to look at its sculptured form, strokes the scarcely perceptible indentations on its surface, finding the nacreous-pink insides as moving to touch as the skin of her new-born twins had been. Tears prick her eyes.

She pushes the shell away and throws the ball for the dog under the wall-eyed gaze of cows. Keeps on until her arm aches more than her memories, as she follows the high-sided corridor Slinky's body makes as he cuts through the long grass. A check of her watch tells her she should start heading back if she's to collect Georgie from school on time.

'Hang on a minute,' she yelps. 'Who's that?'

She squints through the unexpected shafts of sunlight. Someone's in the pub's garden. She bristles with irritation. She knows she'll have to get used to strangers enjoying her home, but not yet, not until they open for business.

Whoever this is, their movements are slow and furtive, and suspicion tightens its grip.

'Who is that?' she narrows her eyes but, despite the

plastic dinosaur and rotting climbing frame being cleared away, she can't make out who it is.

Odd, she thinks, scouting for a tissue in her waterproofs and blowing her nose. It could be Bryn or one of his men but, starting before seven each morning, they're usually gone by now. Odd, she thinks again, deciding, as she breaks into a run, the dog bounding alongside, whoever they are, they shouldn't be there.

NINE

Rain pushes its way along the cliffs. A grey curtain sweeping indiscriminately eastwards over the town. It crackles against the synthetic material of her hood and cold droplets slide down inside her parka. But she doesn't stop, she keeps on running, the dog pulling her along. Down from the headland to the beach, then over the dunes, her needless detour via the pub has made her late. Very late. And it was a waste of time. When she, at last, made it back to the Monkstone Arms, whoever had been snooping around was gone. She should have fetched the car keys; it would have been quicker to drive.

Pounding tarmac, splashing uphill through puddles, her feet inside their thin socks chafe the frayed lining of her boots. Rain slaps her face like a wet flannel as she passes the little park with its assortment of swings and roundabouts, and a brief thought of the sunny afternoon when she'd taken pictures of Gareth pushing Georgie high into the blue sky. Pictures, she posted on her Facebook page to show friends back in Kent just how wonderful their new lives were.

Her skeleton jars against the road, making her jaw ache, but she won't slow down, any more than she will stop to shake out the sharp stray stone swimming around in her boot. Gareth would be impressed with her surge of speed, her endurance; he's the runner, not her. Except impressed is the last thing he'd be. Late to collect their daughter from school, how irresponsible is that? What kind of a mother is she? One with a bad track record, she visualises the black spot on her copybook she can never erase. But — she tries to convince herself, running, running — it will be all right, half an hour won't hurt, it doesn't mean you're a bad mother, that you don't deserve to have children.

The main road at last. She gasps, tastes wood smoke from the tall chimneys of the town's elegant houses. Suddenly too hot for her hood, she pushes it down again and presses a hand to the burning sensation in her chest. A coach sends up a spray of rainwater and a flurry of dead leaves as it pulls into the curb, drenching her already sopping jeans. The hiss of brakes, and she is forced to slow to a walk as it decants the day-trippers who've come to wander the castle, take in the views.

'Excuse me. Excuse me.' She calls through the knot of tourists. Oblivious to anything but themselves, they are barely on the tarmac before snapping out selfies and flashing their new-for-the-holiday anoraks and hiking boots.

Weaving through them, the dog leading the way, his lean, black shape out front, she sees the school. Squat and white, its spreading magnolia tree propped like a drunkard against the white railings. She charges across the slope of playground marked out for hopscotch and netball, secures the dog's lead to a section of vertical guttering and dives into the porch.

'Hello? Is anyone there?' Dripping rainwater on to the brush mat, she pushes her voice down the empty hall, into the vacated classrooms beyond. She hears voices and the closing of a door, but unfamiliar with the layout, she can't place where they are coming from.

She takes a tentative step inside, her wellingtons sliding on the freshly-mopped linoleum, the tang of disinfectant in her nostrils.

'Georgie. *Hello?*' Her voice is absorbed by a cream-walled corridor decorated with a series of A3 sheets of collage. Flakes cut from magazines to form monstrous peaks, their thick ink-black silhouettes jutting against a bilious sky. Strange the way little minds work, she shivers, zipping her damp coat to the chin. 'Is anyone there?' she tries again.

Bolder, the need to find her child spurring her on, Melanie tiptoes over the wet floor, mindful of her sandy soles, she peeps into empty classrooms before opening the door on the cloakroom to scan the wooden benches, the multi-coloured pegs labelled with children's names. Then she spots the back of her daughter's head, her narrow child's body, and along with the huge relief the sight of her gives, comes an unexplained tightening in her chest.

'Georgie!' she cries into the rustle of waterproofs as she spreads her arms wide. 'I'm so sorry I'm late, sweetheart. Your Mummy's such a twit.' She blinks back sudden tears, flicks her wet fringe from her eyes. 'But I ran all the way here. I'm not too late, am I?'

'There's nothing to fret about.' A woman in checked overall answers; partially obscured by a forgotten coat hanging in front of her. 'I've been looking after Georgie.' The little-girl voice declares. 'We've been getting to know one another, haven't we, *cariad*?'

Georgie twists round; her expression is blank.

Melanie hears herself swallow. 'Aren't there any teachers here?'

'Oh, yes, they're having a meeting in the staff room.' The woman emerges and Melanie recognises her. Watches her pick up her mop and bucket, only to set it down again.

'I was walking the dog and I saw someone in the pub garden,' she feels the need to explain. 'I nipped back to check. I thought I'd have time.'

'There's nothing to bother about, I'm here.' The woman's nervous fingers fiddle with the buttons on her overall.

'I thought it was after-school club tonight?' Melanie sees the puddle of rainwater she's made.

'No, that's only Tuesdays and Wednesdays. It's Thursday today.'

'Oh, dear, I can't get my head around the new school timetable.'

'It's easy to get confused.'

'Thanks for looking after her for me.' Melanie helps Georgie on with her coat. 'It's Delyth, isn't it?' She remembers the name Tegan gave her, the one written on the greetings card Gareth threw away. 'I hear you were at school with my husband.'

TEN

'It's still raining, you can't walk in that. If you give me five minutes to finish up here, I'll give you a lift,' Delyth offers.

'But I'm soaking, I'll make your seats wet.'

'Does your Mammy always fuss like this?' Delyth makes Georgie laugh.

'And I've got the dog.' She remembers Slinky out in the rain.

'You can't have seen the state of my car. A wet dog won't make much difference.'

Delyth slips out of her overalls and tidies her cleaning things away in a cupboard that she locks afterwards. Melanie notices that although Delyth's hair is old-fashioned with no style to speak of, it's well cared for. Not a knot, or a tangle, it looks as shiny and heavy as glass. How does she keep it immaculate? A hand to her own short, shaggy cut, doubting she could be bothered.

'Come on,' Delyth, winking at Georgie. 'Let's get you two home.'

Melanie unties the dog from the drainpipe and they all dash through the rain to the car park at the rear of the school.

'Slinky Dog!' Georgie, ruffling his fur, makes her usual fuss of him.

'Come on,' Melanie chivvies. 'You and Murray get in the back. Slinky can sit with me.' And steering the tail of her daughter's coat away from the Defender's muddy sides, she helps her inside and fastens the seatbelt. The interior of the car is surprisingly clean, from Delyth's warning, she'd been imagining all sorts.

Melanie feels enormous beside Delyth, her knees butting up against the glove box, there's barely room for the dog.

'Push the seat back if you want.' Perched on a fat foam cushion so she can see over the steering wheel, Delyth's gaze travels the length of Melanie's thighs in their wet jeans.

'That's better.' Releasing the bar beneath the seat, she stretches her legs.

'I've seen that dog around, haven't I?' Delyth brushes the back of an arm across the already steamed-up windscreen.

'I don't know, have you?' She jerks upright, feels rainwater track over her scalp, tickling like ants.

'I'm sure I have. Where d'you find him?'

'Chained up on the beach.' She scratches her head.

'He belongs to someone, then?' Delyth's hair swings forward when she digs a spectacles' case from the side pocket of the door. When she puts them on, Melanie sees they are ugly, black-framed things that look as if they belong to a man. 'For driving,' the explanation, almost an apology.

'If he did, they didn't look after him very well.' Georgie pipes up from the back. 'Slinky was starving when Mummy brought him home. And his coat was all knotty and dirty. The vet says he belongs to us now.'

'Not quite, sweetheart,' Melanie is quick to correct. '*If,*' she reminds her daughter, 'after twenty-eight days the police still haven't found his owners, *then* he's ours.'

'I'm glad you reported him to the police,' Delyth sounds relieved.

'Oh, yes, we filled out a form at the vets.'

Delyth starts the engine, turns up the Defender's de-misters. With feet just about reaching the pedals, she miraculously reverses out into the road. Melanie, her waterproofs rustling through the thump, thump of windscreen wipers, strokes the dog's damp head and whispers nonsense things, like whether he'd prefer chicken dog food or beef when they get home.

'He's certainly taken to you.' Delyth pushes the heavy-looking spectacles up her nose; but too big, they immediately slide down again.

'He's part of the family now. We'd be heartbroken if it turns out we couldn't keep him.'

'It's nearly dark already.' Delyth switches on sidelights. 'Winter's really drawing in now.'

They drive through a swirl of leaves the inadequate wipers struggle to clear from the windscreen. Melanie stares out through the smeary glass at the steady rain, the wet town beyond. Thinks of the tourists, and how they'll be put off by the weather, so probably won't come again.

'How long have you worked at the school?' she asks.

'Since I left sixth form.' Delyth shifts her boneshaker of a car up into third, and Melanie notices again how coarse and red the woman's hands are. Working hands, she considers, before averting her gaze.

'My mum used to be a cleaner.' Melanie volunteers, omitting: *the times she was sober enough to hold down a job.* 'Hard, isn't it?'

'You get used to it. Need's must, and it's not so bad; there's three of us what do it.'

'You work at the golf club too, don't you? I saw you there the other night.'

'Only when they've a function. I like it there. I wish I could get more hours. The pay's loads better.'

'I suppose it is.'

'I work at the Co-op too.'

'Do you? I've never seen you.'

'I've seen you.' Delyth turns the dark of her eye on Melanie for the briefest moment. 'I was going to say hello.'

'You should have.'

'I will next time.'

'Didn't you want to go to college, university?'

'Couldn't. Not after my father died. Sudden, it was. An accident on the farm. He got trapped in the bailer.' Melanie listens to the sadness in Delyth's voice. 'I came home after sitting my last exam to find the ambulance taking him away.'

'Oh, dear, that's dreadful,' she sympathises, she remembers Tegan talking to her about this. 'It must have been terrible for you and your family.'

'I was all set to go to college. I had good enough A levels, but—' Delyth swings her gaze to Melanie again, then transfers it back to the road, 'there was the farm to run. I couldn't let it go to ruin. And I had Mam to look after. She suffers terrible with depression. Never got over the shock. Drinks, see.'

Melanie nods. She does see. Clearly. With a mother battling alcohol addiction meant a disrupted childhood spent in and out of care; she understands the implications all too well.

'Mam never leaves the farm now.'

'That's a shame,' Melanie says, automatically.

'She used to work for Gareth's father, back in the day. She was one of his top employees. Cut quite a dash, did Mam.' A thin laugh. 'She was a good-looking woman. Good-looking like you.' Another sideways glance at Melanie. 'But she fell to pieces after Da died, she gave up on life, I suppose. It's been up to me to put bread on the table since, and there's plenty of work round here if you don't mind what you do.'

'I suppose there is during the summer, but the winter's a different story.'

'That's why I make hay while the sun shines.' A quick hand to a gold crucifix — shiny and new-looking — on a chain around her neck. 'And there's Andrew to look after. And I'll do anything if it means he gets the chances I didn't.'

'Andrew? Is he your boy?'

'My boy.' Delyth confirms, indicating left into the Monkstone Arms' parking area. 'He's started his A levels himself now. His teachers say he's going to do ever so well.'

'I'm sure he is. All credit to you. It's tough bringing up kids on your own.' Another transient thought of her own troubled upbringing.

Melanie studies Delyth through the rhythmic thud of wipers, the ticking of the indicator. Decides she is a woman who has little or no self-image in her frumpy, mismatched clothes. Poor thing, she thinks, reading the premature lines around her mouth, the set of her wide, brown eyes, the little turned-up nose. She could be really attractive if she got a decent haircut, spent some money on herself. But everything, from the looks of it, is for her son.

'I do admire you,' she says, to be kind. 'It's amazing the way you've coped. Most people would have gone to pieces.'

'There we go.' Delyth doesn't respond to her comment and pushes her foot to the brake to bring the Defender to a standstill.

'Thanks for the lift.' She repositions her hood that with wet hair, is a waste of time. 'Would you like a cup of tea? The kitchen's still mostly rubble but we've a kettle, tea bags.'

'No,' Delyth lifts the handbrake. 'I'd better get back for Mam.'

'Another time then?' Melanie undoes her seatbelt, hooks the lead on the dog.

'That'd be nice.' Delyth smiles for the first time, it instantly softens her features. 'D'you want to swap numbers?'

'Good idea.' Melanie searches her pockets for her smartphone, then reels off her number. 'Cor, that takes me back,' she jokes as Delyth presses the digits into an old Nokia, immediately wishing she hadn't, the woman probably can't afford an upgrade.

'It's Andrew who's got all the latest gizmos. What do I need with that world-wide-web stuff?' Delyth tucks the Nokia away again.

'Thank you for your card and jam, by the way.' She remembers to say. 'I'm sorry if Gareth was a bit short with you.'

'Not for you to be sorry, though, is it?'

'No. I suppose not.' Melanie feels a blush travel up from her neck.

A stilted silence.

'He's been under a lot of pressure lately, what with the move and everything.'

'You don't have to make excuses for him. He doesn't like me. He never did.'

'I'm sure that's not true.'

Delyth turns her head: slowly, deliberately; levelling Melanie with her stare.

'What did you mean in your card?' she asks as she opens the car door and encourages the dog out into the rain. 'When you said you're good at *keeping secrets*? What secrets?'

'I think that's a conversation you should be having with your husband, it's not for me to say.'

'I have, but he says he doesn't know.' Melanie is remembering the grilling she gave him while she helps Georgie out.

'Then he's a bigger liar than I thought he was.'

ELEVEN

Swathed in the eerie hush of morning, Melanie is mindful her breathing keeps strange rhythm with the suck and sigh of the waves. Smart in black jeans and jacket, she walks briskly, following her tall shadow past a string of cottages facing the shore and the church with its crowded graveyard and NO DOGS sign. The glare off the water means she can't see beyond the fishing boats straining on their moorings and is unaware of the large, shadowy figure of a man loitering among the jumble of tombstones watching her.

She is on her way to Plas Newydd. Her mother-in-law's house, where Gareth and Tegan grew up. She is going to show willing, to please Gareth, because these kinds of social gatherings aren't her thing. Melanie takes the coast road that climbs away from the town, comes to a grassy cliff-top perched high above a series of inlets and coves. She stops, leans over the lip of the precipice and gasps at where the sea has chiselled caves as vast as the interiors of cathedrals from the weather-beaten rock.

Plas Newydd is one of Pencarew's finer residences. A detached red brick of Victorian origin set well back from the road on an elevated slope. With high-rise chimneys scuffing the unequivocal Welsh sky, the porthole-like apertures on its upper floors blink blindly on to an unsuspecting town and its imposing castle. While ground floor windows are besieged by prissy nets and floral curtains. What a place to grow up, she sighs as she progresses up the driveway; small wonder Gareth can't understand what it was like for her in institutionalised care. Above the satisfying crunch of gravel, the harsh chuckle of a magpie drops down into the treetops. *One for sorrow . . . the opening line of the superstitious rhyme learnt long ago curls back to her as she tries to work out when she was last here. Was it really eight years ago? It hardly seems possible. She remembers little of that fraught day of Rhodri Sayer's funeral apart from the heavy fatigue that came with being seven-months pregnant and the community of gnomes positioned around the carp pond, which to her amusement, she sees are still here.

The front door flung wide in anticipation of guests, lets in the withering smells of autumn and the eternal chatter of seabirds. Stepping into the passageway, with no sign of Bronwyn, Melanie follows the sound of a television and finds her sister-in-law, bleary-eyed and trying to placate the grizzling Ffion.

'*Teething.*' Tegan says as a form of greeting, switching the television off. 'None of us are getting any sleep.' She looks desperate.

'You poor buggers.' Melanie puts a consoling arm around Tegan's shoulder and ferrets out the flouncy nets with frills, the pelmets with frills, the high-backed armchairs with frills, antimacassars with frills, the velvet-tasselled lampshades. 'Let me take Ffion, you go and have a lie-down. You look bushed.' And she prises the cherry-cheeked baby from her sister-in-law's arms.

'You're a lifesaver.' Tegan flops down on Bronwyn's chintzy sofa. 'Fancy an éclair?' Her eyes dull beneath pale lashes.

Things must be bad; this one's never seen without her make-up. 'No, you have them.' She shakes her head. 'Your need is greater than mine.' And watches Tegan tuck into one of her mother's coffee morning creations.

'They're all through there.' Tegan jabs what's left of the cake in the direction of the hall and licks cream from her fingers. 'Mam opens up the front room on occasions like this. Go on, you go, I'm not really up to it.'

'Shall I take Ffion with me? Give you a chance to have a sleep.' She jiggles the baby up and down, pleased she has, at last, stopped crying.

'You've the magic touch. Try putting her in her cot.' Tegan relaxes on a mountain of frilly-edged cushions and smiles her appreciation. 'She might settle, with any luck.'

Melanie does, and to her astonishment, Ffion's eyelids flutter and close.

'Mam's been telling everyone you're coming. She can't wait to introduce you.'

'She's changed her tune.' Melanie follows a beam of sunshine journey from bookshelf to mantelpiece, over the various photographs of Gareth and Tegan when they were little, ones of Rhodri dressed like Biggles. Until her eyes land on a picture of Gareth's first wife; her pretty heart-shaped face held in a silver frame.

Tegan sees her looking. 'Mam had a card from her this morning.'

'Oh, yes,' Melanie does her best to sound neutral while thinking how different Elizabeth looks in this picture to the time she saw her.

'Starting some new research post at the university. She still works there, and she's still single.' Tegan screws up her mouth. 'For the record, I don't know why Mam bothers with her.'

'Probably to spite me,' Melanie answers too quickly.

'Probably.'

They swap mirthful looks.

'You're good not to mind. I'd have to say something if Bryn's mother behaved like that with me.'

'None of my business.'

'Course it's your business, your mother-in-law fraternising with the enemy.'

'Elizabeth's not the enemy, Tegan,' she sighs. 'I was the one in the wrong.'

'Gareth was the one in the wrong,' Tegan is quick to correct. 'He was the one doing the cheating. And anyway, I can't believe it's even still an issue, it was a lifetime ago.'

'I agree, but your parents adored Elizabeth, didn't they? They're difficult shoes to fill. Maybe if Elizabeth had found someone else.'

'*Someone else?*' Tegan splutters and lifts another éclair to her lips. 'She was lucky to have Gareth for as long as she did. Calling her bloody difficult would be an understatement. No wonder my brother fell in love with you.'

Melanie smiles. Not in the business of scoring points off her husband's ex, she lets it go. 'Want me to bring you a coffee?'

'*Gerroff.* Sleep, I want. Not climbing the walls.'

'I'll leave you to it then. Hopefully,' Melanie leans over the soundly sleeping Ffion, admiring the delicacy of her shell-pink eyelids. 'This little flamer will give you the chance to chill a while.'

A small wave goodbye to Tegan and Melanie is out in the passageway, walking in the direction she believes Bronwyn's front room to be when her mobile rings in her bag.

Gareth.

She presses it against her ear.

'Hi, Mel. What you up to?' Voices in the background: not working voices, it sounds more like he's in a bar. She makes out what she thinks is chart music.

'I'm at your Mum's. Coffee morning. I've just got here, not seen her yet.'

'Nice. She'll be pleased you made the effort.' Melanie hears him swap the phone to his other ear. 'She didn't expect you to do any baking, did she? I did say our kitchen's out of action.'

'No, nothing like that. According to Tegan, she just wants to introduce me to a few people. Which is nice of her.' The words stick in her throat.

'You what?' A shout goes up behind him. 'What d'you say?'

'Where are you?' She can't bring herself to deliver the generosity a second time.

'Client lunch. Come up the West End. Nice place, you'd like it.'

She looks at her watch. It isn't even eleven. 'Early. You eaten yet?'

'Not yet.'

'If it's any good, get a copy of the menu for me, would you?'

'Will do.'

'Useful for the pub.'

'Uh-huh.'

Silence drops between them, peppered by laughter Melanie's end and his.

'Did you ring for something particular, only I'd better go and show my face.'

'*Erm.*' She identifies a tightening in his voice and knows he's got something to say that she might not want to hear. 'Thing is, Mel,' he begins, then falters. 'And I'm sorry about this—'

'What?' She braces herself.

'I'm not going to be able to get back to you this weekend. It's too full-on. I'm snowed under with paperwork. You know how it is.'

'Yes,' she croaks, it's all she can manage.

'You're not too disappointed, are you?'

'No, course not. You do what you need to do. We'll be fine.'

'If you're sure?'

'I'm sure. And Julie and Mike don't mind?'

'Mind what?'

'You, staying the weekend. Because it wasn't the deal. You were supposed to be out of their hair at weekends.'

'They're cool. Julie's taking the kids to see her parents, so it'll just be me and Mike.'

'Boys alone,' Melanie says crisply, she can't help it. 'Takeaways and rugby on the box. Nice for you.'

'I won't have time for telly, Mel. It'll be head down.' He sounds as upset as she is. 'It's only a small sacrifice until we get things up and running.'

She gulps back tears and dare not answer. She was looking forward to seeing him, it's difficult to sound chirpy.

'Mel? You still there.'

'Still here,' she sniffs.

'Aw, don't be sad. I'm as disappointed as you are.' Gareth is firm. 'I'll be missing you and Georgie like mad, but I need to keep earning. We need the money, don't we? At least for the time being.'

'I know, and I'm grateful to you for sticking with it.' Suddenly, Delyth's voice is in her head, taunting: '*Then he's a bigger liar than I thought he was.*'

'Melanie!' Bronwyn is there, clogging the hallway with her permed hair and bolster bosom. She fills her tweed skirt and cashmere pullover to bursting.

'Your mum's seen me, I'd better go,' she whispers to Gareth, waves at her mother-in-law. 'Speak later?'

'I love you,' he says.

'Love you, too.'

'Say hello to Mam from me.'

'I will,' she says and ends the call.

'Was that my boy?' Bronwyn, smelling of face cream and powder, deposits a kiss on Melanie's cheek she isn't ready for. 'How is he, the darling? Not working too hard, I hope.'

'He's on a jolly.' Melanie drags a finger beneath each eye in case her mascara's smudged. 'A client lunch in some swanky joint, by the sounds of it.' She adjusts her handbag on her shoulder and trails behind along the passageway made unnecessarily dark by the mock-Regency wallpaper.

'Good.' Bronwyn drops the word over her shoulder as she sways ahead. 'He deserves some fun. I hate to think of him slaving away at the coalface.'

Hardly the coalface, Melanie thinks, as Bronwyn prattles on.

'Not that I could ever get my Rhodri to take a day off work, mind you. I think Gareth takes after him. Which is just as well, as it's what us women want.'

'Is it?' Melanie says, astonished with how nimble her mother-in-law is on her feet.

'Everyone. Everyone.' A theatrical clap. Bronwyn stops conversations, makes heads turn. 'This is Gareth's new wife, Melanie.'

'*New?* We've been married years,' she mumbles, defending herself: the accused offender appealing to a hostile jury. Bronwyn prods her in the small of her back, urging her forward to shake the hands being held out to her.

Bronwyn's decision to host a MacMillan coffee morning is little more than an opportunity to show off and, once the introductions are over, Melanie sidesteps those being ushered through to admire Plas Newydd's new conservatory and takes herself off for a nose around instead. Wandering the remaining downstairs rooms, their carpets the colour of treacle sponge, she sniggers at the collection of majolica earthenware. Her own mother used to be partial to this kind of pottery, not that she could afford the real McCoy, she reminds herself, touching the spine of a lumpy glazed monkey straddling a yellow teapot.

Back in the main living room, Melanie looks around at the fuss and clobber, the choice of décor. She realises nothing, not even the walls, has escaped Bronwyn's amplified attention. The wallpaper — gilt stripes and bowls of fruits and flowers — is completely over the top. This is a house of mid-nineteenth century origin, with its coving and original fireplaces. Such genuine features are rare and should be harnessed, not smothered; it's what they're trying to do with the Monkstone Arms. The fireplace is a beauty though and Melanie goes over for a closer look. Examines the whimsical William De Morgan blue-green peacocks, dragons and fishes on its tiled surround, before turning to the picture windows to lift the frilly nets obscuring fine sea views beyond the sharp incline of lawn.

'Wow, why would you want to cover that up?'

'Do help yourselves, ladies.' Bronwyn's chime over the thrum of conversation Melanie isn't included in has her spinning on her heels. 'It's all homemade.' The announcement is given to the room: to the conservatively dressed and chapel-going brigade, Bronwyn counts among her buddies. 'I don't want any leftovers.'

Pouring a coffee, Melanie sees there isn't a variant of cake that hasn't been made for this morning's event and can't help but admire Bronwyn's skill. She helps herself to a slice of chocolate cake, its ganache topping shiny enough to see her face in. With her back to the room, the sweetness dissolving on her tongue, she thinks of Gareth. Wonders how his lunch is going, what he's ordered from the menu. She regrets showing any kind of weakness when he told her he wasn't coming home tomorrow because at least he is coming home and she and Georgie aren't on their own. Her thoughts swing to Delyth and she sees the bird-like fluttering of her nervous hands, the frailty of her wren-thin ankles. Cruel for a woman like that to be left to bring up a child alone. Needing to work every hour to make ends meet. She will offer her the hand of friendship and invite her over; try to make up for Gareth's behaviour the other day. Try, if she can, to get her to elaborate on what she meant in her card, and why she called him a liar. Georgie likes her and, with Gareth away all week, Melanie can spend time with whoever she likes, can't she?

TWELVE

Melanie sleeps. An arm flung out to the side. The room is boiling, the radiators no one seems to have the power to turn off are raging. Her lips move. What is she saying? 'Sophie, Sophie, Sophie,' . . . as her baby's fists pummel the air . . . she is waiting to be lifted from her cot in the hot-walled hospital.

She opens her eyes on to the ceiling, tracks a crack from the coving around the light to the far wall. In her dream, she's been back to their old street in Bromley, to a time nearly four years ago. This is a dream she often has: a trauma in her past, of Sophie who appears as alive and real as the grey day leaching in through the bedroom curtains.

It is Monday again already and she's managed a whole weekend without Gareth. She counts the days, only four to go and he'll be home. A sideways look at the alarm clock. 7.15. She removes her tooth guard and sits up, pulls the duvet over her as if someone has come into the room unexpectedly. Muffled thuds and hammering from the workmen downstairs. The lavatory flushes. Then sounds of Georgie padding along the landing. Was she woken by bad dreams too? Through the fraying curtains, she sees that the moon has swapped places with the sun, and there's enough light to see the wardrobe with its musty-smelling insides that have already permeated her city clothes. She supposes their upstairs living quarters could do with updating too, eyeing the tired-looking wallpaper that is flaking where it meets the ceiling. But what stories it could tell, it has a certain appeal, in a dated kind of way. Trapped in time, like the scenery engulfing this place, where the past is strong, pulsing and sinister. Pencarew is home to so much insurmountable beauty and a more historic, dramatic or hostile place, she has never known.

Melanie washes and dresses and looks out over the grey swill of sea moving below the window. Pulls her fleece on and zips it to the neck, her thoughts: a butterfly; flit from thing to thing. A glimmer of the pale-faced junior doctor who came to find them in the waiting room. How he pressed his soft hands together when he told them there was nothing they could do.

Snapping to the present, Melanie leaves the view behind to check on Georgie.

'Oh, I see.' She smiles, spotting Slinky, curled like a cashew nut on the bed. 'That's where he's sleeping now, is it?' The dog yawns and flaps his ears, and Melanie sits beside him on the duvet and strokes his coat.

'We can't leave him in the kitchen, Mummy,' Georgie hands her a brush. 'Not with the workmen.'

Melanie continues to smile as she brushes out her daughter's light brown hair, twisting it into the plaits Georgie insists upon. They don't exchange more than a couple of words during this daily ritual. Choosing, as they so often do, to communicate in looks and gestures, such is their closeness, their deep connection.

'Ready.' She says, securing the final band.

At the landing window, they stop to assess the quality of the morning, the shifting silhouettes of trees against a pale sky. Then they proceed downstairs, hand in hand, the dog between them, into the over-bright kitchen where Melanie opens the fridge and invents breakfast from its meagre contents.

'I must go shopping,' she says to no one, sniffing leftover smells of takeaway bacon rolls along with the vinegary smell of grout and silicone as the last of the floor tiles are laid. She can't be heard above the din of hammers and drills and Radio Two and tiptoes around Bryn's men, some standing, some sitting, legs splayed, head and shoulders lost inside the skeletons of new kitchen cupboards, gaps in the masonry. Dusty-skinned men who help themselves to the biscuits, tea bags and coffee she leaves out for them.

'That sink you ordered has finally arrived,' Bryn, a mug of milky coffee in hand, is suddenly beside her. 'Should be able to fit it today.'

'Brilliant.' Melanie claps her hands. 'And the floor's looking amazing.'

'Everything's taking shape now.'

'Can't believe how quickly it's come together. Those units look fab.' She points to the wall, at the smart marble-finished worktops.

'Still no news on the stove. We'll get on to them again.'

Melanie looks around at what still looks like a bombsite. 'We're waiting on the new fridge and chest freezers too. Any idea how long they're going to be?'

Bryn shrugs. 'I'll get on to them as well.' He rinses his empty mug, shakes out the water droplets. 'How are you enjoying your new school, Georgie?' he asks, setting it down on the draining board.

'I love it.' She grins up at him, twirls a hand over her heavy plaits.

'You making new friends?'

Georgie nods then lists them for him.

'Right,' Melanie checks her watch. 'What d'you fancy?' she asks her child. 'Cornflakes. Toast. Yogurt?' Then, running out of options, she averts her gaze from the mouldy rubber surround of the old fridge door and looks at the gallery of paintings Georgie's already stuck to its front.

Breakfast over and, Georgie's backpack sorted, Melanie

slings it over her shoulder and hooks the wagging Slinky on to his lead to stroll out across the dappled dampness of the town under the clatter of herring gulls, trailing her dream. Melanie and Georgie have a rhythm going, each holding one another's hands; like two parts of the same machine, such is their trust of one another.

'You mustn't talk to strangers, Georgie.' Melanie's voice surprises her. Walking for fifteen minutes, they've almost reached the school and haven't exchanged a word. Both lost in private thoughts that she is now sharing. 'You do know that, don't you?' She squeezes her daughter's hand to accentuate the point. 'I meant to talk to you about it last week, but I forgot.'

'But I don't talk to strangers,' Georgie protests.

'Delyth was a stranger, wasn't she? Yes, I know she was at school with Daddy, but *you* didn't know anything about her before last week, did you?' Melanie injects a nervous laugh into the seriousness. 'And just because this is Wales and we're living in the country it doesn't mean you don't have to be just as careful as you were before.'

'But Delyth wasn't a stranger, Mummy.' Georgie stops to pull up her socks. 'She knew all about Sophie. And strangers don't know about what happened to Sophie, do they?'

Melanie yanks back her hand. The casual way her child drops the name of her dead twin sister into their conversation startles her.

'She knows all about me too.' Georgie adds, borderline gleeful. 'And about you and Daddy.'

'*About me and Daddy*?' Melanie listens to the tremor in her voice. 'What did she say?'

Her daughter swings Murray round in a circle and seems to change her mind. 'I don't know, I can't remember.'

'Well, tell me what you do remember,' she is sterner than she means to be.

'She said Sophie was happy and you didn't need to

blame yourself anymore.'

'*What!* What does that mean?' The pain of grief, something that is never far away, tightens its hold and tears fill her eyes.

'Delyth says that even though Sophie's leg got crushed up by her trike, it was all better now. And that bang she had on her head when the car hit her, she says that's gone away too.'

'How can she know about that?'

'I don't know.' Georgie looks up at her, wide-eyed and innocent. 'But she said Sophie was as good as new. It's what she said, Mummy.'

'What else did she say?' Melanie sees the school railings up ahead and tightens her hold on Slinky's lead.

'That she's gone to a lovely place where Jesus is looking after her, so we don't have to be sad anymore.'

As if they have summoned her, Delyth Powell rattles past in her car, heading in the direction of the harbour. Melanie lifts an arm to wave: robotic, programmed; is faintly aggrieved when it isn't returned.

What a strange woman you are, talking about such things with my seven-year-old; how come you know so much about our lives?

Melanie ponders this as she watches the Defender's downward progress. Delyth's small, dark head, barely visible through the vehicle's smeary rear window.

THIRTEEN

Along the seafront, past smells from a mobile burger van, the road tilts steeply down to Pencarew Quay. Metal rigging from the moored fishing boats clink against their masts in the wind and a dog barks at the door of the site office to be let inside. Without Slinky for a change, she follows it; buoyed along by the improvements the workmen have made to the pub, she must get on with sourcing local suppliers in readiness of opening.

She sniffs the wet fish smell of the docks before banging on the office door. Waiting long after the dog gets fed up and creeps away, she looks around. Sees weather-beaten men made burly in oilskins milling about the netting and wet concrete, slippery with scales and the spent casings of prawns.

'Can we help you?'

Melanie turns. The door she knocked on remains firmly shut and the question comes from a pair of men. One tall and thin, one short and round. Both clad in stereotypical cream-knit fishermen's jumpers, flat caps and waders.

'Yes. *Erm.* I'm here to ask about—' she falters, the grinning pair put her off her stride. 'About buying fish from you direct.'

'Aren't you Gareth Sayer's new missus?' the short one asks.

'Hardly new.' *What is it with people around here?*
'I heard he'd bought the Monkstone.'
'That's right.'

'Bit of a state, isn't it?' The taller one chips in.

'Yes, it needs some work.' Melanie smiles, she knows she needs to be friendly.

'Gonna cost a fair whack, I heard.' The taller one exchanges glances with his sidekick.

'Is there someone I can talk to? Someone who deals with the business side of things?' Melanie hasn't time for idle chitchat.

'Come with us.' The men in harmony. 'You'll want the boss.'

'Right,' Melanie brightening; follows them inside the site office.

'Boss?' One of them says. 'Got someone 'ere to see you.'

'How interesting.' Boss, a man who looks like Santa Claus.

'What's your name?' the short one whispers to her. 'Melanie.'

'Melanie 'ere,' he shouts as if Boss might be hard of hearing, 'has come to buy fish.'

She watches Boss rise from his desk and go to the window to stare out on the industry he's responsible for, before pushing a poker deep into the fire. A fire so low it's nearly gone out. Then he places lumps of coal, handpicked from a tin bucket, lays them over the embers. Flames lick, only two to start with, then more come, yellow and orange ribbons, until it's ablaze.

'I know you.' Close to Melanie, his voice smells of lemon drops.

'Do you?'

'Aye, you're married to Rhodri and Bronwyn's boy. What's his name again?'

'Gareth.'

'Aye, Gareth. Lovely boy. Lovely boy.' Boss, who doesn't introduce himself, sits down again and slides a photocopied form over the desk to her. 'Just sign the top and give us your phone number,' he jabs with a gnarled finger. 'Then tick what you want from the list.' He passes Melanie a pen. 'How will you be paying?'

'Oh, I'm not quite ready to start ordering just yet.'

'No?' The white eyebrows bob like rabbit tails.

'As I was explaining to—' she turns, but Little and Large have gone. 'We've bought the Monkstone Arms, we're hoping to open mid-December.'

'I see.' The broad, ruddy face widens into a grin. 'No problem. You hold on to the form. You can see what we sell. Some things are seasonal, but it's all self-explanatory. Will there be anything else?'

'No, that's great.' Melanie flaps the sheet of paper between them. 'I'll be in touch nearer the time.'

When she turns to go, she collides with a titan of a man whose head scrapes the ceiling of the hut. Craggy and broad like a fallen bough left out in all seasons, this is the man she and Georgie saw the day they went blackberry picking. It's a shock to find him blocking the only exit.

'Excuse me.' Melanie, intimidated by the intensity of his gaze, is keen to distance herself but he doesn't move and, with no choice other than to push against him, she's met by a solid wall of muscle beneath the ripped donkey jacket.

Stalemate.

The situation is faintly ridiculous and she could laugh if it wasn't for his unforgiving stare. Self-conscious under the uninvited scrutiny, she sees sand on his elbows, in the oily deepness of his beard, and up-close the smells of wet wool and seaweed, along with something else, harshly antiseptic. Something belonging to her childhood, but slippery, elusive, she can't bring it to mind.

'Excuse me,' she tries again, dropping her hands to her sides.

The man eventually shifts sideways and she hears the unmistakeable drag of his left leg. Not once does he avert his gaze. Dark and accusing from beneath his brows, she carries his look as she descends the metal steps of the site hut. It's the same look he gave her with Georgie, and she expects him to speak, but he doesn't utter a word.

Striding away, Melanie throws her gaze as high as she can, wanting to fling off the sense of unease this stranger gives her. Then she identifies the smell. Carbolic soap. And her sense of unease intensifies.

FOURTEEN

Days later, Melanie gives the flat a quick tidy before heading out for a walk with the dog. In this clear, sharp light, the steel-green fields hemmed in by a succession of drystone walls, look artificial. Everywhere is the sense of the sea and she sniffs the tangy air, feels the bracing thrust of the tide. Buffeted by the wind, she follows the path that tracks the spine of the coastal shelf, the hollowed shells of chapels and low stone farmsteads break the horizon; evidence this parish has been inhabited for thousands of years. Their innards licked clean by centuries of weather. Their walls reduced to rubble, that in turn have been scattered by sheep so they re-join the landscape.

Overhead, the dark shapes of birds move over a quickening sky. It sparks a memory of Gareth and the time they first met. Not an autumn day at all, but of high summer. Of the sand-blown Norfolk lanes around Wiveton. And strawberries. Taking a fortnight's leave from the Savoy to help cousin Cassie with her business, Melanie had only set out her sign on the verge minutes before, when he pulled up in a sleek, smart car she can't remember the make of.

'Hi,' he'd said, sweeping a confident hand through his dark curls. 'How much for a punnet?'

She fell in love with him then. And confiding this sometime later, he gave it a name. A *coup de foudre*. Loving to classify, teaching her the French. Because it didn't take long for her to admit her feelings, in texts and emails that were to follow, how intensely she felt about him. Correspondence if she was to read now, would make her cringe. Melanie hadn't wanted anyone after Dave — the motorbike-mad boyfriend she met at the care home — dumped her. She hadn't wanted the hassle. Certainly not the hassle that came with seeing a married man. But Gareth: turning up out of nowhere, good looking and confident with his nice car and money he's never been too shy to spend on her; was different. And when he finally got around to telling his wife he wanted a divorce, before Melanie knew it, she'd moved out of her dingy bedsit on the Fulham Road and into his smart, three-bed semi with its glazed portico and bay windows on that Bromley estate.

Not that it was plain sailing. It was a long and difficult journey before they could finally be together. So long, in fact, she thought it would never happen. Early on, they would meet in out of the way places, in the rough woods beyond the footpaths they liked to stroll. Once, in a little B&B with gable windows looking out on the North Sea, where she drank too much and told him she couldn't stand it any longer, that he needed to leave Elizabeth, that she would not see him this way again.

She thinks of those painful weeks when he took Elizabeth away on a road trip around America for her twenty-fifth birthday. How he didn't text or call. She thought they were over. That she'd imagined the whole thing. And how, when he came back, it was as if nothing had happened; that he hadn't been away for a month without so much as a whisper. She didn't mention it. Shared nothing of how she lay awake for nights on end, her mobile under her pillow in case he called. How she'd badgered the postman and made herself sick with worry. After all, what right did she have? He wasn't hers then. He wasn't hers for another two years.

Heading towards home, but reluctant to go back inside just yet, she calls by the deli for a takeaway flat white. Unsure where to drink it, she carries it downhill, beneath the glamorous spread of deciduous trees, marvelling at the flame-coloured leaves dressing the heavens. Passing the black-belled church and feeling rebellious, she ignores the NO DOGS sign and eases open the timber lychgate worn smooth by the hands of parishioners. Almost hidden by the magenta-berried shrubbery, it is with a quick look over her shoulder that she pulls Slinky in after her, letting the gate snap shut behind them.

The dog seems to know where he's going, wagging and eager, he tows her in the direction of the church porch, to where there are several empty lager cans tidied into a pile on the chipped flagstones. The dog sniffs through them, licks the pools of spilt beer, hunting for what, she doesn't know, but she fears the hollow metal clattering might summon unwanted attention, so urges him away. She peers up at the strange gargoyles staring down on her and counts her faults. Doesn't everyone have faults? Maybe. But she's never been all that interested in other people's faults, only her own.

Finding the only bench, she sits down and peels back the plastic lid on her coffee. Brings it to her lips. Too hot, she puts it down and looks about while she waits for it to cool. She loves graveyards, especially ones as chock-a-block with stone angels and cherubs as this. Friends, as well as Gareth, think she's macabre, but she finds the calming quality of these settings comforting. The spaces between the headstones are bolstered by the odd spray of bright flowers and bobbing, black-backed crows and a robust sun shows itself through a tear in the cloud. Its hot eye striking the top of her head. With Slinky panting against her ankles, she listens to the transitory song of a solitary robin and sips her coffee. Quietness drops around her, it has a curious weight to it and fills her ear with its muffled breath.

Coffee finished, she squashes the empty carton into a pocket and removes her parka. Tying it around her middle, she weaves among the listing tombstones, dipping her head to the inscriptions on the sharp-edged stone. She doesn't mind so much when she can see the dead have lived good long lives, it's the children's graves that bother her. And there are plenty in here. Tears come when she sees the sad inscription for little Philip, claiming his all-important eight and a half hours on earth and her thoughts turn to Sophie's grave. Something that is the furthest away it has ever been.

Seeing Slinky is about to cock his leg against a headstone, yanking him away they move deeper into the shadows, over waterlogged grass bouncy with moss. On under the dripping spread of cedars, reading of past lives and the farms they were born in, chiselled into the thick Welsh stone that has turned black from the rain. Tan-Y-Waen ... Ael Y Bryn ... Carreg Goch ... she rolls the foreign-sounding words over her English tongue, thinks of the posters advertising Welsh language classes at the library and how she should sign up for one. She is pulling the dog away from a crop of spooky-looking mushrooms huddled at the base of a tree, when she spots a rather grand memorial of pink speckled marble standing proud and erect among its slanting neighbours.

Erin Meredith Powell of Gweld Y Môr.
Beloved Mother, Daughter, Sister.
Asleep with the Angels.
1988 – 2011

And below it:
Walford Earnest Powell.
Beloved Father, husband, brother.
1951 – 2002

'Gweld Y Môr.' Melanie gathers the three Welsh words she remembers Tegan giving her at the golf club. Kicks through the little drifts of confetti that have gathered here and there. 'That's the name of Delyth's farm,' she confirms to the wind that is combing the bare boughs of trees. 'Who's this Erin, then?'

Gathering up the dates, she guesses Walford Powell must have been Delyth's father and, crouching to read the inscription for Erin Meredith Powell again, she does the sums and works out that whoever she was, she'd have been four years younger than either her or Gareth, four years younger than Delyth.

Was this Delyth's sister? And if so, what happened to her? The inscription says *mother*, doesn't it? Was she a wife, did she have a partner, where's her child now? Did the baby die too?

'Dear me,' she sighs, 'the girl would've only been twenty-three when she died.' And cuddling Slinky, her eyes travelling the backs of other gravestones, she thinks how small life is, how cruel.

A bird flies up, startled by something in the unruly undergrowth at the rear of the cemetery. Slinky barks. Upright, Melanie sees what's set him off. A man: big and dark and loitering in the shadows that are cast by the crippled boughs of apple trees. It's him again. Mr Grizzly. This is the name she gave him after the unsettling experience down at the harbour, and the time before with Georgie. Is he following her? The idea is alarming, but there isn't the time to think with the dog barking and wagging, more insistent than ever; she can barely hold on to him he's so strong. The man turns in their direction and steps free of the obscurities the vegetation provides, out into the illuminating sunshine. And she notices this time, that as well as a limp, his left arm hangs uselessly by his side.

'Bugger,' she swears under her breath. 'He's seen us now.' She blames the dog. 'Hardly surprising with the racket you're making.'

'You're not supposed to bring him in here,' the man booms; his left leg dragging like the tide.

Flustered, Melanie tugs on Slinky's lead. 'Come on, boy. He's on to us. Let's get out of here.'

But the dog refuses to budge: a recalcitrant child; his fox brush tail thumping against her shins.

'Slinky, *please*,' she coaxes, pulling on his leash. 'Quick, come on.'

But the dog won't be moved. His four black paws squarely planted, wagging enthusiastically, extra friendly; Melanie wishes he wasn't so interested in whoever this man is.

Nothing else to do other than pick him up. A dead-weight in her arms, she staggers over the sodden ground. She reaches the gate and is squeezing through it when her fleece snags on a straggle of thorns weighted with rosehips.

'All right, I'm going.' She raises a hand; she wants no trouble. Frantically extricating herself, a brief look tells her the man is gaining on them and she rips her sleeve in her dash to escape.

'Hey! Wait!' he roars at her.

But Melanie doesn't want to wait. She wants to put as much distance between her and this man as possible. But look how bedraggled he is, how sad; she is as sorry for him as she is afraid.

Free of the thorns, she pushes out through the lychgate. Listens to it bang behind her as she sets the dog on the ground. She charges away, Slinky still trailing behind on his lead, she doesn't dare stop to inspect the damage to her top. Desperate to get away from this man and the treacherous wind-blown headland, she darts over the road and into the near-deserted square. Heads uphill towards the old market house with its grand Tuscan columns, Pencarew Fishing Club and shops selling everything from fudge to Welsh love spoons. Races past cobbled ginnels sloping seawards and giving glimpses of the low-tide and bristle-backed dunes.

Out of puff, she slows to a brisk walk up the slight incline that leads to the Monkstone Arms. Repeatedly checking over her shoulder, she is relieved to find no one following.

Safe.

She rounds the stone pillars that pinpoint the

entrance to the pub and its car park. The reassuring crunch of gravel under her boots. Exhaling her relief, she listens to the rattle of rooks and briefly contemplates the dark geometry of their wings. Then, dropping her gaze, she sees something on the doorstep.

'What's that?'

Alien. It shouldn't be there. Inching towards it, trepidation banging beneath her collarbone, she scans around for the person who left it. But the place is empty, even the builders' van has gone for the day. There is only the Mazda, in its usual space between the spreading rose bush and crumbling stone wall.

When she reaches the main door, she sees what's been left for her. A large, square Tupperware container. She bends to retrieve it, peers through the plastic lid at a pile of flat scone-like cakes. There's a message taped to the lid and she reads the familiar sloping scrawl.

Sorry. From Delyth.

'Sorry, for what? For not waving to me yesterday. For feeding Georgie a load of nonsense about her dead sister?'

Melanie stares up at the now bare chestnut tree for answers, but all she sees are its thin arms held out to the clouds.

FIFTEEN

'Sorry, sweetheart, but he's not here.' Melanie puts a consoling arm around her daughter. 'D'you think you could have dropped him on the way home?'

'I don't know,' Georgie begins to cry. 'Can you check again?'

Melanie does, unpacking and repacking her daughter's backpack for the third time. She rinses out her lunchbox, turns it upside down to dry on the newly-fitted double drainer. Takes a break from the drama to stroke the handsome tiled surround, the curve of the stainless-steel taps and the Belfast sink of sparkling-white porcelain. Her mind wanders further, despite Georgie's mounting distress, and she appraises the beautiful floor Bryn's men finished laying the previous day.

'I'm sorry, baby.' A sigh and she's back in the moment. 'But Murray's not here.'

'He must be,' Georgie is distraught. 'Poor Murray, it's going to be dark soon.'

Melanie looks out through the kitchen window. Her child is right, they are pushing on into autumn, the evenings are drawing in a little more each day. 'Look, he can't have gone far. Let's put our coats back on and go and find him.'

A sharp rapping at the pub's front door interrupts them. A sound that vibrates through the empty bar. The dog barks his warning and trots away to see whoever it is off the premises.

'I'll get it,' Georgie, brightening. 'It might be Murray. He might have found his own way home.'

Melanie, close on her daughter's heels, glances out through the patio windows at a sky that is like a crumpled piece of silk being dragged towards the horizon.

'Delyth. Hi.' She opens the door, lets in the bite of cold. 'Come in. Come in,' she beckons, not that the woman moves. Nervy and breathless, her red hands feverishly pushing the dog's snout away. 'Thanks for the cakes you left the other day.' Melanie's pleased with herself for remembering. 'It was very kind of you.'

'It's all right.' The small voice is clipped. 'I made them for Georgie, really.' The dog, still taking an embarrassing amount of interest in the woman, sniffs the greasy hem of her waxed coat. 'She told me you still didn't have your oven.' Delyth, now slapping Slinky's snout away with her rough hands, seems unwilling to step inside. 'But it would have been nice,' she adds, hanging her head, 'if you'd taken the time to text me a thank you.' Melanie, slightly taken aback, hears something of the self-pitying trait Gareth complained of. But there isn't time to respond. 'I found this little chap in the school cloakroom, *cariad*.' Delyth addresses Georgie. She need only bend slightly; the child is already up to her shoulder. 'He is yours, isn't he?'

'Murray! Murray!' Georgie squeals her delight and, taking her toy, presses its soft blue head to her lips.

'What do we say?' Melanie prompts her, fearful Delyth will if she doesn't.

'Thank you. Thank you.' Georgie gushes.

'So, he's called Murray, is he? That's an unusual name.'

'After Andy Murray.' Melanie strokes her daughter's head. 'He's our favourite tennis star, isn't he, sweetheart?'

'Yes, he is.' Georgie, gleeful, spins on her heels and charges up to the flat. 'Me and Murray are going to watch CBeebies.'

'Take Slinky with you,' Melanie calls after her, dragging the dog away from Delyth by his collar. 'I'll bring you up a sandwich in a bit. It'll put you on till dinnertime and Daddy's home.' Then, returning to Delyth, 'Thanks so much for bringing him over. 'Please, come in?' she encourages, opening the door as wide as it will go. 'I could show you around.' A small nod from her caller. 'And I'm sure I could stretch to a cup of tea. Have one of your cakes to go with it.' She throws out a laugh that bounces around the hollow bar; a laugh Delyth doesn't throw back.

'Oh,' Delyth says, finally stepping over the threshold. 'You've ripped everything out.' The tone conveys a disappointment Melanie immediately counters.

'Sorry if it's a bit of a shock, but we wanted a clean sweep. We want—' she pauses, wary of offending, 'to attract a different kind of clientele. And you have to admit the place was stuck in the seventies.'

'I liked how it was.' The disappointment continues. 'And I should think there's lots of others round here that liked how it was too.'

She guides her visitor through the downstairs rooms, over rubble, naked wires, stepladders leaning against stripped-down walls — the usual evidence of workmen who've gone home for the weekend. Dispensing periodic warnings of: 'Don't trip over that,' and 'Watch your step,' as she identifies to a now staunchly silent Delyth, what will go where and building a picture of how it will look when everything's in place.

'There used to be a pool table. In that corner.' The woman stabs the air with a chapped finger. 'Us sixth formers would end up in here lunchtimes. Or when we were mitching.'

'*Mitching*?' Melanie doesn't understand.

'Bunking off school.'

'Oh, I see.' Her face relaxes into a smile. 'I did a fair amount of that myself, as I remember.'

They go into the kitchen and Melanie points out,

that aside from the stove, it's near completion.

'It's all lovely, but it must be costing you a fortune.' Delyth, eyes restless from beneath their hard line of eyebrow. Melanie sees her attention flit across the floor, to the smart new sink and double drainer. 'But I suppose Gareth can afford it.'

'I admit it's a massive outlay, but you've got to speculate to accumulate.' She supposes it must be difficult for Delyth to see such apparent carefree spending when she struggles to keep the wolf from the door.

'It's funny, but I didn't think for a million years he'd come back to this place.' Delyth fixes Melanie with her gaze. 'Always thought he was too good for round here.'

Your opinion, or what you think Gareth thinks of himself? Melanie doesn't ask.

'I mean, he can't have been home more than a handful of times in all the years he's been away. He's seen next to nothing of his mother, or sister, has he? Certainly not since Rhodri died.'

'He's not been back here because Bronwyn used to come and stay with us in Kent. Tegan too.' Melanie sets her straight. 'It's quite a hike from Bromley and Gareth could never get enough time off work.'

'But he must've had holidays?' The look is unflinching.

'Barely. A fortnight a year, tops, plus a few extra days at Christmas.' *Not that it's any business of yours*, her thoughts while maintaining her smile and answering politely. 'If he did, by some miracle, manage a whole week off, he always liked to take us away somewhere hot.'

'Aren't you the lucky one,' Delyth sniffs, undoes her outsized coat.

'D'you want me to take that for you?' she asks gruffly, unsure why she's being given the third degree.

'No, I'll keep it on for now.' The coat is pulled tight around her. 'Did Gareth ever bring you to Pencarew before now?'

'Once. The week of Rhodri's funeral.'

'But that was years back.'

'Whatever.' Melanie shrugs. She's had enough of this. What right has this woman got to question their lives? 'We're here now, and come Christmas, when this place is open, Gareth will be here full-time.'

Delyth shifts her bantamweight to her opposite leg. 'Bet Bronwyn's happy to have him back.'

'She is, yes.'

'You're so lucky. The pair of you.' Delyth: pale, elfin; peeps out through her screen of hair. Her fretful hands set Melanie on edge. 'I wish I'd been able to get away from here and make something of myself like Gareth has.'

'It's not too late.' Melanie, keen to lighten things. 'Andrew's growing up, it won't be long before he's off doing his own thing.'

'Oh, no, I don't want him leaving home.' Delyth looks horrified. 'I don't want him leaving me. I'll have no one if he leaves me.'

God, what is it about mothers and sons? Melanie's thoughts drift to Bronwyn, to what Bryn said his mother was like with Tegan. 'Well, yes, it'll be strange to start with, but you said yourself he's a clever boy, he's going to want to spread his wings.'

'But he's my rock. He knows I can't do without him.' Delyth stares at her feet, all sorrowful.

'I can appreciate it must be hard when your babies leave home.' She studies Delyth: half-woman, half-child; and can't imagine her all round like a peach with a baby inside. Where did she put it? There's nothing of her. 'But I can't imagine standing in Georgie's way. You've got to let them do what they want.' She stops short of calling Delyth selfish. 'We all want our kids to grow up and be independent of us. Dear me, the alternative is unimaginable. And just think,' she adds, as upbeat as she can be. 'You'll be free to do your own thing then. You could go to college; train for something you want to do.'

'Don't be ridiculous, I'm thirty-five.' Delyth gives her a filthy look. 'My life's over.'

'Over?' Melanie laughs without meaning to. 'Ta very much. I'm the same age as you and I don't consider my life to be over.'

'But it's different for you.'

'Is it? How so?'

'You've got Gareth. You've got this place. You're so lucky. Far luckier than me.' Delyth flings back her head and Melanie sees there are tears in her eyes.

What is this? I don't need this.

'Things haven't always been this good.' Melanie, feeling pressurised to justify her good fortune. 'I've had bad stuff happen too. Things were tough for me as a kid, but I got out of that as soon as I could. And yes, you're right, I have got Gareth,' she lowers her voice, 'and he's totally changed my life.'

'He was married before you, wasn't he? Some girl from university.' Delyth rubs her arms through her man-sized coat. 'I heard you two had an affair.' The tone, now disapproving, is accompanied by a little tap of the gold crucifix. 'He got you pregnant, and that's why he left her.'

'*Erm*, y-yes,' Melanie, gobsmacked by this woman's bluntness. 'How did you know about that?'

'I know lots about your husband he'd rather I didn't.' The eyes narrow into slits. 'And this is a small town, don't forget. Word gets around.'

'I suppose it does.' She frowns when Delyth picks the skin around her thumbs, resists the urge to smack her still.

'Must've taken some doing.'

'What did?' She shrinks from the question; wishes they could talk about something else.

'Him. Gareth. Living a double life. *Cheating*.' The woman holds Melanie's gaze. 'They say a leopard never changes its spots. Don't you worry he could do the same to you?'

'No. I don't.' Melanie, resolute, even though she's squirming inside. 'His first wife didn't make him happy.'

'And you do?'

'Course I do.' An awkward laugh. 'He's the happiest he's ever been. And so am I.' Sensing she is under attack, she's on the verge of asking her to leave when Delyth swings their conversation in another direction.

'I used to work here, for the old owners. Cleaning. Working the bar. That sort of thing.'

'Did you? You never said.'

'I know every inch of this place,' Delyth shares in her girly voice. 'I also know it split them up. I hope the stress of it doesn't split you and Gareth up.'

Melanie isn't sure how to answer, so she doesn't.

'Going to be quite a job.' Delyth looks around. 'And I hope you don't mind me saying, but I think you might have underestimated it. D'you know what it takes to run a catering establishment like this?'

'I've some experience.'

Delyth nods. 'You got someone to run the kitchen? You'll need a proper chef if you want to open a restaurant.'

'I'm running the kitchen. I was a chef before I had Georgie.' It feels good to inform her. 'So, I know what I've taken on. I mean, we know what we've taken on,' she corrects herself.

'I can't imagine you as a chef.' Delyth bestows a watery smile. 'I've seen them programmes on the telly, *MasterChef*, that Gordon Ramsay. It's heavy work. And I don't mean to sound rude, but look at you, you don't look robust enough.'

'Don't I?' She straightens her spine; already head and shoulders above Delyth, she makes herself as tall as she can.

'Yes, I know you're tall,' Delyth sees what Melanie is doing. 'But you're not tough, you're too refined.'

'That's a new one for me. I've never been called *refined* before.'

'Well you are,' Delyth insists. 'And those environments, well, they're all swearing and aggressive.' A shudder. 'Oh, no, I can't imagine you doing that.'

'Hah! I learnt to swear along with the best of them.'

'Did you?' The look is of disgust and comes with another touch of the gold crucifix. 'You worked anywhere I've heard of?'

'The Savoy.'

'The Savoy?' Delyth, her mouth widening into an admiring O. 'I've heard of that.'

'I thought you might.' Melanie, happy to have trumped her. 'I was there for years, ended up in the pastry section. But had to give it up when the—' she tweaks what she's about to say. 'Georgie came along. The shifts weren't too bad, I could manage them, but the commute from Bromley was horrendous.'

'You worked since?'

'Not cheffing, no. What with one thing and another, I ended up at a call centre. Which was pretty dire.' She scrunches up her face. 'It was all I could do after—' Melanie shuts her mouth, she doesn't want this woman knowing everything; although, from the things Georgie said she was saying, she already knows about Sophie and the part Melanie played that meant she never made it to her fifth birthday. 'But anything was better than moping around the house.'

'You're a pastry chef, then? I'd best stop baking you cakes.' A chuckle. 'You're bound to be better at it than me.'

The questions Melanie has about how Delyth knows so much about her dead child must wait for another time. 'Not at all,' she says, instead. 'I don't know anything about traditional Welsh recipes, you're going to have to teach me.' She laughs too, but listening to herself, she's ashamed how false she sounds. 'And anyway, Georgie would never forgive me, she loves your cakes. Oh, is that the time.' A check of her watch. 'I promised her something to eat, didn't I?'

Delyth stands beside her as she sets about preparing her daughter's drink and customary banana sandwiches. Measuring herself against Delyth's mousiness, Melanie feels her personality is too big and her mannerisms too dramatic, in the presence of this diminutive woman.

'Would you like a job, when we open for business?' She makes the offer as she cuts the sandwiches into quarters. 'I'd like it if you did.' She makes eye contact with Delyth. 'What with your experience, and the fact you know this place inside out.' She realises she should run this idea past Gareth first, but because it lifts the mood, she's pleased she suggested it.

'Really?'

'Yes, you'd be a huge asset.'

'Thanks.' Delyth looks delighted. 'I think I'd like that very much.'

'Good.' Melanie rubs breadcrumbs off her hands. 'Oops, hang on. Best not forget to give Georgie one of your cakes.' She puts one on the side plate. 'D'you want to come up to the flat?' she says, licking sugar from her fingers.

They find Georgie, TV on, happily playing with Murray and Slinky in the living room. Legs up on the dimpled sofa lost in her own little world. *Just like your father* — Melanie's realisation, no matter how often it occurs, is always potent.

'Here you go, sweetheart.' She sits beside her, strokes Georgie's and Slinky's heads in turn. She doesn't notice Delyth has taken herself off for a wander, so when she eventually joins her, it's a surprise to find her rootling through the last of the crates yet to unpack.

'Two thousand and two. My final year at school. I'm here somewhere.' Delyth eagerly unfurls a two-foot colour photograph. 'Look, that's me, and there's Gareth. And Tegan.'

This is the most animated Melanie's seen her and,

moving closer, she looks over Delyth's shoulder at the rows of fresh-faced youngsters.

'Gareth keeps threatening to frame it and stick it on the wall,' she says, as Delyth continues to identify various children, their names meaning nothing. Until:

'Erin.' Delyth says and swallows: a dry, wretched sound that is strangled at the back of her throat.

Erin was your sister, wasn't she? Your sister who lies in St David's churchyard.

Melanie's thoughts tumble over themselves as she scrutinises the pretty girl in the second row: a girl already more womanly than her big sister two rows back. In fact, she's more womanly than her sister is today. She would love to ask Delyth to explain what happened to Erin but in the same way she can't ask about Sophie, she doesn't know how to broach such a delicate subject. Decides, if Delyth wants to talk about her sister she will, that it's not for her to go wading in with her size sevens.

'Oh, he was popular with the girls, was Gareth. A real heartthrob., Delyth says, returning from wherever her memories took her. 'We all loved him you know. Even the teachers. He was Head Boy and a real star on the rugby field. He's not changed a bit.'

'Neither have you,' she says because it's true — the woman looks as small and childlike as she did then.

'You wouldn't believe how many women would swap places with you, right now.' Delyth heaves a sigh into the lopsided complement. 'But it must be a worry, what with him being away in London and you stuck out here. Bet he gets up to all sorts.' A sly smile that makes Melanie wonder if the woman wants to deliberately provoke her.

She snatches the photograph. Rolls it up and slides it down inside the crate. 'I just need the bathroom.' Fearful of what she might say, she must remove herself from the frame for a minute. 'I'll see you back downstairs if you want. I'll make us some tea.'

Hiding behind the bathroom door, Melanie waits

until the coast is clear, before edging out on to the landing to check on her daughter.

'Are we having fish and chips when Daddy comes home?' Georgie asks, her plate nearly empty.

'Yes, sweetheart.' Smiling broadly at her child's hearty appetite that is not unlike her own.

'Is Delyth staying?'

'Would you like her to?'

Georgie nods. 'I like her. She's kind. Kind to Murray too.' She flies her toy through the air, making whooshing noises.

'She is kind, isn't she?' Melanie echoes, determined to quash the misgivings she has about the woman. 'You're right, it was very sweet of her to bring Murray home safe. You won't be leaving him behind at school again, will you?'

'No way,' Georgie says.

'There we go then. Are you going to be okay up here on your own? I'll be in the kitchen if you need me.'

'Okay, Mummy,' Georgie, finishing the last quarter of her sandwich, is offering the crust to Murray.

*

'Right then,' Melanie says as she breezes into the kitchen. 'How's about a nice cup of tea?'

She is mid-reach for the kettle before she notices Delyth has removed her coat and is crying. Her thin shoulders shaking beneath her flimsy dress.

'Shit!' Melanie drops the kettle she had been about to fill, down on the counter. 'What the hell are you doing?'

A tap to the elbow and she knocks the carving knife from Delyth's hand. Hears it clatter noisily into the sink. Bright red blood on the white ceramic. Melanie could cry herself. The unit, with its state-of-the-art taps, cost over two-hundred quid and, installed that morning, she's barely had the chance to use it.

Melanie takes a few short breaths and smooths the legs of her jeans. She is scared to touch her and watches blood drip on to the floor. Scarlet coins against the new anti-slip porcelain tiles. She hopes they can be cleaned, in the way the sink can be cleaned, and the floor won't be spoilt before they've even opened for business.

Staring at the dark-blue veins on the insides of Delyth's arms, Melanie realises she has intervened in the nick of time. Any later and this would have been a very different story. She assesses the damage: the neat slices, clean and straight; and makes a small noise as if she too has been wounded. All fingers and thumbs, she sluices, then binds Delyth's arms with the only thing to hand: one of the posh new towels purchased for the bed and breakfast guests who've already paid deposits on reservations that steadily fill the diary. Offering hot, sweet tea, Melanie listens to her own voice, but not to what she is saying, as fresh blood seeps through the christening-white fabric.

'I've-got-nothing-everything-ruined,' Delyth babbles, incoherent, in her little-girl voice. 'My-life-too.'

Melanie bites her lip and guides her silently to a chair. Seated, Delyth peers out through her black swathe of waist-length hair that opens like a pair of curtains. Her eyes, beneath wet lashes, dart around as if she is surprised to find herself here.

With no idea how to respond, Melanie stares at the woman's severe centre parting, at the line of gleaming white scalp and her rough, trembling hands.

'Took-my-dreams-from-me,' Delyth rattles on, hiccupping through tears. 'I-was-the-one-made-sacrifices-look-at-me.'

And Melanie does. She regards the thin gold chain weighted with its crucifix lying heavy on her skin. The spray of freckles travelling over her neck and down inside the ill-fitting dress that has slipped over a shoulder.

'I'm-a-wreck-left-to-rot-in-this-dump-I-could-have-been-someone-too.' A deathly-pale Delyth raises her eyes. A slow movement that gives the impression her hair is too heavy for her neck. 'Help me,' she pleads in the same small voice, but with the added tremor of a punished little girl. 'Please, help me.'

Ticky-ticky-ticky sounds behind them.

'Georgie!' Melanie spins around, expecting to see her child; is relieved the only other witness to this horror is the dog who, sniffing out the coins of blood at their feet, licks them clean. 'Slinky, no!' She shouts and shoves him away with her foot. 'No! Slinky, stop it.'

Appalled by the amount of blood, Melanie blots it with another towel to staunch the flow. Such large, coarse hands for such a tiny woman: a passing thought as she presses a thumb to the crude tourniquet. Shocked by very little nowadays, she doesn't ask for clarification, instead, she is patient and kind, reassuring with the same catalogue of platitudes she dishes out to Georgie when applying plasters to her playground scrapes. It isn't that she doesn't have questions — questions as to why this woman believed it acceptable to violently self-harm while her young child was in an upstairs room — she simply keeps them to herself.

'Stay still for me,' her calm demand and Delyth closes her eyes, then opens one to see what it is Melanie's doing. There is less blood then, the cuts bleed more slowly, contained by the towels. 'You hold it here.' She shows her, then dips away. 'Good boy,' she tells Slinky, relieved to see him now dozing on his bed, she crouches to hunt the skeletons of kitchen units awaiting their doors. 'Bandages, we need bandages . . . where the bloody hell?' She waves her arms around inside the gritty, empty innards. 'I'd swear I put them here, for emergencies . . . and this is a bloody emergency.' Melanie, upright, presses a frantic hand to her brow.

'In the bar.' Delyth, head bowed, face hidden. 'The first aid box always used to be in the bar.'

'I'll go and look. Don't move.' *Don't drip any more*

of your blood in my kitchen . . . her thoughts trailing behind her as she runs up the stone steps.

She finds a rusted red tin with a cross painted on in Tippex. Inside, dressings, a sterile bandage still in its wrapper, a tube of antiseptic. Not her first aid box, but it will do.

Back in the kitchen, a rapid wash of hands, then she sits beside Delyth and gingerly unwraps the towels. Nasty and raw, the cuts are dreadful, but she gives nothing away as she smears on antiseptic cream, her movements small and gentle, mindful of the woman's winces, her hissing noises.

'We should get you to hospital. Get you checked out.' Melanie applies the squares of dressing, secures them with strips of bandage.

'I've-got-nothing-ruined-I'm-ruined.' Delyth sobs through words Melanie can't sew into any kind of meaning. 'My life,' she says, tears wetting her cheeks. 'Life-over-took-my-dreams.'

She stops what she's doing to look at the moving mouth and reminds herself this woman was once a child, that she wouldn't have always been this way. Life, with its cruel twists, is what's brought her here. Delyth would have been happy once, there would have been moments, as Melanie herself had moments, when she would have laughed a carefree laugh. But in the same way it's hard to look out on a winter landscape and imagine the flowers of summer, so it is with Delyth Powell.

'I learnt this at Girl Guides,' her turn to prattle, but only because she can't make sense of what Delyth's saying. 'Never needed it until now, but there's a first time for everything.'

Close enough to see the striations on Delyth's forehead, the light from the single ceiling bulb reflected in the curve of her eye, Melanie proceeds to bind the wounds with the length of bandage. Delyth has stopped her gabbling and is now regarding her with the quick, dark eyes of a scolded child.

Finished, she gets up and steps aside. Wanting the woman to settle, she sets about making tea but gets no further than filling the kettle. It's difficult to focus, the questions she wants answers to buzz like flies. Why has she done this to herself? How come she knows so much about Sophie? And if that is her sister's grave in the churchyard, then what happened to her? But now isn't the time, so it's without speaking that Melanie retrieves a bucket from the bar, fills it with hot, soapy water and gets down on her hands and knees to clean Delyth's blood from the floor.

'I've got to take you to A&E.' She straightens up and drags the back of an arm over her perspiring forehead. 'We should let a professional take a look at you.'

'I don't want to go to hospital.' The small voice is surprisingly assertive. 'I'm so embarrassed.' Delyth is crying again. Melanie drops her cloth into the cloudy pink water and goes and puts an arm around her.

'There, there,' she comforts. 'It's all right.'

Delyth tilts forward. 'I'm sorry, I shouldn't have done that here. In your home. Can you ever forgive me?'

'It's okay. There, there.' Melanie repeats herself. What else is there to say? All words are inadequate. 'You're in a very bad place.'

'I am, but I shouldn't have put you in this position.'

'Would you like a shot of something? How about a whisky? I could certainly do with one,' she says, emptying the bloody water away and washing her hands.

'No, I never drink. Not alcohol.'

'I'll make us a pot of tea?' She fits the lid of the electric kettle back on and notices the tremor in her hands; she could think Delyth is more in control than she is.

Melanie's mobile rings from the back pocket of her jeans. She tugs it out, looks at the screen. 'It's Gareth,' she says out loud. 'I'd better answer it.'

'Don't tell him I'm here.' Delyth presses her lips together when more tears sprout. 'And please, please, don't tell him what I've done,' she implores. 'You won't, will you?

Promise me.'

Melanie promises and passes her a box of tissues before activating the call.

'*Gareth*,' she exhales and watches Delyth blow her nose, dab the skin under her eyes, sees her face is red and blotchy from crying. 'Hi, love. Are you far away?' She returns the tissues to the side. 'That soon? Wow, you've made great time.' She shoots a look at Delyth. 'Yes, okay, I'll nip out for them. Same as usual? Great, see you in a bit. Drive carefully.' And she hangs up. 'That was Gareth,' she says as if Delyth didn't know. 'He's on his way home.'

At this, Delyth springs upright. Wobbly on her feet, she reaches for the tabletop to steady herself.

'Whoa,' Melanie leaps forward. 'You're not going anywhere. Sit. Sit down.' And she guides her back to the chair.

'But I've got to get home.' Delyth scrunches the soggy tissue in her fist.

'No, you don't. I'm sure your mum and Andrew can survive without you for an hour or two. Just stay there.'

'No, it isn't that.' Delyth frowns. 'I don't think it's a good idea if I'm here when Gareth gets home.'

'But you're in no fit state to drive.' Melanie switches the kettle on. 'At least stay for a cup of something, get your strength back. One of us can run you home later.'

'No, no, no.' Delyth looks frightened. 'You don't understand. I don't want to see him. I only came because I knew he wouldn't be here.'

'Oh, dear, please don't stress yourself.' Melanie is fearful of upsetting the woman further. 'But honestly, you can't leave yet; not after . . . after that.' She waves at Delyth's bandaged arms. All the things she wants to say, like: *you might try it again and I'd never forgive myself if you didn't make it home in one piece*, dissolve in her mouth. 'Please, stay. Just for a while,' she urges, more for herself. 'I'm sure Gareth wouldn't mind you being here.'

And Delyth feeds her a look that says they both

know this isn't true.

SIXTEEN

'Come on, Georgie.' Melanie grabs her parka and handbag from the peg on the door. 'Daddy will be here soon; we'd better go and fetch our fish and chips.'

'I can look after her,' Delyth, tears dry, her deathly pallor less so, is sitting up at the kitchen table with Georgie. Mid-jigsaw, Delyth is helping fit the background together.

'You don't mind?' Melanie isn't sure, but she can't say she doesn't trust her.

'I don't mind.' Delyth, quite bold, appears to have recovered from the trauma. If it weren't for the bandages, Melanie could pretend nothing had gone on here.

'I'll be about twenty minutes.' She darts a look at her watch, then to Delyth and Georgie; decides how well these two get on.

'But are you sure you want fish and chips?' Delyth, sliding another piece of the sky into place, doesn't look up.

'Sorry, you what?'

'I know you don't need to watch your figure, it's not that. You've a shape like a proper woman, not like me.' A timid laugh. 'I've never had the shape men like. Never had much that men like, truth be told.' Melanie senses Delyth's gaze travel the length of her. 'But *fish and chips*? Haven't you anything better to eat.'

'*Erm.*' Melanie is stumped. 'Well, I suppose there's things in the freezer, bits and bobs in the fridge.'

'Because it's not good for this little one,' Delyth

interrupts, a sidelong smile at Georgie. 'Living on takeaways and ready meals all the time.'

'You are right.' She scans the half-finished kitchen. 'Ordinarily, I'd cook myself, this takeaway thing's only for the short term.'

'Oh, don't take any notice of me, Georgie's your daughter.' Delyth wrinkles her nose. 'You do what you think best.'

'Thing is, we're running low on everything. Me and Gareth, we're going to do a proper shop tomorrow.' Melanie opens the fridge — its up-to-date replacement is another thing they're waiting for. 'I suppose I could make us a salad.' She riffles the scanty contents. 'Look, I've got a bag of lettuce leaves and some tomatoes, half a red pepper. Oh, and here's a couple of onions.'

'There you go then,' Delyth, looking satisfied inside the cheap material of her dress.

'But it isn't enough.' Melanie holds out her hands, shows the meagre offerings. 'We'll need something hot.' She taps a finger against her mouth, thinking. 'Hang on. I've got a lasagne in the freezer. How about that?'

'Shop bought?'

'From the supermarket. I only got it for emergencies.'

Delyth lifts then drops her thin shoulders.

'Might it be healthier than fish and chips?'

'I suppose.' It seems this is all her dinner guest is prepared to say, before refocusing on the cartwheel Georgie's completed at the bottom of the jigsaw. 'Clever girl,' Delyth congratulates. 'You can piece the horse together now.'

'Lasagne it is then.' Melanie slips out of her coat, returns it and her handbag to the peg behind the door. 'Won't be a tic.'

'If you want,' Delyth starts, an engine warming up. 'I could make you something next week. Do you like casseroles?' she directs her question to Georgie, who blithely grins her reply; the idea of something homecooked obviously appealing. 'I thought you would. What would you like, chicken, some beef?'

'Oh, now,' Melanie steps in. 'That's very kind of you, Delyth, but really, no. No, you mustn't, you can't afford to feed us as well.'

'It's no bother. While I'm doing for us, I can do extra for you. Casseroles are mostly vegetables and I grow them in the garden. How about it, Georgie?' Delyth claps her hands, then winces, forgetting for a moment how sore her arms are.

'Yes, please,' Georgie grins.

'It's not that I'm—' whatever Melanie had been about to say, evaporates before it forms.

'No need for you to feel bad,' Delyth reads her mind. 'You do your best, but a microwave is next to useless. Look at it as me helping you out.' Another smile for Georgie, who is now holding Delyth's hand. 'Because it's important this little one gets proper, homecooked food, isn't it, *cariad*?'

Melanie grabs the bloodied towels and leaves Delyth and Georgie to it. Flicking the light switch, she descends the stone steps into the basement to where the new chest freezers and catering-sized cooler are. Cold down here, she shivers, despite her numerous layers. She catches a slice of her reflection in the side of the cooler, decides she should go and tidy herself up for Gareth; at least put some lippy on and pull a brush through her hair, especially now it's not as styled as it used to be.

The thought of three nights and two whole days with him lifts her heart. But remembering the woman sitting in her kitchen and the terrible thing she tried to do, her mood takes a dive. Melanie drops the towels into the stainless-steel sink, runs the hot tap and sprinkles on washing powder. She knows this is futile, that the white fabric is ruined. Experience tells her no matter how many times she might scrub them, she won't be able to wash away the stains. They will haunt the weft and warp like rose-coloured phantoms. They will bloom and swell with each fresh soaking. Poor Delyth, she must be dreadfully unhappy to have done that to herself and in such a small window of time. She can't have been on her own for more than ten minutes. As someone whose own life has brought her down low, so low there was a time she believed it wasn't worth living either, Melanie forgives Delyth's prickliness, her resentfulness, and wonders if there's anything she can do to help her. Letting Delyth cook them a meal might be a start. Maybe this is her way of apologising, because what she did, with Georgie dangerously close by, was a desperate act by anyone's standards. Yes, Melanie decides, what harm could it do?

She leaves the towels to soak and, drying her hands on her jeans, lifts the lid of the freezer to hunt its frosty innards. Moving the bags of blackberries, she and Georgie picked on that sunny afternoon, she finds what she's looking for. Light off, she hurries up the steps, the family-size lasagne cold between finger and thumb and hears Georgie's excited squeals as she approaches the kitchen.

'Gareth! You're home.' Melanie puts down the frozen ready meal and throws her arms around him. But wooden beneath her embrace, she can tell he's not happy.

'Daddy's home! Daddy's home!' Georgie, joyful, has abandoned her jigsaw to dance about the kitchen, pausing to include the dog who, wagging and excited, looks as pleased with Gareth being home as she is.

'What's going on here then?' He passes Melanie a bunch of roses and cocks his head in Delyth's direction. 'You didn't say we had visitors.' And leaning in, as if to kiss Melanie, he whispers through clenched teeth: 'What the fuck is she doing here?'

'Daddy. Daddy.' Georgie hurtles towards him and

Melanie stands aside, watches Gareth lift his daughter up by her middle.

'How's my best, best girl, then.' He kisses her, then sets her down.

'I'll tell you later.' Melanie says, noticing the muscles tighten in his jaw.

'Flowers, eh.' Delyth remarks as Melanie brushes past to place them in the sink. 'He either really loves you, or he's guilty of something.'

'I'm sorry?' She half-turns, unsure if she heard correctly. 'The roses are beautiful, thanks, love.' She calls over to her husband and, stroking the vermillion-red petals, tries not to think of Delyth's blood.

'I see they've finished the floor.' Gareth shrugs out of his suit jacket, folds it over the back of a chair. 'Looks fab.' He removes his tie and undoes his top button, completely blanking Delyth.

'The Belfast sink's in. Look.' Melanie runs the cold tap, hunts for scissors in the rack on the drainer. 'And you want to have a look at the restaurant. They've put the panels in and plastered the alcove.'

'It's coming on great.' He rubs a hand over the stubble she knows he would have shaved clean that morning, inspects his palm as if to find its inky blackness to have been transferred there.

'I've made a start on the website too.' Melanie unwraps the roses, lifts one to her nose to inhale the perfume that isn't there. 'Loaded up those brilliant views we took the day we arrived.'

'The website? Well done.'

'Everything's progressing nicely. Shame about the stove. We could cancel if we hadn't paid a walloping deposit.'

'I don't know what you expect me to do about it?' Gareth, unusually offhand, and she can tell it's because of what he's come home to. 'I've got my work in London.'

'I know that. I was only giving you an update.' Self-conscious in front of their unexpected guest, she glances at Delyth who is doing a noble job of pretending the jigsaw is more entertaining than the conversation she and Gareth are having. 'These roses are gorgeous,' she returns to her stem-trimming. 'I'll get a vase.' And jogging away, Gareth is swift on her heels.

'*Well?* What the fuck's she doing here?' he hisses, angry in the unlit bar. 'It's just supposed to be me, you and Georgie. Christ, Mel,' he grits his teeth. 'What the hell did you have to invite her for? I've not seen you for a bloody fortnight.'

'I know.' She puts an arm around his waist, feels him stiffen and pull away. 'I didn't invite her.' She lets go of him to tug open the swollen cupboard door, wrinkles her nose at the musty smell. 'She called round with Murray. Georgie had left him at school.' She finds a vase. 'I was so grateful, I invited her in for a look around, said she could stay for dinner.' Melanie leaves it there, remembering the promise she made to Delyth.

Gareth grunts. 'I'll fetch us a bottle of wine, what d'you want?'

'I don't mind,' she says before heading back to her roses, placing them in the centre of the table once they've been arranged. 'You'll need to clear that away before we eat.' She explains to Georgie who is fitting together the horse's rump.

'I don't want to.' Her daughter spreads her little hands in a brave attempt to protect the half-finished jigsaw.

'You have to, we need the table, sweetheart.'

'Why are there two of our new guest towels soaking in the sink downstairs?' Gareth, back from the cellar, a bottle of Shiraz in his hand.

'There was a little accident.' Melanie and Delyth swap glances.

'Looks like blood. Did one of Bryn's men injure themselves?'

'Georgie, can you please do as you're told and tidy

that away,' Melanie, fiercer than she means to be; she'd forgotten about the towels.

'Mel? What's gone on?'

'It's nothing. I'll tell you later.'

'And where's our fish and chips? I'm starving after that drive. I had bugger all for lunch, deliberately.'

Melanie, peeling the first of two onions, blinks through wet lashes. 'I thought we should try to eat a little healthier, so we're having lasagne tonight.' She lifts her hand, shiny with onion juice, jabs the sharpened stump of her paring knife at the microwave. 'I'm making a salad to go with it. We had loads to use up in the fridge, it'll only go to waste.'

'What? I thought we agreed.' Gareth drags his mouth south and wanders over to peer through the steamed-up glass at their cellophane-wrapped dinner. 'There's no way that's going to stretch to four. Let me fetch some chips to go with it? Yeah,' his face brightening. 'Chips will do it.'

'Gareth?' Melanie wipes her eyes on a cloth, looks at Delyth again. 'We're not having chips, okay?' The bowl of salad finished, she puts it, and the cruet, on the table. 'Georgie?'

'Yes, Mummy.'

'Stop that now and put it away, please. I've asked you once.'

'Bread, then? A basket of bread.' Gareth suggests. 'Want me to cut some?'

'Sorry, bit stale. What's left is only good for toast. No, come on, there'll be plenty.'

'You are kind but,' Delyth thrusts herself back from the table and makes to go. 'I'm just in the way. I don't have to stay.'

'No, you don't, do you?' Gareth snarls.

'Yes, you do. Sit.' Melanie insists, cutting him off. 'Now, who's for wine?' she asks, ignoring the black look Gareth is giving her. 'I know I could do with some.'

Delyth seals a hand over the top of the long-stemmed glass Melanie sets before her. 'Just water, please. I never touch the stuff. You wouldn't neither if you'd seen what it's done to my Mam.'

'Christ, woman, it's only a glassful. We're not asking you to drink the whole bloody bottle.'

Melanie sees Delyth touch the crucifix at her neck. 'Gareth? Not in front of Georgie.' The excuse of protecting her daughter's sensitivities allows her to shield Delyth's too. But looking around, Georgie isn't here; she's packed away the jigsaw and is returning it to her room.

'Oops, *sor-ry*.' Gareth, mocking, focuses on Delyth for the first time. 'What've you been doing to yourself?' He waves the corkscrew at her arms. 'You're bleeding.'

Melanie, up behind him with cutlery and placemats, sees that blood has seeped through the bandages.

Delyth lowers her eyes.

'What's up? Cat got your tongue,' Gareth persists.

'Leave it, love.' Melanie warns and leads him away once she's set the table. 'Delyth's fine now.' The last thing she wants is him upsetting her, the woman's fragile enough as it is.

Gareth rolls his shirt sleeves to the elbow and pours wine into two glasses. He holds one to the light and turns away from Delyth to take a mouthful. 'Bloody nutcase,' he mutters, swirling a finger at his temple.

'Oh, Georgie, there you are.' Melanie calls exaggeratedly to drown her husband out. 'Good girl for putting your jigsaw away. Come on, you sit up next to Delyth, dinner won't be a minute.'

At the ping of the microwave, Melanie retrieves their meal. She must agree with Gareth, it doesn't look appetising and, tearing off the cellophane cover, finds it smells little better. Why was she swayed by Delyth, why didn't she just stick to the plan and get them a takeaway? They eat in awkward silence; Melanie listens to the scraping of knives and forks against the cold plates that, without a stove, she couldn't even set to warm before serving.

'Remind me again, why we're not having fish and chips?' Gareth drains his glass, pours another. 'Because I don't know about you lot, but this tastes revolting.' He lifts the sodden layers of pasta with his fork, rakes through the unappetising filling, then pushes his plate away. Melanie, watching, wishes he wouldn't, Georgie copies all his bad habits.

'Delyth was saying, and I agree with her.' She notices her daughter has left most of hers too. 'Living off takeaways isn't good for us, never mind Georgie.'

'What! So, we're eating this rubbish because of her?' Looking outraged, he treats Delyth to a good, hard stare.

Melanie puts down her knife and lays a restraining hand on Gareth's hairy forearm. 'We'll have fish and chips tomorrow. Now can we please talk about something else?'

But there doesn't appear to be anything else to talk about, so no one does, for quite some time.

'Who's for ice cream?' Melanie asks while she clears the table. Is surprised that even her daughter declines. 'Are you feeling all right, sweetheart? It's not like you to turn down pudding.'

'I'm all right.' Georgie says, but she doesn't sound sure.

'I'll feed this to the dog, shall I?' Melanie nudges Gareth.

'If you think he'll eat it.' He curls his lip.

'Can I get down now?' Georgie asks. 'I want to go to bed.'

'You tired, baby?' Melanie kisses her child's soft little brow. 'Do you want Daddy to come and read you a story?'

Georgie nods and slips from her chair. A stroke of the dog to let him know she's going upstairs, and he slinks away after her.

'Mind if I use your bathroom?' Delyth rises to her feet.

'Course not. You know where it is,' Melanie smiles.

'Are you going to tell me what's been going on?' Gareth demands as soon as Delyth has gone. 'What are those bandages for?'

'I don't know.' The lie is hard in her mouth: treacherous, the ultimate betrayal. She doesn't understand why she should feel protective towards Delyth; yes, she promised not to tell, but she's made bigger promises to Gareth. Melanie gulps a mouthful of wine, darts a look at the eight-piece knife set in their stunning acacia block and swallows. 'I think she hurt herself at work.'

'I still don't know why you had to ask her to stay for dinner, or how you let her persuade you against getting a takeaway.' Gareth puts an arm around her. 'That was one of the worst meals I've ever had.'

'I'm sorry.'

He hugs her tighter, whispers into her ear. 'As long as you make sure it doesn't happen again.'

'What? — giving you a horrible meal?' she teases.

'No, silly. Inviting her round here.'

'Oh, Gareth, she's all right.' Melanie thinks of the offer of a job she gave Delyth earlier and pulls away.

'Why does she keep calling round, what does she want? The creepy cow.'

'*Shhh.*' A finger to her lips. 'Keep your voice down.'

'God, I hate that look she gives. I always did.' He ignores Melanie's warning. 'All *woe-with-me.* I don't buy any of it.' Gareth makes a fist, punches his other palm. Melanie finds it alarming. 'And neither should you, you don't know her like I do.'

'Tell me what happened with her, then. It's not my fault if you won't talk to me about it.'

'Why isn't it enough for you to do as I say about this? I've asked you to stay away from her, why d'you have to keep on with your bloody questions. She's off her head, Mel; you only have to look at her to know that.' His tone

111

isn't one she has ever heard him use before and she doesn't much like it.

'Gareth, for pity's sake.' She flicks her eyes to the doorway, is relieved to find it empty. 'She's had a rough time and she's got three different jobs and an elderly mother to look after. Who, for the record, sounds a bit of a nightmare. And she's her boy to bring up, don't forget.'

Gareth whips back his head. 'That's another thing I can't get my head around. That kid of hers, he's going on seventeen, yeah? Well,' a cruel laugh, 'that would've made her eighteen and still at school when she got pregnant. And I don't know anyone who'd have been desperate enough to shag her.'

'God, you're vile. Why can't you just be nice, she's not had any of the chances you have.'

A rustling behind them.

'*Shhh*, she's coming,' Melanie cautions.

'I'd better get going,' Delyth, uncertain from the threshold. 'Thanks for the lovely meal.' She addresses Melanie while sneaking a look at Gareth.

'Oh, it was far from lovely.' A forced laugh as she slips to her feet. 'When we've got something to cook on, you'll have to come over for a proper meal.' She sees Gareth open his mouth, about to speak. A touch of his shoulder stops him.

'Well, thanks anyway.' With timid little movements, Delyth retrieves her coat from where she left it and slips it on.

She looks pathetic, her arms aren't even long enough for the sleeves and, with a rush of pity, Melanie dives forward to give her a hug. But the disconcerting frailty of bones beneath the waxy material has her pulling back, fearful of crushing her.

'Come on, I'll see you out.'

'No need,' Delyth lifts a hand. 'I know my way.'

SEVENTEEN

Minutes later, Melanie, elbow-deep in suds, is passing Gareth the plates for him to dry and put away.

'You don't like Delyth at all, do you?' Her question bounces against the kitchen walls.

'No, I bloody don't. And I don't want her having anything to do with our daughter, either.'

'Why not? What's she ever done to you?' She runs the cold tap; the spray soaks her cuffs. 'It's not like you to take against someone like this.'

'I don't trust her.'

'On what grounds?' Melanie passes him a fork.

Gareth wipes it, puts it away, then reaches for his wine. 'Because she's a creepy cow. Come on, you have to admit it.'

'I think she's unhappy.'

'*Huh*,' he sneers. 'She's a moaner, that's what she is. D'you know what we used to call her at school?'

Melanie shakes her head, of course she doesn't.

'Cry baby. Cry baby bunting, daddy's gone a-hunting . . .' he trails the nursery rhyme he used to sing to the twins when they were babies, to the bin and back. It has a sinister ring now and tarnishes her cherished memory. 'Suits her, don't you think?'

'Maybe she had something to cry about.' Melanie thinks of what Delyth told her about her home life, her mother's dependency, her financial worries, the feeling life has passed her by. Circumstances, she believes, that led her to do what she did in their kitchen sink.

'Been feeding you some sob story, has she?'

'She mentioned stuff, yes.'

'Don't get sucked in, Mel. *Please*.' Gareth kisses her. 'You're not her bloody social worker.'

'I don't encourage her; I was only being nice. I can't help it if I find it hard to say no to her, I feel sorry for her.'

'She's like a stone in your shoe,' he snaps. 'Yes, she's small and doesn't take up much space, but she's bloody irritating and there's no ignoring her.'

'You did a pretty good impression of ignoring her,' she reminds him, rinsing the washing up bowl and turning it upside down.

'Why are you defending her?' he shouts. 'Taking her side over mine?'

'Because she hasn't done anything wrong.' Melanie dries her hands.

'You're too trusting, that's your trouble; always seeing the good in people.'

'Until I'm shown otherwise.' She stands her ground. 'Delyth's been kind to me and Georgie, baking us cakes and stuff—'

'That woman bakes you cakes?' Gareth cuts in.

'Yeah, I told you on the phone. She brought some round the other day. Georgie loves her cooking.'

'You let Georgie eat them! I don't want Georgie eating anything that woman's touched. And anyway,' Gareth pauses, something occurring to him: 'Why's she doing that, what does she want? She's not the type to do anyone a favour and not expect something in return.'

'She doesn't want *anything*,' Melanie glares at him. 'She's just being neighbourly. She knows we've only got a microwave—' she closes her mouth, reluctant to rake through the reasons again. Instead, she attempts to shift their discussion in a more positive direction. 'Isn't the kitchen's looking great? I'm glad you love the floor.' A blaze of Delyth's blood. 'And this sink and drainer are the business.' Another image of the bright, red streaks against the white ceramic.

Gareth dries a spoon, holds it up to his face and scowls at his distorted reflection. He puts the spoon away. 'I still don't know why she had to stay for dinner. You knew how much I was looking forward to coming home, I've missed you and Georgie so much. And I end up having to sit there with that muppet, dictating what we eat, the cheeky cow. She hardly said a word and I don't see why I should have to make the effort after the week I've had. Certainly not with her. Christ, Mel, talk about awkward, you could have cut the atmosphere with a knife.'

'All right, I've said I'm sorry.' Melanie winces at his choice of words.

'Just for the record—'

'A broken record,' she butts in.

'Just for the record,' Gareth finishes what he wants to say, 'that was a shit evening, so please don't invite her again. *Okay*?'

Melanie makes a sound, audible enough to communicate without words, how unreasonable she thinks he is being.

'Look,' he drops the tea towel on the side, puts his hands around her waist. 'I'm sorry if I sound hard,' he pulls her towards him. 'But I just don't like her, I never did. Can't you see it? She's a bloody weirdo.' He drags the back of his hand over her cheek: tender, loving. 'She'll only drag you down and you've been doing so well these past few months, weaning yourself off the tablets. You get involved with her and I'm frightened you'll spiral down again. She's bad news, trust me. And this is supposed to be a new start for us.'

But I'm already involved, she thinks, looking over his shoulder, wondering again why Delyth chose their kitchen to do what she did in and what Gareth would do if he knew.

'Oh, come on. I think you're painting an overly-black picture here,' she says. 'She's nice. Bit lonely perhaps, poor thing. Why have you got such a problem with her? She went out of her way to bring Murray back.'

'Greeks bearing gifts.'

Melanie rolls her eyes. 'Talking of gifts, are you going to tell me what she meant in her card? I know I've asked you before, but I want to know.'

'I told you, I haven't the foggiest.'

'I don't believe you. Tell me. What did she mean she was good at *keeping secrets* — what secrets?'

'I've said, I don't know. How can I? I've not seen the woman for years.'

Melanie gives him a look, a look that says she's not going to let him get away that lightly.

'I don't know,' he says, still holding her tight. 'I might have been smoking at school, or she saw me mitching and covered for me. Something childish like that, so what? She's still living in the past, a past she wants to relive now I've come back.' He tugs her closer, gives her the trust-me blue of his eyes.

'There must be more to it than that.' Melanie removes his hands from her hips and steps away. 'She wouldn't still be going on about not telling teacher on you.'

'Not if it's still a big issue in her mind,' he argues. 'It's obvious she's never grown up, never moved on. She's still living with her mother. She's just a silly little village girl, who'd rather wallow in self-pity than pull herself together. I'm sorry, but—' he must clock the look Melanie gives and so softens what he was about to say. 'She's her own worst enemy. It's why people round here don't bother with her anymore, they're sick of her moaning.'

'How would you know what people round here think, you've been gone from the place for years?'

Gareth doesn't answer.

'And anyway, that's not what I heard,' she informs him. 'So far as I can tell, you're the only one who's got a problem with Delyth. Others I've spoken to think she's nice.'

'Yeah, what others? Who've you been talking to?' He looks vaguely alarmed.

'Why are you so bothered?'

'Who've you been talking to?'

'Your sister.'

'*Huh*, like she'd know.' He looks relieved. 'Butter wouldn't melt. Lovely little Delyth. She's hoodwinked the pair of you, hasn't she?'

'Okay,' Melanie sighs. 'Then it's everyone else against you, Gareth, is it? Except it's the majority that wins, I'd say.'

'Look, I don't give a damn about anyone else, I don't like her. And I don't want her coming here pestering you.' That tone again, the one she doesn't like. 'And I don't want her anywhere near our daughter, okay? She's not all there.' He taps his temple again.

'Ooo, you're an obstinate sod, Gareth Sayer.' Melanie, aware that the precious hours they have together are ticking away. 'For what it's worth, I reckon Delyth Powell's still got a crush on you.'

'You what?'

'Yes,' she grins. 'I have got eyes in my head. I saw the way she was looking at you.'

'What are you on about? She *didn't* look at me, that was the problem. It's why our evening was so bloody excruciating.'

'Exactly.' Melanie rinses out the sink, watches water swirl down the plughole. 'That's how I know, because she couldn't look you in the eye.'

'Daft bugger, you are.'

'Tegan said she used to follow you around at school.' Melanie kisses him. 'Is that the Big Secret? Are you afraid to admit it because you think I'm going to be jealous?'

'And would you be?'

'Maybe,' she says, playful.

'*Mm*, you smell good.' His lips against her ear, the

brush of stubble on her cheek. 'Have I told you how gorgeous you're looking?'

'No, because I don't, I look a mess,' she titters, chin in neck, strangely shy all of a sudden.

'You do. And I'd have told you earlier had we not been entertaining the Grim Reaper.'

She giggles some more.

'. . . *she's nearly a laugh . . . but she's really a cry,*' he mumbles.

'You what?'

'Pink Floyd lyric. Sums that nutter up perfect. Anyway, never mind about her,' She feels the weight of his gaze. 'You're looking the best I've seen you since—' he pulls up, skims around the elephant in the room, the unspoken loss they share their lives with.

And it is her turn to look at him. To wonder why, when their lives and experiences are as entwined as the roots of a tree, there should be this glaring no-go area in their marriage? The one thing she can never bring up for fear of distressing him, even though there are times, like now, when she wishes they could talk. Of her. Their dead daughter. But Gareth asked her, didn't he? He asked her to leave Sophie alone, to stop mentioning her, to lay her to rest; saying this was the only chance they had of living what remained of their lives. For Georgie's sake, he said. These are her thoughts, and his too, she guesses. And so much of her wants to tell him it's wrong to box Sophie away. But then his sorrow is different to hers, he's not looking for forgiveness for the part he played. Unlike Melanie, Gareth isn't beleaguered by self-hatred and remorse, or the stomach-churning memory of that moment she let go of Sophie's hand.

'It's because I'm happy,' she says simply. What else can she say? She hasn't seen him for two weeks and, like him, is reluctant to talk of sad things. 'I've been feeling loads better.'

'It shows.'

'It's being out in the fresh air. All the walking I'm doing, I love it. My therapist said that being close to nature was one of the best things for depression, and I do feel brighter, out with Slinky, the scenery's breath-taking. I know it's been a long, slow road for me and how patient you've been, but really,' she wraps her arms about him again, wanting his solidity as she nuzzles the curls that grow over his collar. 'Coming here's the best decision we've ever made.'

'Mummy. Mummy.' Georgie, barefoot in pyjamas and holding Murray, looks up at them through sleepy eyes.

'Darling. What's up?' Melanie releases Gareth and bends to cuddle her. 'Did you have one of your bad dreams?' She tests Georgie's temperature with the back of her hand.

'I've got a bad tummy.'

'Oh, sweetheart. Show me where it hurts.'

Georgie presses her abdomen. 'I feel a bit sick.'

'A bit sick? Oh, baby. You do look pale. You've probably picked up a bug at school.' Melanie scoops her in her arms, shoots a look of concern to Gareth. 'Daddy make you cocoa? Settle your tummy.' A puff of her daughter's breath, sweet as a lamb's, against her neck.

Gareth nods and reaches for a mug, then inside the fridge for the milk.

'Come on, little one. Let's get you tucked up in the warm. Dear me, your feet are freezing.' She folds her palm over her daughter's little foot. 'Get you nice and cosy and read you a story, shall we?' She feels her daughter's nod, the weight of her skull against her collarbone. 'Thanks, love,' she turns to Gareth. 'Are you happy to close up down here, bring Georgie's cocoa and my wine up?'

'No probs. Where's the Calpol?' He drapes the damp tea towel over the curve of the sparkling chrome taps to dry.

'In the bathroom. Can you dig it out?'

With Georgie in her arms, Melanie swaps the

119

brightness of the kitchen for the dark bar. Empty but for its moon-washed walls, the ochre light leaking from the flat upstairs enough to go by. A scuttling sound and a rasp of rubble against the concrete floor. She spins around. Alarmed. At first, she thinks it is Sophie's ghost she sees: so small, so pale; the way she often glimpses her. But this isn't Sophie. This is Delyth. Her crucifix glinting through the indeterminate light.

She's heard it all . . . every single word.

Melanie's realisation is not a comfortable one in the tightening seconds she scrabbles over the contents of her and Gareth's conversation. Feeling queasy and holding on to Georgie who grows heavier by the second, Melanie flicks the light switch to extinguish the gloom.

But Delyth has gone. And rushing after her, desperate to put things right, by the time she reaches the door, all that remains of Delyth is the sting of her Defender's exhaust polluting the night-time air.

EIGHTEEN

'Mummy, Mummy. Look!' Georgie, up at her bedroom window, gazes out on the garden. The sea they both know is out there has been lost to a ribbon of mist. 'It's like a fairyland.'

Half-term has crept up on them already and they wake to their first hard, blue frost.

'It's beautiful,' Melanie, halfway through making her daughter's bed, looks up. 'We're going to need our hats and gloves today.' She strokes the dog's velvety ears, then tucks the duvet in at the bottom. 'I'll have to dig them out.' She relinquishes Slinky to test the radiator, that for once doesn't scorch her hand.

Minutes later, sitting side by side at the pine kitchen table, sharing a breakfast of mashed banana on toast with the dog, they map out their day.

'How's about this for an idea—' Melanie projects her voice over the clatter and bang of workmen. 'What if I,' she begins, sprinkling cinnamon over the banana and cutting the round of wholemeal into triangles, just how Georgie likes it. 'What if I come and collect you from Nia's at two.' She puts the plate in front of her daughter and licks her fingers. 'We could drive to Pwllglas?' Georgie is gathering the dead rose petals that have dropped to the table. 'You like Pwllglas, don't you?' The kettle comes to the boil and she springs up to pour a little water into the teapot, swills it round.

'I'd say that was perfect timing,' Bryn's voice from

the doorway, his head made white by plaster dust. 'You making a brew?'

'Hi, Bryn. How's it going?' She pours on water, squeezes the goodness from the tea bags.

'Great,' he says, looking far from great himself: his red-rimmed eyes and unkempt beard tell her he isn't getting much sleep.

'Ffion still teething?' she asks, reaching for another mug from the hooks above the new marble-effect work surface.

'How can you tell?' he yawns. 'Tegan's worse. She won't let me get up to see to the baby in the night.'

'It does get better,' she glances at Georgie.

'Tom's worked out how to control the heating, so you won't be needing a new boiler.'

'Gareth will be pleased.' They trade smiles and Melanie hands him a mug of tea.

'Ta.' Bryn blows on it, takes a sip. 'Think you've got a mouse problem. Not surprising in a place like this, but you'll need to sort it before you open.'

'*Mice?*'

'Yep,' he grins, drinks more of his tea. 'Oh, nearly forgot,' he wipes his mouth with his hand. 'Tegan told me to say that we're house-sitting for Bronwyn next week and you're to come over.'

'Where's she galivanting off to?'

'Some women's institute trip to . . .' Bryn screws up his face. 'France, or Finland? Sorry, can't remember.'

'Nice for her.'

'Nicer for us,' he winks, mischievous.

'I'll give Tegan a bell.'

'You do that. She's finding it a bit hard stuck with Ffion all day on her own. Anyway,' he jabs a thumb at the bar. 'Best get on with it.'

Melanie watches him go, the turn-ups on his overalls dragging through the rubble.

'Right, little one,' she pours herself a mug of tea and

sits back down. 'Where were we?'

'You said we could go to Pwllglas,' Georgie plays with her food.

'That's right.' Melanie, her mind wandering, fearful her daughter might be suffering from another tummy ache. 'We could see what's on at the cinema.'

Her daughter pushes her half-finished breakfast away — a habit of her father's she's copied despite Melanie's best efforts.

'Come on, eat up.' Melanie slides the plate towards her and brushes crumbs from her top. 'You'll never have curls like your Daddy if you don't eat your crusts.'

'But I don't want curls.' Georgie twirls her heavy plaits over her hand.

'I was desperate for curly hair when I was little,' Melanie bites off a corner of toast, chews it slowly. 'A friend of mine gave me a perm once. That was a shocker, I can tell you.'

'Why aren't there any pictures of you when you were little?' Georgie, round-eyed, picks through the banana. 'Nanna Bronwyn's got loads of Daddy and Auntie Tegan.'

Melanie takes another bite of toast and thinks how best to explain. 'I suppose,' she swallows, 'there wasn't anyone around to take them.'

'Didn't your mummy have a camera?'

'No, cameras were too expensive.'

'Couldn't she have taken some on her phone?'

Melanie laughs. 'People didn't have mobiles back then.'

'Didn't anyone in the care home have a camera?'

'I don't remember. If they did, they never gave me copies.'

'Poor Mummy, with no one to take care of you.' Georgie slips from her chair and puts her arms around Melanie's waist. 'But I'm taking care of you now.'

'Yes, you are, my darling,' she gulps back her emotion.

'Don't be sad, Mummy,' Georgie is on to her. 'You don't have to be sad anymore. You've got me, now.'

'I have, haven't I?' Melanie tips her head to the ceiling to stave off tears. 'But I'm worried about you not wanting your breakfast. You're not feeling bloaty again, are you?'

'No, I'm loads better.'

'Why don't you want your toast?'

Georgie shrugs.

'You would say, wouldn't you?'

'Yes, Mummy.'

'Come on then, see if Slinky wants that piece you've left. He's rather partial to bananas.'

The dog responds by thumping his tail against the floor, and Georgie passes him her unfinished toast. 'Can I have one of those cakes Delyth made me?'

'The raspberry muffins?'

Georgie nods.

'I suppose.' Melanie finishes the last of her breakfast while Georgie retrieves the Tupperware box. 'You love her baking, don't you?'

Another little nod.

'It was ever so kind of her to bring them to school. You did thank her properly, didn't you?'

'Yes, Mummy.' Georgie prises the lid and lifts one out. 'She told me if I give her the box back when I've finished, she'll make me some more.'

'That's sweet of her. Did she happen to say why she didn't bring them here herself?'

'No.' Georgie, eating with gusto.

'I think I've got a fair idea,' Melanie says to herself, as she makes a start on the washing-up.

*

Melanie waves a gloved hand to Nia's mother as the blue-glossed door of number seven Castle Row closes. Such a lovely family; they've gone out of their way to make Georgie feel welcome. The tide is out so she heads to the beach, lets the dog off his lead as soon as they reach the dunes. She loves the way he bounds alongside, his eagerness and zest for life is cheering. Until her thoughts curl back to Delyth Powell and blacken at their edges. She still hasn't recovered from the shock of what she did in their kitchen, but as Delyth is clearly avoiding the pub — and who could blame her — Melanie's thinking she should be the one to extend the hand of friendship. A text to thank her for the muffins would be a good way to start, Gareth doesn't need to know.

With barely a stir of wind, the freeze of morning catches her lungs. This is her favourite kind of weather, sliced as it is between the rain that's sure to return, she's determined to make the most of it. The cold burns claret-red whorls on her cheeks and, reaching the foaming shallows that skim the rubber toes of her boots, she sees Slinky dart off up the beach to make friends with another dog. He's all right, she decides, returning the ball to a pocket, happy to see both sets of tails wagging.

The only sound is the resonance of the sea and, with purposeful strides, holding the faux fur collar of her hood to her jaw, she makes light work of the near-empty stretch of shore made ready for her footprints. She lifts her gaze to the wildness of the headland, sees the Monkstone Arms rising against its patchwork of hedged fields on the fringes of town. Its high slate roof, beaten back by the weather, has taken on the shapes of the waves and looks frozen solid on such a cold day. Can she and Georgie actually rattle around alone in such a huge place after dark? She shudders, pushing away the uncomfortable feelings its isolated setting brings whenever she thinks about it. Going by her lengthening shadow, she knows she needs to be starting back soon. Even if she didn't have to get ready to take Georgie out later, the sun at this time of year barely shifts beyond the rim of the horizon and sets so suddenly, the temperature dips to below zero in seconds. Melanie doesn't like the dark of these early winter nights when the moon is up and surrounded by such impenetrable blackness. The same moon that Slinky howls at the sight of as if to tell her it is the most unnatural of things. Reminded of the dog, she calls him, sees her breath steaming before her. Amazed at how quickly he's learnt his name, it makes her smile to see him look up from his investigative snuffling and abandon the little pug he found to play with, to hurtle back towards her over the sky-reflecting sand.

'Good boy,' she praises him when he pushes his salty nose into her gloved palm. 'Good boy for coming when I call you.'

She secures his lead to his collar and they walk up the beach. Her eyes travel the spread of buttery sand interspersed with the blanched bellies of upturned fishing boats that have been pulled high on to the dunes to be safe from the tongue of the tide. She thinks she identifies the boat she found Slinky chained to on her first morning here.

'Oi! You!' A loud cry goes up behind her: powerful, commanding; lifted high as the wheeling seabirds above. 'Wait!'

She does as she's told and turns. Sees the man who chased her out of the churchyard, the man she's been calling Mr Grizzly. Big and dark, the sight of him in his donkey jacket frightens her, and her initial impulse is to flee. But something in his look won't let her, this isn't someone she can ignore; and the way he drags his left leg to walk, it would be cruel to run away just because she can.

'That's my dog.' He shouts when, at last, he joins her on the dunes. 'You've got my dog.'

Close enough to see the accusation burning in his eyes beneath his dense facial hair. Her mouth falls open, yet she has nothing to say.

'It was you.' He points with his good arm. 'You took my dog. I saw you. I was watching, so don't bother to deny it.'

NINETEEN

A rattling from downstairs. Melanie turns off the shower. Waits in the drip, drip, dripping, for whatever it was to sound again. When it does, she grabs a towel and wraps it around her. Out on the landing, the moon's orbicular stare through the skylight is bright enough to go by, and she stops at Georgie's half-open door to lean inside. She is met by a little draught of her daughter's sleepy smells and the slow turn of the night light sprinkling soft pink stars over the ceiling and walls. A favourite of Sophie's come bedtime that since her twin died, Georgie always asks for. Everything is as it should be. Her child is sleeping. Except where's Slinky? And as if on cue, he barks from somewhere downstairs.

Barefoot, her wet hair trickling into her eyes, she tiptoes down through her shadow to stand among the rubble in the moon-spilt bar. This place is spooky after dark and her imagination is in danger of running wild. Shivering beneath her damp towel, she hunts the dimness for whatever set Slinky off. But there's nothing, and no sign of the dog either. Eerily quiet; only the scratching sound of the mice Bryn warned about. She makes a mental note to ask Gareth about getting a cat as she breathes back smells of raw wood and fresh plaster that has diluted the reek of stale beer. Prickling with goose-bumps, her skin contracting as it dries, Melanie will never admit to Gareth how vulnerable this place makes her feel and that the weekends when he's home, can't come quick enough.

The dog is suddenly by her side. His wet snout seeking out her hand. He lifts his head and gives her a quizzical look, the whites of his eyes caught in the moonlight.

'What are you doing down here on your own, boy? Come on, let's get you back up to Georgie.' She strokes his head, rhythmically, her heartbeat slowing to normal. 'It was probably only the wind. This is an old place, there's bound to be noises.'

A clattering from outside. Slinky barks and she jumps, but neither move. Melanie crushes the edge of her towel into a tight ball and holds her breath. When she hears it sound again, the two of them bolt for the kitchen.

'Who's there?' she calls, her voice cushioned by the blackness.

Looking around, she traces the familiar shapes of electric appliances, the new floor to ceiling units streaked in moonlight. Then she identifies the smell of cigarette smoke. None of the builders would smoke inside and anyway, they left hours ago, and this is fresh. Her thoughts as she sees the vase of wizened roses from Gareth, she couldn't bring herself to throw away, lies smashed on the floor.

'Was that you?' she blames the dog — easier to blame the dog. She bends to pick up the broken pieces, is putting them in the bin, when she spots the back door has been left slightly ajar. Weird, she thinks, closing it; she swears she locked it before going to bed. Something crunches underfoot. She yelps and lifts her foot to inspect the damage but, reluctant to put a light on, fearing there may be eyes looking in from outside, she can't see. A flash of white against the blackened windowpane. Torchlight. It strikes the glass, then bounces away.

'What the?' Ignoring the pain in her foot, she flings the door wide on to the night.

Nothing. Only the puff of her breath and Slinky tearing away down the side of the pub and the car park beyond. Dead leaves skid in across the floor tiles. Her mother was someone who believed the wind carrying dead leaves into a house brings bad luck and unhappiness. But that was her mother, wasn't it? Full of small, useless facts, that despite Melanie's best efforts, continue to jingle in her head like loose change at the bottom of a handbag. She inhales the briny breath of the sea and looks up at the wide, Welsh sky salted with stars. The cold wind against her skin is almost human and she listens to it nudge through the dry-stalked honeysuckle. Shivers. Could it have been that bloke from earlier? The one who shouted at her on the beach, accusing her of taking his dog. She hopes not, she shivers again, she wouldn't stand a chance in hell against him.

An owl answers the moon. Into the spookiness, Melanie does her best to persuade herself she has nothing to fear, that she and Georgie are perfectly safe here alone. But only when the dog returns, reassuring and wagging, his bright eyes telling her all is as it should be, does she believe it.

'Come on, boy,' she smiles, grateful for his company. And with the back door locked, the new window blinds pulled down, she feels safe enough to flick on the light switch at her shoulder.

What the string of halogen ceiling bulbs illuminate makes her suck back her breath in horror. A trail of bloody footprints. Red and wrong against her gleaming floor. She screams in terror.

TWENTY

A day or so later, home from dropping Georgie at school and a quick walk along the headland with the dog, Melanie, in an old rugby jersey of Gareth's and a tatty pair of jeans, is on her hands and knees. With smells of paint stripper, wood dust and varnish in her nostrils, she is glossing the skirting boards and dado rails now the wallpaper has gone up. The bar is near completion and the transformation is remarkable.

'Hey, Mel.' One of Bryn's men with a mop of ginger hair and a name she can't pronounce. 'D'you hear the news?'

News?'

'Yeah.' He nods exaggeratedly. 'Tom and Sian have finally decided to tie the knot.'

'Have you, Tom?' Melanie rocks on her heels. 'That's wonderful. Congratulations.'

'Yeah, she's finally ground you down, ain't she, mate?' Another of Bryn's crew joins in.

'When's the big day?' Melanie asks.

'Depends when we finish here.' Tom, a drill bit between his lips.

'How d'you mean?'

'Sian wants to have the reception here.' He secures another wooden panel to the opposite wall.

'Wow, that'd be brilliant. Our first wedding.'

Tom grins sideways at her. 'We can christen the place for you.'

'Trash it, you mean.' The redhead again.

'Then you'd better pull your bloody fingers out and get it finished,' Bryn breezes in, winks at Melanie. Smart in suit and tie, she wonders where he's been. 'That's right, isn't it, Mel?'

'Certainly is.' She dips her brush into the pot of plum-coloured paint. 'D'you want me to pencil something in the diary?'

'Nah, Sian will sort the dates.' Tom flicks his head back, poised to screw another wall panel into place. 'She's the one in charge.'

A cheer goes up from his workmates.

'You're learning, boyo,' the Ed Sheeran lookalike laughs.

Melanie doesn't rise to it, she wants to finish this job today and, half-listening to their banter, humming along to Radio Two, before she knows it, she's completed an entire length of skirting and finished all four dado rails.

'You okay?' Bryn asks, returning to her after a quick inspection.

'Okay? Yeah, I'm fine.'

'Only Tegan said you phoned the other night in a bit of a state.'

'I'm sorry about that. I didn't mean to scare you.' She gets up off her knees. 'I thought I heard something, but it was probably just the wind. I'd stupidly left the back door open. And then there was all this blood on the floor, I just freaked.'

'Blood?'

'My foot,' she explains. 'I cut my foot. It bled all over the kitchen floor. Frightened the life out of me.'

'Not surprised. Is it all right now?'

'Bit sore. Serves me right for going around with bare feet.'

Bryn nods and loosens his tie. 'You don't think anyone could have broken in, do you?'

'No,' she says, then feeling a little unsure. 'But I

was thinking, the previous owners, or someone that used to work here — they couldn't still have a key, could they?'

'It's possible,' he grimaces. 'You could get the locks changed, just for peace of mind.'

'Yes, okay,' Melanie agrees with a smile. 'Can you sort it for me?'

'No probs.'

'Thanks, Bryn.'

'Catch you later, yeah,' he says, before walking into the sounds of hammers and drills.

*

Melanie is stiff from being bent over for so long and decides to have a break and finish the job later. Cleaning the brush against the tin and resealing the lid, she gets paint on her fingers and heads to the kitchen for the turps and paper towel she left ready on the side.

A glance at the clock. Almost midday. Coffee-time. She washes her hands and is mid-reach for the kettle when something shifts beyond the window.

She jerks her head to it. Sees a face at the glass.

'Delyth,' she mouths through Slinky's barks, throwing the window open. 'Hi, how are you? I've not seen you in ages. D'you want to come in? I was just about to make a coffee.'

The question isn't answered. Delyth thrusts forward a spindly forearm instead. And with the cuff of her coat pulled back, Melanie sees the dressings and bandages have gone and only plasters remain.

'You can cut us a slice of this to go with it if you want?'

'Oh, you've been baking again.' She accepts the clingfilm-wrapped offering. 'Wow, it's heavy. Looks delicious. Smells delicious.' She unwraps it, sniffs its knobbly, glossy top. 'D'you want to come in?' Melanie repeats the invitation.

A timid shake of the head. 'I'd rather stay out here if it's okay?'

'Isn't it too cold?' A glance at the bright, blue day going on outside.

'Not with your coat on.'

'All right, I'll join you in a minute. You go round the side, there's benches and tables . . . lovely view, now we've cleared that eyesore of a dinosaur away,' she chatters, preparing a tray. 'Hopefully, the seats aren't wet . . .' She looks up, but Delyth has gone.

'You're right, it is warm in the sunshine.' Melanie, carrying the tray and zipped into her perky red parka, joins Delyth on a bench positioned against the rear wall of the pub. 'Bit of a suntrap.'

'We've got to make the most of it. Days like this are rare, now the clocks have gone back.'

She passes Delyth a mug of coffee and a generous slice of her fruit loaf. 'Help yourself to milk and sugar.'

'Thanks.'

'*Mm*, terrific cake.' She bites off a corner.

'It's called *bara brith*.' Her visitor spoons two heaped sugars into her mug and stirs noisily. 'Speckled bread. It's Welsh. You soak the fruit in tea.'

'Delicious.' Its fruitiness dissolving on her tongue. 'You should go on *Bake Off*.'

'Don't be silly,' Delyth sniggers but Melanie can tell she's flattered.

'I'm serious.' She takes another mouthful, looks down at the dog who's followed her outside. 'Sorry, boy,' she strokes his head. 'This is way too good for you. Honestly,' she turns to Delyth, 'that dog's a walking bin.'

'You spoil him.' The opinion is non-negotiable.

'I suppose we do.' Melanie fetches up an awkward laugh. 'But the poor thing was in such a state when I found him, I can't help it. Who could resist those eyes?'

'You found out who he belongs to yet?' Delyth answers the question with one of her own.

'No.' Melanie chews through her lie; loath to share her strange exchange with Mr Grizzly.

'You can spread butter on it if you like.' Delyth points at what's left of Melanie's bara brith as she nibbles her own.

'Oh, no. It's plenty rich enough. You're going to have to teach me how to make this, and those other flat cakes with the currants in.'

'Welsh cakes.' Delyth informs her and, with an irritated shove, pushes the dog's snout away.

'Welsh cakes.' Melanie echoes, frowning at her impatience, Slinky's not doing any harm. 'You did get my text to thank you for the muffins, didn't you?'

Delyth nods as she rummages through her bag. 'I found you this.'

Melanie takes the slim volume being handed to her. 'Welsh recipes,' she smiles, flicking over the illustrated pages. 'Thanks.' A grateful hand on Delyth's sleeve. 'Not that I can compete with you.'

'Nonsense. You're the qualified chef, I'm just an amateur.'

'Hardly. You won't know it, but it's a job to get Georgie to eat anything else now she's sampled your baking.'

'She's such a sweet little girl.' Delyth drinks her coffee and Melanie follows her gaze as it travels the beer garden, away to the blue band of sea beyond the boundary fence. 'I said I was going to make you a casserole, didn't I? I'm sorry.'

'*Sorry*?' Melanie polishes off her cake. 'With the goodies you've been sending Georgie home with?' She dabs up the last of the crumbs. 'I don't want you going to any more trouble, you've been way too generous already.' *Far more than we deserve, considering the awful things you must have heard Gareth calling you.*

'It's no trouble. I like cooking.' Delyth rifles the pockets of her coat and pulls out a battered packet of cigarettes. 'You don't mind, do you?'

'Course not.' Melanie's relieved to see the woman has some vices.

'I've managed to cut down to a couple a day.' Delyth lights up, shakes out the match. 'But I can't totally give them up.'

'One or two won't do much harm.' Melanie sniffs the chemical smell: it doesn't conjure happy memories. 'My mum's a chain smoker. Everything to excess, my mother. It'll kill her in the end.' And then suddenly, Melanie remembers with a shudder when she last smelt cigarette smoke . . . in the kitchen in the middle of the night when the door she knew she'd locked was open.

'I started when I was at school. Did you ever smoke?'

'You what?' Melanie, miles away.

'Just wondered if you'd ever smoked?'

'Er . . . no, my mum put me off it.'

'Lucky you.' Delyth takes a deep drag, flicks ash on the grass.

They sit on, listening to the creep of the tide.

'How's Georgie?' Delyth asks.

'Oh, um, actually, she's been feeling a bit off-colour these past few weeks.'

'Has she?' Delyth exhales a grey snake of smoke.

'Yes.' Melanie watches it disperse into the crisp clear air and drinks her coffee. 'She's been complaining of stomach cramps and gripes on and off. I don't think it's serious, it's just a bit uncomfortable.'

'I could give you some herbs for that. Peppermint's good. I grow it on the farm. Mam suffers terrible with indigestion and she swears by it.'

'If you think it would help.' Melanie isn't sure.

'You can make tea with the leaves. It's very effective.' Delyth, finished with her cigarette, leans down to screw it out on the leg of the bench.

'I suppose it's worth a try.' Melanie, a little annoyed with her, hopes it doesn't burn the wood; this garden furniture cost a fortune. 'Although, I think I should take her to see a doctor. I've been meaning to get us registered at the surgery.'

'Ask for Dr Cassidy. He's the best.' Delyth traces the rambling rose-pattern on her mug with a forefinger, spots a tiny beetle on her hand and swats it. 'He's the only one with an imagination, put it that way.'

'I will, thanks for the advice.'

'Surprisingly toasty in the sun.' Delyth gives a glimmer of a smile.

'Gorgeous.' Melanie closes her eyes and tilts her face to breathe in the last of summer. 'How's Andrew doing? Your mum?'

'They're fine.' Is all Delyth gives, absentmindedly cleaning her nails on the corner of the cigarette box, the grubby crescent moons floating to the ground.

She studies Delyth. Thinks she can see beneath her skin, down to the truth of this unhappy, haunted, half-lost soul. She wonders if this could be why she feels strangely connected to her; because Delyth Powell isn't the kind of person she'd usually associate with.

'I am sorry about what Gareth said the other night.' Melanie breathes against the steam rising from her mug. 'It must've hurt to hear him say those horrible things about you.'

'No matter.' Delyth shifts in her seat. 'I'm kind of used to it. I've had it all my life.'

Melanie sees the way her lips press against themselves, while the eyes: lonesome and blank; have a look of someone who is sick of seeing.

'Really? That's awful. You shouldn't be, you

deserve better. Loads better. I know it's no excuse, but he didn't know you were there. We thought you'd gone home.'

'Look, Melanie,' Delyth holds her gaze. 'I've said to you before, you don't have to apologise for him. You're not accountable for his actions.'

'No, I know that.' Melanie puts the recipe book on the tray. 'But even so, I am sorry if he upset you.'

'He didn't.' Delyth turns away.

'Okay, but just to say, it's not like him. Not like him at all.'

'You're sure about that, are you?' The voice is hard.

'Yes, I am. And I know, deep down, that he's sorry.'

'Sorry I overheard him, or sorry he thinks like that about me?'

Melanie can't answer and they slip into an awkward silence that is now and again perforated by birdsong.

'I'm the one stuck in the middle here,' Melanie breaks it. 'Because unless one of you tells me what's gone on between you two, I can't be expected to understand, can I?'

Delyth, fidgety, reaches up and under the cuff of her coat, picks at the edge of a plaster. It sets Melanie's teeth on edge and it takes everything she's got not to smack her fingers still.

'Are your arms still sore?' She surprises herself for bringing up the subject, even if it is from this oblique angle.

'Not now, no. They've healed up good.' And much to Melanie's relief, Delyth drops her hands into her lap.

'That's great to hear.'

'I'm sorry about what I did that day. It was wrong of me to involve you.'

So softly spoken and combined with her mild Welsh accent, Melanie must lean forward to hear all Delyth is saying. It is a voice that would be lost among others and she half-wonders if it could be deliberate on Delyth's part. A clever tactic if it is. Forcing you to listen, forcing you to give more attention than you would ordinarily do. But that would make the woman calculating, cunning even, and Melanie's sure this isn't the case. She is someone who's always prided herself on her ability to read people. A useful tool, and one she honed during her childhood. Shunted from care home to foster home and back to her mother, she needed to be able to pick out the liars from the sincere. And Delyth Powell is definitely the latter. Such a gentle, vulnerable person. A truly troubled soul. It's why she can't understand why Gareth is so cruel about her.

'It was shameful of me, so weak and shameful.' Delyth continues to harangue herself in her quietly-spoken way. 'I'm so embarrassed.' Her flap of hair, black as the sloes in the surrounding hedgerows, is blown open by a sudden gust of wind. It reveals her woebegone expression. 'You won't tell anyone what I did. You haven't said anything to Gareth, have you?'

'I've not breathed a word. It can be our secret.'

'Thank you.' Delyth wrings her hands. 'What must you think of me?'

'I don't think anything of you,' Melanie promises. 'Only that you're obviously very sad about something, about life.' She hesitates, unsure whether to share what's on her mind. 'Have you ever thought about talking to somebody?'

'What d'you mean?'

'A professional. A counsellor.'

'Oh, no,' Delyth is firm. 'I don't need anyone like that, I've got God.' And her fingers fly to her neck, forage under her layers to touch the crucifix.

'It's great you've got such strong beliefs, but—' she is about to say: *Where was God when you decided to slice into your arms in my sink? He didn't do anything to talk you out of that. It's help from the corporeal world you need.* 'There's no shame in it. I saw a counsellor for a while. She was the loveliest woman, she helped straighten me out. I was a complete wreck after—' she stops, she can't bring herself to speak her dead daughter's name.

'After Sophie?'

'Y-yes . . . after Sophie. *Erm*,' Melanie thinks she might as well just come out and say it, there's been enough pussyfooting around. 'I've been meaning to ask how you know so much about her?'

'It's not a secret, Melanie. I'm sorry if you thought it was. Most of the town knows.'

'That's as maybe, but don't you think it was a bit irresponsible to—' she pauses, approaches it in another way. 'I mean, what was that nonsense you were telling Georgie at the beginning of term?'

'Nonsense? It wasn't nonsense.' Another touch of the crucifix.

'No?'

'No. I see things.'

'*You see things*?' Melanie splutters. 'I don't understand.' And she doesn't. How would this kind of thinking fit with this woman's obvious strict Catholic faith?

It goes quiet for a minute. Melanie isn't sure she's going to get an answer.

'I see things. Things beyond this world,' Delyth says, at last. Enigmatic and dark, she gives Melanie a look she can't push past. 'I know you blame yourself,' the tone is impassive. 'I know you're ashamed. That you think it was your carelessness that caused it. That if you hadn't been so selfish Sophie might still be alive today. If you hadn't stopped to chat with your neighbour. If you hadn't let go of the trike . . .'

'*What*? What did you say?' Horrified, Melanie gawps at her. *How does she know? How does she know?* She stares in disbelief at this relative stranger who, in turn, is staring fixedly out to sea. 'What are you talking about? You don't know the first thing about me.'

'It's why you came to Wales. This is your chance to start again. To wean yourself off the anti-depressants, to give up your crummy job. The only job you could hold down after Sophie's accident.' The words are delivered slowly and Melanie wants to grab hold of her, make her look her in the eye. But she doesn't. Too stunned to move, she lets Delyth talk. 'I know what it feels like,' the voice continues, speaking thoughts Melanie believed had been buried deep. But here they are, tumbling out of this other woman. This puzzlingly, perceptive woman. 'You can't believe the sun keeps setting and the dawn keeps rising, that days roll over into seasons, years, so that before you know it, nearly four years have gone. And people are so selfish, aren't they?' The speaker doesn't wait for an answer, answers aren't required. 'They're oblivious to our suffering because they're too wrapped up in their own problems. It mattered little how shocked they were at the time, it didn't take them long to forget your dead child, for her to slip from view. Because we both know the world doesn't stop turning just because you're suffering, does it?'

'You're right. I do blame myself,' Melanie admits, refusing to cry. 'But how d'you know?' A floating image of Erin Powell's gravestone.

'I know because it's what I think about myself and the people I've lost. If only I'd done that, if only I'd done this.'

'In the weeks following Sophie's death,' Melanie continues with her confession, 'I could tell Gareth looked at me differently. Or I imagined he did, believing I deserved it. I'd failed as a mother, you see, so he's bound to love me less. I love myself less.'

'Have you talked to him about it?'

'I want to, but,' Melanie swallows. 'I'm frightened it will widen his pain and mine, beyond all measure.'

'Speaking of a death doesn't worsen it, your daughter can't suffer again.'

'No, you're right. But I can't remember the last time we spoke about her.'

'You must. Your girl is gone, but by speaking of her you give her a second life. A life she can live alongside yours and Georgie's.'

'D'you think?' She blinks through the surprising

sunshine, her chest heaving beneath her winter clothes.

'Be gentle with yourself, Melanie,' Delyth says kindly. 'Don't try to understand God's mystery or wisdom, none of us can know that. And don't count the years. I know you must because I'm the same. But don't.'

Melanie supposes Delyth is talking about her sister; but again, it doesn't feel right to ask.

'Think of the child you've got, the curiosity that is Georgie. Thank the Lord daily for her little life.'

'Yes, I know.'

'The Lord's unfailing love and mercy will still continue if you go to Him and ask for His forgiveness for whatever badness you do, as sure as the sun sets each evening.'

Melanie bristles, she can't help it; it is how she reacts whenever someone pushes their religious beliefs on her. And yet so much of what Delyth says makes sense, and she's grateful for her guidance, even though she can't help thinking it doesn't quite come from the heart. That the phrases she uses are second-hand and learnt from the reading of religious texts. That they sound rehearsed.

'But you say you see things? How does that fit with the church?'

There isn't time for Delyth to answer.

'Mel! Mel!' One of Bryn's workmen opens the patio doors. 'Someone's trying to get hold of you. Your mobile's been ringing and ringing.'

'Oh, bugger.' Melanie gets up and, with Delyth and the dog following, goes inside.

On their approach to the kitchen, her mobile rings again. Vociferous and demanding, she dashes away to answer it.

It's Gareth. A nervous smile at Delyth who is close on her heels.

'Hey, Mel. Where've you been? I've been calling and calling.' The voice she loves sounds far away.

'Sorry, Gareth. I've been in the garden.'

'God, I've missed you.' She hears him sigh. 'It's been a hell of a slog so far this week, I can't wait till I'm home,' he whispers. 'Tell me what you're wearing?' His question, the way he delivers it, she can tell he wants to talk sexy. 'What underwear have you got on? Mel . . . tell me, tell me. I need you to give me a picture, I miss you so much . . . so much.' Flirtatious, it reminds her of when they were first together: the text messages, lustful, exciting; except now there's no Elizabeth to worry about. But she can't engage in this with him now, not with Delyth listening. 'Two more days, Mel. Only two more days . . . and I've been thinking,' she hears him grinning, 'are you gonna let me do whatever I want with you when I get home? Just like last weekend?' A gravelly chuckle. '*Mm*, Mel, I can't wait to get my hands on you. I can't wait to—' He pulls up short, sensing her reluctance, her muted response. 'You're not on your own, are you?'

'No.' Melanie shoots a look at Delyth.

'Who's there?'

'*Erm.*'

'Mel?'

'Delyth.' She says nonchalantly. 'Delyth's here.'

'What? She's there now?'

'Yes. That's right. She called round with a beautiful cake.' Melanie hears Gareth's irritation rasp against her ear and, conscious Delyth is staring at her, she does her best not to show it in her expression.

'I don't believe it, after everything we agreed.' He is angry. Horribly angry.

'Yes, she just called over,' Melanie continues calmly for Delyth's benefit. 'We're just having a coffee in the garden. It's glorious here, I don't know what it's like—'

'Get rid of her,' Gareth bellows, cutting her off. 'Get fucking rid of her. *Now!*'

TWENTY-ONE

The mountain of a man Melanie has been calling Mr Grizzly, invites her and Slinky into a cave-like room tacked on to the rear of the church. Swapping the bright day for the gloomy interior with its stale water and damp root smell, she realises, not only is it little larger than her larder, but it's barely high enough for either of them to stand up in.

'Thanks for bringing him to see me.' The man who asks to be called John, motions with his good arm to the only armchair. 'Sit. Please, sit.'

She does and, gripping her knees, tries to make as little contact with the motheaten material as possible. What is she doing here? Is she crazy? He could be anyone. He could be some knife-wielding madman, for all she knows. She shouldn't have come; she was stupid to let him persuade her. No one knows she's here. Nervously watching him play with the dog, Melanie sees him dig through the tatty pockets of his jacket for the scraps he says he's been holding on to in the hope she would keep her promise.

'Paw.' He booms in the same voice that stopped her in her tracks on the beach.

Slinky needs prompting, needs a little tap against his front leg, but when, at last, he obliges, Melanie can't help but smile.

'He remembers.' That deep baritone again, it fills the limited space much as he does. John raises his eyes in time to catch her smile and returns it. It's the first time she's seen him smile and it instantly softens him; his fierceness

144

melting. 'Putting on weight, I see.' He strokes the dog's well-covered ribs.

'It hasn't taken much; he was pretty thin.'

Melanie absorbs her surroundings. The condensation-wet walls that were she to spread wide her arms she could probably touch both sides at the same time. A shredded rug under her boots. A narrow camp bed with a mattress no thicker than a slice of bread, its sheets and blankets folded into a regimented square at one end. No ornaments, no photographs. His only luxuries, from the looks of things, is a single bookcase stuffed with old paperbacks. How does he manage? With no television, radio, internet, or any other of the twenty-first century trappings the likes of her and Gareth couldn't do without. You can't live here, surely? Not with your bad arm and stiff leg. What's brought you down so low? She longs to ask but curbs her curiosity and considers him instead. Sees that although his clothes are shabby, he is clean: his hair and beard both washed and brushed, his scant quarters orderly.

He twists to the rickety sideboard. The rasp of a match and he lights an outdated gas lamp fashioned into the shape of a toadstool; instantly throwing his giant shadow against the lumpy whitewashed walls. He transports the lit match to his makeshift kitchen, lights the camping stove, then blows it out, distributing its sulphur smell. His troublesome leg collides with a tin bucket positioned in the centre of the room, and when it clatters, she jumps at the sound.

'There's no need to be scared, I'm not angry with you.'

'No?' she croaks, looking up to a crack in the ceiling, at the yellow stain on the plaster where rainwater leaks in.

'No, I'm happy he's got a good home. As you can probably guess, I've barely enough to feed myself.' She watches him wipe out two enamel mugs with the stiffened tail of his jacket. 'I was ashamed how thin he'd got.' John stoops to give the wagging Slinky the attention he craves.

'He's a great dog. My Georgie's besotted with him.' Melanie says, then instantly regrets it; she shouldn't have given this man her daughter's name. 'But—' she trails her gaze along a line of lager cans cooling on the only windowsill, 'I suppose you're going to want him back now.'

'And break your little girl's heart?' John gives her a lopsided smile. 'Nah, he's better off with you.' And proceeds to fill a kettle from an old copper tap fixed to the wall. 'You'll have tea?'

She nods, watches him place the dumpy kettle on the blackened camping stove and adjust the flames. 'What have you called him?'

'Slinky. My daughter's choice. It's a character from *Toy Story*.' His look is blank. 'A Disney film, computer-animated?' A quick laugh, anxieties ebbing. 'If it wasn't for her, I wouldn't know about it either.'

'I like it.' Kneeling, his good leg taking the strain, he strokes the dog who obliges by rolling over, giving John his tummy. 'Slinky suits you, doesn't it, mate?'

'Why did you keep him chained up on the beach?' Melanie's bluntness seems to startle him, and he doesn't answer right away.

'You've seen the sign on the gate,' he says, at last. 'They allow me to live here, just, but not with a dog. They wouldn't stretch to a dog. They'd have everyone bringing their dogs in here, otherwise.'

'I suppose. But why didn't you just take him to the RSPCA?'

'Because,' he says and struggles to his feet. 'B-because h-he was all I had in the world.'

And he bursts into tears. The water in the kettle bubbling over his shoulder, filling the tiny space with steam.

Melanie doesn't move, at a loss to know what to do. Instinct tells her to comfort him, console him, but it also tells her to keep her distance.

'But it's worked out okay, hasn't it?' He rights

himself, sniffs against a fraying cuff. 'You're only at the pub.' He flings back his head, narrowly misses the ceiling. 'It's not like he's gone miles away.'

'You know we're at the pub?' Melanie is surprised.

'Yes. You've bought the Monkstone.'

'How d'you know that?'

'I followed you. After I saw you take—' he hesitates, rubs a hand over his beard, '*Slinky,*' he says, testing the dog's new name. 'Then there was another day. I came to see you, but you weren't in. I had a good look round your garden, but I couldn't find him.'

'That was you? I was up on the headland, I saw you.'

'Guilty as charged.' His eyes, dark beneath their dense brows. 'You're Gareth Sayer's missus.'

'That's right.' She twirls her wedding ring around her finger, realises she hasn't told John her name. 'I'm Melanie.' She taps the front of her parka.

'Melanie,' he repeats. She likes the way he says it; likes his accent, his deep, rumbling voice.

'So,' she clears her throat, 'how d'you know Gareth?'

'I was in his class at school.'

'Oh, right,' Melanie smiles but notices the smile is not returned this time.

'He definitely hit the jackpot with you.' John, awkward, looks away. 'But then he always was a jammy bugger.'

Lost in his private thoughts, he appears to have forgotten the kettle and is oblivious to its high-pitched screaming. Rising from her seat, Melanie goes to lift it from the heat.

'Careful.' He steps up behind her. She smells the carbolic soap again, and something else, a mustiness, like an old cupboard that hasn't been opened for a long time. With his face close to hers, she sees the tenderness held in his mouth beneath the beard. 'Hope you don't mind it black. I haven't any milk.'

'That's okay, as long as it's not too strong.' She returns to the armchair. 'You work down the docks, don't you?'

'Now and again. When my leg's not playing up.'

'What happened to you?' She takes the mug he passes, noticing again his left arm hanging limp and useless by his side. 'If you don't mind me asking?'

'Afghanistan. I served two terms.'

'Right. I see.' Except she doesn't. How could she possibly imagine the horrors he's undoubtedly lived through. 'Is that how you hurt your arm?'

'My arm and my leg. An exploding bomb. Well, they're the injuries you can see.'

Melanie nods, sympathetic to the subtext. 'You must've been terribly traumatised.'

'I was. *Am*. They debrief you but it's not enough, you can't be unprogrammed. It's why I don't trust myself now I'm back in civvy life, it's t-too . . .' She can tell he has to hunt around for the right way to explain. 'It's too hard living in a normal house, in a normal street. I'm like a coiled spring, I'm fearful I could blow at any moment.'

'Is that why you live here?'

'Yeah, I've got to tuck myself away. I'm not part of society. I tried but I just don't fit in anymore. I tried living with my sister when I first came back from Afghanistan, but she just wouldn't leave me alone. Nagging, you know. She means well but she doesn't understand and I didn't trust myself, not after what I saw, what I did . . . what I'm trained to do.'

'Oh.' Melanie stares at her tea, at a bubble travelling over the surface. What else is there to say?

'It's not Nerys' fault,' John is quick to explain. 'I was impossible. I couldn't stand the kids, all that noise and screaming. She couldn't cope with me, which is hardly surprising, I can hardly cope with myself.' He lifts then drops his good arm. 'But don't feel sorry for me, this is my choice. Being too close to people and their pity; I can't stand it.'

He looks old, but he isn't old, he's the same age as her and Gareth, she reminds herself, reading the premature lines around his eyes. 'I can sort of understand that.' She takes a tentative sip of tea.

'I sort of can tell.' His tea untouched on the sideboard.

'How did you end up living here?'

'The vicar. Have you met him?'

Melanie shakes her head, the enamel mug almost too hot to hold.

'Him and his wife, they're the kindest people. They let me stay here for free, no questions asked, no pressure.'

'But what d'you do for meals? Have you got a bathroom?'

'It's a bit primitive, but they let me use the washroom in the vestry. And Mrs Evans—'

'The vicar's wife?'

He nods. 'She brings me meals. The odd box of tea bags.'

'Lager?' Melanie eyes the windowsill.

'Now and again.' He lowers his gaze. 'I need it sometimes; it helps me sleep.'

'They sound lovely people.' Melanie scrunches her lips. She's sorry she mentioned the cans, it's none of her business. Always moved by the generosity of others, she wishes she'd thought to bring him the rest of Delyth's bara brith. 'Don't you want your tea?'

'In a minute. I can't swallow if things are too hot.'

'You make a nice cuppa,' she says to be kind.

'Good. Does that mean you and Slinky will come and see me again?'

'If you like.'

'I would. Very much.' His eyes sad again.

'It's funny,' Melanie begins, 'but you frightened me to start with, shouting like that in the graveyard, then again on the beach. You're pretty formidable, you know?'

He laughs, for real this time. 'That's my army training.' He pauses, his expression etched in concern. 'But you're not frightened of me anymore, are you?'

Melanie's mobile rings from inside her coat pocket.

'Hang on,' she says, pulling it free. 'It's my daughter's school.' She frowns before answering. 'Mrs Jenkins? Hello,' she greets the woman caller. 'Oh, dear,' her hand flies to her mouth. 'Oh, dear. No,' she pushes her alarm through her fingers. 'Yes, yes. I'll come right away.'

TWENTY-TWO

'Slinky! Stop it.' Melanie yanks the lead, fearing the dog is about to cock his leg against one of her mother-in-law's garden gnomes.

'It's all right.' A laughing Tegan in the doorway of Plas Newydd is jigging Ffion in her arms. 'Mam's away. Didn't Bryn say?'

'He did, yeah,' Melanie, breathing hard after her climb from the beach. 'But she might still have her spies out.'

'How's Georgie? Did Hop Along say what it was?'

'Hop Along?' Melanie's turn to laugh. 'D'you mean Doctor Cassidy?'

Tegan nods. 'It's what Mam calls him.'

'He reckons it was gastric flu. Said it's doing the rounds. He told me to keep her home.'

'But she's not with you?' Tegan kisses her baby's head.

'No. I kept her home Wednesday and yesterday, but she got up this morning, full of beans, saying she felt better. That she didn't want to miss more school.' Melanie joins her sister-in-law on the step, unfurls her scarf. 'I've just dropped her off.'

'Bit late. It's almost half ten.' Tegan steps aside to let Melanie into the hall.

'I've been walking the dog.' She explains as she bends to check Slinky's paws, decides he's clean enough for Bronwyn's fussy hall carpet.

'I thought you might've gone to see John Hughes again?'

'John Hughes?' Melanie unzips her parka, slips it free of her shoulders.

'Ex-squaddie. Lives in the churchyard.'

Melanie senses the weight of Tegan's gaze as it searches her face. 'Oh, him.' She pegs her coat up. 'How d'you know about that?'

'I saw you coming out of there on Tuesday.'

'Blimey. I didn't know I was under surveillance.'

'I just happened to be passing.' A flash of her sister-in-law's occasional sharpness.

Melanie shakes off her wellingtons, leaves them in the porch. 'I haven't seen him today, no.' She straightens her socks. 'But as I said, Slinky used to belong to him, so I'll be taking him to see him now and again. Not that it's anyone's business.'

'I'm just saying to take care.' A little wriggle of the hips as Tegan repositions Ffion. 'This is a small town. People gossip.'

'Obviously.' On her walk along the beach, Melanie had been wondering about asking Tegan if Bryn would mind doing some maintenance on John's roof but changes her mind. 'You got the kettle on? I'm gasping.' She says this with a forced cheeriness to hide her irritation.

'I like your hair. Are you letting it grow?' Tegan compliments when Melanie removes her bobble hat.

'Not deliberately.' She runs her fingers through it. 'Just not got around to getting it cut.'

'Well, leave it. It looks nice with you.' Tegan, poised to turn. 'Sian's here. She managed to get the morning off work to talk *weddings*.'

'Great, I hope she's got some dates in mind.' Melanie returns to her coat, pulls out a notebook. 'The diary's looking quite full.'

'You must be getting fit, all this walking you're doing.' Tegan leads the way along the hall, her pale-blue slippers clashing with the mocha-swirl of carpet.

'It's the dog, he won't take no for an answer.' She unfastens Slinky's lead and they watch him trot daintily off to the kitchen.

'Hi, Mel.' The scrape of stool against the floor, and Sian rises to her feet. The movement threatening to topple a vase of tiger lilies over the sea of wedding magazines spread out on the table. 'You look all rosy and fresh. Have you been walking?'

'She does look lovely, doesn't she?' Tegan, generous as always; it's difficult for Melanie to stay irked with her for long. 'She doesn't need make-up like the rest of us. She's one of those naturally beautiful people.'

'Get away, you two, you're making me blush.' And she gives Tegan a jokey shove. 'Hi, Sian. Yes, a good yomp to wear him out. Nice day, windy but nice. How are you?'

'Excited.' Sian giggles.

'I bet. Many congratulations by the way, it's fabulous news about you and Tom.'

'Thanks, Mel.'

'I love this room.' She sighs and looks about her at the rustic wooden island, the matching units, the handsome Aga. The polka dot cotton curtains hanging above windowsills busy with robust houseplants. No fuss, no frills, just homely and welcoming. 'I told Bryn this is how I want our kitchen to look.'

'You stand more of a chance than me, you're paying him. I want him to give ours an overhaul, but he says he's too busy.' Tegan lays Ffion in her carrycot.

'D'you mind if I wash my hands?' Melanie steps up to the sink, peeks in on her baby niece; at her fluttering eyelids, the webbing of delicate blue veins. Gorgeous, she thinks, turning the tap.

'That's another thing I love about her,' Tegan whispers to Sian. 'She's so polite.'

'Handsome dog.' Sian, perched on board her stool again, reaches over her comfortable middle to stroke

Slinky's black head. 'Tegan says you found him.'

'Did she?' Melanie turns the tap off, darts a look at her sister-in-law.

'Turns out he belongs to John Hughes.' Tegan avoids her gaze.

'Who's he?' Sian, bemused.

'He's a tramp. Lives in the churchyard.'

Sian is still none the wiser.

'He's not a tramp,' Melanie sets them straight. 'He lives at the back of the vestry.'

'He is a tramp, Mel,' Tegan, emphatic. 'With good reason, I know. Poor dab.'

'Why poor dab?' Sian is all ears.

'Ex-army. Injured out. Suffering from PTSD, most probably.'

'What's that?' Sian again.

'Post-traumatic stress disorder. Screwed his mind up a bit, I think, poor thing. But I suppose he's harmless enough, he wouldn't be allowed out in public otherwise.' Melanie dries her hands on a tea towel, drapes it over the Aga.

'Why's he living at the back of the church?'

'It's a long story.'

'I bet it is,' Tegan says.

'Ok-ay,' Sian frowns. 'And what? This John's cool with you taking his dog, is he?'

Melanie pulls up a stool and sits down. 'He says he's grateful to us for giving him a home.'

'Huh,' Tegan grunts and pours a kettle-full of boiled water into the cafetiere.

'You don't have to go to all that trouble for me, I'd be just as happy with instant.' Melanie ignores whatever the *huh* means.

'Yes, I do. I'm living the highlife with Mam away. Got some nice bickies to go with it.'

'You're enjoying yourself.'

'You bet. Being here's way better than home. I've

decided I'm going to encourage Mam to go away more often.'

'Your place is lovely, what are you going on about?' Sian enthuses. 'Wish me and Tom could afford our own home.'

'Something'll turn up.' Tegan sweeps aside the magazines and sets three dainty cups with matching saucers down on the table with a clatter. 'You know there's talk of extending the estate we're on? There's a percentage to be given over to affordable housing.'

'Yeah?'

'Bryn went to a council meeting the other day, put a bid in for some of the work.'

'D'you reckon we'd be able to afford something?'

'Don't see why not. But you'd better get your name down quick. If they do build, they're gonna go like hot cakes.'

Sian sighs. 'Probably a waste of time, doubt we'll get a look in?'

'Don't be so negative.'

'I don't mean to, but we've been disappointed before.' Sian turns to Melanie. 'Honestly, we thought it'd be better here, but it's as bad as Cardiff.'

'All them people buying holiday homes by the sea, it is,' Tegan adds.

'House prices have gone mental over the past few years,' Melanie agrees. 'I don't think we'd have got the pub if it hadn't needed a complete overhaul.'

'Come off it, Mel. You and Gareth are loaded.'

'Hardly.' The state of their finances isn't something Melanie wants to discuss, not with Sian in the room. 'Anyway, whatever happens,' she says to the bride-to-be, 'we'll make sure you have the most wonderful day and not bankrupt you at the same time.' She takes a biscuit from the plate being offered to her. 'You'll be our first.'

'Guinea pigs, then?' Sian laughs.

'*Erm*, I don't think so,' Tegan nips in. 'You're

looking at a top-notch chef here, mind.' She tips her head at Melanie. 'Head pastry chef at the Savoy.'

'Not quite head,' Melanie bites the biscuit in two.

'Might as well have been.' Tegan sits opposite, pours the coffee with one eye on her baby.

'Sweet of you to brag me up,' Melanie smiles. 'But no, I was second in command.'

'But at the Savoy. That's really something.' Sian sounds impressed. 'Would you be able to make our cake?'

'Sure, I can.' Melanie crunches on the last of her biscuit.

'Oh, that's brilliant.'

Melanie motions to her baby niece. 'It'll be your turn next.'

'I hope,' Sian grins.

'It's a great place to bring up kids,' Tegan says. 'Are you and Gareth going to have any more? Gareth said he wants to.'

'He said that?' Melanie nearly chokes.

'Yeah.'

'He's not said anything to me.'

'No?'

'No.'

'You don't sound keen.' Tegan rakes a freckly hand through her auburn waves.

'I'm not, that's why. How can we have a baby now? We've got a business to get off the ground.'

'People manage.'

'But I don't want to just *manage*.'

'I'm only saying what Gareth said.'

'No, Tegan. Our priority has to be Georgie; she's been through enough upheaval already.'

'That's why a little brother or sister would be good for her.'

'Why do I feel like I'm under attack?' Melanie blinks back sudden tears. 'You're a bloody terrier, Tegan. When you get on the scent of something—' she stops, mid-flow, conscious of Sian shifting uncomfortably beside her. 'You want the truth? I'll give you the truth. I'm afraid to have more children. I can't trust myself. How can I trust myself?'

The awfulness of her question and all it implies spins through the disturbed silence.

'Don't upset yourself,' Sian puts a comforting arm around Melanie.

'You're right, it's none of my business.' Tegan, colouring, slips from the table under the pretext of checking on Ffion. 'I'm sorry, Mel. Me and my big mouth. I didn't mean to upset you.'

Melanie doesn't know how to answer, she isn't sure how much Sian knows. 'You got a date in mind for your wedding?' she says instead, feigning brightness.

'Can you fit us in between Christmas and New Year?' Sian pulls back her arm.

'Great. I love winter weddings. The pub will be looking extra pretty too, with all the Christmas decorations.' Melanie sneezes.

'Oh, dear.' Tegan passes her a box of tissues. 'Hope you're not coming down with the dreaded lurgy?'

'No, I'm fine.' She takes one, points to the spray of lilies. 'I'm allergic to those beauties.'

'I forgot. How is Georgie?' Sian asks while Tegan moves the vase to the furthest window ledge.

Melanie blows her nose. 'She's much better, thanks. Hell of a shock when the school phoned me.'

'I can imagine.'

'Thing is, she's been feeling a bit off-colour for a while. Complaining of tummy aches, off her food.'

'She probably takes after Gareth.' Tegan, seated again, takes a biscuit, then another. You take after Gareth too; Melanie thinks with a half-smile. 'He was always a picky eater. It used to drive our Mam up the wall.'

'Georgie never used to be fussy, she's like me, eats anything. It could be a protest thing because we've only got a microwave to cook in.'

'But Hop Along didn't seem bothered, did he?' Tegan, crunching.

'No. He said schools are incubators for all sorts. But I have to say, if it weren't for Delyth's baking, I don't know what she'd be living off. It's all she seems to want to eat.'

'Delyth? Delyth Powell.'

'Yes.'

'She bakes things for you?'

Melanie nods.

'Wow, you're honoured.'

'Am I?'

'Well, yeah. She keeps herself very much to herself; definitely not one for mixing, let alone making cakes for people.'

'Really? Well, she often pops over. Always bringing me and Georgie goodies.'

'You're honoured. Seriously, Mel, she doesn't bother with anyone. Does she Sian?'

Sian purses her lips and shakes her head.

'Well, well,' Tegan eyes her. 'Fancy Delyth taking a shine to you. I'd take that as a big compliment if I were you.' The tone is venerating. 'She's a nice person . . . very *ddiniwed*.'

'Very what?' Melanie doesn't bother to try and pronounce the Welsh.

'Innocent, *erm*, guileless . . . not very worldly.'

'Yes, she strikes me as that too.'

'I don't know her very well but from what I can tell, she never lets anyone close. So it's nice she's found a friend in you. Poor dab's not had much of a life.'

'Delyth's talked about how hard it's been. Talked about her mother too.'

'Norah? Aye.' Tegan gives her a look. 'I've heard she's a load of worry. And that farm of theirs, I don't know how they've managed to keep it going. Place is crumbling to bits. Better for them if they moved into town.'

'Fetch a tidy sum,' Sian adds when Tegan is alerted to the grizzling Ffion. 'Amazing position, overlooking the sea like that.'

'Maybe they like living there,' Melanie says. 'Maybe it suits them being out of it.' Away from gossips, she thinks but keeps it to herself.

'I suppose.' Ffion settled, Tegan rinses out the cafetiere, spoons in more of Bronwyn's best coffee. 'It doesn't suit everyone to be in the thick of things.'

The thick of things — Pencarew? Melanie stifles a giggle.

'They'll probably sell up after Andrew's left home.'

'Andrew, leaving home? I can't imagine Delyth agreeing to that,' Sian interjects. 'She dotes on that boy something terrible.'

'I told her it would be a perfect time to go to college. Do something she wants to do.'

'Good for you, coming up with something positive for her future,' Tegan grins. 'No wonder she likes you.'

'Gareth told me off. He says I'm too soft. According to him she isn't someone who wants help, she likes moaning and I'm to stay away from her.'

'He said that?' Tegan, in a voice of pure amazement. 'Take no notice. He can be a funny bugger, my brother. It's Mam's fault, she spoilt him rotten.'

Sian laughs.

'I'm serious. He used to be a right arrogant sod when he was younger. All the girls fancying him, the boys in awe of him, I suppose it would go to your head.' Tegan refills the kettle, sets it to boil. 'Delyth spoils Andrew too,' she laughs, 'but he's such a nice kid, fair play. She's done a great job bringing him up.'

'It's no joke being a single mother.'

'Mother?' Tegan blurts. 'Oh, no, Andrew's not hers, he's not Delyth's.'

'Not Delyth's?' Melanie echoes. 'I thought he was her son?'

'Whatever gave you that idea?'

'I thought Delyth did, but I must've got the wrong end of the stick. Whose boy is he then?'

'He was Erin's.'

'*Erin's?*' A flash of the pink marble headstone. 'She was Delyth's sister, wasn't she?'

A nod. 'She got herself pregnant when she was fourteen. Pretty shocking at the time.' Tegan transports the coffee to the table. 'The shame of it, you know, what with her being so young. Well, she was just a kid, really.'

'Must've been worse again with them being such a religious bunch?' An image of Delyth's gold crucifix comes to mind.

'Are they? I didn't know that.'

'Catholics.'

'News to me.' Tegan pushes the heel of her hand to the plunger and refills their cups.

'Erin died, didn't she?' Melanie asks.

'Yes, it was very sad. She was only twenty-three.'

'What happened to her?'

'I'm not entirely sure, but I was away working in Cardiff at the time. From what I remember, it was just after Dad died, so it's all a bit of a blur. A few rumours were doing the rounds but the goings-on at Gweld Y Môr, well, it's always been a bit of a closed shop.'

'What was Erin like? Did you know her.'

A sharp laugh. 'Nothing like Delyth, that's for sure. She was dead popular at school. Great fun, you know? And so pretty, the boys all loved her. No wonder Delyth was jealous.'

'She was jealous?'

'Definitely, *yeah*. Delyth was such a plain little thing, still is, isn't she?' Tegan says this in a way that suggests the thought has just occurred to her. 'Even I was jealous of Erin.'

'Was she in your class at school?' Melanie can't remember the dates on the tombstone.

'Two years above. I looked up to her, I did, she was so special. It's sad, she never came back to school, didn't take her GCSEs or anything. I heard she struggled terrible with the baby. Was depressed and unhappy being stuck at home.' Tegan gets up to check on Ffion again and smiles when she sees she is sound asleep. 'Poor girl tried running away a few times, so people round here reckoned. Ended up in some squat in Swansea. Doing drugs, I heard. Police found her, brought her back to the farm with her tail between her legs.'

'Not with the baby?'

'No, I think she'd left him at the farm.'

A whimper from beneath the table and three pairs of eyes go to Slinky who is lying stretched out under their feet. They watch him for a moment, see he's dreaming, his back legs moving.

'Look, he's riding a bicycle,' Sian chuckles.

'Didn't you go and see her?' Melanie wants to get back to the topic of Delyth's sister.

'I tried, but I never got very far. You'd know what I mean if you went to the farm, it's a weird set-up.' Tegan drinks her coffee. 'It was like Erin suddenly changed from this fun-loving, popular kid, to someone who hid herself away.'

'Or *they* hid her away?' Sian drops the sinister suggestion into their conversation.

'Maybe.' Tegan appears to consider the idea. 'There's a lot of Welsh families like that. Batten down the hatches when stuff happens. Specially them in the rural farming community.'

'And Delyth, *what*? She just stepped in to look after Andrew after Erin died?'

'Yes, she did.'

'That was good of her. I can't imagine many who'd put their lives on hold to bring up someone else's kid.'

'Hardly someone else's, Mel. Andrew is her nephew.'

161

'Even so.'

'Didn't the boy's father want to get involved?' Sian wonders.

'I don't think Erin ever let on who he was,' Tegan answers.

'Then it's doubly admirable of Delyth.'

'There's them who say she tried to legally adopt Andrew when Erin was still alive. Apparently, she got social services round, claimed her sister wasn't a fit parent.'

'Bit mean.' Sian pulls a face.

'But didn't you say Erin abandoned him and buggered off to Swansea to live in some squat?' Melanie reminds them. 'Well, I'd say Delyth was putting Andrew first, wouldn't you?'

'Yeah, she's a good person. And you can tell she's always put Andrew's needs before her own,' Tegan, thoughtful. 'That's why it's odd about Gareth telling you to stay away from her.'

'I don't suppose either of you know what went on between the two of them, do you? And I don't mean some silly teenage infatuation, because I know it's more than that.'

'Between Gareth and Delyth? Why would you think anything went on?' Tegan, in a chair pulled up to the window, is unbuttoning her top to give Ffion a feed.

'Because of the way Gareth speaks to her . . . about her. I've never heard him be this nasty about anyone.'

'I can't imagine your Gareth being nasty.' Sian folds back the cuffs of a raspberry-pink jumper that clashes with her home-dyed hair.

'He is to Delyth.'

Neither Tegan nor Sian reply. Melanie looks past them, out through the picture windows at a blustery day by the sea; imagines what these two would say if they knew what Delyth did in the pub kitchen.

'I know she used to wind him up at school,' Tegan, from her window seat.

'But that was, *what?* — seventeen-years-ago. Why

would he still have a problem with her now?'

'Have you asked him?' Tegan: the personification of motherhood; is haloed by the pale light dripping in through the window.

'I've asked them both, but they don't want to tell me,' Melanie explains. 'I didn't tell you, did I? But that first weekend we arrived, Delyth called over with a pot of jam and a homemade card.'

'Aw, that's nice of her.'

'It was. But what she wrote in it was strange.'

'Yeah, what?' Tegan and Sian chorus.

'Something about her being good at keeping secrets.'

'Weird.'

'It is, isn't it?'

'She used to have the hots for Gareth at school, I told you that, didn't I?' Tegan says, and Melanie nods. 'He used to think she was a bit of a pest. Well, you've only got to look at yourself to know the sort of girl he goes for, Mel. He's a good-looking guy, and little mousy Delyth, well, she wouldn't be his type at all.'

'Oh, come on, all that was when they were kids,' Melanie reasons. 'He should have a bit more understanding now. She's not a love-struck teenager anymore.'

'You are quite a bit younger than Gareth and Delyth though, aren't you, Tegan?' Sian chips in. 'You might not have been all that clued-up on the ins and outs of it. Six years is a big age gap when you're a kid, and if they were in the sixth form when you were just starting secondary school, they'd have seemed miles away.'

'I suppose,' Tegan rebuttons her top, settles Ffion in her carrycot again. 'But I definitely saw the way she used to trail around after him, I wasn't too young to know that.' Melanie watches Tegan reach for one of Bronwyn's precious majolica earthenware bowls from a shelf and fill it with water and give it to the dog. 'But I agree, it's strange for him to still be holding it against her now,' she says, over sounds of Slinky's lapping. 'Maybe he's got a lot on his mind. Maybe he's just being protective of you.'

'*What?*' Melanie, bewildered. 'Why would I need protecting from Delyth? What harm could she possibly do?'

TWENTY-THREE

arefoot and in her pyjamas, Melanie is brushing her teeth over the basin. She turns off the tap, listens to the weather throw its weight against the exterior walls. The ferocity of the lashing rain and high winds is alarming. The pub feels like a ship out on a sea churning like a washing machine. She is grateful she's not married to a fisherman, listening to every wave coming in, fearing the worst. All day, Met Office warnings of gale-force winds and flash flooding along this stretch of Welsh coast. Blaming it on the tail-end of a hurricane they christened with a child's name. It's why Gareth isn't here. He's holed up in a hotel somewhere beyond Pwllglas and, with the local radio talking of roads into Pencarew still being impassable come morning, she's worried he might not make it home at all this weekend.

While she is relieved Georgie's tummy ache eased enough to tuck her up in bed, without her company, Melanie is feeling acutely alone. The pub's interior is eerily still and, melting into a matt black beyond the yellow bathroom light, feels especially strange tonight. She rinses her mouth and stares at her reflection in the cabinet mirror. Her face — naked now the make-up she put on in readiness of Gareth's homecoming has been removed — looks sallow and she applies her night-time moisturiser in firm, determined circles, refusing to be spooked by the fact she and Georgie are cut off and totally alone.

She is about to put her tooth guard in and head to

bed, when the electricity fails. The bathroom light snaps off, casting her into a blackness so solid she could push her fingers against it.

'Oh, now what?' she speaks to the gloom, to the amplified sound of rain thrashing the night-blackened windows, as apprehension bubbles in her stomach.

Lightning: a stark sheet of lilac falling between breaths; illuminates the bathroom for a heartbeat. It is quickly followed by a violent crack of thunder that clatters against the roof slates, making her jump. Panic strikes her and she gropes forward, stumbling out on to the landing. Everything is pitch black, inside and out. She isn't sure what to do and stands for a moment, listening to the rain. Its ferocity waxing and waning in a hurried cyclical tempo with several seconds of calm dropping between the violent surges. Then it's her mobile she hears, its ringtone summoning her to the bedroom. She follows the sound and pushes on the open door, is guided to the bedside cabinet by its winking blue screen.

'Gareth.' She dives on it when she sees his name flag up. 'Oh, God, it's so good to hear your voice.' She slumps on the bed. 'The power's just gone out here.'

'Are you all right? Is Georgie all right?' He sounds a frighteningly long way away.

A whimpering from somewhere nearby. Then another flash of lightning and she sees the dog cowering; the startled whites of his eyes seized in the split-second brightness. She taps her leg to beckon him to her.

'Slinky's terrified. I haven't had the chance to check on Georgie.'

'Do it,' Gareth urges. 'Take me with you.'

'I can't see anything,' she blinks on to the dark. 'Where the hell did I put the torch?'

'Try the bedside cabinet. Top. My side.'

Melanie stretches over the duvet; tugs open the drawer and fumbles its contents.

'Brilliant. Got it.' She switches it on and shadows

bloom and swell against the walls. 'Come on,' she tells the dog and Gareth. 'Let's go check on Georgie.'

A few steps and she is at her daughter's bedroom door. A tentative shine of the torch shows Georgie is asleep with Murray on her pillow. She is making little whimpering noises as if she might be chasing a rabbit across the illustrated pages of her Beatrix Potter book.

'She's fine,' she whispers and transports Gareth back to their bedroom. 'Out for the count, thank God.'

She plonks down on the bed, pats the space beside her for the dog. But he won't be persuaded to join her.

'I miss you,' she says to Gareth, her voice fraying at the edges.

'I miss you too.'

She hears him swap his phone to his other ear, the clunk of the handset against his wedding ring. 'What's your room like?'

'Lonely.' The word hovers between them. She hears him take a mouthful of something and swallow. 'Got a bottle of the house red to keep me company.'

He laughs a quick laugh: hollow and empty. A fierce beeping from her mobile severs it.

'Oh, no.' She activates the dozing screen and stares at it. 'Battery's nearly out.'

'And nothing to recharge it with.' Gareth finishes her sentence. 'You'd better save whatever juice you've got left, Mel. For emergencies.'

'You're right,' she sighs. 'Oh, great, now the torch is dying on me.' Melanie bangs it up and down on her thigh. Watches it bounce into life, before fading again.

'Switch that off too,' Gareth advises. 'You might need it.'

'I have,' she smiles through the dark; at what she carries of him in her heart. 'I'm going to need candles. D'you remember where we put them?'

He pauses and into the silence, she hears him take another mouthful of wine. 'In the kitchen, under the sink.

I put a box of them there. I think we've got another torch there too.'

'Great. Okay. Look,' she assesses the battery indicator on her phone: twelve percent. 'I'd better go.'

'Love you,' he says and hangs up.

She sits on in the darkness, the dog's black shape cringing at her calves. The nights are when she misses Gareth the most.

'Are you frightened, boy?' she asks the unanswerable question and strokes his ears to the accompanying drum-roll of thunder bouncing over the pub. 'We'll be all right.'

She yawns and slumps on the pillows, pulls the duvet over her. She should go and find the candles but, suddenly overwhelmed by tiredness, she closes her eyes and listens to the bang and clatter of the storm instead. This centuries'-old building is a sounding box, even on quieter nights its rickety windows are no deterrent to the wind that pesters to be let inside. Often, lying in bed, unable to sleep, is when the night-time motorbike riders come. Their headlamps scribbling dazzling pictograms across the ceiling. Young men in black leather, she imagines; clanking with buckles, their hair flying out behind like party streamers. They'd be like Dave, her long-ago boyfriend, these lads from nearby towns who come to race along the shoreline. She likes listening to the thrum of their engines, their shouts floating up from the shore. Feels less lonely to think of them scoring figures of eight in the sand just as she did astride Cassie's pony on Hunstanton beach in the summers before her grandmother died and her mother drank herself into oblivion, forcing concerned neighbours to call social services who had no choice but to take Melanie into care.

But there are no motorbike riders tonight. And tonight, she feels lonelier than ever. Another flash of lightning that is quickly replaced by the inscrutable blackness of a night by the sea. A blackness she doubts she will ever adjust to. It presses its face to the window along with the pulsating rain. The cold moves in between the bedcovers and her nightclothes, extinguishing all sense of tiredness. Melanie holds her breath for the next clap of thunder that, when it comes, is the most violent yet. She sits bolt upright and reaches down to comfort the dog. Wide awake and accepting she isn't going to be able to drift off to sleep now, has her pushing her toes into the moulds they have made inside her slippers, peeling back the curtain and looking out on a sea that has transformed itself into a deep and unfathomable violet blanket.

She decides to venture downstairs for a glass of wine in the hope it will help her sleep. She switches on the torch. Barely there. She thumps it against her thigh again, and it bounces into life. Might it be enough to get her to the kitchen and find the candles? She is half-wondering whether to risk it, when a loud and rapid pounding on the front door reverberates up through the floorboards.

'Who the hell?'

Trepidation thumps in her throat. A stark memory of the police officers who called to take statements after Sophie died. Wanting to hear her side of things. Wanting to know if she blamed the driver of the car, and if so, why wasn't she interested in pressing charges?

More knocking: insistent, pervasive.

'Gareth?'

A spark of hope through her quivering unease. Has he made it home after all? The possibility is enough to galvanise her into action.

'I'm coming, I'm coming,' she whispers, fearful of waking Georgie. 'But he'd never have made it through this weather and she's only just spoken to him, he's miles away . . . never mind the wine he's drunk.' Muttering to herself, she pushes out on to the landing, gropes for the bannisters, her pulse banging wildly in her wrists. 'And if he did, he'd have used his key to get in . . . but not if I put the bolts on.'

Speaking in disjointed sentences, she trails her fear, along with the dog and the waning torchlight, down the stairs to the empty bar. Raising dust and grit under her slippers, she grabs the giant wooden peppermill from its home with the cellophane-wrapped serviettes and brand new cutlery. Just in case.

'Hang on,' she calls, her voice wobbling through the frigid air. 'I'm coming.'

TWENTY-FOUR

She takes a deep breath before sliding the bolts and tugging open the heavy door. Rainwater spills along the guttering and Melanie stretches out, torch in one hand, brandishing the peppermill in the other.

'Hello?' she calls, mindful of the dog trembling against her pyjama bottoms. 'Who's there?' A gust of wind drives hard, dappled rain over her feet. 'Is anyone there?'

The torch finally gives up the ghost. She can't see a thing and is about to close up again when lightning charges the sky. A face, clarified by the flare of light: deathly pale and framed in wet hair hanging down like black rat's tails.

Delyth.

'*Jesus*!' Melanie yelps her surprise. 'You scared the shit out of me hammering the door like that. I thought you were the bloody police.' She steps back, but only enough to allow Delyth as far as the welcome mat; the woman's movement emitting the tell-tale whiff of a recent cigarette. 'How the hell did you get here? I thought the roads were flooded.'

Delyth, dripping rainwater, switches on the torch she's carrying and pokes its yellow beam beyond Melanie and into the bar.

'I guessed the power would be down with you.' She shakes her wet hair off her face. The movement flicking cold water over Melanie and the dog. 'The houses from the school to here are out too.'

'I don't know how you made it? Gareth's stuck out

on the coast road. He can't get home. It's a bloody nightmare.'

'Please don't swear, Melanie.' Delyth, her small voice competing with the downpour going on over her shoulders. 'I don't like to hear you swear. It doesn't suit you.'

Piqued at how readily she allows herself to be ticked off like a naughty child, Melanie tells herself she should be the one calling the shots, setting the rules, not this woman who thinks it's perfectly acceptable to turn up here late at night and scare her half to death.

'I came to see if you were all right, I didn't like to think of you and Georgie alone.'

How did you know we were alone? She thinks but doesn't say, asking instead: 'Why would we be a concern of yours?' She knows this is ungracious, but she can't hide her irritation at the intrusion, at the way she's been so swiftly brought into line.

'Because we're friends?'

This woman's way of moulding what ought to be a statement of fact into a question is clever, it shames Melanie into an apology.

'I'm sorry,' she says and leans her redundant torch against a skirting board. 'But it's ever so late, I was on my way to bed.'

Water droplets from Delyth's sodden coat splash to the floor; Melanie isn't going to get an answer.

'Well—' she moves to close the door, hoping Delyth gets the message without the need to spell it out. 'Thanks for coming over, but you can see we're all right.'

'Oh dear, you've cut yourself?' Delyth exclaims, pointing at Melanie's foot. 'Are you all right?'

'Oh, that was a while ago,' she flaps away the unwanted concern.

'This place is a death trap,' Delyth tuts, then bends to retrieve something from the wet doorstep. 'I brought you this. Been promising Georgie a casserole for ages, haven't I?' She passes Melanie a lidded Pyrex dish.

'What? Oh, no, y-you shouldn't have bothered . . . the stove's fitted now.' Melanie's sputtered protest as she takes what is being offered to her. Its wet sides, still warm, are slippery in her hands. 'It's very kind of you, but did you need to bring it over now?' She can't believe it, what this woman must have risked getting it here; there's no way Melanie would have ventured out in weather as atrocious as this. 'They said on the news the roads were all flooded, however did you manage it?'

'I drive a Defender, Melanie,' Delyth says as if this explains everything.

'You'd better come in.' She steps aside for her, then forces the door shut against the storm. 'Take that wet thing off, peg it up there.' Delyth does as she's told and shrugs out of her coat. 'Come on through, I'll find you a towel.' She turns, but without her own torch, she needs Delyth to lead the way. 'Not that I've anything to offer you,' she mutters, following along behind with the casserole, the peppermill tucked under an arm. 'I can't even boil a kettle.'

With the help of Delyth's torch, Melanie locates the box of fat altar candles from a cupboard under the sink.

'Matches? Where did we put the matches?'

'Here,' Delyth pulls a box from her trouser pocket, then switches off her torch.

A candle lit, Melanie places it on a saucer in the centre of the table. Sees how far it throws its light. Not far. The room around them dissolves into obscurity, the spent match smell evoking Christmas as their shadows flicker like giants against the walls.

'This is so kind of you,' she thanks Delyth again, lifting the lid of the Pyrex dish. 'Smells delicious, what's in it?'

'Beef and carrots and onions.'

'Lovely, we'll have it tomorrow. Gareth should be home by then.'

'I didn't think he'd be able to get through in that

silly car of his.' Delyth gives her opinion. 'Too low up. That Porsche of his might be okay in the city, but it's hopeless for round here.'

'I won't put it in the fridge,' Melanie talks to herself. 'They say to keep the doors closed in a power cut, don't they?'

'Not that your Mazda's much better.'

Melanie ignores the comment and retrieves what she hopes isn't one of her best tea towels.

'To dry your hair,' she passes it to Delyth who stands within arm's reach. 'Sit down,' she urges. 'Try not to trip up over him.' The dog's dark shape sneaks between them, before parking himself on the toes of Melanie's slippers. 'He's terrified, poor—' she pauses, substitutes her choice word of *bugger*, for one Delyth will prefer: '*Thing*. He's been stuck to me all night.'

Another blaze of lightning is followed by a distant rumble of thunder. The storm is finally moving away.

'Scary for you too. Here on your own.' Delyth tips forward in her chair: a dark, winged moth drawn to the candle flame.

'I was all right until the electricity went.' She encourages Slinky on to his bed, shakes out some of his biscuits.

'What about Georgie?' Delyth gives her head a vigorous rub, then jiggles her mane of hair back into place.

'She seems to have slept right through. How's things up at the farm? You're really remote out there.'

'We're fine. We've got our own generator. You might want to think about getting one yourself.'

'D'you think?' Dog settled, Melanie looks about for a bottle of wine and finds two of the long-stemmed glasses they use on special occasions. Is this a special occasion, then? Her silent question as she thanks God Gareth's not here.

'Definitely. You don't want this happening when you've guests staying.'

174

'You're right. I'll have a word with Bryn. *Brrr*,' Melanie shivers, pouring out the wine. 'It's gone cold in here.'

She retrieves her parka from behind the door and zips herself into it. When she sits down, she notices Delyth hasn't touched her wine. She assumes it's because she's driving, not that Melanie bothers to ask, but then she remembers the woman's reason the time she stayed for dinner and how she blamed her loathing of alcohol on her mother's addiction. If anyone should be deterred from drinking, it's Melanie; her own mother's ruinous dependency destroyed her childhood.

Hail against the window: a deafening round of applause. With it comes a cold draught of air which has the candleflame ducking and dancing, throwing liquid, shadowy shapes beyond their circle. They talk small talk to cover the boredom. It isn't something she needs to do with Georgie or Gareth. With Georgie, especially, their talk is honest and always of important things, otherwise, they are silent and happy to be so. Her daughter hasn't learnt the art of small talk, this is an adult's complaint; not that Melanie has ever been particularly good at it.

She yawns. The wine is soporific, and she wants her bed. She wants the cool, white linen. She wants Gareth. He should be the one here with her, not Delyth. Melanie's tired, her limbs ache, it's been a busy day what with one thing and another. She peers through the gloom at the dog, identifies his prone, black sleekness on the almost luminous blanket. He looks as if he might be sleeping, his legs are twitching like they do when he's dreaming. Such a darling, she loves that he appreciates his home comforts. John said he was way too soft to live a harsh life and that she had saved him. Melanie, lost in private thoughts, forgets herself and smiles. Dear John, she thinks, hoping he's keeping dry in the vestry's back room and its already failing roof doesn't give out on him tonight.

'Penny for them?'

Delyth's accent, unlike Gareth's, hasn't been diluted by the Thames Embankment and coupled with her softly-spoken manner it means Melanie doesn't always understand what she says.

'You what, sorry?' Surfacing from her daydreaming and her concerns for John.

'Penny for them. Your thoughts, isn't it?'

'Mummy? Mummy?' Georgie calls to her from upstairs. It saves her the need to share. 'I'm frightened. Where's the lights gone?'

Melanie springs to her feet and grabs the saucer with its candle. 'I'm here,' she rushes into the bar. 'Don't worry, the electricity's gone down for a minute.'

'Where's Slinky?' Georgie's voice filters through the guttering candlelight. 'I can't find him anywhere.'

'It's okay, sweetheart. He's with me. He was a bit scared of the thunder.' A few purposeful strides and Melanie reaches the foot of the stairs. 'You stay where you are, I'm coming up.' She calls to the dog, and together, with Delyth in tow, they head up to the flat.

'D'you mind waiting here? I won't be a minute,' she says to Delyth who hovers at her back. 'She had another of her tummy aches earlier, I hope it's not come back.'

'Poor Georgie. I should've brought some of that mint tea.' Delyth's face floats pale as a moon in the dimness. 'I'll bring some next time.'

'You got your torch?' Melanie checks, her concern is for her daughter — she's only half listening to what this woman says.

Delyth answers by switching it on.

'Good, okay. I won't be minute.' She leaves her at the top of the stairs. Walks away through the dark, haloed by candle flame: a pyjama-clad Florence Nightingale.

After a quick rendition of Peter Rabbit, mostly from memory because there is little more than a flickering flame to read by, Georgie settles down. Happy the storm is easing, Slinky, now curled at the foot of her bed, is fast asleep. When Melanie emerges from Georgie's room, Delyth isn't where she left her. The landing is empty. But there's a muted light leaking from the living room and she carries the stubby candle towards it, pushes open the door to find her standing in a hoop of torchlight.

'Do you mind if we call it a night?' Melanie yawns and hopes her unwanted visitor gets the hint.

There is no resistance and Melanie escorts Delyth out into the rain. Waits on the step until the Defender reverses between the pillars and the red tail lights disappear into the road. She learnt her lesson and won't risk a repeat of what happened the last time she thought Delyth had gone home. As she closes the pub door, Melanie thinks how Delyth's visits don't end. That like the vague waft of unhappiness she leaves behind with her cigarette smell, they hang in the air and eventually evaporate.

What was she doing in here? Melanie, upstairs in the living room again, extends her candle-holding arm out through the dark. The gambolling flame shows the contents of the last of the crates left to unpack has been rummaged through. Her books have been taken out and not put back properly. Blaming Georgie, or Gareth, she bends to tidy them, but she knows this isn't true. Georgie wouldn't be interested and Gareth hasn't been home for a week.

'Ouch!'

The sting of hot wax has her pull back her hand. It's a waste of time, she can't see enough anyway. But hang on, a thought nudging into view — wasn't this the box Gareth's old school photo was in? And hadn't Delyth been especially interested in looking at it the first time she invited her inside the pub?

The electricity clicks into life. Lights: sudden and stinging her eyes. Yes, she realises, eyes adapting to the brightness — Gareth's photograph has gone.

TWENTY-FIVE

L ate the following afternoon, Melanie stands looking out through the tall glass patio doors. What a view. It never fails to amaze. She shifts her gaze beyond the beer garden, to the melodramatic white-tipped breakers. And higher, to slow, fat clouds, pink as corn cockles floating over a whale-grey sky. Calmer now the thunderstorm that raged all night has blown away inland.

Gareth has spent most of the day erecting a swing and now it's finished, he is lifting Georgie on to the blue plastic seat and pushing her higher and higher. Sounds of excited laughter finds her through the glass. They have no idea she's here. Guilty pleasures. As watching them play together is one of her favourite pastimes. This is what fathers are, she thinks, they are for the small things, the practicalities in life, like tying shoelaces and stringing kites. A pang for her own father and wherever he might be in the world, if indeed he is still in the world. Because Melanie has never met him, her mother always maintained she was too drunk to remember who he was, so he doesn't even have a name. It used to make her sad, imagining him looking up at the same moon she was and knowing nothing of her existence. But not anymore. Since meeting Gareth, she rarely thinks of her father at all. Her heart surges with love for her little family and tears fill her eyes. Happy tears, grateful tears, she wipes them with a thumb and backs away to go and prepare dinner. Which thanks to Delyth, means there is very little to do.

*

'*Mm*, that smells good.' Gareth, fresh from the shower, nuzzles into Melanie's neck.

She puts down her paring knife and the cooking apple she's peeling, breathes in his aftershave.

'What are we having? I'm starved.' He peers through the glass doors of their newly installed kitchen range.

'After the lunch we had? You can't be.'

'I can't help it,' he taps his midriff. 'I'm a growing boy.'

She giggles, tugs on oven gloves and, to a hot blast of air, lifts Delyth's Pyrex dish out on to the iron trivet.

'Delicious,' Gareth grins when she lifts the lid for him to see. 'What's in it?'

'Beef, I think.' Melanie, instantly realising her mistake, returns the casserole to the oven. 'I mean, beef.' She asserts. 'Yes, it's beef.'

'You don't sound sure.' He eyes her quizzically.

'Yes, I am. It's beef.' She resumes her apple peeling. 'And there's tarte tatin for pudding.'

'You spoil me.' Gareth kisses her. 'D'you want me to fetch Georgie?'

'Would you?'

'I don't like it.' Georgie sucks the end of a plait and turns her nose up at the serving Melanie ladles on her plate. 'What sort of meat is it?' She pushes the cubes of pork-like protein around with a spoon.

'Beef, darling. It's beef.' It's what Delyth told her, so she's sticking to it.

'What d'you think, Gareth? Is it okay?'

179

'I'm sorry, Mel, I'm with Georgie.' He pulls a face and pushes his plate away. A look from Melanie has him drag it towards him again.

'I'm not eating anymore.' Georgie spits out what's in her mouth and makes a face in the upside of her spoon.

'Have you got a tummy ache again?'

Georgie shakes her head.

'Okay. Good girl. We've probably just not got our appetites back after that enormous lunch, eh?' Melanie puts her fork down; she has to agree with her family, the casserole is inedible.

'It was a bit of a blowout, wasn't it?' Gareth rubs his stomach, stretches back in his chair.

'You said you were hungry.' Melanie reaches for his hand and squeezes it. 'Okay, well, who's for pudding?'

'Better not tell Delyth we didn't like her dinner,' Georgie says sweetly. 'Because we love her cakes and stuff, don't we Mummy?'

'*Delyth* — what's that about Delyth?'

'No, sweetheart,' Melanie avoids her husband's question and replies to her daughter. 'There's no need to say anything because that would be rude, wouldn't it?'

'You're not telling me Delyth cooked that?' Gareth's expression is darkening.

'I don't think savoury is her forte.' Melanie's stomach clenches. Stupid of her to think he wouldn't find out, and stupid to think he'd let it go if he did. 'But not to worry, I've made us a nice pudding, and Slinky will do the casserole justice, won't you boy? Come on,' she rallies the dog. 'Dustbin that you are, here you go.' And she slides the uneaten meal into his bowl.

'Do I have to have custard?' Georgie whines. 'I don't like custard.'

'Are you going to answer me?' Gareth isn't going to let this drop.

'How about ice cream?'

Georgie responds with whoops and cheers.

'Melanie!' Gareth secures her attention. 'Tell me.'

'Yes, yes, okay. Delyth made the casserole. She brought it over last night. I didn't tell you because I knew you'd go off on one.'

'*Go off on one?* I don't go off on one.'

'You do when her name comes up in conversation.'

'So what? She brought it round. You didn't have to cook it.'

'I didn't want to waste it, it smelt perfectly lovely, you said so yourself.' Hands on hips, determined not to argue in front of their child. 'Would you like some pudding?'

He nods grimly. 'But only because you made it. I told you before, I don't want—'

'I know, Gareth, but *please*,' a sidelong glance at Georgie. 'I didn't ask her, did I? She just turned up with it.'

'All right. I don't want to argue about it either. But honestly, Mel . . .' Whatever he was going to say, he keeps to himself.

She smiles her thanks and turns the tarte tatin out on to a plate. Hot and glossy-topped from the oven, she cuts three slices. 'I don't want anything to spoil our time together. I honestly didn't think you were going to make it home at all this weekend.'

'Me neither,' his voice is gravelly. 'Hardly slept a wink all night.'

'Me neither.'

'Make up for it tonight?' he winks. 'Have an early one, shall we?'

Dinner over, it is with her hip pressed to the sharp-edged kitchen work-surface that Melanie rinses the dinner plates and casserole dish and loads the dishwasher that was only plumbed in a day or so ago. She listens to her chattering daughter. A sound that should be coming from two little girls. Was Sophie punishment for what she and Gareth did to Elizabeth? Is that how it works. The unanswerable question is accompanied by a memory of those distressing phone calls early on in their marriage. Brandy-fuelled tirades deep into the night. Then the solicitor's letters: fake and threatening, that Elizabeth would type out and push through their letterbox. Threatening what? Melanie can't remember now, but she can remember feeling sorry for her. But not sorry enough to let her in the time she turned up when Gareth was at work, shortly after the twins were born. A wreck of a woman, flabby and overused, nothing of the girl in the photograph Bronwyn keeps. It had been hard for Melanie to see what the attraction for Gareth had been as she watched her wobbling mouth, her sunken, dry-eyed stare. The woman looked wrung out. But she would, wouldn't she? She'd lost her husband, the man she loved, and any chance of having a family with him.

It was why she paid for Elizabeth's taxi home. Why she took two twenty-pound notes from her purse and pushed them between her husband's ex-wife's fingers, telling her she was sorry, that she hadn't set out to hurt her. Elizabeth stopped hounding them after that, according to Bronwyn, she immersed herself in her academic world and has been there ever since. Not that Melanie can relax, the fear there is yet more trouble to come — whether from Elizabeth or elsewhere, has never left her. She suspects she will spend the rest of her life holding her breath for it.

'Mummy . . . Daddy!' Georgie shrieks. 'It's Slinky, look, he won't get up. His mouth's gone all bubbly.'

'What?' Melanie, snapping back to the present, rapidly dries her hands and spins to find the dog slumped against the legs of Gareth's chair. 'What's going on? What have you done?' she shouts at her husband and child, dropping to her knees to cradle Slinky's head in her hands.

'It's not me,' Georgie shouts back.

'No, we've not done anything.' Gareth is beside her on the floor. 'It's that horrible stuff Delyth gave you. I told you something was wrong with it.'

TWENTY-SIX

The waiting room at the veterinary surgery is crowded with every conceivable pet. Melanie, Gareth and Georgie, tacking their way across the darkened car park, still in their slippers, push through the swing doors and into it. Melanie's shoulders ache under the weight of the dog who lies like a colossal baby in her arms. Refusing all offers to carry him, she babbles nervous nonsense to the woman on the desk.

'If you could hang on for me, just a minute,' the receptionist sees the situation and is on to it. 'I'll get someone to look at him right away.'

Within seconds they are guided into a consulting room.

'You best wait here with Georgie. Just in case,' Melanie says before she and Slinky disappear beyond the rubber-coated door.

She lowers the dog, frothy-mouthed and shaking, on to the examination table. A tall, bearded man in a white coat snaps on a pair of latex gloves and sets about examining him. Melanie shifts from foot to foot in the silence, her anxiety intensifying amid the antiseptic smells and posters warning of lungworm and ticks.

'It looks to me, Mrs Sayer,' the senior partner lifts his gaze to hers. 'Like he's been poisoned.'

'Poisoned!' she shouts her alarm.

'I believe so,' the tone is heavy. 'Can you tell me what it is he's eaten, where he's been?'

'He's not been anywhere,' Melanie is confused. 'Only the usual. A walk on the beach, or was it up on the headland?' Her head is hurting under the fierce light. 'Hang on, I remember now,' she strokes Slinky's rich, dark coat. Neck to tail, neck to tail. His violent convulsions frightening her. 'We had to stay on the beach today, didn't we, boy,' she talks to the dog. 'It was too windy, really windy. After the storm, I suppose.' She knows she's rambling, that this is useless information. 'But that was hours ago, and I watched him all the time. I threw his ball for him, that was all.'

'All right. The beach you say?' the vet is keen to clarify. 'Which beach was this?'

'Pencarew. We live in Pencarew. Me and my husband. We've bought the Monkstone Arms . . . we're in the process of—' she closes her mouth, realises this too is unnecessary information. 'Yes, the beach at Pencarew.' She focuses on the top of the vet's head as he takes Slinky's temperature; sees his dark hair is flecked with grey.

'Now, tell me, what's he eaten?' The vet rootles the cupboards behind him, returns with a syringe of something in his hand.

'*Erm*. Well, he had his food. *Burns* food.'

'Good. Nothing wrong with that.' The vet strokes Slinky's juddering body, then administers the injection of clear liquid into his neck without explaining what it is. 'What else?'

'*Erm*,' fingers against her mouth, then remembering, 'Oh, yes, some casserole. Nothing wrong with that either, is there?'

'There could be. What was in it?' The vet, calm and steady, strokes the dog.

'I don't bloody well know,' she snaps: panicky, forgetting herself. 'I'm sorry. I didn't mean to shout. But can't you do something? Stop him shaking?'

'The casserole? Mrs Sayer,' he pushes.

'I don't know what was in it, a friend made it,' babbling again. 'But my husband and our little girl, we didn't fancy it, and Slinky, well, you know what dogs are like? We gave it to him. *Please*, do something. You've got to help him.'

'We'll do all we can. We'll keep him in overnight, flush him out. See how he responds.' The vet has finished injecting whatever it was, and her dog goes limp in her hands.

'He's going to be all right, though, isn't he?' It is Melanie's turn to shake. 'Y-you see, m-my husband, our little girl,' she begins to cry. 'We've grown ever so fond of him, and-and we've-we've only . . . Sophie . . . not long ago. We can't lose Slinky too.'

'We'll do our best, Mrs Sayer, but you must prepare yourself for the worst. The prognosis doesn't look good.'

'Oh, please . . . please. You can't let him die. You can't let him die,' she wails, grabbing the sleeve of his white coat.

The vet takes her hands in a way you might a hysterical child, squeezes them gently and returns them to her.

'What would be good,' he says. 'Is if you could bring us a sample of what he's eaten . . . a sample of the casserole. It would greatly help his chances if we could analyse it. We'd know what we were dealing with then.'

'Right,' she agrees, grateful to have something constructive to do. 'We'll nip home, be back soon as we can.'

She rushes out into the waiting room, to a sombre Gareth and a teary-eyed Georgie. Forgetting — as her husband presses his foot to the floor of the Mazda, skipping at least one red light — that any remnants of Delyth's casserole have either been eaten by the dog or washed away.

TWENTY-SEVEN

November. A time of rotting windfalls and the swallows long gone. Melanie identifies autumn's melancholy breath when she drops her passenger window to look out on the town netted in a fine sea mist. The Co-op car park, with its stunning sea views, is enveloped by low cloud and is surprisingly full for a Sunday morning. Gareth, already in a foul temper after the shock of the evening before, must do a double lap before he finds a parking place.

'We could drive to Pwllglas and make a day of it,' Melanie suggests, to lift the mood.

'I'm too knackered to do much more than this,' he yawns and slumps in his seat.

'Might have been better than moping around waiting for the vet to ring. And you won't like it in here,' she warns, quickly doing up her window before he cuts the engine. 'There's never much left on Sundays.'

'I don't care, it'll have to do.' Gareth secures the handbrake. 'I can hardly keep my eyes open.'

'Terrible night.' She checks her mobile for the umpteenth time.

'I hardly slept a wink.'

'That's two nights on the trot,' Melanie's turn to yawn. 'Are you going to be okay for work tomorrow? For the drive back, I mean.'

'Going to have to be.' Gareth sighs and undoes his seatbelt, but he still doesn't move.

'It's been one thing after another.' Melanie swivels in her seat to check on Georgie, her parka rustling in the tight metal void of the car. 'You're looking better, sweetheart.' And she is, her dimpled cheeks are swirled with pink. 'How are you feeling?'

'I'm okay,' Georgie says, her eyes like two wet pools. 'I just want Slinky home.'

'I know, you do. So do I.' Melanie reaches behind her, rubs her daughter's legs to jolly her along. 'We should hear something soon.'

'D'you think it was the casserole that made him sick, Daddy?'

'Course it was.' Gareth rubs an irritable hand over his thick, dark stubble. 'What else could it be?'

'We don't know that, love,' Melanie frowns at him. 'Not for sure.'

'Don't we?' His fierceness makes her jump. 'What other explanation is there? One minute he's right as rain, the next, wallop.'

'But if it was the casserole, it doesn't mean Delyth did it deliberately.'

'Course it was sodding deliberate.'

'That's one hell of an accusation.'

'I keep telling you that she's dangerous, that she's a nutter. But you won't listen, will you?'

'For goodness sake,' Melanie's conscious that Georgie's listening and wishes they could have this conversation out of her earshot. 'Have you heard yourself? That woman couldn't hurt a fly.'

'You just can't see it, can you? You're so gullible; always seeing the good in people. It's a-a,' he bites his lip, and she can tell it takes everything he's got not to swear again. 'It's a flaming annoying habit. Cos you're forgetting something crucial here—'

'And what's that?'

'That casserole was meant for us.'

Melanie considers this cold, hard, fact for a

moment. Pretends it doesn't bother her. 'Oh, come on, she wouldn't.' A vehement shake of her head. 'She wouldn't.'

'Yes, Daddy, Delyth's our friend,' Georgie pipes up. 'She wouldn't want to hurt us.'

'I'm not so sure.' Gareth slides his gaze to Melanie. 'How much more proof d'you need?'

'Gareth, please.?' She really doesn't want to have this discussion in front of their child. 'We need to wait, hear what the vet has to say. Georgie's right, Delyth's our friend. Let's not get carried away, yeah?'

'The vet said *poisoned*, didn't he? Well, that casserole was poisoned.'

He's right, the vet did say poisoned, Melanie thinks but fearful of stoking his fire, says nothing.

'I know she's trying to poison us.' His eyes are hard. 'Why else has Georgie been having these tummy problems *all of a sudden*. You thought about that?'

'What?' Melanie stares at him — has he finally lost the plot? 'I've taken her to see Dr Cassidy. Twice. I'll make another appointment next week. He's talking about running some allergy tests, he's as flummoxed as we are, but he doesn't think it's anything serious.'

'Blasted doctors. What d'they know? I'll tell you what's wrong with her, shall I?' Gareth smacks his palms against the steering wheel. 'It's those cakes that woman brings round.'

'Oh, come on. I eat them too, and I'm all right.' Melanie tries to reason, then adds, 'Look, Gareth, I'm not having this conversation now,' a glance at their daughter. '*Please*, we need to wait. We need the facts.'

'And we'd have had them by now if you hadn't washed the evidence away.'

'Oh, I wondered how long it would take you.' She unclips her seatbelt, tips herself out of the car. 'That's it, put the blame on me.' She talks to the back of his head while she opens the rear door to help Georgie from her car seat.

Gareth reaches behind him for his sweater, tugs it

on over his head. Whatever else he says is lost to the muffle of mouth on material.

'Come on, let's get this over with,' he says, locking the car and jogging away through the hiss of the supermarket's sliding doors. Pausing to collect a basket on the way.

'Don't worry, Slinky's going to be fine,' Melanie fastens Georgie into her silver puffer jacket. 'I don't know why Daddy's got such a problem with Delyth. She's a nice person, isn't she? She's been very kind to us.'

'I like her,' Georgie squeezes out a smile.

'There we go then. We're not going to listen to any more of your Daddy's nonsense.'

Georgie holds out her hand for her mother to take, and they look up at the unexpected rhythmic flap of a heron as it passes low overhead: a bird so huge, it momentarily blocks out the light.

Melanie grips Georgie's hand and jigs it up and down. 'Come on, let's go and get something nice for dinner. Something nice and easy.' At the entrance, Melanie puts a ten-pound note into the poppy appeal box, takes three poppies. 'What d'you fancy?' she asks, pinning one to Georgie's lapel and one to her own.

'Pizza. Can we have pizza?'

'Let's go and have a look, shall we?'

They find Gareth halfway down the bread aisle, flapping his list. Melanie pockets the third poppy, deciding now isn't the time. The store is still dressed for Halloween and Melanie trails the strings of skulls and plastic spiders journeying the polystyrene ceiling tiles that nobody's taken down. The usual piped medley of Eighties' music is more irritating than usual, although, it won't be long before it will be wall-to-wall Christmas jingles, she thinks gloomily, unable to decide what's worse.

'Would you credit it?' Gareth, too loud, rubs a hand over his thinning crown. 'They haven't even got a wholemeal loaf. It's totally useless in here.'

'I did warn you. They always run out of stuff on Sundays.' Melanie surrenders Georgie's hand and squats to check the lower shelves. 'They've got a sliced Hovis. Thick cut. That'll do, won't it?' Upright, she shakes it under his nose before dropping it into the basket.

They turn their heads to the sound of clanking and see a high-sided trolley roll towards them.

'Can I be of any help?' the tiny voice from behind it asks. 'What are you looking for?'

Gareth spins on his heels. '*You?* What are you doing here?'

'I work here.' Delyth, swamped by her Co-op uniform, is filling shelves from the large metal trolley that is an obvious struggle to manoeuvre.

'Hi, Delyth,' Melanie smiles at the woman who looks as vulnerable as a child on her first day of school.

'Useless shop.' Gareth sulks, picking up a tin of something, inspecting the label, then slamming it back down.

'If you tell me what you're looking for, maybe I could help.' Flicking her long black hair over her shoulders, Delyth returns Melanie's smile.

'I think you've done enough, don't you?' Gareth growls at her.

'Things are a bit fraught at the moment, Delyth,' Melanie steps between them, keen to explain.

'Too right,' Gareth pushes his wife away and drops his face dangerously close to Delyth's. 'Since you poisoned our dog.'

'Poisoned your dog?' Delyth looks blank. 'That's horrible, what are you saying?' She lifts her eyes to Melanie: helpless, pleading.

'That casserole you made.' Gareth swings the shopping basket at the end of his arm: a pendulum in the dangling moments it takes Delyth to answer.

'The casserole?'

'Yes. It was so disgusting, we fed it to the dog. And now, thanks to you, he's on a drip at the vets and is probably going to die.'

At the word 'die', Georgie's face crumples and she bursts into tears.

'Now look what you've done,' Melanie bends to comfort her. 'Daddy didn't mean it, sweetheart. Slinky's going to be just fine.'

'We don't know that,' he says, then returns his attention to Delyth who cowers and backs away.

'I'm sorry about this,' Melanie apologises to her. 'Gareth's convinced—'

'Stay out of this,' he warns before refocusing his anger on Delyth: 'You meant for us to eat that stuff. It's us you want dead.'

'I don't know what you're talking about?' The woman scans the aisle, nervously fretting the hem of her dark-grey tunic.

'Liar!' Gareth flings his head back. 'Try telling that to the police.'

'The police?' The voice is small and pleading. 'What are you talking about the police for?'

'Don't come the innocent with me. You know what you did.' Gareth is oblivious to the small crowd of shoppers that have gathered to watch. But Melanie isn't and, abandoning her daughter, steps up beside him.

'*Gareth*. Stop it. Stop it.' She tugs his arm. 'We don't know this is what happened, not yet.' But he throws her away, determined to have his say.

'You can't stand it, can you?' Gareth to Delyth. 'You can't stand to see other people happy. You were a miserable cow at school and you're even more of a miserable cow now.'

'Gareth!' Melanie, consoling Georgie, who is visibly distressed by her father's behaviour, shouts at him from the side-lines. 'Why are you being like this?' His aggression frightens her. 'Delyth's done nothing wrong. Not wittingly, anyway. For goodness sake, stop it. Leave her alone.'

Melanie watches Delyth. Wonders why she doesn't kick back and defend herself? There's no way she'd let someone speak to her like this. But not Delyth, it seems her nature won't permit her to be bold. Perhaps she thinks she can win him round, that this show of self-effacing goodness will ultimately disarm him. But why would she want to win him round? It's obvious Gareth despises her; he makes no attempt to disguise it. And now, with whatever might have happened to the dog, he feels he's got a legitimate excuse to treat her badly. What does she want? Melanie asks her silent question. Is she as besotted with him as an adult as she was as a teenager?

Delyth grips her gold crucifix, her large, dark eyes welling with tears.

'Look at her.' Gareth challenges the shoppers who've gathered to see what the fuss is about. 'Playing the sympathy card. It's pathetic.' He crosses his arms. 'Convincing though, isn't she? She's always been good at playing the *Poor Little Me* card. But it's an act . . . it's all a bloody act.'

Someone must have fetched the manager, because he is suddenly amongst them, threatening to remove Gareth from the premises. Not that Melanie thinks he is equipped to carry out his threat. He only looks about sixteen, with his spots and bum fluff; he's certainly no match for her burly husband when he's as pumped-up as this.

Delyth is sobbing openly now. Melanie reaches out to Gareth but again he shoves her away. Delyth sees it, the crowd of shoppers see it too. And they whisper about him behind their hands.

'I'm sorry, sir, but we're going to have to ask you to leave if you don't calm down.'

'Calm down!' Gareth wags an angry finger. 'I'd like to see how any of you lot would react if she'd tried to poison your family.'

The store manager gives Delyth a questioning look. She returns it with a shrug, her mouth wobbling through her tears.

'Sir, I do have to warn you,' the young man tries again. 'If you don't do as I ask, then I will have to call the police.'

'Good,' Gareth, forceful. 'It'll save me from having to.'

'I don't think you're listening, sir. The abuse of staff is something we take very seriously.' The store manager briefly closes his eyes and Melanie can tell he knows he's out of his depth but perseveres anyway. 'So, if you would please—'

'It's okay,' Melanie does what he can't, and grabs hold of her husband; feels the tautness of his bicep, the power beneath his pullover. And perhaps for the first time, understands his potential for violence. 'We're going.'

Holding Georgie's hand and steering Gareth, she marches them out of the store. Dumping the basket with the sliced loaf they need for breakfast at the exit, they stride out into the blustery car park.

'Have you completely lost your mind?'

'No. I'm just saying what needs to be said.' Gareth stomps away, forcing Melanie and Georgie to run to catch him. 'She riles me up.' He clenches his jaw. 'Standing there, all-all . . . she makes me sick.'

'What you did, it was horrible. *Horrible*,' she shouts. 'Gareth, stop. Listen to me. *Listen to me*. You can't go hurling accusations around. You made her cry. You're nothing but a bully.' Melanie clutches Georgie's hand and feels like crying herself.

'Ouch, Mummy.' Georgie grizzles. 'You're hurting me.'

'Am I? Oh, dear, I'm sorry.' Melanie loosens her hold and looks behind her at the store's entrance. Sees Delyth hovering by the buckets of flowers. 'She's there.

Look. She's followed us out. Go back and apologise to her.'

'Apologise to her?' Gareth turns when he reaches the car, his expression indignant.

'Yes.'

'No way. She's probably enjoying this — us, arguing.'

Melanie drags an exasperated hand through her hair.

The mist they woke to has blown away to reveal a sparkling blue day and something, probably the dark undercarriage of a seabird, has her jerk her head to the vast bow of the cliff. She sees John, alone on one of the salt-crusted benches, staring out to sea. When he turns his head, she forgets herself and lifts an arm to wave in his direction. Not that he signals back and, feeling an idiot, tells herself he was too far away to see her.

'Who are you waving at?' her husband's question is automatic.

'No one.'

Gareth gives a cursory nod before starting up again. 'She's jealous, isn't it?' His Welsh accent is stronger than ever. 'She probably wants you to leave me, so she can have me all to herself.'

Melanie searches his face for the irony that isn't there.

'Why the hell would she want you? You're horrible to her.'

'Well, all right then,' Gareth rejigs his argument. 'She wants to split us up. She wants to destroy our marriage.'

'Is that right?' Melanie laughs: brittle, derisive. 'I don't think you need anyone else's help in that department, I think you're managing that perfectly well on your own.'

'She is,' he insists, wringing his hands. 'She's trying to split us up.'

Melanie glances around, is grateful no one from the town is close enough to hear the contents of their argument.

'Why can't you see her for what she is?' Gareth

again.

'I don't know who you are anymore. You're frightening me.'

'You're frightening *me*,' he says and looks more pitiful than angry now. 'You're so *gullible*. You're everyone's flaming friend.'

'Why are you being so nasty? I've not done anything wrong.' Melanie fights back tears. 'What is it with you and that woman? Did you two have something going once?'

'What! With that? Don't be ridiculous.'

'Ridiculous now, am I? Why? Because I refuse to buy the drivel you keep feeding me. I'm not stupid, Gareth, I know something's gone on.'

He says nothing. He simply turns and walks to the rear of the car park. Hands in his jeans' pockets, fixed on the sea.

'If you don't tell me, I'm sure Delyth will.' Melanie threatens, following on behind with Georgie. 'I could tell she wanted to talk.' A burst of the blood on the kitchen floor, the cold feel of the steel blade. She winces into the memory. 'Delyth was on about some bloke who'd ruined her life. That was you, wasn't it?' Melanie accuses. 'Yes, I get it now,' she says, even though she plainly doesn't. 'She was on about you, and that's what all this is about.'

'Don't be so bloody stupid.' He turns and marches back to the car. 'D'you honestly think someone like me would've been interested in her?'

'You don't half think a lot of yourself, don't you?' she tuts, cradling Georgie's head in her hands. She's given up trying to curb his bad language, but she worries for her daughter and wishes again that they could have had this conversation away from her. 'Georgie thinks you're being unreasonable, don't you, sweetheart?'

Their daughter nods, plays with her plaits.

Gareth unlocks the Mazda, bounces the keys in his hand: dice he is about to cast. 'Look, I don't know what it is, I just can't stand her.'

'You want to get a grip. You're not in the playground anymore.' She senses the weight of his gaze but refuses to receive it. 'We're going to be opening up for business in a month. Do you think people are going to want to patronise us after that performance? Half the town was in there today; in case you didn't notice. And you were vicious, Gareth. Vicious.' The accusation is heavy, too heavy for the wind shuffling up from the shore to disperse. 'This is a small place, word gets about,' she echoes the warning Tegan gave her about her friendship with John. 'You can't go behaving like that. And anyway, what sort of example are you setting our child?' She bends to guide Georgie into the back of the car and fastens her seatbelt. 'Are you even listening to me?'

From her position in the front passenger seat, Melanie looks sideways at her husband: a man she is struggling to recognise. Gareth drums his fingers on the steering wheel and she comes to realise he is a person of empty gestures. His habit of jangling loose change in his pocket, the way he clears his throat. Who is he? — this man she married and fell in love with. The father of her child.

'You can't blame me for being suspicious,' she says finally.

'Suspicious of what?'

'Of the two of you.' Melanie follows his gaze as it travels the horizon. 'Because something's gone on, you've definitely got history.'

'She tried to poison us, Mel,' his tone is reasonable. 'Isn't that enough?'

'No, it isn't. Not when we don't know that for sure.' She squints through a sudden shaft of sunlight spearing the windscreen. 'There's something more going on here, I know it.'

'You know it, do you?' The look is nasty.

'Okay,' she says, relenting a little, wanting to give him the chance to redeem himself. 'I know she can seem a bit odd.' Another flash of the blood against the floor tiles, the raw cuts on the tender insides of Delyth's arms. 'But she's got a good heart, she's been—'

'I want you to stay away from her.' Gareth cuts her off: a boulder thrown into a stream. 'I mean it, Mel.'

She turns her head, stares out at the last of summer's leaves being blown around the car park. Thinks again how they shouldn't be having this discussion in front of their child.

'You telling me to stay away from Delyth's not going to work, you know. Being like you were just now, it's only making me more suspicious. Why won't you just tell me? What are you hiding?'

Her questions go unanswered and, wary of pushing him anymore, the three of them sit in frost-bitten dumbness.

Then Melanie's mobile rings. The violence splinters the silence.

She looks at Gareth, then at Georgie, and pulls it from her coat pocket. Stares at the illuminated screen in alarm.

'It's the vets.'

She closes her eyes and takes a deep breath before answering the call.

TWENTY-EIGHT

'M rs Sayer?' The voice, a young woman's, competes with canine whimpering and yelps. 'Sara, it is. From Bishop Lane Vets?'

'Hi, Sara.' Melanie tries to keep the trepidation hammering in her chest out of her voice. 'Have you got news for us?'

'Slinky's fine, Mrs Sayer.'

'Sorry, you what?' Melanie's unsure if she heard correctly and activates the loudspeaker for them all to listen.

'He's out of the woods. He's off his drip and doing fine.'

'He's fine! Oh, that's wonderful.' She whips her head to Georgie who is squealing and clapping her hands.

'Yes, he's breathing normally, and he's comfortable.'

'Oh, thank goodness,' she exhales, looks down at Gareth's hand that has found its way on to her thigh. She squeezes it and grins at him.

'Yes, Mrs Sayer,' the voice is solemn. 'Your dog was lucky to survive.'

'W-was it . . . poison?' Melanie is scared to ask.

'Of a sort, yes.'

'From the casserole?'

'No, it was nothing you fed him.'

'Right,' she says, and sees Gareth smack his skull back against the headrest.

'Test results show he ingested some algae.'

'*Algae?*'

'A blue-green algae found in stagnant water. Brackish water. It can be lethal.'

'But how? How's that possible?'

'It's been traced to a pond at the north end of Pencarew Bay.'

'A pond?' Melanie struggles for breath. 'I didn't know about any pond.'

'It wouldn't usually be a problem, but with it being milder than normal for the time of year . . . the algae, well it contaminated the water.' The young woman explains. 'There've been other dogs showing similar symptoms, we've been inundated today.'

'Sounds dreadful,' Melanie frowns.

'It is. We've had problems like this before. Stagnant water isn't a hazard many people appreciate. And as a dog owner, you do need to be aware.'

'Right, okay, I've never heard of that before.' Melanie removes her hand from Gareth's and presses it to her chest. 'So, just to make sure, it wasn't anything he ate, nothing we gave him?' she lifts her eyes to Gareth's, wanting him to hear, to understand. 'The thing is you see; we rather jumped the gun. Blamed the friend who made us the casserole.' She is enjoying this, enjoying rubbing it in.

'No, nothing he ate. It was the algae,' Sara confirms. 'Cyanobacteria. That's the proper name for it.'

'Okay, good. I'm just glad we didn't call the police because as you say, no one's to blame.' This is for Gareth's benefit. 'It's easy to jump to the wrong conclusion in the panic of it all.'

'I suppose so,' the veterinary nurse agrees.

'When can we come and fetch him?'

'*Ooo*, let me see, I think we'll want to observe him for a little while longer.' Pages being turned. 'Shall we say midday tomorrow?'

'Tomorrow's great. Thank you so much for calling and for everything you've done for him.'

'It's a pleasure. We'll see you tomorrow.'

Melanie hangs up. Returns the phone to her pocket.

'Right,' she says to Gareth. 'You're going to have to go and apologise to Delyth. Go on,' she pushes, sensing his reluctance. 'She's still outside.'

Gareth unclips his seatbelt and gets out of the car.

Melanie watches him in the wing mirror. She might not be able to hear what is said, but going by his frantic hand gestures, he's most certainly raising his voice. She admires Delyth: her composure, the dignified way she holds her ground; as Gareth undoubtedly dishonours himself yet again.

'What did you say to her?' she asks when he's back in the driving seat.

Not that he answers. His mouth set in a thin, grim line as he reverses out of the car park space. And thinking how this demonstrates how little she knows him; Melanie is too scared to demand that he tell her.

TWENTY-NINE

Over a fortnight later, on a day when winter has well and truly blown in, Melanie listens to a sudden shower of hail drum the roof and imagines the wind scouring the bald hills above the town. Home from taking Georgie to school and a walk with the dog along the beach, she sets about tidying the kitchen, now and again lifting her head to look about her. A small smile curves her lips as she appreciates the gleaming walls and marble-topped units. Bryn's team have worked magic turning this from bombsite into the luxurious space it now is. With only the extractor fan to fit and the electric fly zapper to secure to the wall, everything is finished in here. She counts the weeks until Christmas, lists the jobs still left to do in readiness of opening and realises she's on track, there is nothing to fret about.

Tantalising smells of warm chocolate and sweet amaretto remind her of the second batch of biscuits. The ones she's made for John. With Delyth conspicuously absent since that unpleasantness at the Co-op, Melanie's been putting in some practice of her own. And she's been busy. Pleased with this morning's creations, she hopes these sugared offerings will lift John's heart. She turns off the oven and transfers the biscuits to a wire rack, tears off a sheet of greaseproof paper in readiness of wrapping them. She inspects the biscuits, presses one to check it's firming up the way it should. Quite why she wants to please John this much, she doesn't know, but in the ticking-down sounds of the cooling oven, she admits she is especially drawn to him. Yes, it's partly to do with feeling sorry for him, but it's also that he's kind-hearted and gentle. Qualities she loved in Gareth that, since moving here, seem to have evaporated. Her eyes follow a rare splinter of winter sunshine vault from wall to counter. It reflects off the vase of flowers she bought to cheer herself up once he'd left for work after yet another fraught weekend. She gulps down its dazzle as if this is to be the last of it. And it is, the light she stands in suddenly changes. All is cast into a strange apricot as the sun disappears again. Swallowed up by the hunchbacked clouds that blacken to a bruise beyond the kitchen windows.

Remembering the jar of coffee she bought for John, Melanie digs it out of a cupboard and finds a carrier bag to put everything in. Needing the biscuits to cool properly before she can wrap them, she nips to the basement to put a load of washing on. Down in the chilly bowels of the pub, she nearly trips over the laundry basket. Sophie and Georgie used to play in that. Melanie would sing them the *row, row, row your boat* song . . . such a small thing, a snapshot in time. They can't have been more than two. Their remembered laughter has her pressing her palms to the cold stone walls to steady herself. Even now, she thinks, her mouth dry. Even now. And exchanging the fizz of excitement she had about seeing John for sorrow, tears sprout.

Half an hour later, her parka zipped to the chin, Melanie leaves the gorse-sheltered path that runs adjacent to the pub, to cut down through the slips to the town with its smart stucco-clad houses. The streets, washed in a curious light, are eerily still. It has her wondering if the mood might be an indication of snow. Thoughts of snow bring a rogue thought of the hospital waiting room and the young doctor with those purple half-moons under his eyes. The fourth anniversary of Sophie's death is only a matter of weeks away and she has no idea how she is going to get through it. She just has to keep busy, there is no alternative; there is no going back, only forward. But in moving forward, Melanie has learnt that not mourning her child is impossible. As her therapist said, she must learn to find a way to live alongside it.

Swinging the bag of goodies, Slinky knows the way and, tugging her downhill, tail at half-mast, they reach the lychgate in no time. She knocks on the dark timber door at the rear of the vestry just as the rain, now falling as sleet, begins in earnest. Pulling up her hood, she shelters beneath the blue-green layering of a mighty cedar and waits. Nothing. She puts an ear to the door, but the only distinguishable sound is the wind pushing through the dripping trees. It seems no one's home. Disappointment spears her to the spot. What should she do? Leave the coffee and biscuits for John to find later? But that will mean she misses out on seeing him.

Rooks. High above. She hauls her gaze to their scythe-black shapes stencilled against the low-hanging cloud. Then she looks down to where the dog should be and finds he's gone. She must have accidentally let go of his lead.

'Slinky!' she calls, circling the graveyard with the carrier bag looped over her arm, clapping her gloved hands against the cold. 'Come on, boy. Don't bugger about.' She lifts her eyes to the drama of a shifting grey sea, then up and over the belt of sad green fields huddled with ponies, their bums to the weather. 'Come on, daft dog. Where are you?'

'Hello, again.' A deep baritone close to her ear.

She spins to receive it.

'John.' His big, broad body blocking the limited light. 'I've lost Slinky. I only let him go for a second.'

'Don't worry.' His hand is heavy on her wet sleeve. 'He can't come to harm in here, it's all enclosed.'

'Oh, look—' she points to a darkened knot of nettles in the wildest corner of the churchyard. 'There he is.'

They watch him scamper over, dragging his lead through the dead leaves.

'Were you looking for me too?' John's look is hopeful as he bends to fuss the dog.

'I was, yes. Coffee?' She lifts the carrier bag. 'Good boy,' she praises Slinky, collecting his lead.

'Come on. Let's get inside.' John smiles through the raindrops running over his oil-dark beard.

*

John's room is smaller than Melanie remembers from her previous visits and the whitewashed stone walls look wet to the touch. With all that winter still has to bring, she worries about what effect the damp might be having on him; she heard him coughing the last time she was here.

'D'you want to take your coat off?' John fills the metal kettle from the only tap while Slinky shakes himself and lies down on the frayed rug, once again owning the tiny space.

'No, it's okay.' She removes her gloves, rubs her cold thighs through her jeans to generate some warmth. 'How d'you manage? You don't seem to have any kind of heating in here.' Bolder today, she crosses from one side of the room to the other, counting it takes less than five paces before butting up against his wretched little camp bed.

'I like the cold. It makes me feel alive. After the suffocating heat of that Godforsaken desert.' He gives her a look. 'I'd rather put on extra layers.'

Washed through with a watery light that drips in through the single window, the air is cold enough to see her breath as she drags her fingers over the tatty spines of paperbacks crammed into the bookcase.

'You've read all these?' Her observation sounds feeble to her ears.

'Yep. Some more than once. Most of them are falling to bits, but I couldn't part with them. They're like old friends.'

'I'm the same, I love reading,' she says, watching him bend stiffly to ignite the flame on his camping stove. Seeing it's a struggle for him with his one good hand, it is on the tip of her tongue to ask if he needs help, but stops: this is a proud man, a man who's survived conditions she can't possibly imagine. 'I drive Gareth up the wall with my books.'

John coughs. A dry miserable sound that leaves him hoarse. 'Doesn't he read?'

'Not novels. He'll read the sports pages and the biography of some rugby legend if I buy him it for Christmas.'

John gives a look she can't interpret.

'You and me, we could do swaps?' she suggests brightly.

'I'd like that. I used to have a mate in the army I'd swap books with. Not that I've seen him for years. He moved to France to open a second-hand bookshop.' John gestures to the armchair, while he perches on a wooden chair, he's far too big for.

'We're refurbishing our guest rooms next week.' She eyes the camp bed again. 'You could have one of the single beds if you like?' *He'd never fit a double in here.* 'The mattresses are as good as new.'

'Why replace them then?'

'I know, it sounds like a waste.' She glances at Slinky, now spread-eagled between them, cleaning his paws. 'But the Tourist Office said nowhere has single beds anymore.' Such trivia, she thinks, a little shamefacedly; especially when John has so little.

'Thanks for asking.' The look is dignified, it makes

her like him even more. 'But I think I'll stick with what I've got.'

They listen as the water rises to the boil. Its bubbling competes with the sleet that has reverted to rain hammering the roof and John's occasional coughing. Melanie wonders whether to ask if he's seen a doctor about it but remembers his complaint about his sister's interfering and changes her mind.

'D'you know how to cut hair?' John shoots his question across the room.

Melanie, surprised by it, needs a second to arrange her answer. 'I'm not professional but I cut Georgie's.'

'D'you think you could cut mine?' he asks, shy from beneath his hedge-thick hair.

'If you like,' she agrees, thinking again how sweet he is, how gentle. A gentle giant.

'I meant to ask you last time.'

It's clear to Melanie why she's attracted to him. She's responding to the qualities her husband once had. Qualities she fell in love with, that for some reason have been replaced with anger and a desire to control. The qualities that drew her to Gareth are being shown to her in this other man: a man who has nothing but seems to need her in a way Gareth no longer does.

'If you've a decent pair of scissors?'

'Scissors are the one thing I have got.'

The kettle whistles and fills the room with its steaming breath. John rises to his feet and shuffles forward; the movement makes him cough again.

'Thanks for bringing coffee.' The clink of a spoon and he hands her an enamel mug, reaching over the dog who is up on his haunches, nosing the carrier bag Melanie pulls on to her lap.

'Would you like one of these to go with it?' She unwraps the greaseproof parcel, holds it out to him. 'I made them 'specially.' He takes one and she takes one herself. 'And,' head down in the bag again. 'You said you liked marzipan.'

'So, you brought me marzipan.' The look is warm. Melanie can't remember the last time Gareth looked at her like that and, for a treacherous moment, half of her wishes he'd stay up in London and not bother coming home at the weekends anymore.

'This is delicious.' John lifts his biscuit as if saluting her. 'You're a wonderful cook.'

'Make you some more, if you like?' she offers, bathing in the glow of his approval. 'I've loads of recipes I want to try before we open,' she adds to make it clear she doesn't think he's some charity case.

'You seem a bit down today,' he says as the dog nuzzles into his hand, rolls over for a belly rub.

'Aw.' Melanie blows on her coffee, liking the warm steam against her face. 'I've never seen him do that for anyone but Georgie.'

'Is everything all right? You can tell me anything, you know.'

She makes a face. Her biscuit finished. 'I wouldn't know where to start.'

'From the beginning?'

An automatic smile as her thoughts slide to Sophie's anniversary . . . Georgie's worrying tummy aches . . . her husband's aggressive treatment of Delyth . . . the knock-on effect that means the two of them are at constant loggerheads. She would love to share her troubles with John, he'd be easy to confide in. 'You went to school with Gareth?'

'That's right. Same class.'

'You said something about him being a jammy bugger. What did you mean?'

'Just that he's always been lucky.' He stares at the ceiling, then drops his gaze to the floor. 'Gareth Sayer could do no wrong in certain quarters.'

Melanie can tell John doesn't much care for her husband. She detected it the first time his name came up in conversation.

'Why don't you like him?'

John laughs. 'You're perceptive.'

'I'm right then. Can I ask why?'

He returns his attention to the dog, his coffee seemingly forgotten.

'Come on,' she urges. 'You can tell me.'

Still nothing.

'Is that why you didn't wave when I saw you at the Co-op a few weeks back? Because I was with Gareth?'

A shrug.

'I'll keep on until you tell me,' she teases, searching out his eyes through lashes that are as long as a girl's.

Met with stubborn silence, Melanie wonders if he would be more inclined to talk if she wasn't looking directly at him.

'Shall I cut your hair now?' She places her mug on the floor and gets up.

'You don't mind?'

'Not at all.'

She takes the scissors he finds her. 'D'you have a towel and a bowl? To catch the hair.' She explains. 'Oh, and a comb?' John reaches around, passes her a shallow plastic basin and a damp-smelling towel. He locates a comb from somewhere in his jacket. 'You sit there and hold the bowl.' She motions him back to the chair and puts the towel around his shoulders, tucks it into his collar.

It isn't warm enough to remove her coat, so she folds back the cuffs instead. Concentrating on the back of John's head, she works methodically, carefully, combing his hair that, unlike his beard — toughened by a life spent outdoors in the salt sea spray — is easily as soft as Georgie's.

'It's in great condition.' She says as it falls through her fingers, her thoughts returning to Gareth and how, despite his best efforts, the shampoos with outrageous claims he spends a fortune on, he is still thinning on top. 'How much d'you want me to take off?'

'Enough to make me look respectable.'

'*Respectable?* Who wants to look respectable?'

'I do.' His voice is serious. 'I'd like to look respectable for you.'

John's declaration sets her insides fluttering and she's relieved he can't see her blushes. She makes a start on his beard, noticing, up close how it's threaded with silver. The beauty Melanie finds beneath it unsettles her further. The sharp cheekbones, the sensitivity held in his mouth once the heavy black growth is trimmed away. She sees his earlobe, is moved by the tenderness of it. And the smell of carbolic again. Hurling her back to the horrors of the care home that is never far away.

Melanie will often wake to the dusty dark corridors of her childhood, the taste of cod-liver oil in her mouth. Thick with sleep, it will take her a few minutes to realise time has moved on and she no longer has anything to fear. Like a prison camp, the only way to describe her years in institutionalised care. The routine, rules and noise. What she'd needed was love and protection, but the world she went into was no safer than the home she'd been removed from. It was a brutal, abusive regime. Not that she discusses it with anyone, even Gareth has only been given the bare bones of her perceived incarceration. Perceived, because as a grown-up there are moments when she will grill her younger self as to why she didn't run away. Life on the streets, her only alternative at the time, was surely preferable to the endless drudge and lack of privacy. The passing of years and meeting Gareth have undoubtedly changed her life beyond recognition, and fortunately, much of what she was made into between the ages of nine and sixteen have been well and truly eradicated. She no longer flinches at raised voices and doesn't chew her nails, but there are still aspects of the old routine she clings to.

'Were they really dreadful?' Preferring to have John's story than her own memories. 'Your experiences in Afghanistan?'

He doesn't immediately answer. Then, after a moment, admits, 'I still have nightmares.'

'Do you ever talk about it?' Out of his eye line, she hopes he will be more inclined to talk.

He shakes his head.

'Do you want to talk to me? I'm a good listener.'

'I can tell that.' His voice: rich and deep and rumbling.

'Tell me then.'

Again, a solid silence.

She listens to him breathing.

'It's the nightmares. Same ones. Most nights,' he says, at last, leaning sideways for his mug. 'I had some counselling but not much. They said I was suffering from PTSD, but I couldn't stand it, talking to people who weren't there and didn't know what it was like.'

'I wasn't there.' Melanie cuts his hair slowly, fearful of making a mistake.

'I know, but you're not judging me. The counselling was only so they could work out what to pension me off with, it didn't prepare me for civvy street. It didn't help me to undo what they turned me into. What I've become, through that stinking war.'

'No, I don't suppose it did.' She looks around at his meagre belongings. 'Tell me how you got your injuries, it might help stop the nightmares if you can get it off your chest.'

'You sound as if you have nightmares yourself. Do you?'

'We're talking about you.' Reluctant to share the sorrows in her heart, fearing they will sound paltry in comparison.

'It was a bomb. Strapped to a young mother. She had a baby in her arms.' He pauses, and she hears him heave down air, fighting back tears. 'It was a split-second decision: it was all I had. My lot were shouting orders to shoot, but I couldn't, all I could see was that baby. Such huge black eyes, innocent, you know. I see them every time I close my eyes. I can see them now.' John sniffs, wipes his nose with the back of his hand. 'I didn't think the mother would do it, but she did. She detonated the bomb that was strapped round her middle.' He falls silent again and snipping sounds splinter the chilly air. 'They kept shouting "shoot, shoot", and she was babbling stuff I couldn't understand. But how could I shoot? She had a baby in her arms. I'm not a monster.'

'No, you're not a monster.' She soothes as she combs his hair, cutting a little more each time.

'But people died. Some of my battalion were killed when the bomb went off. I was one of the lucky ones.' Hardly lucky, Melanie thinks, but doesn't say. 'And the woman and her baby died anyway. It was cowardly. They thought I was cowardly.' He rubs his eyes, sniffs again. Melanie doesn't falter, she keeps on with her trimming.

'I think you were in an impossible situation. No one had the right to call you a coward. How could you have lived with yourself if you'd shot that mother, killed her child?'

'I don't know,' he says, limply. 'But I'm struggling to live now.'

'Why did you join up?'

'Join the army?' John takes a breath before answering. 'Because of your husband.'

'Gareth?' Melanie stops what she's doing, holds the scissors aloft. An unexplained chill, colder than the room, tracks through her. 'Why, what did he do?'

'I'm not sure I should—'

'*John*?' she cuts in, impatient. 'You can't say something like that and not tell me.' She squeezes his shoulder through the thick wool of his jacket to push him on.

John sucks back his breath for a second time, seems especially reticent. 'Well, you must know he's got a problem with any kind of weakness. Any physical weakness.'

'Has he?' Melanie sifts through what she knows of

her husband. 'I'm sure he hasn't.'

'If he hasn't got a problem with it now, he certainly used to.'

'Not with you, surely?'

'Believe it or not, I was puny as a kid. And Gareth hated puny. If you weren't one of the gang; if you weren't like him,' he pauses, rubs his chin through what remains of his beard. 'I'm sorry to have to say it, but he was a bully. If he took against you, he made your life hell.'

Bully.

Melanie unfurls the word. A bully is what she accused him of being after his abysmal treatment of Delyth.

'Is that what he did to you?' she asks, unsure if she wants John's answer. 'He made your life hell?'

'Put it this way, I signed up to get him off my back. To prove to people round here that the rumours he was spreading about me were wrong.'

'What rumours?'

'That I was gay. That I wasn't a proper man.' John sniffs. 'I know it doesn't sound much now, but back then it was a big deal. I used to get beaten up regular for it.'

What John says lodges inside her like a shard of ice. She could pretend he was talking about someone else, had she not witnessed Gareth's cruelty with Delyth. He doesn't know it, but John isn't telling her anything new. Recent events have opened her eyes to what her husband is capable of and it frightens her. Could she have been hoodwinked by him all these years? It's possible. Because although they only have weekends together here, it's a solid chunk of time and far more than either of them is used to. Their Bromley life was hectic, most of it spent apart and, aside from a few snatched hours on weekday evenings, weekends were for socialising with friends or golf. Until Sophie was killed and they were consumed in other ways.

'I'm sorry. That's a horrible way to behave.' It occurs to her she's been doing rather a lot of apologising on her husband's behalf since arriving in Wales.

'Thank you, but it's not for you to be sorry.' John inadvertently echoes what Delyth said. 'But would I be right in saying you don't seem surprised by what I'm telling you?'

Melanie drops her scissor-holding hand to her side. 'I might have been, a few months ago.' She hesitates, weighs up whether to say more. 'But I've sort of seen him in action for myself.'

'He bullies you?' John twists in his chair, his eyes brimming with concern.

'No, not me,' she assures and repositions his head to continue with her trimming. 'It's Delyth he's got the problem with.'

'Delyth Powell? Why would he have a problem with her?'

'No idea, but he really laid into her at the Co-op the other week. She ended up in tears.'

'What an awful thing to do,' John sounds appalled.

'It was shameful, I don't know what's got into him.'

'She was another one he was cruel to at school. I used to think it was because she wasn't pretty, and because of that, of no use to him. Yeah, Delyth . . .' John lost to whatever his memories dredge to the surface. 'Gareth used to be especially vicious to her.'

'It seems as if he still is.' Melanie ruffles John's hair into place, pleased with how neatly the shortened layers follow the contours of his head.

'But why, what trouble could she be to anyone?'

'That's what I say.'

'She's had a tough life.'

'I know, poor thing. I told Gareth about her struggles but he doesn't care, he's so unfeeling,' she sighs. 'I hate to admit it, but I've seen a side of my husband lately that I don't like.'

John doesn't respond.

'Gareth says everyone hated Delyth at school.'

'Hated Delyth? No, that wasn't true.' John sets her straight. 'She was shy, that's all; kept herself to herself.

From what I remember, it was only Gareth who had the problem with her.'

'D'you know why? I don't mean about how they were at school, I think I sort of understand that, I mean now. Why would he still have a problem with her now? Because for some reason she sure brings out the worst in him.'

'That's his shame, that is.' John replies, thoughtful. 'Shame and guilt. Seeing her again after all these years. She probably just reminds him of what a shit he used to be.'

'You might be on to something there because I'm telling you, I'm struggling to come up with any logical explanation for his irrational and unprovoked attack of the woman.'

John drinks his cooled coffee. 'Your Gareth drives a black Porsche, doesn't he?' he says when he's finished.

'Yes.' Melanie brushes stray hairs from his collar.

'I saw him. Monday morning. Out on the coast road. He turned off at the entrance to the Powell's farm.'

'Powell's farm . . . Powell's farm.' The penny drops. 'What, Delyth's place?'

'That's right,' John nods. 'Gweld Y Môr.'

'Monday, you say? Do you remember what time?' Doing her best to sound casual, she offers him another biscuit.

'First thing. I was on the bus.' John feeds a chunk to Slinky who is salivating against his calves.

Melanie's thoughts, snapping like dogs . . . *What was he doing there?* — *he was supposed to be on his way back to London.*

'Are you sure it was him?' She tucks a strand of her own hair behind an ear, absentmindedly testing its length.

'It was a black Porsche. Latest model. I'm pretty good with motors, it's a sort of a hobby.' John rubs the dog's head, whispers sweet nothings against his silky ears. 'And I can't think of anyone else round here with one like it, can you?'

214

'No, they're a bit impractical for these parts. It's a company car, he doesn't own it.' Melanie is quick to add. Sensitive to what a vehicle like that costs and how little John has. 'Whereabouts is Delyth's farm?'

'Remote. Way out on the coast road, towards St David's.'

'That's going in the complete opposite direction to Pwllglas.' *And London*, she thinks, opening the box of marzipan and offering them to John.

He takes one fashioned into a banana, pops it in his mouth. 'You didn't know, did you?'

'No, I didn't.'

'Delyth had a hell of a crush on your husband when they were at school.'

'So I keep hearing,' she says, a little more sourly than she intends.

'You can't be jealous?' he smiles. 'A woman as attractive as you?'

She laughs. 'No, I'm not jealous.'

'Good, because me saying Gareth thought she was a nightmare, would be the understatement of the year.'

'Yeah, I've heard that too.'

John swallows the last of his marzipan, his breath an almondy sweetness. 'But Delyth was a bit of a sad case. I don't mean to be unkind or anything, but she wouldn't accept that he wanted nothing to do with her. It was a bit humiliating, to be honest.'

'There.' Melanie announces, pleased with the job she's done. 'I think you'll do. You got a mirror.'

'No. Mirrors aren't allowed.' He grins, more handsome than he realises.

'Hang on.' She dives into her handbag, retrieves her vanity mirror. 'There,' she passes it to him once he's set the basin on the floor. 'Have a look at the new you.'

He holds the mirror up, moves his head from side to side. 'Look at that. Am I going to lose all my strength now, Delilah?' They laugh. 'Bloody grand job, that. You should go into business.'

'I am, remember,' she giggles, and returns the mirror to her bag.

'Thanks. I feel almost human again.' He uses his good hand to feel her handiwork.

'Not too short?'

'Perfect.' John gives way to more laughing, this time showing a row of surprisingly neat, white teeth. 'God, Melanie, I can't tell you the last time I laughed. I honestly thought I'd forgotten how to. See how good you are for me?' He shoots her a look: so good-looking, her insides turn to jelly.

She returns to the armchair, sits opposite him, her hands in her lap. 'She cut herself in our sink.' Melanie says with no preamble.

'You what?' John gasps. 'Cut herself? Who did?'

'Delyth.' Barely recognising him, she is acutely shy under his gaze.

'I don't understand, are you telling me she tried to kill herself?'

She nods. 'But I don't think she meant to do it.'

'Didn't mean to do it? I should think she did,' John is resolute. 'I've come close myself, more times than I care to remember. I nearly managed it once,' he says, twisting away to hide his emotion. 'But my sister found me in the nick of time.' He slumps back in his wooden chair.

'Oh, John,' Melanie presses her fingers to her lips. 'I'm so sorry you were driven to that. You must have been in a bad way.'

'Like Delyth must be,' he sidesteps her observation.

'Yes, like Delyth must be,' she nods.

'Where was Gareth when this was going on?'

'In London. It was just me and Georgie.'

'Good God. Your daughter saw it?' He looks aghast.

'No, thank goodness. She was upstairs in the flat.'

'And she did it in your kitchen . . . in your sink, you

say?'

'Bad, isn't it?' Melanie pulls a face. 'But I could tell she didn't want to do it. Kill herself, I mean—' she breaks off. 'The cuts were deep, yes, but if she wanted to do it, if that had been her true intention, she'd have done it where there was no chance of being found.'

John coughs into his hand. 'What the hell was she thinking?'

'I don't suppose she can have been thinking. To me, it seemed like a desperate cry for help.'

He grimaces. Coughs again.

'Has she done anything like this before?' Melanie asks.

John's look is thoughtful. 'I don't know. She was an unhappy kid, and then with everything that happened. You've probably heard that her father was killed just after we finished our A Levels,' he waits for Melanie's nod. 'The mother hit the bottle, big time, or so they say . . . well, Delyth says actually, I don't think anyone's seen Norah for years. Rumours are, she's not left the farm since she retired. What did Gareth say, when you told him what Delyth did?' John wants to know.

'I haven't told him. She swore me to secrecy.'

'But you're telling me?'

'I am, yes. I knew you wouldn't dismiss it as being an attention-seeking stunt, like Gareth would have . . . because I'm sure he would have,' she adds to justify her decision. 'Going by what he already calls her. No,' she swings her gaze to his. 'I'm telling you because I know you'll be sympathetic, that you might help me to understand.'

'Have you talked to Delyth about it since?'

'Once. Yes. I asked if she'd ever thought about getting help, talking to a therapist, that kind of thing. But it fell on stony ground. She just kept telling me how sorry she was.'

'It might be something in her makeup, you know. In her genes, or whatever.'

'Why d'you say that?'

John clears his throat. 'You know what happened to Delyth's sister, don't you?'

'Her sister? Erin. No, I don't. I've been meaning to ask you about her. I know she died, I found her grave, but no one seems to know what happened to her. Or if they do, they're not saying.'

'They're probably not saying, because Erin killed herself, Melanie.' John's words knock her back. 'She was so young and pretty,' he sighs. 'So you can sort of understand why no one round here has the stomach to talk about it.'

THIRTY

Saturday morning has somehow come around again. Melanie opens her eyes to find Gareth standing at the bedroom window, peering out through the parted curtains at what promises to be a sunny day.

'What's up?' She turns on her side, presses her back to the glare.

'Can't sleep.'

'What's the matter?' Her voice is husky above the rustle of bedcovers.

'Stuff on my mind.'

'Want to tell me?'

He doesn't answer and, closing her eyes, Melanie drifts off to sleep again.

'What time is it?' She wakes with a start, imagining she's been sleeping hours when it was probably only seconds.

'Half eight.'

'Early for a Saturday. Come on,' she lifts the duvet, pats his side of the bed. 'Little lie in?'

He drops the curtains and the room goes dark again. She feels the mattress shift when he gets in beside her.

'That's better,' she says, cuddling up behind him and kissing the available skin between t-shirt and hairline. 'Let's try and have another half hour.'

It is their daughter who finally wakes them. Not to complain of stomach cramps for a change, but to present them with a milk tooth on the cushion of her outstretched palm.

'Look at that, Mummy.' Gareth sits up, rubs his eyes. 'You put that under your pillow and the Tooth Fairy will come and give you something.'

'Show me.' Melanie yawns, not quite with it. 'You tricked me last time, using the same one.'

Georgie giggles and, using a finger, peels back her lip to show the gap in her teeth.

'Daddy's right.' Melanie, now fully awake. 'Go on, quick. She might come for it before breakfast if you're lucky.'

Georgie goes and Melanie snuggles into Gareth; his arms tight around her, not letting go. She smiles, happily imagining his red Welsh dragon tattoo pressed against her back. Things have been good between them since he arrived home yesterday and, closing her eyes to whoever's listening, she prays for it to stay that way.

Later, with breakfast almost over, Melanie and Gareth drink what's left of their tea and finish their toast standing up.

'There's long your hair's getting,' he smiles at her.

'D'you like it?' She does a little twirl.

'I do.' He kisses her. 'It suits you.'

'Good, because I fancy a change.'

Georgie skips into the kitchen with the post and Slinky trotting alongside.

'She's looking loads better than last weekend.' Gareth lifts the teapot, directs the spout at Melanie's mug.

It is a bad habit of his, talking about their child in the third person as if Georgie wasn't there. But for the sake of a weekend free of disagreements, she lets it go.

'How long before we get her test results back?' He drains what's left of his tea.

Georgie is divvying out the mail. 'One for Daddy.'

She reads the name on a brown envelope, passes it to her father. 'Looks like a bill.' She grins, showing off the asymmetric spaces between her teeth.

'Electricity.' A groan, and he slides a finger under the flap.

'Thursday.' Melanie answers. Her toast and tea finished; she places her crockery in the sink to rinse before loading the dishwasher. 'I'm to ring the surgery.'

'That long?' Perplexed, but not by her, with the bill he's reading. 'What tests did they do?'

'Bloods. Loads for different allergies. They were very thorough, weren't they, Georgie?' Melanie strokes her child's hair that, still to be brushed and braided into plaits, fans over her narrow shoulders. 'And you were such a brave girl, weren't you?'

'Yes, I was.' Georgie frowns in concentration, she is taking her role as postmistress very seriously. 'One more for Mummy. One more for Daddy.' Job done; she steps back to admire the two tidy piles of envelopes on the work surface.

'Thank you, sweetheart,' Melanie smiles, proud of her daughter's efficiency, her ability to read so well. 'Have you checked under your pillow? Maybe the Tooth Fairy's visited you.'

Georgie sucks on her bottom lip.

'Best go and look then. We'll have to get going in a minute. I booked your riding lesson for eleven,' Melanie says, her mind galloping to the pound coin Gareth hid under Georgie's pillow before coming downstairs.

'I hope you booked yourself one too?' He looks up at her.

She watches Georgie bounce away, then nods. 'If that was okay?'

'Definitely. I think it's fantastic you're getting into it again,' he sounds genuinely enthusiastic about the idea. 'I know how much you loved horses as a kid.'

'Let's hope the doctors get to the bottom of it, once

and for all,' she says, pulling their conversation back to their child now she is out of earshot. 'Great thing is, she's been feeling loads better. I don't think she's complained about a tummy ache for a couple of weeks now.'

'Bit of a coincidence, don't you think.' A smirk curves Gareth's mouth.

'What d'you mean?'

'That Georgie's tummy aches stop when Delyth finally gets the message and stays away.'

'Oh, Gareth.' Melanie slumps against the counter, crosses her arms.

'*Oh, Gareth*, nothing,' he snaps, looking pleased with himself. 'Georgie's feeling well because she's not eating the stuff that woman cooks. I told you, didn't I? I told you she was bad news.'

Melanie sighs into the sourness that always accompanies any mention of Delyth Powell. But she refuses to respond. If she doesn't respond, they might be able to get through to Monday morning without falling out.

She uncrosses her arms and picks up an envelope from the top of her pile. Something from the bank. She rips it open, scans November's payments, the standing orders, the direct debits, before realising. 'Oh, no. Sorry, Gareth. This isn't mine, it's yours.' And she is about to hand it over when she notices a three-thousand pound cash withdrawal halfway down the first sheet. 'What's this?' she yelps. 'What the hell did you need to take all that out for?'

Gareth tries to snatch the statement from her grasp but, quicker than him, she whips it behind her.

'Give it to me,' he demands, hand outstretched.

'Not until you tell me what you needed all that cash for?'

'It's none of your business.' The hand opens and closes with impatience.

'Erm, I think it is my business.' She flaps the statement at him.

'I just needed it, *okay*? I needed it for London.

There was something I had to do.'

'Oh, right. London, was it?' She refers to the printout again. 'So why does it say the cash was withdrawn from the NatWest branch here in Pencarew?'

'You what?'

'On the statement. It says Pencarew.' She repeats, the blood rushing to her face. 'On the thirteenth.' She looks up. 'That was a Monday, wasn't it?'

'So what if it was?'

'You always leave at the crack of dawn Mondays, to be back at your desk, you say. What were you still doing in town?'

His expression clouds and he moves away. She follows him, thinks that less than an hour ago they were making love, and now they are on the brink of yet another argument.

'Is that all you've got to say? I'm asking you a question; I want to know. Jesus, Gareth, you'd want to know if I'd withdrawn that much. Three grand's a lot of money.'

'Give it to me.' He snaps his fingers.

'What were you still doing in Pencarew?' She hands him the statement reluctantly. 'The bank doesn't open until nine?'

He refolds the sheets back into their torn envelope, pushes it into the back pocket of his jeans. Melanie remembers something John said, decides to approach things from another angle.

'Your car was seen up at Delyth's farm. Has this mysterious need for a walloping load of cash got something to do with her?'

'What d'you mean my car was seen? Who says?'

'Does it matter? You were seen at the turn off to the farm.'

'Rubbish.' He butters himself a cold triangle of toast, bites it in half.

An unexpected image of John floats before her. Is it any wonder she's attracted to him when she's met with this kind of hostility from her husband; it's natural to want the closeness she and Gareth enjoyed with someone else.

'You've got a very distinctive car,' she challenges, while carefully keeping a safe distance.

'But it's not the only one in the world,' Gareth chews through his words.

'Around here it is.' Firm, she refuses to let him intimidate her, she wants an answer. 'What were you going to the farm for, if you hate her so much?'

'I told you, it wasn't me. Whoever said they saw me; they must've been mistaken.'

'I don't believe you. You told me you were heading back to London, why didn't you say you were going up there?'

'Because I didn't.' He takes another bite of toast, then gives the last of the crust to the dog: another habit of his Georgie copies.

'Stop lying. I'm not an idiot.'

'What is this? Twenty bloody questions?' He licks butter from his mouth.

'Because you've drawn out a huge amount of money and you won't tell me what it's for? We can't afford to be spending that amount of cash.'

'Look,' he stops munching and swallows. 'It's a surprise. Okay.'

'A surprise? Oh, no, Gareth, I'm sorry, but that's not good enough.'

'Well, it's all you're getting.' He smiles, irritatingly reasonable; it makes her want to thump him.

'Tell me.'

'Doh,' he makes a face. 'It wouldn't be a surprise then, would it?'

'A bit of a theme this.' she folds her arms again.

'What is?' He wipes his hands on the tea towel and turns away. She sees his little bald patch. The unexpected vulnerability of it has her wanting to reach out to stroke it; wanting their marriage to be put back to what it was.

'This brick wall you put up whenever Delyth's name gets mentioned.' She dives in front of him, shuffles backwards until her heels bump up against the steps separating kitchen from bar. 'And you wonder why I'm suspicious? What is it with you and her?'

'What is it with you and your bloody questions?' He pushes her aside, lifts a foot to the first stone step: a flash of the aggression she saw him dish out to Delyth that day in the Co-op.

'Excuse me? I don't think I'm being the unreasonable one here. I'm not the one withdrawing thousands of pounds from our account.'

'*My account.* And you weren't supposed to see it,' he sniffs.

'Obviously.' Hands on hips.

'Just leave it, will you?' He moves past her into the bar; his voice unequivocal in the near-empty rooms.

'I don't know you at all, do I?' Melanie shouts after him. 'What did you do to Delyth when you were kids?'

'I said, *leave it.*' A muscle twitches in his jaw. 'You'll find out soon enough what the money was for.'

'I don't like what I'm seeing, Gareth.' She follows on behind. 'This isn't you? Or is it, and you've just managed to keep it from me all this time? Because I tell you, I don't like what I'm seeing, I don't like it at all.'

'Tough.' He turns, lifts an arm. She ducks, believing he's about to strike her, but he smacks the wall instead. 'You can keep on all you like, but I'm not telling.'

Something communicated in his eyes makes Melanie recoil. The mask slips, and again she sees his potential. Her insides go cold and for the first time in their lives together she is afraid of him.

Georgie is suddenly there. The pound coin her father left under her pillow held high above her head.

'Are you all right, Mummy?' Her little face drains of colour. 'What's the matter?'

'Nothing, darling.' Melanie puts a protective arm

around her child and guides her out of harm's way. Throwing Gareth a look she hopes communicates her disgust, rather than the fear that is knocking against her ribcage.

THIRTY-ONE

More than a week later and disaster strikes. A severed water main in the downstairs cloakroom means the pub is under a foot of water. It also means Melanie is late collecting Georgie from school. Over one hour late. The luminous-green clock on the Mazda's dashboard blinks accusingly on the drive through town. It's okay, she tells it, swinging into the near-deserted car park. It's Wednesday, they'll have let Georgie join in the after-school club. Admittedly, she didn't book her a place in advance, but they're not going to mind.

What a day. She grabs her handbag and locks the car. It's been nonstop since she woke that morning, with problem after problem, culminating at three o'clock this afternoon when one of Bryn's men sawed through a pipe they shouldn't have. She had to leave them to it in the end, pray it didn't flood the kitchen. Thankfully, the parquet flooring in the bar, unlike the restaurant and guest lounge, has yet to go down, otherwise, it would have been catastrophic.

Handbag banging, she runs to the entrance of St Ishmaels Primary School. The metal doors are stiff on their hinges and screech when she pushes them wide: a sound that settles into an unnerving silence. For there is nothing of the children's laughter she was anticipating, only an emptiness made bleaker by the fluorescent strip lights.

'Hello?' she calls and, serenaded by the heels of her boots, moves deeper into the building; dipping in and out of the vacated classrooms, alarmed by the rapidly descending fog, which is now rubbing itself against the wide, school windows.

'*Hello?*' she tries again, her despair intensifying when she peers into the main hall and finds it deserted, save for its rubber and polish smells.

She is met by a set of large double doors at the end of the corridor and tests their handles. Locked. Squinting through the safety glass into the unlit canteen and abandoned rooms beyond, there seems to be no sign of life.

'Where the hell is everyone? Where's Georgie?'

Panic: a butterfly caught in a jar; flaps inside her.

'Stay calm. Stay calm. She has to be somewhere,' she gabbles, throwing her head from left to right. 'Please? There must be someone around. Why else are the main doors still open? Is anyone here?' she pleads loudly, then holds her breath for the answer that doesn't come.

With little choice other than to turn back the way she came, she dashes out under the lowering sky to circle the empty playground. Hunting the shadows, the darkened spaces between the dormant spread of magnolia tree and boundary wall.

'Georgie! Georgie!' she yells, the markings for hopscotch and number mazes, a muddle of colour through her mounting desperation. 'Where are you?'

She veers off sideways, in the direction of the car park. Sees a vehicle, the only one apart from hers. It means someone is still here. And a surge of hope has her sprinting towards a yellow light leaking from deep inside the building. Scrabbling through a thatch of nettles, Melanie must slide between a steep bank of grass and grip a series of flaking windowsills to haul herself along the rear school wall. Panting, out of breath, she is about halfway along when she identifies where the light is coming from and, clarifying a nub of corridor with a large classroom beyond it, she makes out what she assumes is the back of a cleaner dragging a mop from side to side.

'Georgie!' Melanie shouts and raps the glass, believing her daughter is with them. The woman looks up, turns momentarily in Melanie's direction, but with a frown of annoyance returns to her mopping again.

She bangs the glass a second time, harder, keeping on until her knuckles hurt. It works, the woman drops her mop in the bucket and sways towards her. Another bulb is flicked on and Melanie waves her arms, flashes the screen of her mobile like a torch at the glass. The window is thrown open, toppling her against the bank.

'Oh, thank goodness,' she gushes, fumbling upright. 'I'm Georgie's Mum. Melanie . . . Melanie Sayer?'

'Hello.' The woman gives a bemused smile. 'Whatever are you doing? The main door's open, you know.' Whey-faced and as wide as she is tall, the woman pulls a tissue from her sleeve and blows her nose.

'I tried that,' Melanie says, waiting for her to finish. 'I came in, but I couldn't find anyone. I was getting worried. But it's okay, it's after-school club this evening. Sorry, I'm a bit late collecting Georgie, we had an emergency at home.'

'I'm afraid you've got the wrong day, *bach*.' The woman tucks her tissue away. 'After-school club's Tuesdays and Thursdays. It's Wednesday today.'

'What? It can't be. I was told Tuesdays and Wednesdays.'

A shrug. 'Then you must've been given duff information.'

'Okay.' Mind racing, Melanie could swear those were the days Delyth told her, but accepts she must have misheard. 'Are there any teachers about? Is Mrs Jenkins here? Can I speak to her, please?'

'She's gone home, all the teachers have gone home. I'm the only one here.'

'Where is she then? Where's Georgie?' Panic bubbles in her throat.

'I'm sorry, *bach*, I'm just the cleaner.'

'Is Delyth here?'

A stiff shake of the head. 'Gone home for the day, I'm afraid.'

'But someone must know, Georgie has to be somewhere.' Melanie hears herself shout. 'Where's my daughter? I thought this school had a strict safeguarding policy. Her class teacher said she wouldn't let her go with anyone unless I'd given her verbal or written confirmation.'

'Oh, dear, please don't upset yourself,' the cleaner's hand flutters between them. 'Your daughter can't have gone far.'

'Can you get me Mrs Jenkins' number? I've got to ring her, find out where Georgie is.' A sob has invaded her voice, and she wrings her hands.

'I'm sorry, the office is locked for the night. I haven't access to that kind of thing.'

Melanie isn't listening, with her mind racing ahead to the places Georgie might be, it is without another word, she struggles back between bank and wall to the car park. Stinging her hand on a nettle along the way.

A glance at the sky, to where a thin moon claims its space in what remains of the dun-coloured day. Colder now, a fine drizzle through the fog settles on her hair, on the sleeves of her parka. She must find her child, get her into the warm, it's going to be dark soon. She chants this as she drives around the town, keeping close to the curb, not accelerating above second gear. The engine growls in protest when she speeds up to pass alongside the string of benches lining the seafront.

'Georgie!'

She slams the brakes and lurches forward in her seat. Lucky no one's behind her. But no, this isn't Georgie, this is another child with honey-coloured plaits and a Smiggle backpack walking hand in hand with what she supposes is an older sibling. She gulps down her spiralling anxiety and freewheels as far down as the harbour wall, before circling back up to the playing field with its empty swings and vacated climbing frame on the fringes of town.

A burst of that happy, sunny afternoon, when she, Georgie and Gareth played in there, taking photos on their phones to share with the friends they'd left behind. Her face crumples, preparing itself to cry. But she won't cry, there isn't time, she must find Georgie. She must find her. Now.

Melanie stops the car whenever she sees someone. Strangers mostly, black-clad, androgynous figures fastened into winter coats. Some she half-recognises from her walks along the headland, on the beach. She doesn't care, wild with worry, she buttonholes anyone and everyone, asking her desperate question: 'Have you seen her? Please, you must've seen her.'

She catches sight of herself in the side mirror: frantic, feverish, leaning over the passenger seat to appeal through the open window.

'Excuse me, excuse me?' she tries not to shriek. 'But have you seen Georgie? My little girl. She's seven, nearly eight. She's got light brown plaits and she's wearing a silver puffer coat . . . No? Are you sure?'

Met with little more than a series of befuddled faces, it terrifies her, do they even know who her child is?

She drives on past brightly-lit shop interiors, transparent as goldfish bowls with windows already dressed for Christmas, searching street after street. Until she reaches the terraced houses on Castle Row. Nia. Could Georgie have gone there after school? She sometimes does. Melanie scratches her hand, her fingers tracing the loop of raised bumps from the nettle sting. Did Georgie say this is what she was doing this evening and Melanie, increasingly distracted by the countdown to opening night, wasn't listening? She parks outside the Wilson's house, ratchets up the handbrake and slips out from behind the wheel. A spark of optimism as she sprints up the garden path to slam the ram-head knocker against the blue door. But any rosiness she has finally located her child is quickly snuffed out when she presses the tip of her nose to the cold windowpane. Nothing. The rooms beyond Mrs Wilson's bleach-white nets fall away into black.

'Where the bloody hell is everybody? The place is deserted. Where's Georgie?' A hand to her mouth, her muffled entreaty as she backs away.

The pub, she thinks, letting number seven's gate snap shut on her heels. It is possible Georgie went home, that she missed her by minutes and her daughter is there. Where she usually is at this time of day: in front of CBeebies with Murray and Slinky. She might be . . . *oh, please, please have gone home, Georgie, please.* Tyres skid on gravel, she leaves the motor running in the pub car park, unlocks the door and goes inside to check.

A smudge of a gibbous moon hangs mellow and low beyond the pub's darkened windows. Its pale face filtering through the thickening fog is mirrored back in what remains of the flooded bar. She tiptoes inside, dark except for a single light spilling out from the kitchen. At least the electricity's not out, she thinks, following her shadow over what has dried to shallow pools of water, to plead with the perpetual gloaming of the stairwell and the flat above.

'Georgie? Georgie?'

But Georgie isn't here. She isn't anywhere. And when Melanie reaches the kitchen, apart from the dog, she finds it is empty too.

'You seen Georgie, boy?' she interrogates Slinky who doesn't shift from his bed: understanding her agitation, he barely lifts his head and doesn't wag his tail. 'Bloody hell,' she curses, sprinting back outside.

'Georgie, please? Where are you?' she wails through the dripping dusk, then it occurs to her. 'Of course you're not here, you don't have a key, you're too young. You're not a latchkey kid like I was. I've got a bloody cheek criticising my mother when I'm such a shit one myself.'

Her mobile rings from inside her coat pocket, it severs her self-recriminations. She tugs it free, along with the British Legion poppy she never did manage to fix to Gareth's lapel.

'Oh, please, *please*—'

It's Gareth. The chink of brightness dims. She can't speak to him, not now, not until Georgie's been found safe and sound. Safe and sound. She churns the words until they become a sickening sludge and stares at her phone. She can't, she can't. Tears sprout, she wipes them away. She can't tell him Georgie's missing. Not when it's her fault their other daughter died.

In the pub car park, the late afternoon dark of a day that never grew properly light enfolds her like a wing. Not that it provides comfort. Quite the contrary. With dusk threatening, the town, shrouded in thin grey cloud, is eerily quiet, there isn't even the snuffle of the wind. Filmed in a layer of drizzle that has now extinguished the moon, Melanie doesn't move. Can't move. She has run out of places to try and is going to have to ring the police . . . who will then notify Gareth . . . Tegan . . . Bronwyn. These thoughts spear the cottonwool feel inside her head until an idea jostles its way forward. Could Georgie be with Tegan? And if so, should she drive there or phone? Quicker to phone. But her fingers won't work. Clumsy and wet, sliding over the screen of her handset, she eventually activates the number and listens to its hollow ringing through the textured miasma that has engulfed the town.

It rings and it rings. At last Tegan picks up.

'Oh, thank God you're there.'

'What's up?' her sister-in-law asks brightly.

'Is Georgie with you?' Melanie rubs at her nettle-stung hand.

'Georgie? No.'

'*No?*' Melanie's legs give way and she topples backwards. 'You were my last hope.' She slumps against the wet car.

'What are you on about, Mel?'

'Shit, Tegan. She's missing . . . Georgie's missing. I was late collecting her from school, the pub was flooded, didn't Bryn say? Georgie wasn't there, she isn't anywhere.

Oh, God, Tegan, I don't know what to do.'

THIRTY-TWO

'Calm down, Mel, she can't have gone far,' Tegan tries to reason with her. 'This is Pencarew, not Bromley.'

'But she's nowhere,' she wails and grips a handful of her hair. 'I've tried the school . . . I've driven all round town.'

'D'you want me to call the police?' Tegan offers.

'I don't know, I don't want Gareth finding out . . . because they'll need to tell him, won't they?'

'And what's wrong with that?'

'Oh, Tegan, he'll bloody kill me.' She grips her hair harder, hurting her scalp.

'Could Georgie have gone home with someone from school?' Tegan sounds far away.

'I've tried Nia's, no one's home. I've tried everywhere. Oh, God, Tegan,' Melanie is in danger of losing it completely. 'This is all my fault. I was forty minutes late . . . *forty* minutes. We were up to our calves in water . . . Bryn's lot hit a water main.' She paces the darkened car park, the Mazda's engine still running. 'I can't believe I forgot about her. I thought Wednesdays was after-school club.' Melanie, shaking, scrubs a frantic hand over her face and tries to get a hold on her escalating emotions, but the tears keep coming.

'Melanie . . . *Mel?*' Tegan again. 'Calm down, please. You sound all funny, your breathing's all funny.'

'My chest hurts.' She squeezes the sudden shooting

pain in her shoulder.

'You've got to try and stay calm. You'll give yourself a heart attack.'

'How can I stay calm,' she shrieks. 'I've lost her . . . how can I have forgotten my own daughter? What kind of a mother am I?'

'Come on. Everything's going to be fine, you'll see.'

'You don't know that.' Melanie, still pacing around, helpless and agitated, is way fiercer than she means to be. 'Georgie could be dead in a ditch for all I know. And it's my fault.'

'D'you want me to come over? Where are you?'

'At the pub. I thought she might be here, but she's not.'

'She's got to be somewhere. Mel, listen to me, she can't have gone far. *Think* — where could she have gone?'

'I don't know . . . I don't know.' A dreadful pause and into it drops a dreadful thought. 'I'm going to have to call the police. I've got no choice.' Melanie bawls, flings her head from side to side. 'The likes of me don't deserve to have children.'

'*What?* Don't be ridiculous.' Tegan's quick to set her straight.

'This is punishment for Elizabeth, for Sophie.' Melanie doesn't give Tegan the chance to interrupt. 'Don't tell me it's not, because it's punishment for something,' she rambles. 'Gareth's been ringing, but I can't talk to him. You won't tell him, will you? Not yet.'

'Mel, listen to me. I'm coming over—'

'No, Tegan, don't. What if Georgie turns up at yours? Oh, God,' a fresh cold wave of panic sloshes through her. 'It's happening all over again. We're going to lose Georgie too.'

'What happened to Sophie was an accident, Mel. It wasn't your fault. You're an amazing mother. Georgie's evidence of that.'

'An amazing mother? I don't know how you can

even say that, after what I did.'

'You've got to stop beating yourself up. If anyone was to blame it was the speeding motorist, not yours.'

'I'll tell you just how amazing I am as a mother, shall I?' Melanie listens to the bitterness in her voice, hears the self-loathing, and knows her sister-in-law hears it too. 'I was late collecting Georgie before. We'd only been here a week.' She blinks through wet lashes. 'It was lucky Delyth was there to look after her. She's a good woman, she's been so kind to me.' Melanie reminds herself as she continues to pound around the gravelled car park. 'So,' she gulps down a lungful of damp, sea air, her chest feeling desperately tight. 'That's how I know I'm not responsible enough, that I can't be trusted. After everything that happened with Sophie, I still haven't learnt my lesson. I still screw up.'

'Georgie was with Delyth that day, you say?'

'Yes. She loves Georgie, they get on really well.'

'Could she be with Delyth now, d'you think?'

Tegan's suggestion: a lifeline through the thickening sea fret.

'*What?* Where?'

'At the farm, maybe?'

'The farm?'

'Yes.'

'But why?' Melanie isn't totally dismissing the idea. 'If she'd seen I hadn't collected her, wouldn't she just have brought her back here?'

'Maybe she tried, and you'd already left.'

'Yeah, but,' mind whirling. 'She'd have told me, wouldn't she? Phoned the pub? She wouldn't just take her.'

'She might've been trying to, for all you know.'

'Do you think?' The nettle-sting is still smarting, she gives it a vigorous rub.

'Have you got her number? I don't think I have.'

'I'm not sure.' Then she remembers. 'Yes, I have. We swapped them ages ago. Yeah, bloody hell, you might be on to something there.'

'What's that?'

'Georgie came home from school the other day, all excited because Delyth told her they had kittens up at the farm. Yeah, Tegan, honestly, I think that's where she is.' The pain in her chest easing a little. 'I've not seen Delyth for ages, not since the Co-op when Gareth had a go at her . . . I think she's been avoiding me.'

'Yeah? What was that about?' Tegan is keen to know.

'I'll tell you another time. Let me ring her . . . I've got to ring her.'

'Yes, yes. Go on, quick. I'll hang up. Let me know what's happening, okay?'

THIRTY-THREE

'It keeps going through to bloody voicemail. I've left two messages.' Melanie, back behind the wheel of the Mazda. 'Can you give me directions to the farm?'

'What — you're not driving there?' Tegan sounds alarmed.

'I've not got a choice.' Melanie straps herself in, starts to reverse out of the pub car park.

'You could ring the police?'

'Let me try this first. It's not far, is it?'

'I still think we should still call the police, Mel.'

'All right, but you do it, will you? I need to get there. Talk me through how to find it.' She doesn't tell Tegan that in between dialling Delyth's number, Gareth called again and she didn't pick up. Not so long ago, Melanie could tell him anything, no matter how bad. She recognises a change in herself, a change in the dynamics of their marriage and she takes it as a clear indication of the distance that's growing between them.

She's frightened of him. There, she's admitted it. And telling Tegan he'd kill her if he found out about Georgie may only be a figure of speech, but remembering his recent hot-faced aggression, his volatile temper, the threat of violence, it has a maleficent ring.

Melanie abides by Tegan's directions and heads north. Up

high, with Pencarew far behind, the A487 follows the jagged bow of the cliff. In her driving mirror, lights from the town throw a tangerine belt across the sky and ahead, a sliver of orange, as the sun goes down red beyond the sea. Other than this, the world beyond the Mazda's windows is leached of colour and into this realisation, an unwelcome thought unfurls. This is winter. This colourless existence will be her life if something has happened to her child. If she doesn't bring Georgie home safe. This is how things will be from now on: nothing will ever bloom again, everything will be trapped in this grey, barren drabness.

Delyth's number is on redial but there is still no answer and with mobile reception intermittent, then disappearing completely, she is forced to give up. Why won't the woman pick up? If Georgie is with her then surely she'd appreciate Melanie's need for reassurance. The road dips sharply. Flanked by a tunnel of ravaged hedgerows and wind-licked trees, their black and crippled limbs stamped against the dusk. Melanie bites her lip. Realises just how hard when she tastes blood. She drops the window an inch and the sound of tyres on wet road fill the car. Darker now, she switches on sidelights, then headlamps. With nothing more than patches of cloud showing lighter on the horizon, she doubts there is more than fifteen minutes of daylight left. Her expression grim, she's too anxious for the company of the radio and, closing the window, she plugs the silence by chanting the directions to Gweld Y Môr. Listening to her voice bounce around her, she's terrified she will forget, with no way of calling Tegan back to clarify. She throws the redundant mobile on to the empty passenger seat, not daring to think beyond the journey to Delyth's farm; the possibility her daughter isn't there is unimaginable.

The road soars up into the rain again. Thoughts of Georgie, cold and alone and out in it somewhere, butt up against the thump, thump of windscreen wipers. Supposing Melanie doesn't find her? A sense of dread has her tighten her grip on the steering wheel, the whites of her knuckles showing through the skin. She glances at her wedding ring, wonders whether Tegan's telephoned the police yet, whether Gareth knows the terrible thing she's done. This is madness, she shivers despite the car's cosy interior, Georgie isn't going to be with Delyth; this is a wild goose chase and one she is going to come to regret. She shudders and clamps her jaw tight against the trepidation she holds in her mouth.

At last, the way ahead opens out. She makes the most of it and, foot to the floor, she pushes the car up into fifth, then sixth, for the first time. But not for long. Red tail lights snaking ahead, the spray from other vehicles drenching the windscreen, she is forced to squeeze to a stop and join a queue around the next bend. Road works. The usual assortment of signs: the Welsh that must be read first, an English translation given beneath.

'Just my bloody luck.' She bangs the dashboard, desperate. 'Come on. Come on.' Her pulse thumps in her neck as she inches forward in first gear, only to jerk to a standstill moments later.

Everything is wet and dank and heavy. She drops the window a fraction, wanting the little air there is. Stares out on the disappearing world, breathing into the flaccid moments of eerie calm. What was that? She's sure she saw something scurry up the bank. But too quick and far away to be certain, she locks her doors as a precaution and swallows, hears the Jurassic creep of the tide in her ears and waits for confirmation; for whatever it was to show itself again. But nothing does. The high-pitched keening of a buzzard has her looking up to a floating shape above the filigreed branches. Mimicking the cry of a baby, the bird sounds as distressed as she is. She watches it land on a nearby telegraph pole and settle inside its feathers.

Roadworks. She sniffs the acrid burn of asphalt. No one's working; they've all gone home for the night.

'Bloody pointless,' she curses, as the red traffic light turns green and she is finally on the move again.

The rain eases to a drizzle and she cuts the

windscreen wipers, swaps their squeaking for the spooky stillness going on beyond the car. The rain-blackened boughs of deciduous trees sprinkle the way ahead with what remains of their yellow leaves, they spiral down like gold sovereigns through the gloom. At last, she picks up speed, the tail lights thinning as she passes a series of triangular road signs warning of hairpin bends and blind spots. Slowing to 30 for a smattering of low-slung cottages, their stone faces turned to the road. She wonders fleetingly who lives in these places? There's nothing here. No shops, no pub, only banks and banks of blue-green conifers dissolving up into the cloud. Wide timber gates leading off into dark, lonely woodland, littered with 'land for sale' signs. There are other notices too, advertising, 'eggs for sale', 'hay for sale' . . . 'Shetland ponies for sale.' Would Georgie like a pony? The idea stabs her tightly-knotted concern for her daughter's safety.

'When I find you and bring you home,' she whispers, sending something of herself out to wherever Georgie is. 'That's what we'll do. We'll buy you a pony. Would you like that? A pony to love.' The painful prickle of tears has her biting her lip again, wanting them to stop, but they fall regardless. 'We will, we'll get you one.' She wipes the tears away, continues to talk to her missing child. 'Must be easy enough to rent a field nearby, there must be loads of grazing.' She tries not to think of the gorse-thrown hills squatting behind the mist, or that Georgie could be out there somewhere, lost and frightened, cold and wet. 'Don't worry, baby,' she says, pressing a hand to her abdomen in a way she would when she was pregnant. 'Mummy won't let anything bad happen to you.'

As she says this, a powerful memory of Sophie heaves into view. Her sweet face, vivid as ever, shines lantern-bright above the bonnet. Enough to make her gasp. To have known the colour of her eyes, to have touched her skin . . . what a brutal end. Black thoughts rise and fall with the contours of the road. To have let go of her hand .

. . she may as well have pushed her into the path of that car herself. Melanie picks over her dream, the one she has most nights, when she gives birth to twins. Sees again how they fit into the palms of her hands: one perfect, the other disfigured; until someone comes and takes them away. Tegan pushing her to have more children, she should tell her this, give her the images that haunt her night after night.

The sight of a white Luton van hurtling towards her at breakneck speed ruptures her dismal contemplations and snaps her into the present with a jolt. Blinded by the sudden headlights, Melanie swerves. The danger of the water-logged verge bouncing beneath her wheels. She pulls her mouth wide in silent scream as shrubbery scrapes the metal sides of the car. A blare of her horn and she follows the van's momentum in her driving mirror, only looking back at the way ahead in the nick of time.

Cows.

Blocking the road.

Nothing more than shifting shapes through the mist. Until she is almost upon them.

She slams the brakes and skids to a stop. In seconds, the Mazda's surrounded. High walls of muscle jostle the car and cattle breath steams into the air.

'This is a main road, and it's nearly bloody dark,' she yells, pushing her fingers to her collarbone to feel the heightened force of her heartbeat. 'Who in their right mind moves livestock in these conditions?' She sees the blood-red mud the cows trail from field to tarmac. Smacks the steering wheel over and over, until her hands hurt. 'Bloody, selfish idiots,' she screams, borderline hysterical. Not that she can be heard above the herdsmen's shouts, the mooing protest. Farmer and son, she guesses, unfurling a memory of her grandmother . . . the grandfather and the dairy herd she never knew. She tells herself to calm down, to have a little sympathy. Sharing ruddy complexions and identical blue overalls, these two, positioned on opposite verges, are unperturbed.

'I've got to find my child . . . I've got to find my child.' She pleads to no one. These men are as indifferent to her distress as they are to the weather.

The placid, liquid-eyed creatures mosey ever-closer to the car. Trapped and tense behind her seatbelt, Melanie's thoughts: curdling to a blackened muddle; are accompanied by that pain in her left arm again. Is this what extreme stress does to her now? she thinks and, rubbing what remains of her nettle sting, checks her phone for the umpteenth time.

'Oh,' she pounces on it when she sees a single bar of mobile reception. Uses it to dial Delyth and listens to it ring and ring. Breathe, she reminds herself, there is nothing she can do. She lets it ring out, looks past the illuminated handset to her frightened face reflected in the slope of side window. Half-mad and helpless, the woman she sees is unrecognisable.

The older farmer brandishes a stick, threatening. He barks orders to the sheepdogs that, slinking and weaving, run the gauntlet between the mud-splashed hocks. The cows are the colours of those pebble sweets in clear glass jars she would now and again win at the funfair in Hunstanton. Black, brown, fawn. Their rope tails swinging, their rubbery muzzles smearing the Mazda's bonnet. Nothing she can do. She cuts the engine. A car pulls up behind her. Headlamps blinding. Another beyond the cows. Sharp green smells from their dung waft in through the partially open window. Dung that splatters the insides of their hind legs. Warm again, she drops the window further, feels the chilly clamminess slap her cheeks. How uncannily still it is. Without a breath of wind, the fog has draped itself over the land like a damp, grey blanket.

The cows saunter on into the farmyard, udders swaying. Then she is on the move again, but only to part-exchange the dairy herd for a Land Rover tugging a rusted trailer.

'Bastard.' She swears when he pulls out in front of her at the next junction. 'You could have waited, there's sod all behind me.'

Crawling along, the trailer rattling and bumping, its red tail lights blinking on and off as the driver repeatedly slows then accelerates for no apparent reason. This is purgatory, she repeatedly smacks the dashboard. She just wants to get there . . . she just wants this agony to be over.

'Drive to the road,' she bawls her exasperation. 'Go on, you moron, some of us have to be somewhere.'

Slowing again, she uses the opportunity to recheck her mobile. But there is no signal. Emergency calls only. But this is an emergency. She should have telephoned the police herself, not left it to Tegan, she could be making the biggest mistake in her life. Supposing all this is a waste of time, then what? The same unanswerable questions, a relentless carousel in her head.

'Finally,' she inhales through her nostrils when the person in front turns off down some mud track. 'A clear road.'

The world beyond the Mazda's windows has darkened to an impenetrable indigo blue and she presses her foot to the floor, accelerates. She knows she is driving too fast, but the urgency of finding Georgie outweighs any fear she'll end up in a hedge. Then, veering around the next bend, she is met by a wall of pulsating ice-blue lights. They puncture the dark, mimicking her racing heart.

An ambulance.

'Oh, God, no. It's Georgie, I know it is!' she screams. 'Oh, please . . . *please*, don't let it be Georgie?'

THIRTY-FOUR

Melanie abandons the Mazda in the middle of the road. Engine running. Deaf to the blare of horns, her boots sliding against the wet tarmac, she hurtles towards the ambulance.

'I can't lose her too?' she shouts through the rain she doesn't notice. 'Please, don't let me lose her too.'

She jumps at shadows carved out by car headlamps. At the sharp shapes thrown up and over the blackened hedgerows.

'Georgie. Is it Georgie?' her desperate cries as she leaps over puddles.

Up close, a sweaty-faced paramedic. His mouth a wide, black hole as he steers her away.

'Madam, please.' He grabs her by the forearm. 'Go back to your car. There's nothing to see here.'

But there is. And wrenching free, she twists backwards, nearly losing her footing again. A red motorbike is buried in the briar and thorn-choked undergrowth, smoking. Its rear-wheel spinning in the mud. With it, a flash of the boys who come to ride along the beach at night, the sounds she listens to when she can't sleep. A memory too, of her motorbike-mad boyfriend from years ago. Then it's a stretcher she sees. Transported by the paramedic who told her to get in her car and his female colleague. It grazes past her, catching the hem of her parka. She shouldn't be here. She's no rubbernecker. But Melanie can't avert her eyes. It means she inadvertently sees the injured rider.

Leather-clad and bleeding, an oxygen mask fixed to the battered face. This is a man. Someone's husband, brother, son. Not Georgie.

On her return to the car, under the blaze of headlights, she eavesdrops on the conversations of drivers leaning out through their open windows.

'Took the bend too fast. Didn't stand a chance.'

'Hellish black spot for bikes.'

'Emergency services probably got here too late.'

A squeal of sirens and the ambulance disappears down the tunnel of trees. When the traffic eventually picks up speed, she swings the car from left to right. The centre road markings have faded to a chalky scuff and there are no cat's eyes to lead the way. Fields of sheep, partly engulfed by fog, whizz by. Shrunken trees straddle the road, their parasitic ivy and artificially bright moss are picked out by the Mazda's headlights, before fading into obscurity again. A fox tucked into the verge; his red eyes unblinking.

'Stay there,' she breathes. 'Don't step out.'

She passes side roads and crossroads, but with Tegan's warning: 'Don't turn off anywhere . . . the sign for the farm will be clear from the road.' She does as she was told.

'Keep going, keep going,' she chants into her escalating distress. 'You've not come far enough yet.'

Stone-fronted farmsteads, stern as Welsh chapels, rear up beyond high metal gates. Their wet yards lit by searing security lights show corrugated barns crammed with vast, black-wrapped haylage bales in readiness of snow. Farm names . . . Tan-Y-Waen . . . Bal Mawr . . . Caer Eithin . . . hurtle by. None of them Gweld Y Môr. A long-abandoned tea shop, its windows boarded against the seasons. A sign for a stud farm boasting Dutch warmbloods she remembers Tegan telling her to watch out for. It means she must be close . . . keep looking . . . keep looking.

Heavy raindrops strike the windscreen like a shower of bullets. She jumps, flicks the wipers on again. Then she sees it. A large wrought iron gateway just as Tegan described. Wide enough for a car, but so enveloped in ivy, she could easily have missed it. A quick check in her driving mirror before indicating and pulling into a lay-by. Lurching to a standstill, she identifies the mouth of the entrance: a tunnel made darkest green by slippery-backed rhododendron leaves. She gets out to investigate, uncovers a corroded metal plate nailed to a crumbling gatepost, reads: Gweld Y Môr, as the rain slaps her face.

Back behind the wheel, she turns on to the dirt track, focuses on the central spine of green weeds growing between the tyre tracks. Ghostly. The murky sulphur tubes of the car headlamps flinch with each pothole. Mind-numbing in its endlessness, the trail is overarched by the buckled boughs of trees and scales what she supposes to be a high-sided cliff. Eyes peeled, a momentary lapse in concentration could be fatal. She is imagining what sliding down the sheer drop that is alarmingly close to where the hardcore ends and fields begin would mean, when the rattle of a cattle grid under the Mazda's tyres has her jerking the wheel. The car veers suddenly to the left. She screams into the hammering panic and manages, just, to right the car in time.

'Please?' she prays to the dark, with a fierce determination. 'Let Georgie be here.'

The track snakes on, rising higher and higher. This is steep, impossibly steep, she responds to the strain of the engine, unable to push up into second gear. Another fear she has is that the Mazda won't make it to the top. She'd be better off on a horse and wonders what vehicle could manage this day-in-day-out? Not many. She thinks of Delyth's bashed-up Defender, a boneshaker like that, she decides, or a tractor. She remembers what John said about seeing Gareth's Porsche heading off up here. *Really?* She can't envisage him risking his gorgeous motor along a track like this.

On and on, nudging past a series of large, corrugated iron sheds with heavy bolted doors and sagging barbed wire. Her body jolts at the sight of an owl, it lifts her from the wandering dread of her thoughts. The wonderment of its white, angel spread of wings as it follows the updraft of the car, floodlit by headlamps. Then, a final push over the withers in the track and a row of lofty Scots pines loom into view. Bent to the wind and working as gateposts, they mark the entrance to the surprisingly palatial farmstead up ahead.

'At last,' Melanie breathes her relief and steers in through a double set of grand metal gates.

She skids to a halt, scattering chickens which flap and wheel away. Free of her seatbelt, she leaps from the car and charges out across the muddied twilight of the yard. Head down through the downpour, smelling wood smoke from a nearby fire, she is drawn like a moth to a thin light from the porch. Its guiding beam rendered almost useless in the moisture-laden blackness.

THIRTY-FIVE

The door of the farmhouse opens and there stands Delyth, all smiles and backlit by the hall light.

'Is Georgie here? Is Georgie with you?' Melanie shrieks.

'What?' Delyth, evidently surprised by her question. 'Course she's here, I texted to tell you.'

'Georgie's here? She's definitely with you?' Melanie's body sags. At the end of her reserves she wobbles, unsteady in the dripping porch.

'I told you. In a text message.' Delyth stares at her as if she's stupid.

'But I didn't have it.' Melanie bursts into tears. 'And I've been ringing and ringing.'

'Oh, dear, don't upset yourself. Georgie's here, she's fine.' Delyth takes her hand, pulls her out of the rain. 'Come in. Come in.'

She stumbles over the threshold, into a fug of floral-smelling perfume. *Delyth's wearing perfume?*

'I've left you loads of messages; didn't you get them?' Melanie sobs, too relieved to be properly angry. 'Look,' she holds up her phone with its miraculous full five bars of reception, wanting Delyth to see. 'I've had messages from Gareth, one from Tegan, but nothing from you. I've been frantic with worry, Tegan's rung the police.'

'I'm sorry, I did send it. I didn't think for a minute you'd be worried.' Delyth replies mildly. 'The school must've told you she was with me. Where did you think she was?'

'I didn't know,' Melanie blows her nose on a tissue and glances sideways at a serene plaster figurine of the Madonna and Child, it's an image she's always found disturbing. 'I thought, I thought,' but she can't formulate her thoughts, bleak as they are, into any kind of order.

'Oh, well, never mind. You're here now.'

'And you're sure Georgie's safe?' Melanie, still disbelieving, wipes tears that have mixed with rainwater from her cheeks. 'She's really here? She's really safe, with you?' She keeps on, automatically scraping her boots clean on the heavy-duty doormat.

'Course she is, silly.' Delyth continues to smile calmly into Melanie's anxiety. 'Come on, she's through here.' And she leads the way along the hall. 'I'd have brought her straight back to the pub, but she was so insistent, she wanted to see the kittens. And you weren't around to ask.' She turns and gives Melanie a look. 'So, I brought her back with me.'

When the kitchen door is eased open, they are greeted by a blast of warm air, along with the smells of rising bread dough.

'Georgieeee!' Melanie surges forward, scoops her child in her arms and squeezes her hard. 'Oh, thank heavens, you're all right.'

'Ow, Mummy, you're hurting me, and you're all wet.' Georgie laughs, not the least perturbed as to where her mother's been.

'Sorry, baby. Sorry.' Melanie, still holding her tight, is not letting go.

'Delyth's got kittens.' Georgie wriggles free and, round-eyed, legs swinging, is oblivious to her mother's distress. 'Can we have one? Please, can we have one?' She jumps down from the scrubbed wooden table and leads Melanie over.

'Aw, they're adorable.' Still weeping with joy that her daughter is safe, she crouches for a closer look. 'Is it okay to touch them?' She transfers her blurry gaze to Delyth.

'Fine. Yes. Georgie's been playing with them, haven't you *cariad*? Their mam doesn't mind, I think she's had enough of them.'

A blue plastic crate has been pushed up against the warm side of the Aga. Inside it, a bundle of fluff-balls and an attentive tabby with steel-green eyes. Melanie counts two greys and three gingers but can tell her daughter's heart's been lost to the most affectionate of the bunch: the prettiest black kitten with a puff of white on his chest.

'Oh, please?' Georgie jigs up and down, flaps her arms like the chickens Melanie nearly flattened in the yard. 'Delyth says we can take one home today, if we want. She says they're ready to leave their mummy.'

'Are they?' Melanie is doubtful. 'They look too small to me.'

'Oh, yes. It's perfectly fine.' Delyth assures. 'They're almost twelve-weeks-old, been on solids a fortnight.'

'I don't know, sweetheart,' Melanie says. 'I think we should at least ask Slinky what he thinks first, don't you?'

'Oh, he'd love a kitten. He told me he wants a little friend. Can we, Mummy? Can we?'

'Well,' Melanie hugs Georgie. The trauma of the drive and the dread she was never going to see her child again, is at last ebbing away.

'Please, Mummy. Please.'

'D'you think he'd be any good at keeping the mice down?' she asks Delyth.

'It's why we have them on the farm.'

'I don't know. I should check with Daddy first.' Melanie dithers, letting go of Georgie and straightening up. 'I love that smell.' Standing, she looks around her at the production-line of white-lobed masses. Warmed by the Aga and nudging free of the little steel tins, the bread dough, plump and oven-ready, are like the wet-nosed calves

Melanie imagines Delyth's father once bred and fattened for slaughter.

Sudden thoughts of soft, fresh-baked bread thickly spread with butter, has her knees shift beneath her. Hungry, she realises she hasn't eaten anything since breakfast.

'D'you want some?' Behind her, Delyth is close enough for Melanie to smell her perfume again.

'Um.' Fingers combing her wet hair, she looks directly at Delyth, tries to work out what's different about her.

'It's delicious, Mummy.' Georgie, seated up at the table again, is about to take another bite of the slice she's been given.

'I'm sure it is, sweetheart. But I hope you're not spoiling your dinner?'

'Let her have it.' Delyth overrides her concern. 'She could do with it; she's looking thinner to me. Is she eating properly? She shouldn't be this thin at her age.'

'She's like me, burns it off in a second.' Hating the way Delyth, as is Gareth's habit, talks about Georgie when she is perfectly able and old enough to answer for herself.

'If you say so. But perhaps,' Delyth begins, 'as you're with Georgie all the time you might not have noticed.'

'I think I would have.' Melanie is already feeling a bad enough mother.

'I wondered if it might have something to do with those tummy aches you said she was having?'

'We've been back to the doctors, haven't we, Georgie?' She makes a point of including her child in their discussion.

'Dr Cassidy?'

She nods. 'Test results came back negative.'

'That's good. Maybe it was just a phase she was going through.'

'Let's hope.' Melanie smiles stiffly. 'Because you've not had one of those bad tummies for a while, have you,

Georgie?'

'No.' Her daughter says, licking butter from her wrist. 'Not for ages.'

Remembering Tegan and her need to ring her, to let her know everything is all right, Melanie pulls out her mobile and scrolls through her list of contacts. Perhaps it would be enough to just send a text for now, tell her Georgie's safe and well and ask her to let the police know. Gareth too. Say she hasn't had clear reception and she'll phone as soon as she's home. And with more than enough mobile signal, she dashes off two quick messages.

'Thanks for looking after Georgie,' Melanie sighs, twisting to Delyth. 'I'm sorry if I was a bit short with you when I got here. None of it was your fault. I was the one who was late collecting her.'

'Bread?' Delyth, a fleeting smile, seemingly uninterested in her excuses. 'Fresh from the oven. Go on, you look like you could do with something.'

Melanie listens to the serrated knife saw open the crusty-topped loaf.

'There you go.' Delyth holds out a thick slice of bread on a side plate, the butter melting in shallow yellow pools. 'There's jam. Homemade.' She wafts the knife over a jar that is waiting, ready with spoon. 'Of course, you do,' she answers for her, still holding the plate. 'Here you go.' And dropping the breadknife into the sink with a clatter, she languorously spreads on jam.

The sharp sound of metal against ceramic sparks an image of Delyth slicing into her arms in the pub kitchen. And fighting through what remains of that traumatic afternoon, is when Melanie realises what is different about the woman today.

'You've cut your hair.'

'You what?' Delyth screws up her face. A face — Melanie is seeing, now she's looking properly — that's been sensitively enhanced with a silvery smear of eyeshadow, a blush of lipstick.

'Wow, only now I'm noticing.' She lifts an admiring hand to the chic, black bob that's as shiny as tar. 'You look lovely.'

'Oh, this?' Delyth touches the tantalising bounce of her newly styled hair. 'I got it done this afternoon.'

'And your make-up?' Melanie appreciates. 'Did you have that done professionally too?'

Delyth nods.

'You look lovely. The best I've ever seen you.'

'Thanks.' The woman responds as if she's been complimented about one of her pastries.

'Did you get your outfit today, too?' Melanie clocks the designer jeans, the gauzy material of the shirt — nothing of the jumble sale here.

'Thought I'd treat myself.'

'Good for you. Are you off somewhere special?'

'A works Christmas do at the golf club. D'you want to be my plus one?'

'Best not.' Her eyes slide to Georgie.

'Your coat's wet through. Give it to me, I'll dry it on the Aga.' The request is more of a demand.

Melanie's does as she's told and takes off her parka. 'Best not tip it up,' she warns, handing it over. 'There's shells in the pockets.'

She wanders the kitchen, eating her bread and jam. This hub of the house reminds her of her grandmother's farm and it is to take a trip down memory lane to see the ever-drying washing, the kettle on perpetual boil. Chewing on the last of the crust, she spots a crop of framed photographs balancing on a shelf. Interested in Delyth's life, her family, she peers at a young couple on their wedding day.

'Are these your parents?' She sets the empty plate aside.

The woman, no older than twenty and as petite as Delyth, shows off a headful of flame-red hair. The man beside her is tall with eyes as dark as Delyth's.

'Yes, that's them.' A mug of milky tea is pushed into Melanie's hand.

'Your Mum's very beautiful.' She glances at the fawn-coloured liquid, unsure if she can drink it. Already queasy from her angst-ridden drive. She hates milky tea.

'It was taken a long time ago.' The voice is dry. 'You can meet Mam, if you like?'

Melanie consults her watch. 'Maybe another time, we ought to be getting back.'

'A few minutes more won't hurt. She's been looking forward to meeting you.'

'Has she?' The way Delyth described her, coupled with what John said, Melanie isn't keen to meet a woman who behaves like the mother she grew up with.

'Very much so.'

'All right,' she relents. 'I don't suppose another half hour will matter.'

'That's the spirit.' Delyth bends to retrieve a set of golden-topped loaves from the oven. 'Just give me a minute to finish up here.'

Waiting, Melanie's gaze returns to the photographs. She focuses on a family portrait in which a young Delyth is sitting in a home-spun jumper beside another girl.

Is this Erin? Melanie assumes it must be. Sandwiching their offspring, a noticeably older Mr and Mrs Powell wear weather-weary complexions made ruddier under the stark studio lights. How stiff and gawky they look in their Sunday best. Delyth's mother in a cattle-red dress with pearls about her neck. The father in suit and tie.

'You are nosy.' Delyth swoops up behind her.

'You take after your dad,' Melanie shares her observation. 'It's the eyes. Very attractive,' she adds to soften it. Appreciating, even though she's never known her own, daughters don't necessarily want to hear they resemble their fathers. Then she spots something else. 'Hey!' she yelps, reaching to the back of the shelf. 'That's Gareth's school photograph. You didn't have to take it; I'd have got you a copy if you'd asked.'

'I was going to give it back.' Delyth, sheepish beneath her elegant haircut. 'It's just that I haven't got many photos of my—' Hearing her voice crack, Melanie fills in the gaps.

'I don't suppose Gareth will notice. You can give it back at some point.'

Still waiting for Delyth, Melanie tries her tea again. She must drink it, if only to be polite. Doing so, her eyes land on another framed photograph of a young woman. A girl, really. Her glorious red hair gleaming bright as her smile in the high summer sunshine. She is wearing a light cotton sundress and is standing barefoot on a patch of grass. The man Melanie recognises as Delyth's father stands beside her, his hands around her waist. Both are laughing into the camera.

'She's beautiful. Is she a relative of yours?' Melanie's already guessed the girl is Erin but she wants the excuse it gives to ask questions. Questions like: Why would a gorgeous girl like that kill herself? A girl with her whole life ahead of her.

'Sorry?' Delyth stands at the sink, the cuffs of her top folded back to the elbows.

'The girl in this,' Melanie points to the photograph. 'She's beautiful. She looks just like your mother in her wedding photo. Who is she?'

Delyth turns off the taps and dries her hands. 'Come on.' The look is enigmatic as she twiddles the crucifix gleaming at her neckline. 'Let's take you to see Mam.'

THIRTY-SIX

'**M**ammy. *Mam?*' Delyth snaps at the woman who's asleep in an armchair in the adjacent room. Melanie is about to say, *Don't wake her, let her sleep*, when Delyth shakes the bony shoulder. 'This is Melanie, Mam. Gareth's wife.'

The woman judders awake and blinks like a rodent might in unaccustomed light. She looks like a rodent, Melanie decides, something that sleeps a lot during daylight hours. A dormouse perhaps. Her eyes are dark and huge enough. Their lustre and size exaggerated in the face of such a small person. And the way her long white hair, worn in a single plait between her shoulder-blades, swishes around, it could be a tail.

'What, what did you say?'

'*I said*, this is Melanie.'

The face, unclouded by thought, stares out at them blankly.

'You remember me telling you about her?' Delyth prompts.

'Oh, Del, you do look nice. You off somewhere?'

'Yes.' An impatient sigh. 'I told you. Christmas bash at the golf club . . . oh, I give up.' Delyth tosses Melanie a hopeless look. 'Melanie,' a hand on her arm. 'I won't be long; I've just got to lock my hens up for the night. Are you happy to stay with Mam?'

'No probs.' Melanie plonks down opposite Mrs Powell, whose flickering eyelids suggest she might have drifted off to sleep again.

'Shall I take Georgie with me? She said she wanted to see the chickens.'

'If you like.'

'Great. Be back in a minute.' Delyth tugs on the padded jacket she carried from the kitchen, zips her smart, new clothes away inside. 'I'll call Andrew down; I'd like him to meet you.'

The room is large, falling away into shadow. Items of heavy oak furniture stoop in its unlit perimeters like elderly relatives. The glow from a handsome log fire is cosy, as is the pink blush of a single tasselled lamp and, when an outer door slams, she wonders just how keen Georgie is to be tottering out with Delyth into the rain she can hear thrashing the windows. The flames in the hearth fling crumpled shapes across the floorboards and, throwing one leg over the other, she leans into the couch to trace its floral pattern with her fingers.

Melanie could fall asleep herself and, tilting her head to yawn, sees a Constable-like scene framed in white plastic on the wall above the ancient-looking TV. It is the kind of landscape depicting impossible skies and cliffs and yellow sand, along with the usual fishing boats on an absurdly blue sea. Yet something about it is oddly familiar. Hunstanton. She recognises the layered cliffs she used to think looked like the Battenberg cake her gran would make at Easter: vanilla and strawberry, sandwiched together with apricot jam. Staring into the imagined scene, she lets the fist of her memories push her back to that time like a playground bully. A time when Uncle Pete would take her and Cassie fishing on that very beach. The three of them, clanking down to the shore when the tide was right, for what he termed: 'A spot of sea-fishing.' He would have them making diagonal slashes along the tideline in a hunt for sand eels. Then they would take turns casting, standing in waist-deep water until it grew too cold. Cassie landed a sea bass that they cooked over an open fire once. They stood around the flames eating with their fingers, picking out the bones.

This is a difficult memory and one Melanie tries to push away. Uncle Pete tried to explain — with her sobbing her heart out on the return journey, fearing the inebriated state she was going to find her mother in — why the holidays had to stop after her gran died. He said Aunty Shelia 'Couldn't cope' and didn't want to take on her drunken sister's child. Even if it meant that child going into institutionalised care. Melanie liked her uncle and could imagine a life with him and Cassie. But not Aunty Sheila, with her assistant manager job at Barclays. A woman with perfect hair and lipstick, who wore tailored jackets and high-heeled shoes, even on the beach.

Melanie's mobile beeps and she drops the upsetting feelings that always rub alongside happier memories of golden childhood holidays. A text from Tegan, sending her a smiley-face emoji and seven kisses. Melanie smiles herself and, lifting her gaze, finds Mrs Powell, eyes open, smiling back at her.

'Hello, I'm Melanie.' She extends a hand.

'I'm Norah,' the woman croaks, lips ungluing themselves. Norah holds her hand and stares into her eyes. 'Sorry to fall asleep on you.'

'Don't be silly. Soporific, aren't they?'

'You what?' Norah fiddles with the tartan rug she has spread over her knees.

'They make you sleepy,' Melanie points at the flames.

'Oh, I'm terrible. Fall asleep on a drawing pin, my Wally used to say.'

'Lucky you.'

'You have trouble then, do you?'

'You could say that.' Melanie, reluctant to elaborate, steers the conversation elsewhere by asking: 'Am

I right in thinking that's Hunstanton?'

Norah looks up through glassy eyes. 'How clever of you to recognise it. Wally and me had our honeymoon there. Lovely it was.'

'I used to think it was the best beach in the world.' Withered memories of her and Cassie splashing in the shallows fall like petals. 'Until I came here.'

'Oh, yes. Home is best.' Norah tilts sideways, tugs the little brass handle on a rickety sideboard. 'You'll have a drink?'

'Oh, no, I'm fine. Delyth made me tea earlier.'

'I mean a proper drink,' Norah twinkles.

'Better not, I'm driving.' Melanie scratches her nettle sting which is still smarting.

'I'll give you something for that,' Norah, noticing. 'I swear by sage and comfrey.'

'Oh, no. It's fine.' She tucks her hand away.

'But you'll have a small sherry?' A swish of the tail of hair. 'Go on, keep me company. Delyth's such a stick-in-the-mud, she never touches the stuff.'

'No, I'd better not.'

'Help get you down the track. You need nerves of steel to do that in the dark.'

They laugh.

'All right,' Melanie uncrosses her legs. 'But only a tiny one.'

'There's no need to be frightened.'

'*Frightened?* Sorry, what?'

'Yes, just push them away.' Norah wags a thin wrist.

'Sorry, push who away?'

'The dogs. If they're a bother.'

Melanie twists in her seat, peers into the darkened corners of the room. There aren't any dogs.

'We've always had sheepdogs, see. Lovely breed they are. My Wally,' a sigh, 'he loved 'em. Such dear, faithful dogs. And such energy, they keep me on my toes, I can tell you.'

'They're a popular breed.' Melanie, while a little concerned, doesn't want to insult her host by pointing out the obvious, and takes the dainty glass being handed to her.

'Now.' Up on her feet and surprisingly agile, Norah bends to stroke her imaginary companions. 'Now, boys . . . boys,' she warns, wagging a finger. 'That's enough. On your beds.' She claps and points to a pair of beanbags beside a dark Welsh dresser. 'On your beds.' She repeats the command, lowering her voice to a growl. And seemingly satisfied the phantom dogs have done as they're told, she returns to her chair. 'They do take liberties. You've got to keep on at them. All the time.'

'I'm sure you do.' Melanie plays along, her thoughts spinning to Slinky and how quickly he's learnt certain commands. 'They're cleverer than we give them credit for,' she says, half-believing there are a pair of boisterous sheepdogs in the room.

'Oh, they are.' Norah sips her sherry and Melanie does the same; feels the welcoming warmth of it spread through her. 'Brothers they are.' Norah stares fondly into the darkness, at whatever it is she sees. 'Great company for me, stuck here on my own.' She speaks with her hands. 'Since I retired, well, I don't get out no more, see.'

'That's a shame.' She remembers what John told her. No wonder the woman's inventing dogs for company, it sounds a grim existence. 'Couldn't Delyth take you somewhere now and again?'

'Too busy working, the girl don't go nowhere herself, not socially.'

'She's going out tonight.'

'*Hah*!' Norah splutters, licks her lips. 'Is there a blue moon behind them rainclouds?'

Melanie watches Norah and finds nothing of the woman Delyth made her out to be. So what? She enjoys a drop of sherry, there's no harm in that. Familiar with how miserable life is with a drunk, she decides to have a word with Delyth when she gets the chance. Engulfed by the big leather armchair she sits in, Norah, like Delyth, is doll-like, and with elbows as sharp as the corners of her furniture, Melanie guesses the woman can't weigh more than six stone.

The sound of logs collapsing in the grate has Norah motioning to the hearth. 'Be a love, shove a log on.'

Melanie puts her glass down on a dinky felt-topped table, is pleased to have something to do.

'As a girl, my Del used to have a map of the world on her bedroom wall and dream of all the places she was going to go.' Norah chuckles while Melanie jabs the flames into life with the poker. 'But shame of it is,' the chuckling stops, 'she never got to go nowhere. All the poor dab does is cook and clean. Keep house. Play mother.'

Satisfied with the fire, Melanie returns to the couch, wonders what Norah would have to say if she knew how Delyth went about painting her to the outside world.

'I wanted her to get married, to have her own babies,' Norah's voice is sad. 'She never goes nowhere. Nowhere further than Pencarew,' she repeats herself. 'And what kind of life is that for a young woman? She should have seen something of life, gone out into the big world like you have, *bach*. Not slaving away at three jobs for bugger-all money. I want her to find a nice man, someone to take care of her. It's not natural being on your own.'

Melanie spins her head. *Did Norah just swear?* But there isn't time for private thought.

'Talking of nice men,' Norah winks. 'How's your lovely Gareth doing? What's he up to nowadays?'

'Oh, he's fine.' Melanie picks up her glass, considers the amber liquid. Thinks how the woman sitting opposite once had hair this glorious if those photographs in the kitchen are to be believed.

'Bit of a catch, if you don't mind me saying.' The voice is admiring. 'He was such a star at school, everybody loved him.'

Melanie forces a smile. 'Yes, I know.'

'She'd make someone a lovely wife, my Delyth.'

Norah fiddles with her plait of long, white hair and Melanie's grateful Gareth seems to have been forgotten. 'I suppose, if things had turned out different . . . if Wally hadn't died . . . if Erin hadn't got herself pregnant.'

Melanie doesn't move. This is the first time Erin has been mentioned and she doesn't want to do anything to distract Norah; she wants to know what went on.

'But at least Erin got to spread her wings and experience a few things. I know she fell in with the wrong crowd and that, but it was loads better than living a nothing kind of life like Del. Yes, she could be selfish and irresponsible, but it took guts to run away like that. I didn't mind her leaving her boy with me. She was too young to have a babby. I told Delyth, I said for her to go too. Using me as an excuse, I can look after myself, thank you very much. I could've looked after Andrew too. But she wouldn't have it. Besotted with him from the moment he was born, she was. More besotted with him than Erin.'

'How long was she gone for?'

'Two years, or so.'

'Long time to leave your child.'

'Nah, the boy was always more Delyth's than hers. Erin knew that, I think it's why she ran away.'

'Andrew's going to be doing his own thing soon. Delyth will be free then.'

'Not how she sees it,' Norah snorts. 'She says she's missed the boat, that no one will want her now.'

'That's rubbish.'

'Try telling her that.'

'I have.' Melanie says.

'Then you're wasting your breath, *cariad*.' Norah rolls her eyes. 'Del doesn't want help. Give her a solution, she don't want it. You can't fix her, she's *unbloodyfixable*.'

Norah has no idea but she has echoed Gareth's complaint: about Delyth, about her. And it has Melanie wondering if this is what she does? With Delyth, with John, with people in her life before now. Does she try to fix people's lives because in so doing it makes her feel better about the wrongs she's done? Like stealing Gareth from Elizabeth, Sophie's death; the fact she can't do anything to help her own mother, who is rotting away in a horrid little bedsit on the other side of the country?

'How did you two meet?' Norah's question slices between her deliberations.

'Me and Delyth?'

'No, you and Gareth.' Norah tugs on her plait then drops it over her shoulder with a satisfying thump.

Melanie spends the next few minutes glossing over their affair, talks of Gareth already being married. 'I'm not proud of hurting Elizabeth like that, it wasn't fair.'

'Ain't nothing fair in love, *cariad*. It's got everything to do with luck, and I was very lucky with my Wally. We were very happy. But I was still relatively young when he died . . . I had needs.' She lifts her watery eyes, lets Melanie fill in the gaps, which she can't quite do. 'It's why Delyth had such a problem with what happened to Erin. A strictly no sex before marriage girl, is our Del. Me? —' Norah winks. 'I'm a woman of the world.'

Melanie's gaze wanders beyond the comforting crackle of the fire, to the heavily-beamed ceiling that is flaking and cobwebby at the corners. Sees where damp patches have stained the wallpaper brown like the liver spots on the backs of Norah's hands.

'How d'you manage it all here? It's a big place to maintain,' Melanie asks.

'I don't think we do.' A weak smile.

'Have you ever thought about selling up? She remembers the conversation with Tegan and Sian.

'Oh, no, all my memories are here. Delyth's always on at me. Saying we should sell up, move to town, but I can't. She's a good girl, Del, but I think her wanting to move has more to do with the bad memories she has of her Da. He never bothered with her, see. Erin was his favourite. It was, Erin this, Erin that. Soft as butter, my Wally, he wouldn't let the wind blow on her.' Norah drains her sherry while Melanie's remains relatively untouched. 'That's why I'm glad my Wally weren't around to see what became of her. Erin, I mean. It would have broken his heart. Spoilt her rotten, he did. And there was Delyth, doing for him more than me when I was flat out with my job,' she pauses, 'You know I used to work for Gareth's father, didn't you?'

'Yes. What was he like? I never met him.'

'Rhodri?' Norah aghast. 'Didn't you know, Rhodri?'

'No, he didn't approve of me. Blamed me for splitting Gareth and Elizabeth up. Him and Bronwyn,' a tight laugh. 'They didn't even come to our wedding.'

'Well, I never.' Norah's thin eyebrows shoot up. 'Was he really like that? I always thought he was broadminded about matters of the heart.' She floats away on her memories for a moment. 'He took me up in his plane once.' Norah's eyes moisten with what Melanie supposes is remembered appreciation of the father-in-law she never knew. 'Ah, we used to have some laughs, me and Rhod. Anyway,' she focuses on Melanie again, 'Where was I?'

'You were saying how busy you were at work.' Melanie helps her out.

'That's right. Wally and Del. Oh, my memory's going terrible. Don't be telling her, she worries about me enough as it is.' A click of her false teeth. 'Poor Del, cooking for him, pouring his tea, ironing his best shirt for Chapel every Sunday. But he barely noticed her.'

'That must've been hard.'

'To tell you the truth, it was. And I'd like to say Erin was deserving of her father's doting, but she weren't.' Norah, surprisingly candid from her armchair. 'I have to say, I couldn't cope with Erin. Not after my Wally died.' Pulling no punches, she pours herself another sherry. 'I loved her, course I did, but she was always trouble.' She takes a sip. 'I tried to bring her up right, like I brought Delyth up right, but Erin was so rebellious, with her make-up and short skirts. Oh, you're not to mind me. Silly old woman going on about stuff.' The expression borders on apologetic. 'You don't mind, do you?'

'No,' Melanie, enthusiastic. 'It's lovely listening to you.'

'Thing is, see, I couldn't do no more, I washed my hands of her. I'm not proud of it, but my Wally, he was the only one who could get her to see sense, to do her homework, to leave the boys alone, but after he died, *uch*,' Norah, squeezes the stem of her sherry glass. 'She went completely off the rails. Drinking, staying out all hours. I never knew where she was half the time.'

'What happened to her?' Melanie asks gently.

'She threw herself out of her bedroom window.' Norah says, bluntly. Her thin arm jabbing upwards through the firelight. 'Top floor of the house it was, cos this place has got a third floor. All closed off now, mind. Nice and high for Erin, shut off from the rest of us. We thought it'd be good for her to have her own space when the babby came along. A bit of privacy. You know?'

The words *shut off* have a sinister ring. Especially as it echoes the suggestion Sian made when Erin came up in conversation at Plas Newydd that morning. But there isn't the time to ask Norah to elaborate. The rasp of carpet when it snags against the rough-bottomed door interrupts them. Melanie spins to see who it is.

'Andrew! There you are.' Norah greets the teenager loitering on the threshold, his face lit by the ten-inch screen in his hands. 'Come and meet Melanie.'

'Hiya,' he mumbles, without raising his eyes.

Melanie looks at him. How tall he is. Tall and lanky in his ripped jeans and grey hoodie. When at last he lifts his face, she hunts it, wanting the young man he almost is. She finds him for a moment and tries to hold him there, but he slips away again. How oddly familiar he is, she thinks, judging him to be at least as tall as Delyth's father in the photographs Melanie saw of him, but with the same auburn hair as Erin, and Norah before her, he seems to be a hybrid of the two.

'Can't you put that thing down for a minute?' Norah sighs. 'Come and be sociable. Melanie's been dying to meet you, haven't you Melanie?'

'I have, yes.'

'Sorry. Only had it today. It's new.' Andrew grins his excuse, dazzling them with his smile. 'Del bought me it.'

'Lucky you.' Melanie returns his smile. 'Is it an early Christmas present?'

'Something like that.' A shy glance, up through his conker-shiny fringe. Such a good-looking boy.

'I got myself a new smartphone not so long ago. I love it, couldn't do without it now. I'm not sure how I'd get on with those,' she gestures to his portable PC with its LCD touchscreen.

'I've got a smartphone too,' he says, blowing air up through his flap of hair. 'But this is awesome.' Eyes down, he stretches the adjective like a piece of bubble gum.

'Andrew!' Norah is sharp from her chair. 'Put it away, I won't tell you again.'

He does and, moving into the room, takes the seat beside Melanie on the couch.

'I think I need to change my network provider.' She winks when she catches his eye. 'I had dire reception all the way here.' Then adding, to keep the conversation going: 'How are you liking the sixth form?'

'Not much. I don't even need A levels to join the army. There's tests and stuff you've gotta pass, but I reckon I'd do them easy.'

'You're going to join the army?'

A spirited nod. 'I'll go off my head if I have to stay here.' He sneaks a look at his grandmother.

'I suppose it's a great way to see the world.'

'Too right.' Andrew, drawn to his tablet, is, within seconds, scrolling through the glossy lives on his Instagram page again.

The door behind them wheezes open a little wider and Delyth, trailing Georgie, steps into the room.

'Ah, there you are,' she addresses Andrew, her mobile held close to her chin. 'Melanie must've been wondering if I'd made you up.'

'Andrew's been telling me about his plans to join the army.'

'Over my dead body,' Delyth snaps, dropping the smartphone to her side. 'He's going to university. And not too far away from home, neither.' She focuses briefly on Melanie, then back to her mobile. 'He's such a whizz with technology, I don't know how he keeps up with all the latest gizmos.' Delyth talks for Andrew, even though he is perfectly able to talk for himself. Melanie wonders if it's a Welsh thing.

'Come by the fire, *cariad*.' Norah, tapping her thin knees, beckons Georgie closer. 'You must be freezing. Fancy Delyth making you go out in that horrible weather.'

'But I wanted to,' Georgie informs her. 'I wanted to see the chickens.'

'Chickens.' Norah scoffs. 'Mangy buggers, the lot of them.'

'Mam!' Delyth barks from her standing position by the door.

'Well, they are.' Norah takes Georgie's hands and rubs them between her own. 'Oh, dear, they're like two blocks of ice. That's it, you sit there. Close to the fire. Delyth used to sit on that when she was little.' Norah uses a foot to shift a small tapestried stool in Georgie's direction. 'And never mind the dogs. It's only because they like you.'

'What dogs?' Georgie sits down. 'There aren't any—'

A hand on her child's arm, Melanie stops her from saying what everyone, apart from Norah, is aware of.

'I've tried to teach them, since they were puppies,' Norah babbles. 'Not to lick faces, but will they listen? No,

269

they will not.'

Georgie giggles, but plays along with what she supposes is a game.

'Beautiful, just beautiful. The pair of you.' Norah, turning her head from Georgie to Melanie. 'Oh, they're such naughty dogs. Just push them away, *bach*,' her attention swivelling again. 'I've told them not to lick faces, but they won't listen?'

Delyth points at a photograph of two black and white Border Collies on the mantelpiece then drags a finger across her throat.

'What pretty hair you have, *cariad*.' Norah compliments Georgie, the dogs forgotten. 'Does Mammy brush it into those plaits for you?' Georgie nods, curiously coy under this woman's kindly interest. 'I do my own. It's been a long time since I had a mammy.'

'You don't do so bad,' Delyth sounds hurt.

'No, you look after me lovely.' Norah angles her head at Georgie. 'She does, mind.' She drops her reedy body back into the mound of cushions. 'Delyth and Erin both had long hair when they were little. I used to love brushing it for them too. How old are you again, *cariad*? I know you told me already, but my memory's going terrible.'

'Seven-and-three-quarters.' Georgie pushes her tongue through the gaps in her teeth. 'Delyth had long hair until today, didn't you Delyth? Long hair like you.' She points at Norah's.

Norah picks up her long white plait, pretends to be surprised by it; it makes Georgie giggle again. 'Indeed, she did. And now she's cut it all off. What a clever little one you are.'

'What are you trying to do?' Andrew leaves the sofa to give Delyth whatever instructions she seems to need with her phone.

'Oh, look, Melanie. Here's that text I sent you. It's still in my outbox,' Delyth announces. Casual and breezy, she shows her the screen. 'Honestly,' she leans forward, crucifix swinging, 'I'm having real trouble working out how to use this new-fangled machine.'

'She is hopeless,' Andrew concurs, pulling faces behind her back.

'Oi, less of it, you. I can't help if I liked it better when you had buttons to press.'

'You're still hopeless.' Andrew laughs. Everyone except Melanie joins in.

'Give me a chance, I only got it today.'

'Came into a little windfall, didn't you *bach*?' Norah tells her.

Yes, and I know where from. Melanie thinks of Gareth's three-thousand-pound cash withdrawal.

'Delyth fetched me new slippers today, too.' Norah wriggles her toes, shows off a pair of expensive sheepskin ankle boots. 'Early Christmas presents, they are, aren't they, Del? cos we need 'em here. Place is so flaming draughty.'

'You decided whether you're having a kitten?' Delyth puts Melanie on the spot. 'Because I think a certain someone's set her heart on it.'

'Oh, please, Mummy. Please.' Georgie chimes in.

'You're not helping.' Melanie squirms. 'Talk about being pushed into a corner, but,' she exhales heavily. 'All right, you can have a kitten.'

'Yes, yes, yes.' Georgie, squealing, is up on her feet.

'Have you decided which one you'd like?' Delyth asks Melanie.

'No, I'll let Georgie choose.'

'Go on then. You as well, Andrew.' Delyth ushers Georgie and her nephew out into the hall. 'Help sort a box or something for them to take it home, would you?' She pats him on the arm. 'Oh, and check the loaves. Take them out if they're done, put a couple more in. There's a good boy.'

THIRTY-SEVEN

'Right,' Delyth says, once Andrew and Georgie are out of earshot. 'You've told Melanie then, have you Mam?'

'Told her what?'

'What we agreed.' A final look along the hall, Delyth closes the door.

'Oh, we don't want to go raking all that up again, Del, leave it alone,' Norah floats a bony hand through the flickering firelight.

'No, I'm sorry, Mam. We agreed, she has to know.'

'*Has to know what?*' Melanie is bewildered by the sudden frostiness between mother and daughter.

'Just what kind of a man you're married to.' Delyth gives her a black look.

'Erin . . . it was Erin . . . she was besotted with him,' Norah starts to explain. 'None of it was Gareth's fault. The girl played him like a fiddle.'

'Gareth's fault?' Melanie, more than a little alarmed. 'What wasn't Gareth's fault?'

'I wanted you to go to the police, but you wouldn't have it,' Delyth, her face flushed and angry. 'Quick enough to call them when she fell out of the window, though, weren't you? Happy to have them crawling all over our lives, all over the farm then,' she snipes at Norah. 'Gareth forced himself on Erin, Mam, why won't you listen. He as good as raped her.'

The appalling accusation hangs in the air.

Melanie is winded by it. And with two sets of eyes watching her, poised for her reaction, she gulps it down and feels it splinter her precious life apart.

'Forced himself on her? Bah, don't give me that.' It's Norah who speaks, saving Melanie the need to respond, which she can't. 'Your sister knew exactly what she was doing, especially where boys were concerned.'

'Mam!' Delyth wrings her hands. 'She was barely fourteen. She was a child.'

'Goin' on thirty.'

'None of that excuses him. Not when he was eighteen.'

'*Pfff,*' Norah laughs: a dry, empty sound that spirals around the room.

'I saw what he did. I saw it, Mam. Plying her with drink at our end of school party. Erin wasn't even supposed to be there, but he fixed it so she was. He engineered the whole damn thing.' Delyth is the boldest and most assertive Melanie has ever seen her. 'But we all know why you didn't do anything about it, don't we? We all know where your loyalties lay. With his father.'

'Don't be ridiculous, girl. My relationship with Rhodri Sayer had nothing to do with my decision about not going to the police.'

'You reckon? He was always more important than the family you had left. If it was anyone's fault Erin went off the rails, then it was yours. You were always at work. It was, *Rhodri this, Rhodri that.*'

Norah stares across the room at Delyth who, in turn, keeps her spine pressed to the door; fearful, perhaps, of Andrew or Georgie bursting in on them. 'Delyth, *bach*, you saw what you wanted to see that night at the party.' The voice is calm. 'And you can go on kidding yourself if you like, but I know different. That sister of yours was out of control. Yes, Gareth was naughty to take advantage of her, what with her being so young, but she gave herself willingly, I'm sure of it.' A glance at Melanie who remains too dumbfounded to speak.

'You weren't there. I was the one who witnessed it, not you.' Delyth refuses to back down, her cheeks flushed in the pinkish lamplight.

'You saw what you wanted to see,' Norah dismisses her. 'And I'll tell you why, shall I? Because you was jealous. It screwed you up to see Gareth with Erin, knowing you'd never have no chance with him.'

'My feelings for him had nothing to do with any of it. Okay. He forced himself on Erin that night, and if you'd been any kind of mother and taken me seriously . . . if you'd gone to the police,' Melanie hears Delyth's voice break under the weight of her grief. 'Then Erin might still be here now.'

Melanie doesn't move. Can't move. The shock of what she's heard has rendered her speechless. Watching the flames in the hearth throw disorganised patterns on the opposite wall, she tries to keep pace with their argument.

'Come on, Delyth. Stop being so silly, it was years ago, you've got to let it go. You've got to forgive, it's not healthy.' Norah frowns: life's geometry mapping her face.

'*Forgive him*? He destroyed Erin's life. Getting her pregnant, then disappearing off to university. None of it impacted him.' Delyth is vehement. 'So, no, I can't forgive him.'

'Not very Christian of you,' Norah replies, deliberately provocative. Then whispers to Melanie: 'Got the heart of a lion, that one. Fiercely protective of her little sister, even now. That's why she can't forgive your Gareth.'

Sickened by the first revelation of Gareth forcing himself on a fourteen-year-old girl, when she hears he got her pregnant, she's incredulous. 'What?' she gasps, slapping a hand to her throat. 'Are you saying Andrew is Gareth's son?'

'That's right.'

Melanie flops back into the sofa. Too shocked to speak. Discovering the man she has built her life around is

Andrew's father explains why the boy looked so familiar.

'Your Gareth's not a bad person.' Norah shuffles forward in her chair, takes Melanie's hand in hers. 'I'd hate for any of this to go causing trouble between you both.'

'Oh, that's right,' Delyth, strident from the sidelines. 'The Golden Boy must be allowed to get away with it scot-free. Yet again.'

'B-but, d-does he know?' Melanie stammers to Norah. 'Does Gareth know about Andrew?'

'No, *bach*, I don't think he had the first idea. You know what boys are like when they're that age? Gareth was just your typical teenager; he didn't mean nothing by it. Erin made herself available to him. End of. Delyth's problem is that she can't bear the thought that her sister was sluttish,' Norah speaks as if Delyth isn't there. 'I've tried, but I'll never make her see otherwise. It's easier for her to blame it all on Gareth.'

'What he did, it really doesn't trouble you, does it?' Melanie can't believe what she's hearing.

'Oh, it troubles me, but you can't keep living in the past. What's done is done, none of us can change nothing. You just have to make the best of things, which is what we did. Because by the time any of us knew, Gareth was long gone. He wouldn't have had the first idea Erin was expecting, or that Andrew was his.'

'You reckon, do you?' Delyth plays with her new hair. 'I wouldn't bet on that, if I were you.'

'How could he know?' Norah shouts at her daughter then turns to Melanie. 'Erin swore us to secrecy, we couldn't tell his parents, nor no one from the town. She wouldn't even let us fetch a midwife when the babby came. Andrew was born here, me and Del delivered him.'

'Of course, Erin told him,' Delyth is adamant. 'She must've been in touch with him all along. It's not a coincidence, her killing herself that week he was back for his father's funeral, you know. She must have seen him. He could have come here. How would you know? You were never home.'

'What rubbish, you silly girl,' Norah argues. 'You never let her go anywhere. After the police brought her back from that squat that time, you never let her out of your sight.'

'You make it sound like I kept her prisoner. I was only looking out for her, keeping her safe. Keeping her safe for Andrew's sake. She never wanted for nothing.'

'If you mean booze and fags,' Norah drops her voice a notch. 'No, she weren't never short of them.' She says, then turns to Melanie. 'Don't be too hard on your Gareth, *bach*. Honestly, take no notice of Del, he weren't in touch with Erin. I bet he clean forgot about her as soon as he left Pencarew.'

Norah's vehement defence of Gareth bothers Melanie. As a mother, she should be on Erin's side, no matter how troublesome or provocative her daughter might or might not have been. There's no way she could imagine showing this kind of disloyalty to Georgie, regardless of what she'd done because whatever blame Norah thinks she can put on Erin, Delyth's right, she was only a child and blameless because of it.

'Don't you think about her then?' Delyth speaks to her mother from the shadows. 'Does she never cross your mind when you're in here watching *Coronation Street* and *EastEnders*?' Melanie listens to the anger tighten in her voice. 'I don't know how you do it, living here, in this house. *This house!*' She is almost shrieking now. 'If I had my way, I'd take a flamethrower to this place,' she stares up at the ceiling, raises her palms to whatever horror went on in the rooms under the eaves. 'So, I'm sorry if it affects your sensitivities, that it makes me *silly.*'

'Don't you judge me, Delyth. Don't you dare judge me. I wanted Erin to have an abortion.'

'How can you even say that? Shame on you, Mam.'

'It was you what talked her out of it. I didn't want her getting tied down with a babby at her age, it was so-so .

. . unnecessary.'

'*Unnecessary!* That's my Andrew you're talking about.'

The log in the hearth splits open with a firework of sparks. Delyth pitches from the room, leaving Norah behind in the bloated aftermath of their argument. Melanie doesn't move. Frantically filtering all she's been told and struggling to believe it; she thinks she might be about to be sick.

THIRTY-EIGHT

Friday, five o'clock. A glass of what will be the Monkstone Arm's house red in her hand, Melanie wanders where the late afternoon shadows fall into the vacant downstairs rooms. She is celebrating. Alone. It was the workmen's last day today, the refurbishments are complete and aside from a few last-minute touches and a final trip to the cash and carry, they are set to open for business in less than a fortnight.

Flicking on the main switch in the bar, her heart soars with pride at the chrome pendant lighting, the glamour of the high leather stools, the Bur oak counter with its polished beer pumps and glasses. The huge inglenook fireplace, restored to its former glory and cleared of rubble, has been installed with a chunky wood burner that looks the part, especially with the ox-blood leather fender she sourced on eBay for next to nothing.

She thinks how pleased Gareth is going to be until she remembers the shock of what Delyth and Norah revealed, and her insides cartwheel with dread. She ambles into the restaurant, moseys around the wooden tables decked with potted ferns and glass cruets, the soles of her slippers sliding over the beautiful parquet floor. Looking up, her eyes travel the reconditioned beams, the Victorian-red papered walls dressed with shabby-chic menu boards and vast ornate mirrors. On to the wide picture windows with the disappearing view. She walks the length of the room, fingers trailing framed-sepia prints of the horse-drawn town and local rugby sides dating back to before the Great War. All that remains of the pub from before they came.

Her mobile beeps in her jeans' pocket. It's a text from Gareth telling her he's about two hours away. She doesn't reply, she's been avoiding his messages since Wednesday's trip to Gweld Y Môr. How things have changed in a few short weeks. When they first bought this place, she used to count the days, desperate for the week to pass quickly so she could have him home. Now she spends the weekends willing Monday mornings to come around and for him to be gone again. She is dreading his homecoming tonight more than usual, knowing full well, with the bombshell she is about to drop, there will be a fight. He's got a lot of explaining to do, she thinks, draining her wine and returning to the kitchen for a much-needed refill.

Minutes later, seated at the kitchen table, her fingers caress the stem of her glass without letting any single thought dominate her mind. She pours herself another and works through her list, ticking things off, clearing the way. Even though she's not looking forward to seeing Gareth, he still needs feeding, as does Georgie, who, because she's feeling better after another bout of tummy ache that kept her off school for the last two days, Melanie thought she'd try out one of Nigella's chicken tray bakes as it might be an option for the restaurant menu. With tantalising smells of vermouth and dill filling the kitchen, she finds it difficult to concentrate on her list, so pushes it aside and slumps in her chair. Her eyes close and imagined images of her husband cavorting with that pretty, red-haired girl . . . child . . . in those photographs in Delyth's kitchen, flicker behind her eyelids.

When she opens them next, it is on to Gareth throwing a dark shadow over her.

'You're home.' Melanie, disorientated, has no idea how long she's been asleep, all she's conscious of is the cold and empty sensation in the pit of her stomach. She used to think, when she and Gareth first got together, that he looked like a man who could do anything: climb a tree, jump a gate. Her saviour. Her knight in shining armour. She thought she knew him inside out. But looking at him now, with the awfulness of what she learnt two evenings ago, it is as if to gaze upon a stranger.

He leans down for a kiss. His inky-black stubble close to her face, the tang of the Tube still clinging to the fibres of his suit.

She twists her head in time, she can't bear to have him touch her. She'd hoped they would be able to find a way through this mess together, that he would explain and help her to understand why he did what he did to a fourteen-year-old girl, and everything would be right with them again. But now he's here, standing in their kitchen, the reality is that she can hardly bring herself to look at him.

'Some dream you were having,' he says.

'Yeah.' She yawns and rubs her eyes. It's been a while since she bothered applying make-up in readiness of his homecoming. 'I was on my way to Manderley again.'

'You what?'

'Nothing,' she says, up on her feet, avoiding eye contact. 'Good journey?'

'Not bad.'

'Much traffic?' Sidestepping him, she opens the door of the oven, checks inside. Even though she's no good at it, small talk is about all she can manage, until she can find a way to ask him to explain. But appalled, outraged and disgusted with what she discovered less than forty-eight hours ago, it's a struggle to maintain even this bland civility. The awfulness of what she is trapped into rears its head again: they are married; they have Georgie; they have risked everything by selling their house and piling their savings into this business. The worry of it has been keeping her awake at night because, as she reminds herself, they must make this work; there is no alternative.

'Reasonable.' Gareth removes his tie, undoes his

top button. 'Where's Georgie?' he asks, apparently not the least bothered by Melanie ducking his advances.

'She's upstairs, playing.'

'Has she been feeling all right this week?'

'Great until Wednesday night, I had to keep her home yesterday and today.'

'And now? Is she better now?' She listens to the alarm in his voice. 'Because you haven't exactly been keeping in touch with me the last couple of days.'

'She's fine now.' Melanie ignores his complaint; she has bigger ones of her own.

'You're going to have to take her back to the doctors. Start demanding answers. This has been going on for too long.'

'I called the surgery. I'm to take her back to Dr Cassidy on Monday. He says he'll run more tests.'

'*More tests*? Why didn't they just do all the tests in one go?' Gareth looks tired, the skin around his eyes is purply under the halogen lights. 'I'm going up to get changed. Will dinner be long?'

'Not long.' She moves to follow him, oven cloth in hand. 'Gareth? Can you hang on a minute, there's something we need to talk about.'

He yawns. 'Can't it wait? I'll be down in a minute.'

'No, it can't,' she says, firm.

'Get on with it then. Going all cryptic on me, what's the matter?'

She steps back, hands reaching for the work surface, needing its support. 'I was up at Gweld Y Môr on Wednesday.'

A shift of his feet informs her he's familiar with the name of the farm. 'Where?' he asks, giving a tiny flick of his head.

'You heard me.' She chucks the oven glove down. 'And now, I want you to tell me about Erin; I want to hear your side of things.'

'Erin?' He throws a sharp laugh into the room,

waits, as if hoping for her to lob it back to him. 'Am I supposed to know who that is?'

'Erin Powell.'

'Sorry Mel, you're going to have to give me more of a clue than that.'

'Delyth's sister.'

He looks at her, his expression vacant.

'Come on, Gareth, I'm not an idiot. Erin's why you've got a problem with Delyth. It's why you didn't want me spending time with her. Admit it. I can see why; you were afraid she'd spill the beans. Well, the beans have been spilt now, so you might as well come clean.'

'I'm sorry, Mel,' he rubs his eyes. 'I haven't the first idea what you're on about.'

'Tell me what happened the night of your end of school party. You know, the one you had to celebrate your A level results.'

'End of school party? B-but that was years ago.'

'Tell me what happened the last night you were in Pencarew, before you left for uni.'

'What d'you mean, tell you about it?' he yawns again, his eyes watering from the effort. 'It was a lifetime ago. How am I supposed to remember?'

'Tell me.'

'All right.' He lifts a hand: some kind of surrender. 'I was pretty wasted, is what I remember.' Another laugh she can tell is false.

'You're going to have to do better than that.' She folds her arms and props her weight against the counter. 'I'm giving you a chance here, can't you see, I already know what you did, Gareth. Delyth told me.'

'I'm sorry, what?' he scowls. 'Whatever I'm supposed to have done that night, I don't remember. As I already said, I was proper wrecked.'

'But you remember Erin, right? You remember Delyth's younger sister.'

'I don't think I do, no.'

'Come on, Gareth, we both know that's a big lie.'

'I don't remember any sister, okay?'

'Delyth saw you, don't you understand? She saw what you did.'

'Spying on me, was she?' The tone is both hostile and belligerent, and again, Melanie is more than a little frightened of him. 'If she didn't like whatever it was she says she saw, why didn't she stop me?' His countenance unyielding as usual gives nothing away. 'Look, Mel, I don't know what Delyth's told you, but she probably just made it up because I wasn't interested in her.'

'If you're so sure she made it up, then tell me why you've been adamant I stay away from her?'

'Because she's a moany old cow. I was frightened she'd drag you down again, just when you'd started to feel better about things.'

'I don't believe you. It's way more than that, and you know it. What did she see, Gareth, what did Delyth see you do to her sister that night? Did you make sure Erin got wasted too, as you so eloquently put it, so you could force yourself on her? Please tell me, because honestly, I've had enough of you pissing me about.'

Gareth drags a chair towards him, sits down at the table, head in hands. 'All right, all right,' his declaration muffled by his fingers. 'I remember her, I remember Erin.'

'And?'

'And nothing.'

'*Gareth* — tell me.'

He closes his eyes, and she listens to him breathing. He remains silent for so long she isn't sure she is going to get an answer.

'It was a one-night stand,' he says, at last. 'Me and Erin, we'd both had too much to drink. It was nothing. God knows why Delyth's still going on about it, the saddo.'

'Recovered your memory all of a sudden, then?' Melanie, as acerbic as she can be. 'Delyth's still going on about it because Erin was her little sister. She was a child. A fourteen-year-old child. She's saying you raped her. That you raped her little sister.'

'*Raped her!*' Gareth holds his hands up: the innocent. 'For fuck's sake, Mel.' His look is desperate. 'This is me you're talking to. I didn't rape her. She came on to me.' He gets up, reaches out for her arm, but she yanks it away. 'You've got to believe me, Mel . . . Mel.' He pleads, but seeing he gets nowhere, gives up and sits back down again. 'You didn't know what she was like, you never knew her. Come on,' he holds his hands out to her, but again she recoils. 'She handed it to me on a plate. Show me an eighteen-year-old who'd have refused that?'

'You disgust me. She was just a child!' Melanie flies at him.

'Who went about looking like a twenty-five-year-old woman.'

'And, what? Because you were so used to getting your own way, getting everything you wanted, you took it, is that it? You took her?'

He exhales, braces himself. 'Look, I can see how bad it looks now. But not then. You can't judge me for what I did then. I was only a kid myself.'

'You were *eighteen*. And you should have known better. What d'you think it was like for me, having to sit there, listening to that? It shouldn't have been Delyth and Norah telling me what you did, what you caused, it should have been you. I'm your wife.'

'I didn't tell you because I'd forgotten all about it. Jesus, Mel,' he slams his palms against the table-top, violently, enough to knock her glass of wine over. 'D'you seriously think if I'd remembered doing that, then I'd have wanted to come back here?' Aggressive, arrogant; everything she hates in a person. Everything she hoped she'd left behind in her childhood.

Who is he? She asks herself again, staring at him, barely recognising him.

She grabs a dishcloth and mops up the spilt wine.

'At least I understand why you didn't want me spending time with Delyth now. Why you've been so hostile with her from the moment we arrived. You didn't want me finding out your dirty little secret.' She rinses out the cloth. 'Is that why you went to the farm?' she says, drying her hands on a tea towel. 'I told you someone saw your car. You've given her money, haven't you?' An image of the new Delyth: chic bobbed hair, designer clothes and mobile. 'Hush money. You were trying to shut her up.' Anger curls its fist behind her ribcage. 'Well,' her turn to laugh, jagged and brittle; a sound that separates them further. 'Let me tell you, it didn't work.'

Gareth makes no response and doesn't shift from his position at the pine-topped table.

'You're pathetic, d'you know that? Pathetic.' She backs away from him, alarmed by the menacing gleam in his eye. 'Because you're not telling me if that happened to Georgie when she was only fourteen, that you'd dismiss it as easily. I think you'd insist she was still a child, just as I'm insisting Erin was a child. Double standards, if you ask me. I know you; you'd string him up if a bloke did that at the age you were. If he defiled your daughter. And let's not forget one major fact here, shall we?' She is shouting now. 'It's against the bloody law for a reason.'

She studies him, unsure if they are going to be able to get past this. If only he would say he was sorry, it would be something, but he won't be made to see what he did was wrong. She knows she has got to make their marriage work, for Georgie's sake, for the business they're about to launch. But how? When their marriage is little more than a charade and so easily dissolved, with her unable to bear the idea of him anywhere near her. All it would take is the stroke of a pen. But is a future without him even possible? If she wants out, how will she do it? She hasn't the finances to support her and Georgie alone, and where would they go?

'Delyth wanted to report you to the police, you know?'

Gareth gawps at her, open-mouthed.

'You've got Norah to thank that she didn't. She's the one who stopped her. I don't know why, but Norah never blamed you. You're like Teflon man in her eyes, wipe clean, apparently.'

'But not in Delyth's?'

'No. And I'm sorry, Gareth, but I'm with her on this.'

'If it's such a big deal, why's she waited until now to tell you?' He scratches his stubbly chin.

'How do I know?'

'She wants to split us up,' he says darkly.

'What? So she can take my place.' Melanie splutters. 'You seriously think she's still got a crush on you, don't you?'

'Course she has. And she's spiteful and vindictive. She always was.'

'You're deluded, d'you know that? Deluded.' Melanie, fists on hips. 'Delyth hates you, don't you understand that yet? She hates you for destroying her sister's life . . . for destroying her own life.'

'Destroying her life? For Christ sake, Mel, anyone'd think I'm a monster.'

'Well, aren't you?'

'I can't believe you're even asking that. Why are you siding with her? You're my wife, you're supposed to be on my side. I was a kid, for crying out loud, and what I did, was it really so very wrong?'

'Yes. It was wrong. Very wrong. On every count. And what you did, it had far-reaching consequences,' she informs him. 'You knew how young Erin was and yet you still did it.' She takes a breath, feels her blood slow. 'Don't you take any responsibility? What kind of a person are you?'

'But I didn't do anything, not deliberately.'

'It doesn't matter whether you did it deliberately, it had consequences. Everything's got consequences. Don't you understand that yet? Erin killed herself because of what you did to her, she was too young, she couldn't cope.'

'What?' Gareth is up on his feet, heading her way. 'You what?'

'Didn't you know?'

'Course I didn't fucking know.'

'Didn't your mother fill you in? Or Tegan? She seemed to be up on a lot of the details.' *Is this true?* Melanie can't remember.

'No, they didn't.' The look is baffled. 'When did it happen?'

'Not right away, poor kid, she didn't kill herself right away, she struggled on for nine years. Norah told me Erin tried to make the best of it, but in the end, she just couldn't see a way to go on.'

'A way to go on? What the hell d'you mean? I'm not taking the bloody blame for that.'

'I don't see why not. What you did, tore that family apart. Delyth—' Melanie takes a second to think of Delyth, perhaps understanding, with particular clarity, what drove her to slice chunks out of herself in their kitchen sink. 'Thank God for dear, dutiful Delyth. Picking up the pieces when you'd cleared off. Because she was the one who brought that boy up. And he's a lovely kid. All credit to her. You owe her, big time.'

'Boy? What boy?'

'Aw, pull the other one.'

Gareth seizes her roughly by the shoulders, makes her wince in pain.

'What boy? What bloody boy?' He shakes her roughly and she feels his bruising finger-ends through her clothes.

'Andrew,' she says, defiant, despite her trembling. 'He's yours. That time with Erin, you got her pregnant. But you probably already knew that, didn't you? Delyth thinks you and Erin never lost touch. Did you go and see her that week we were here for your father's funeral? You could have snuck off; we weren't together all the time.'

Gareth shoves her away with such force that she falls to the floor. Smacks the side of her head against the sharp-edged work surface. The world spins and slows in the quivering aftershock and for a moment Melanie is unable to move. Too frightened to move in case he comes for her again. Realising he isn't, that he's probably as stunned as she is, she puts a tentative hand up to where it hurts. Brings her fingers away and sees blood. Gareth sees it too.

'Mel, Mel. I'm sorry.' Contrite and pleading, he sinks to his knees beside her.

'Get off me,' she screams, blood trickling into her eye. 'You're nothing but a bloody bully. A bloody bully.' And as she scrambles to her feet, she thinks of what John told her about Gareth's treatment of him at school: indignities that had floated in the abstract until now.

'Mel, please,' Gareth sobs from the floor, his arms spread wide, desperate, begging. 'Are you all right? Let me . . . I-I didn't mean to hurt you, p-please . . . *please.* I'll do it, I'll make amends with Delyth and her mother, I'll make it up with the boy. I can put things right.'

'It's too late.' She turns away, reaches for the dishcloth to stem the flow; the purple stain of wine mixing with her blood. 'The damage is done.' She means her and Gareth. She means Erin Powell and the family she left behind. 'I never knew you, did I? But I sure as hell know you now.' She sees herself reflected in the blackened glass of the windowpane. The skin around the nasty cut above her eye already blackening to a bruise.

Then, over her shoulder, it's her daughter she's seeing. Drifting into the kitchen, the thin light of the bar, pale as a lemon, in her hair.

'Daddy, Daddy. Look what I've got,' Georgie squeals excitedly, the fluffy black kitten she refuses to let out of her sight, in her arms. 'I've called him Bingo.'

Melanie follows her daughter's gaze as it leaps from Gareth then up to her. Then the tick-tick-tick of claws and

Slinky is there, following Georgie downstairs, he makes a beeline to Gareth and licks his hand.

'What's happened to Mummy's face?' The enthusiasm about her father being home for the weekend, along with a week's worth of things she's been waiting to share with him, crackle with uncertainty. 'Why's Daddy on the floor?'

Then Melanie smells their burning dinner.

'Shit!' She leaps forward, remembering the oven gloves just in time.

The kitchen fills with acrid, black smoke that stings the back of her throat. She lifts the blind to the accompaniment of Gareth and Georgie's coughing, throws open a window and listens to the rain patter on what remains of the leaves.

She heaves down a lungful of salty air, sensing somewhere, out beyond the night and her burgeoning despair, the constant sway of the dark, silver sea, and gives way to hopeless tears.

THIRTY-NINE

The sickly light of dawn licks the edges of the curtains but doesn't penetrate the bedroom. Melanie, watching the lime-green minutes on her radio alarm clock roll over themselves, gathers them up through the gloom. The clock is one of the few possessions she's retained from childhood and the thought makes her sadder than she already is. She turns her bruised head to the side and makes out Gareth's hump-backed silhouette stretching out like a mountain range. Flanked by darkness and daybreak, she rolls over, away from him, feels the gulf between their backs grow as wide as the universe itself.

She knows he's awake, she can tell by his breathing. Neither of them slept last night, each keeping to their own sides of the bed. Lying stiffly along the edges of the mattress isn't without its problems, the reinforced stitching digging into their stomachs, the tender underside of their arms, and yet no matter how uncomfortable, it's easier than if the two of them should accidentally touch. Because then what?

Her body stiffens at the sound of rustling sheets. The bed creaks as Gareth sits up. He's cold, she thinks, resisting the desire to reach out to him. The sudden feeling of helplessness this brings makes her gasp.

'You awake?' his whispered accusation rasps against the bedlinen. She can smell him: the remnants of his aftershave, the vague vinegary smell of his feet.

She unsticks her tongue from the roof of her

mouth. 'Yes.' Her fingers curl themselves into agitated fists, another hangover from her childhood.

'Shit night.'

'Me too.'

'I hope you're not about to blame me for that as well.' The tone is unreasonable. 'I think I've taken the blame for enough.'

'No, I'm not blaming you,' she says but only because there's no way they can have a row with Georgie asleep in the adjacent room.

'I've been going over and over it in my mind.' She can tell he wants to shout, that it's the hardest thing to stop himself. 'I just want to know why you took that woman's side before even talking to me?'

She turns her aching head, sees the curve of his spine as he bends low over the side of the bed.

'Because,' she says, her voice neutral, 'whenever I asked you about her, you said it was nothing. Because you lied to me.' A tentative hand to the injury on her brow and she winces in pain.

'How many more bloody times. I didn't lie to you,' he speaks as if he is quite literally stuffing his fists into his mouth. 'I couldn't sodding-well remember. I still don't. Not fully.'

'Okay. Okay.'

Melanie's learnt there's no point pursuing things with him when he's in this mood, she will just have to lie with her suspicions on her chest, watching the minutes flick by. Is it possible they've been reduced to this? She and Gareth used to be so close, their deep connection was the envy of all their friends. She sobs into her pillow. It was horrible to hear Delyth say those things about him, then the way he reacted when she tried to make him explain. But what did she expect? For them to be able to patch things up, for things to go back to the way they were? Get real girl, this is how it's going to be from now on and when the pub opens and he's here full-time, things are going to get a whole lot worse. She'd better keep her mouth shut from now on. *Put up or shut up*, a favourite saying of her mother's and because Melanie hasn't exactly got a choice in the matter, that they have come too far to go back, she'd better just knuckle down and make the best of it.

*

Up and dressed, with the pretence of breakfast no one can eat, a lid of silence has closed over the Sayer family. It seems now so much has been said, there is nothing left to say. Gareth looks as if he's about to speak, but then gives up, no longer seeing the point in whatever it was. Melanie avoids his bloodshot eyes and doesn't bother making him toast, doesn't bother pouring his tea, and it doesn't look as if Gareth cares. Talk of the pub's opening night, what still needs to be done, when Gareth intends to hand in his notice. All forgotten.

Someone is knocking at the main door. Three heads dart to the sound. But only Melanie springs to her feet. The wooden legs of the chair screeching against the floor.

'Dear me,' Delyth gasps on the doorstep, a tin decorated with blue peacocks in her hands. 'You've been in the wars.'

'It's fine.' Melanie's unsure whether to let her inside, she doesn't think she has the strength if Gareth kicks off again.

'It doesn't look fine.' Delyth fiddles with her shiny cap of hair, it's obviously still a novelty.

Melanie lifts a cautious hand to touch the cut with its purple bruise that's already hardened to a rind of congealed blood.

'Looks nasty, how did you do it?' Delyth keeps on with her enquiry.

'Daddy pushed her,' Georgie has squeezed between them. 'He didn't mean to; it was an accident.'

'Was it now?' Delyth passes Georgie the pretty blue tin. 'These are for you.' She winks. 'A little bird told me you'd had another bad tummy ache last week.' She glances up at Melanie. 'The same little bird who told me my cakes are the only things you like to eat when you're feeling poorly. And you've got to keep your strength up.'

'Look how pretty they are, Mummy.' Georgie admires the twelve fairy cakes with runny pink icing.

'What do we say?' Melanie prompts, smiling with difficulty; the muscles in her face are sore.

'Thank you. Very, very much.' And with a little bow, Georgie skips away.

'Thanks, Delyth,' Melanie echoes her daughter's gratitude. 'It's kind of you to think of her.'

'My pleasure. Although,' Delyth's expression clouding, 'she's still looking a bit peaky, are you sure she's okay? I must say, I was concerned to hear she was off school again, I thought you'd got to the bottom of all that.'

'So did I,' Melanie groans. 'She was great, was great for days, but that night we came home from you with the kitten.' She screws up her face. 'Not so good. It's why I'm taking her back to the doctor first thing Monday. She's okay today, but still off her food a bit, so the cakes are lovely, she'll eat them.'

'Let's hope they help get her appetite back.' Delyth keeps playing with her hair. 'How's the kitten settling in?'

'Bingo? Oh, he's gorgeous.' Melanie briefly forgets her troubles and laughs. 'Georgie's utterly in love with him, keeps pestering me to let her take him to school.'

Delyth turns away from her for a moment, her gaze wandering the gravelled car park, to the glassy sea beyond.

'D'you want me to call the police?' Delyth, refocusing on Melanie again, asks in her small voice, a hand fluttering at her temple.

'What I want is for you to clear the hell off.' Gareth, swooping out of nowhere, shoves himself between Melanie and the outside world; his body spread across the entrance. 'Happy now, are you?' he snarls at Delyth, and Melanie listens to his breathing change the nastier he gets. 'Happy we're now as miserable as you. The damage you've done, you evil witch.' His temper, in danger of bubbling over. 'I thought I made it clear when we arrived that you're not welcome here.'

Delyth gawps at him.

'Are you deaf?' he shouts. 'I said, clear off. Go on, get outta here.'

So much for him wanting to put things right, to make it up to Delyth and her family, Melanie thinks gloomily. She watches him, appalled. What a fake he is. Contrite in the shock of the moment, fearing he'd gone too far and she was seriously hurt, but she can tell from the way he's behaving now he didn't mean it, that nothing will change.

'*Erm*, Gareth. D'you mind?' Melanie is surprisingly emboldened by Delyth's presence. 'Since when do you get to tell me who I can or cannot see? I've said before, Delyth's not the problem, you are.' And clasping Delyth's coat sleeve, says, 'Come on, let's get out of here.' Surrendering Delyth, she swaps her slippers for wellingtons and lifts her parka from the peg; hurriedly checking its pockets for her purse, keys and mobile. Happy she has everything she needs; she calls for the dog. 'You can look after Georgie for an hour or two, can't you?'

She doesn't wait for Gareth's answer. Once Slinky's joined them, which he does in an instant, she walks off without bothering to close the door.

Recent rain means the steep track from pub to beach is too slippery to negotiate safely, so Melanie and Delyth saunter side by side, barely speaking, down through the windy town to the seafront. Slinky tugging them along like a sail.

'You'll be all right with him, won't you?' Delyth asks when they reach the dunes. 'You and Gareth, I mean.'

Melanie doesn't answer immediately. Head down, over the braided river channels now the tide has gone out, their boots crunch the pleat of seashells left behind by the high-water mark.

'I don't know,' she says limply, inhaling wet sand and seaweed. 'Because it's not just what you told me he did to Erin, it's the way he's behaved with you since we got here. I don't even know if I like him anymore.'

They stop for Melanie to shake a stray stone from her boot.

'You and me,' she starts up again, 'I know we've not talked about it since, but the way he spoke to you at the Co-op, in front of all those people, it was terrible. Shameful. I'm so sorry, Delyth.'

'I know you are, and it's not your fault. But you and Gareth,' Delyth's nose is pink with cold. 'You are going to be all right?'

Melanie doesn't have the words to express the leaden feeling she's been carrying around inside her, and dabs away tears with the cuff of her coat.

'Don't cry.' Delyth puts an arm around Melanie's middle. The sudden contact, although meant to be a comfort, is awkward. 'Please don't cry.'

'It's the wind,' she sniffs, knowing it isn't. She could sit down here, on the sand and never get up again. 'I don't think I can trust him, I'm not sure I know who he is.' She says, pulling away. 'He's not the person I thought he was, he's not the man I married.'

'But you're going to be all right? You're not going to split up over it, are you?'

'I don't know,' Melanie repeats herself.

'I should never have told you,' Delyth sounds distressed. 'This is all my fault.'

'Your fault? No, Delyth, this is Gareth's fault. He

should've told me. Letting me find out like that, it was awful. But we can't split up, can we? We've too much at stake. The pub's set to open the week after next and there's no way that can't go ahead, we've got to start clawing back some of the money.'

'But if he hit you?'

'It's not what it looks like, Delyth, really it isn't.' They walk to the lip of the sea, stop to look up at the sky: a perilous blue page punctuated by seabirds. 'Things got out of hand . . . a bit heated.' Her skin tightens when she thinks how quickly their argument unravelled. 'It wasn't the easiest thing for us to talk about, as you can imagine.' A sideways look at Delyth. 'I fell, that's all. He didn't mean it. I know he didn't.'

'Isn't that what all women say when their husband's abuse them?' Her little voice is almost lost to the wind bucking in off the sea.

Melanie watches clouds being blown sideways over the horizon. The word abuse, anchor-heavy and dangerous, swings above their heads. Melanie, well-accustomed to abuse, touches the scar above her other eye, traces the knotty bow that is luckily hidden under her eyebrow. Not from Gareth — until this move to Wales they barely exchanged a cross word — this is an injury from her mother. A time during one of her binges when she lashed out, determined to damage, then claiming, during her calmer periods of sobriety, that she had no recollection of the harm she'd done. An easy get-out clause Melanie was happy to go along with, as to admit the alternative was too dreadful. 'She didn't mean it.' The refrain she'd supply her teachers should anyone bother to enquire about her injuries. 'Oh, yes, Miss, I walked into a door . . . I tripped over the cat. No, Miss, it's nothing. It was my fault, really it was.' As fiercely loyal to her mother as she is now being about Gareth. It's what you do, isn't it? But inside her head, it's a different story.

'He wouldn't admit to even knowing Erin to start

with,' Melanie confides.

'But he owned up eventually?'

'Yes, eventually.' The wind frisks her hair, playful, not that she's in the mood. 'But not to, to . . .' her mouth dry. 'I can't get him to admit that he forced her into anything.'

'Well, he wouldn't, would he?' Delyth blows her nose noisily on a shredded tissue.

'No, I don't suppose he would.'

'And Andrew? Let me guess, he knew nothing about him either?'

'He says not.'

'And you believe him?'

'I want to.' Melanie lifts her gaze to an arrow of geese flying north. 'But he says he wants to make it up to you and your mum.' Another sidelong look at Delyth. Melanie hopes she might say something about the three-thousand pounds Gareth gave her, but she doesn't. 'He says he wants to make it up to Andrew.'

'Got a funny way of showing it.' Delyth bends at the waist and picks up a seashell. She passes it to Melanie to admire.

'It's made you very sad, hasn't it? Erin, taking her own life.' She rolls the shell over in her gloved hand. 'What Gareth did, it ruined your life too, I can see that now. It's what drove you to do what you did in our kitchen, you poor thing.' Melanie, half to herself, she doesn't expect an answer.

With almost no sound to disturb the moist morning air, Melanie's thoughts drift to how happy she'd begun to feel here. But since Delyth's revelation about what Gareth did, everything's been spoilt. They walk without speaking and, unpacking what remains of her marriage, Melanie realises how little there is of it left.

'I miss him, you know. I miss how we used to be. But even if we could be put back together, how can I trust him?' She closes her mouth, is grateful Delyth gives no indication she's heard what she can barely bring herself to admit.

Melanie snaps back her neck. The stark realisation she is frightened of him smacks her squarely on the chin again. Could she have been seduced by his offer of protection, by his power, his money? Blinded, where others with more self-belief would have seen straight through him and understood what he is capable of? But Gareth had been a piece of driftwood at the time, something for her to cling to; needing him, and only him, to keep her afloat after the messy breakdown with her first boyfriend, the misery of her childhood. It was easy to buy into his promise, easy to exchange an unhappy life for one with him; she can't blame her younger self if she was duped. But since moving here, witnessing his appalling treatment of Delyth, and her, whenever she dares question him. Whoever she thought Gareth was, it was a fantasy; a fantasy that's taken the likes of Delyth and John to show her the truth.

'I should get going,' Delyth says, tipping Melanie out of her introspection.

'Sorry, what was that?' Lost in private thought, she tucks the pretty shell into a pocket.

'I'd better get going.'

'Oh, right, yes. I'll walk you to your car,' she replies and calls for the dog.

A crunch of gravel as the Defender edges out between the pillars and into the road. Darker now rain has begun to fall, Melanie pulls up her hood and listens to the wind piping discorded notes through the gaps in the metal gates they never close.

She looks up at the half-timbered sides of the pub, at the newly commissioned sign with its squatting Friar Tuck and, despite the cold nibbling the rims of her ears, is unable to go inside. There was a moment — she tugs it back, wanting to feel it again — when everything shifted and slotted into place. She thinks it was when she saw John's face for the first time, coming home from blackberry picking with Georgie. Or was it at the harbour, seeing him in his sandy-sleeved jacket, wearing his bruised, lack-of-sleep look. Or how he struggled to keep it together when he first talked of his traumatic time in Afghanistan, when she could tell, without the need for words, how broken he was inside. She pulls John's face towards her. Sees again that lopsided smile, his neglect. Something rushes at her, making her want to hold him close. Maternal? Lustful? She isn't sure it's either. All she's sure of is that something of him swims out to her, waving its arms, wanting to be saved. In the same way she wants to be saved. So, with Slinky fully extended on his leash, Melanie turns her back on the Monkstone Arms and Gareth, and heads for the church. For the little stone room tacked on to the back of the vestry and the comfort she hopes she will find there.

FORTY

J ohn stands with his broad back to her, busy with whatever it was she interrupted. 'I don't know how you could hit the face of someone you love.' Melanie listens to the quiver in his sonorous voice.

'He didn't hit me, John. He pushed me and I fell, that's all.'

'That's all?' He curves his big body, tests the seat of the only other chair in a way that suggests he doesn't trust it to hold his weight. Then, sitting opposite, his dark eyes hunt her expression, wanting the truth.

She trembles with emotion, her hand absentmindedly stroking Slinky. 'It was a horrible argument that got out of hand.'

'Can I ask what the argument was about?'

It is some time before she can answer. Seated in the armchair, as usual, she stares at the untidy bundle of her hands in her lap. Focuses on her wedding ring: the plain band of gold she doesn't think she believes in anymore. Then she opens up to John, tells him everything she learnt about Erin and what Gareth did or didn't do. As she speaks, other thoughts crowd in. Thoughts she struggles to keep to herself: *I love him . . . I love this big, gentle, man . . . I want him to shelter me in the deep, dark folds of his heart and keep me safe. Forever.*

Amidst the seraphic light falling on the condensation-dripping walls, she must remind herself she is a mother, a married woman — even if it's only to someone who bullies and frightens and was capable of exploiting a fourteen-year-old child, without thinking he has anything to apologise for.

'And that's about the long and short of it,' she concludes, jerking to a stop.

In the silence that falls between them, she stares as intensely at him as he does her.

'You seem to have taken Delyth's side in all this,' John comments at last.

'Are you saying you don't think I should?' She frowns.

'No, it's not that.' His eyes still resting on hers. 'It's just, well,' he pauses to cough, a hand covering his mouth.

'That sounds nasty.' She tips forward over her knees. 'Don't you think you should go and see about it?'

'It's nothing,' he sidesteps her anxiety. 'Because,' he returns to what he wanted to say, 'this is Gareth we're talking about and I can't imagine he's taking it too well, the fact you're siding with her, even if he is the one in the wrong.'

'I'm siding with Delyth because what he did was despicable. And look at the damage it went on to cause. It's why Erin killed herself. It's why Delyth did what she did in my kitchen, I'm sure of it. No, he can come up with as many excuses as he likes and believe me, he has. Blaming it on the drink, some nonsense about Erin coming on to him. But I'm sorry, nothing excuses what he did. Nothing.'

'What did Norah have to say about it?'

'Funny thing is . . . not that I'm sure how reliable Norah is, she did seem rather confused.' Melanie is remembering the phantom sheepdogs. 'But she doesn't seem to blame Gareth at all.'

'Doesn't she?' John's turn to frown, worrying at the dog's ears, his fingers collide with hers.

'No. Delyth said she wanted to go to the police at the time, but Norah stopped her.'

'Did she?'

'Yeah, and I might just have a theory as to why that is.'

'You do?'

Melanie nods. 'It involves Gareth's father.'

'Rhodri Sayer?'

'Delyth said, well, Norah said some things too, actually.' Melanie takes her time. 'She implied, and I don't think I got it wrong, that Norah and Rhodri got pretty close during the years she worked for him.'

'That's interesting.'

'It is.' Melanie smiles at him, momentarily forgetting the troubles at home. 'From the way she spoke about Rhodri, it was plain she had a soft spot for the man. Perhaps it was enough for her not to rock the boat so far as Gareth was concerned.'

'I remember some rumours doing the rounds. But like all the other rumours in this town, I thought it was nothing more than that.' He gets up, lights the only lamp. It turns the tiny space a warm yellow. 'She was a looker, was Norah. In her day, like.'

'I know. I saw photos of her up at the farm. Erin looked just like her, didn't she?'

John coughs his answer. 'D'you think that all this has got something to do with why I saw Gareth's car up by the farm that morning?'

'Yes, I do. And what's worse, is that I think Gareth gave Delyth money to keep her mouth shut.'

'Gave her money? Are you sure?'

'He withdrew a large sum from our account and wouldn't tell me what he needed it for.' Melanie is reluctant to tell John how much. 'And when I went to the farm it was pretty obvious Delyth had been spending big time.'

'Gareth must be gutted because the money didn't stop her telling you, did it?'

'No, it didn't.'

'So,' John sighs heavily and leans back in his chair. 'Andrew's Gareth's kid then?'

Melanie nods.

'How d'you feel about that?'

'I don't know really.'

'What I don't understand,' John pulls a face. 'Is why we're only hearing about this now? Pencarew's a small place, it never usually takes long for news to do the rounds.'

'Not if they kept shtum. And it sounds as if they did. All of them. People would have got to hear that Erin had given birth, but not who the father was. They said Erin swore Norah and Delyth to secrecy. Even Gareth's sister, Tegan, didn't know. She didn't even know how Erin died.'

'And that one knows everyone else's business.' John rolls his eyes.

She feels herself smile. Presses her fingers to it and considers what she believes is her washed-out reflection in the only window. She will cook John pasta and casseroles, she decides, her plan taking shape with the day that darkens to night beyond the small square of glass. His pain is something she can ease. Is it as ridiculous as it sounds? She tries to push these ideas away, but they keep jogging back. She smiles again, she can't help it, there is something comical about the way she's feeling, it's bordering on the absurd. She should be devastated, discovering her husband's filthy secret, but instead she feels elated. Elated that her future is going to be with John. John Hughes: the ex-squaddie who opened his heart, let her cut his hair; a man who hasn't a vain or deceitful bone in his body.

Melanie is beaming openly at John now. Warmed by the idea he can probably see right down inside her, to her most intimate part, that now belongs to him. And as if reading her mind, he holds out his hand for her to take. Big and broad, she reaches to claim it. Neither saying a word. They sit in silence for a long time, Slinky sprawled between them on the rug. The cold, damp room, clinging to their clothes.

Then she rises to go to him. Takes the two paces necessary, still holding his hand. Only then does he let her go, but only to slip his good arm around her and pull her to him. A frisson at his touch, yet still they don't speak, the power of him rendering her speechless. On his knee, she bends close to his ear, lips brushing the soft, delicate earlobe that nestles beneath his shorn, dark hair.

'John,' she whispers into the charged air. 'Kiss me?'

FORTY-ONE

Two days to go until opening night. Melanie, Georgie and Slinky are on their way home from Pwllglas. The Mazda's boot chock-a-block with last-minute supplies.

With big wet trees looming either side and telephone cables sagging dangerously low to the verges, Melanie drives through what looks like sleet, taking care to keep to her side of the road. Up ahead, a row of larches, their feathered tops touching the amorphous-grey rainclouds as they whizz past open gateways leading to lonely footpaths strangled with bramble. She loves driving, the feeling of freedom it gives. The only downside was seeing roadkill. It upset her. It upset Georgie more. And there was so much of it on these rural roads. Not that its frequency lessens the effect, her body jolting at the horror of seeing each fresh mound of bloodied fur or feathers. Noting, with the passing of days and flattened by tyres, they become desiccated discs embedded into the tarmac. All she can do to console herself is hope that whatever was hit by a vehicle travelling at speed, equalled a swift and painless death. That the dozens of hedgehogs, foxes, pheasants and squirrels, didn't suffer.

Dark enough for sidelights, she switches them on. But catching sight of her face in the driving mirror: the fading bruise and the semi-circular cut that has almost healed over; her eyes drift from the road.

'Mummy!' Georgie screams from the back seat.

'*Stop!*'

A badger. Its saffron eye reflected in the Mazda's headlamps makes her scream. Too slow, she applies the brake, but without enough conviction. Believing, as she half-heartedly presses her foot to the floor, that the animal has time to cross. She hits it. A sickening thump. Then nothing. A hush beyond the ticking down of her engine and the cry of a faraway owl.

'Stay there, sweetheart,' she instructs Georgie and parks up in an adjacent lay-by. With hazard lights flashing, she slips from the driver's seat to investigate.

Sees the sheen of fresh blood streaked on tarmac. A trail that leads her eye up the bank and into the tenebrous undergrowth. Nowhere. Nothing. Only the badger's sour smell, trapped in the space that hangs between the parallel channels of light radiating from her car. She calls out for it through the steadily falling sleet. Her voice sounding feeble, stupid, ringing in her ears. The animal was hardly going to respond, it wasn't a dog. If — and it was a big if — the creature was still alive, it would be badly injured and only the pain of a protracted death awaited it.

She takes this thought back with her to the car. Sits with the bleakness of it, cold between her and the wet material of her parka. She sees herself as she was only moments before, pacing the road, the white puff of her repeated regret: inadequate and dissolving into the icy evening air.

'I'm so sorry,' she apologises to Georgie, to the dog, blinking back tears. She twists in her seat to kiss her daughter then buries her nose in the denseness of Slinky's neck. The dog, in turn, enjoying the attention, licks her face, cleansing it of guilt. Don't worry — his black eyes shining — he wasn't a relative of mine. She wants to believe him, her thoughts turning again to Gareth's anger. And cradling Slinky's skull in her hands, understanding its fragility with stark clarity, an unwelcome thought elbows its way into her head.

It would be easy for Gareth to kill her. All it would take is one blow, correctly placed, to despatch her. She shivers and touches the crust of black blood above her eye. Realising just how dangerously close she came and that next time she might not be so lucky.

FORTY-TWO

The bar at the Monkstone Arms is filled with the penetrating heat of those who've been invited to celebrate its opening. Smartly dressed friends from London mixing with Pencarew dignitaries and local businesspeople. The spill of guests even includes the town's mayor, her well-upholstered figure more heavily chained than the Christmas tree that has gone up extra early. Tegan and Bryn, along with Sian and Tom, are huddled with unknown others by the bar. Where Gareth — excelling in his role as bon viveur by keeping them entertained and keeping up the pretence — is ladling mulled wine from a huge crystal bowl he unearthed in the cellar.

Melanie stops carving the thin slices of cold roast beef and glances over at her husband. How convincing he is, in his dark blue shirt and crisply ironed chinos. Who would guess the trouble their marriage is in, she thinks, almost admiringly. She is grateful to him for playing along, for the sake of the business, for the sake of whatever their future might be here. This is a small town and, as John said, bad news travels fast, the last thing she wants is people — potential customers — knowing their lives have capsized and they have no clear idea how to set it right again. But how long can they keep it a secret? Even if Gareth's expression, as usual, gives nothing away, it's only a matter of time before the hawk-eyed Tegan sniffs them out. She's already been asking questions. The fact Melanie's been steering clear and wearing concealer to disguise what's left of the cut above her eye, it isn't fooling her.

An explosive laugh: firework-loud from somewhere in the crowd. Melanie whips her head to it, sees Bronwyn. Head flung back, mouth open to the dark-beamed ceiling, she is sporting a brand new hairdo for the occasion, and is, as usual, surrounded by her sycophantic coffee morning tribe. Women, hot inside cashmere knitwear and snug tweet skirts, their ankles spilling over their patent-leather shoes. Women who seem to flush a beetroot-red whenever Melanie addresses them. She listens for a moment to their mordent chatter rise above the music she carefully selected and set to play on the sound system. Then head down, she continues with her carving.

'Do help yourselves to cutlery and plates,' she invites those who have formed an orderly queue, jabbing her knifepoint at the end of the trestle table with its Christmas-red cloth. She looks down at the blade, her thoughts wandering to Delyth for a moment. She was invited along tonight, but she hasn't come. Not that this is any great surprise. Dropping by with a beautifully iced chocolate cake she decorated with Smarties. 'For Georgie,' she said. 'For her not to feel left out of the celebrations.'

How kind Delyth is, always so thoughtful. Melanie never ceases to be amazed by her generosity towards her and her daughter, especially when she thinks how abysmally Gareth has behaved. But whispering her good luck for this evening's event, saying she would drop by on Monday when Gareth was safely back in London — his last week of work, because he's handing his notice in next week — Delyth wouldn't be persuaded inside, even though Gareth had taken himself off for a last-minute game of golf with Bryn.

Poor Delyth, she thinks, lifting her head to the Chinese lanterns that float like pretend moons at the windows. She probably hates parties as much as Melanie. But, looking around the bar, at the Christmas tree and the fairy lights she pinned up along the beams, the amazing feast she's spent the last week preparing, she's thrilled with how everything's come together. That her hard work has paid off and their party guests appear to be enjoying themselves.

'Delicious spread you've done us, *bach*.' A silver-haired man in a maroon jacket, works his way along the buffet table. 'Done us proud, you have.' He takes a homemade golden-topped sausage roll, bites it in half.

'I'm glad you're enjoying it,' she smiles, trying not to stare at the crusty food stains on his tie.

'Make it all yourself, did you?' As he chews, flakes of pastry drift like dandruff to his jacket lapels.

'I did, yes.' Another smile. She is getting good at pretending.

'Me and the wife, we love what you've done with the place. Used to drink here when the Morgan's had it. Bit of a dump then, I can tell you.'

'Thanks.' Melanie, awkward under his compliment, fiddles with the clip she needs to wear to keep her ever-lengthening hair off her face. 'Although, Bryn's the mastermind behind the refurbishments. Him and his crew, they did a super job.'

'Well I never,' the man spins his head, takes an exaggerated look around. 'And you're to do Sian and Tom's wedding, I heard.'

'That's right,' Melanie nods.

'Lucky me, I'd say. Cos I'm invited to that too.' He grins, showing off a set of teeth that would look better on a string around his neck.

'A lot to manage on your own though, isn't it, love?' A woman: Melanie presumes is his wife; pushes to the front of the queue. 'You're doing bed and breakfast too, I heard?'

'That's right. We've got four doubles, all en-suite, all kitted out. We've been awarded four stars from the Welsh tourist board.' Melanie reels off her condensed sales pitch. 'Got bookings in the diary already.'

'Aye, but on your own? You won't be able to do it all on your own . . . she won't be able to manage, will she, Aled?' the woman prods the man in the stomach.

'Bit ambitious,' Aled, a splayed hand floating over a salver of mini quiches, dutifully chimes in.

'I'm not on my own, I've got Gareth.'

'But not in the week. You're going to be on your own in the week.'

'Oh, no.' A forced laugh. 'That was while the renovations were being done. Now we're open, Gareth's going to be here full-time.'

'But what about his London job?'

'He's given that up. Running this place with me is his job now.'

'Not what he's been saying.' The woman gawps at her as if she's stupid. 'Not what Bronwyn's saying, neither.'

Melanie wipes her hands on a tea towel and picks up her empty glass. 'Do excuse me,' she says, smile sliding. 'There's things I've got to fetch from the oven.'

She thought the couple of mulled wines she's drunk had softened her, but en route to the kitchen, pausing at the bar for a refill, she finds she needs more than a couple of further sips to loosen her tongue.

'Gareth?' Melanie, fingers twitching, smiles hello to Tegan and the others. 'Can I have a word?'

'What, now?' Gareth, midway through some hilarious anecdote, his audience in raptures, is now seated on one of the high bar stools. Flushed in the face, a tumbler in his hand, it appears he has moved on to the whisky and if she's going to get any sense out of him, she'd better act soon.

She drinks from her glass and puts an arm around him. So much of her wants to forgive him, wants their old lives back; in many ways she still loves him.

'Yes, Gareth, now. If that's all right?' she coaxes, smiling, keeping up the charade, aware of eyes. 'In private, yeah?' She cocks her head, indicating the stone steps that lead down to the kitchen.

But he stiffens under her touch. 'Oh, so you want to talk now, do you?' Way too loud, breaking his word;

blatantly displaying the trouble between them to his immediate audience. Melanie gapes at him in disbelief, she knows it won't take long for it to ripple through the remainder of their guests.

'You promised you wouldn't do this,' she noses through his curls, finds his ear.

'You should've thought about that before you sided with that woman over me,' he hisses.

'Please don't do this. Not here, not tonight,' she urges, persisting with her smile for the benefit of those who are looking.

He swivels away on his stool, turns his back to her; lets his body communicate what he can't be bothered to articulate.

Melanie shrinks from him, despising herself for relenting. He's the one in the wrong, not her. Humiliated, her thoughts spin to John, to the secret she keeps. A floating recollection of their kiss. The intoxicating charge when he touched her. John, she breathes, striding away to the safety of the kitchen, her head held high for the eyes she knows are watching. If she is being forced into the arms of another man, whose fault is that? A glance back at the bar, at the gathering of people who've already closed over the gap she left behind, keen to hear whatever else Gareth has to say. Such a small thing yet glaring in what it communicates. She is the outsider here, if push came to shove and she and Gareth did split up, she knows where loyalties would fall, and this sad realisation leaves her feeling the loneliest she's done in her life.

Melanie finishes her mulled wine and transfers the final trays of savoury pastries, hot from the oven, on to a doily-covered platter. Is wondering whether to take a couple up to Georgie, when Tegan leans around the doorway, motioning for her to come back into the bar.

Gareth is on his feet, a slight wobble. A crash as his bar stool topples over. He drains whatever whisky he has left, then gropes the bar top for something, finds a teaspoon, taps his glass. He is going to make a speech.

'Quiet everyone.'

Someone turns the music off. A thickening silence swells through the room.

'I'd like to start—' Gareth breaks off, drags his fist across his mouth and stares at his shiny brown brogues for a second. 'I'd like to start . . . by thanking you all for coming here tonight to celebrate the opening of—'

He breaks off again, this time because of a disturbance at the rear of the pub.

'Help!' a shout goes up. 'Someone, help. Quick! She's collapsed.'

Melanie, propelled into action, pushes through the ballooning commotion.

'Give her some air.' Another shout goes up. 'Step back, get back. All of you, give her some space.'

Melanie wades through her party guests who stand around squawking and squabbling like the gulls down on the shore and eventually reaches the foot of the stairs leading up to the flat.

'*Georgie!*' she kneels to hold her sticky little hand. 'Someone, call an ambulance,' she shouts, ignoring the grit on the rug grinding into the flesh of her knees. She strokes the soft skin of Georgie's forearm, speaking gibberish in hushed, reassuring tones. 'What happened, sweetheart?'

'I've been sick again, Mummy.' A single fat tear rolls down Georgie's flushed little cheek.

'Oh, darling.' Melanie, crying too, tests her daughter's clammy brow with the back of her hand. 'You're baking . . . oh, Georgie, I'm so sorry, I meant to come and check on you, I'm sorry, baby. I'm so sorry.'

'My hands and feet have gone all funny,' Georgie mumbles, her eyes strangely bright. 'They've got pins-and-needles.'

Melanie spots a dollop of chocolate icing on Georgie's jumper, the giveaway rainbow stain of Smarties on her baby fist.

A hand on Melanie's shoulder. She looks up, expecting Gareth but it's her mother-in-law who comforts her.

'Hang on in there, *cariad*,' Bronwyn, kinder than Melanie's ever known. The pallor beneath her powder and paint, washed to grey. 'The ambulance is on its way.'

'I t-tried to c-come to tell you,' Georgie slurs and, running out of puff, her eyelids flutter and close.

'No, no, no. Don't close your eyes.' Melanie, watching it on some hospital TV drama, shakes her awake. 'You mustn't sleep. Stay with Mummy.'

'Get out of my way. Get out of my way.'

Melanie hears her husband before she sees him.

'Georgie.' A swaying Gareth towers over them. 'What the hell's wrong with her? What's she lying there for?' He throws Melanie a desperate look.

'She's had another funny turn.' She stares at the toes of his shoes. 'Says she's been sick.'

'We saw her come down the stairs, then she just dropped down there. Right there in front of us.' Someone, on the edge of the circle that's formed around them, tries to be helpful.

'We can't lose her too, Mel. We can't.' Gareth wrings his hands: the gesture shrieks of despair.

'Try to stay calm, boy,' Bronwyn talks to her son. 'The ambulance is coming.'

'What's that stuff round her mouth?' Gareth jabs a frenetic finger. 'That's chocolate. Chocolate icing off that cake that bloody woman brought round. Look at her fingers.' He shouts and guests scatter, nervous as birds. 'That's it. I'm going over there . . . I'm going to sort her out. Right now.'

'Gareth, please,' Melanie appeals to him from the floor. 'This has nothing to do with Delyth.' Her eyes skim the crowd before refocusing on her daughter, fearful she could slip into unconsciousness. 'Remember what happened when you jumped the gun about the dog?'

'This isn't about the dog!' he screeches. 'This is our child.'

'I know, Gareth, but please.' Up on her feet, reluctant to turn from Georgie. 'This has got nothing to do with Delyth,' she grapples with him, trying to get him to see reason. 'Let's just get Georgie to hospital. Okay?'

'Yes, Gareth. Come on, let's just get Georgie to hospital,' Bronwyn slips an arm through his.

'Get off me.' He pushes them both away. 'It's that woman's fault, I'm telling you. I've been telling you since we got here . . . but you won't listen, will you? She won't listen to me, Mam.' The ring of spectators flinches in unison. 'I'm going over there. I'm going to put a stop to that fucking woman once and for all.'

'Gareth, stop it. You're frightening Georgie . . . you're frightening me.' Melanie — admitting this to half the town, to her in-laws — ducks down to her child, then up again. 'You're not helping, please calm down.' She reaches out to him a second time.

Gareth, eyes wild and staring, shoves her away: violent, brutish; slamming her against the wall to the gasp of partygoers.

'You've sided with that woman over me from the off. I've been telling you; she wants to damage us. I told you she's evil. She's done this to Georgie. I can't believe it's taken this to prove to you exactly how evil she is. I'll never forgive you, not if our child dies. Never. Not this time.'

'Gareth! Calm down, boy.' Bronwyn, appalled, steps between him and Melanie, but whatever she sees in her son's eyes makes her shrink away again.

'Oh, let him go,' Melanie, exasperated. 'He's no use to anyone in that state, he's just making things worse.' And kneeling beside her daughter again, she picks up Georgie's clammy hand. 'Shush, shush, now baby,' she whispers.

'Don't worry about Daddy, it's you we've got to take care of. Come on, little one, don't fall asleep.'

From her kneeling position, Melanie watches Gareth go. She sees the way the crowd parts to let him through, their eyes accusing. A man, she can't see who, steps forward to dissuade him, insisting he's way over the limit, that it would be madness to drive. But he throws them off too, determined as a freight train in his quest to damage.

All goes quiet. Quiet enough to hear the outer door slam and what she thinks must be the Mazda's engine start up. Melanie fears for Delyth and wonders, in the tightening seconds, whether she should ring and warn her of what's coming. But unlike Gareth, she can't abandon their daughter. It speaks volumes that his primary concern, through anger, is Delyth Powell, rather than his own child.

Poor Georgie. Feeling ill on and off for weeks, listening to her parents arguing whenever they were together, the way things have been since they came home with Bingo and the vile news of what Gareth did to a fourteen-year-old child. Melanie is still clasping Georgie's hand when the cool-blue lights of the ambulance splinter the dark beyond the pub's windows.

'It'll be all right, I promise,' she soothes her child. 'It will be all right.'

Melanie murmurs platitudes she doesn't believe about the seriousness of her daughter's health or her marriage. But her marriage is going to have to take care of itself for the time being; her priority is Georgie, not Gareth. Melanie doubts it will ever be Gareth again. She thanks the paramedics, energetic and efficient in their kelly-green uniforms, and oversees Georgie's safe transference from stretcher to ambulance.

'Can you look after things for me here? I've got to stay with Georgie,' she asks Bronwyn, who has been stuck to her side. 'I'll ring as soon as I know anything.'

'Yes, yes, Mel. Go . . . go,' her mother-in-law gives her an affectionate kiss on the cheek, then waves her away.

'Don't worry, I'll take care of things here.'

FORTY-THREE

I n the days that follow, making the drive to the hospital in Pwllglas twice-daily, Melanie sees the same dead badger again and again. Its black and white stripes stiffening on the verge of the route she took with Georgie returning home from the cash and carry last week. Is it the one she hit, was she to blame? She doesn't dare think about it. Except there it is, on each journey, working like a burning reminder of the crime she committed against the animal kingdom. Nothing eats it. Nothing of the wild goes near it. It just lies there, its black snout pointing accusingly dry and hard into the road.

It is just about dark by the time Melanie gets away from the pub. Charging back there at lunchtime to give Slinky his quick once around the block and dinner bowl, within an hour she is racing off to see Georgie again. Taking the third exit off the roundabout on the outskirts of Pwllglas, it is clogged with traffic lights and road works all along the dual carriageway. When she finally reaches the turn off for the Princess Diana Hospital, she is forced to join an already lengthy queue for the car park. The car park costs money and she's never organised enough to have the correct change. So, along with the stress and worry over the last seventy-two hours, she has the added worry of being clamped.

Jotting down a note to leave on the dashboard, explaining why she hasn't purchased a ticket, Melanie scrambles around for the bag of her daughter's things.

'Bloody hell,' she curses, as it empties itself into the footwell. Then her mobile beeps; insistent, through the dim interior of the car. A text from Gareth.

HOPE GEORGIE AND YOU ARE OK. GIVE ME A RING WHEN YOU GET THE CHANCE X

She thinks about replying but can't bring herself to. He should be here, at Georgie's bedside, not swanning off back to London. Let him wait, the selfish bastard, leaving her with Georgie before the ambulance even arrived. Yes, she told him to go, but even so. Besides, she hasn't the time, the consultant paediatrician telephoned just before she left the pub, said she needed to speak to them as soon as possible. She'll text him later, when she's something specific to convey; after all, she and Gareth aren't exactly exchanging niceties anymore.

It's raining. A cold mean rain that slides down inside her collar. It promises the winter still to be lived through before spring comes around again. By the time she's walked the length of the car park and in through the automatic sliding doors, her parka is soaking. The children's unit is on the fourth floor, so she takes the lift. Shares it with a male nurse wheeling an elderly gentleman in striped pyjamas. Leaving them behind, she pushes through a stiff set of fire doors decorated with stars and walks the length of corridor embellished with rainbows and giant, brightly-coloured butterflies, her wet boots striking the lino. The jolly-looking reception desk looks empty and, conscious of her dishevelled appearance, she uses the seconds available to tidy her hair in the reflective sides of a medicine trolley.

'Can I help you?' A nurse she hadn't seen, prises her eyes from the computer screen.

'Hi, yes. I'm Mrs Sayer, Georgie's Mum. Mrs Brookes asked me to let her know when I arrived, she said she needed to talk to me?

'Okay,' the nurse smiles. 'She should be on the ward somewhere; I'll bleep her for you.'

'Thanks, that's great.' Melanie taps the desk with fidgety fingers. 'Do you want me to wait here?'

'If you like.' The nurse lifts the receiver of a telephone, presses in a series of numbers. 'But I've no idea how long she'll be.'

'Would you be able to tell her I'm with Georgie, that I'll see her when she's ready?'

'No problem.' The nurse smiles again.

Melanie takes the first right into Georgie's unexpectedly noisy room, stopping briefly at the hand sanitiser for a squirt of foam. She rubs her palms together and sidesteps a huge, red octopus transfer stamped to the linoleum, its tentacles groping into the ward. Bypassing rows of little children rigged up to monitors and tubes, their pale green hospital beds huddled with relatives, Melanie reaches the window end and pulls back the screen that isn't usually drawn.

Georgie's bed is empty.

Stripped back to the plastic under-sheet, the cards and sweets on the bedside table, cleared away.

Her hand flies to her mouth. She can't breathe.

'Georgie!'

She whips her head to the eyes that have turned to her.

'Where's my daughter?'

She runs, handbag swinging, back to the reception desk. Slaps the counter, loudly, startling the brigade of nurses who have now gathered there.

'Where's Georgie?' she chokes on desperate tears. 'What's happened to her?'

'Mrs Sayer.' A voice at her shoulder. She spins to receive it. Mrs Brookes: wire-haired and bespectacled; pressing a clipboard to her chest. 'Georgie's fine.'

'Where is she then?' she shrieks. 'It's her father. He's taken her . . . he's taken my baby away from me?'

'No, no. She's fine. We moved Georgie to another room, that's all.' A hand on Melanie's arm, the weight of it ominous. 'I'm sorry if we gave you a fright.'

She slumps against the reception desk. 'Oh, thank

God.' A nurse passes her a tissue and she wipes her eyes. 'So, she's all right?'

'Yes, don't worry.'

Melanie recovers a little. 'Can I see her?'

'Of course, but shall we go through to my office and have a little chat first?'

'Y-yes.' Melanie follows the white-coated woman into a small room.

'Do have a seat.' The consultant paediatrician points with a biro to a long, low sofa.

'Is Georgie getting worse, is that it?' Melanie, her heart pounding, is anxious for reassurance.

'Georgie's doing well, Mrs Sayer.' The pressure of that hand again: scrubbed and pale and ringless; before it's released.

'If that's the case then why was she still connected to a drip this morning? I was told she was coming off that today.' This is the first opportunity Melanie's had to talk to the consultant, and she has a string of questions.

'It's just a precaution. Your daughter was very dehydrated when she was admitted Saturday night. We'll be able to take her off it soon, especially now she's started eating again. You knew she managed a little of her lunch today, didn't you?'

'No, I didn't. Is that a good sign?'

'Very much so. She's been generally more comfortable this afternoon, she even managed to sit up for a while.'

'That's good,' Melanie's heartrate slowing. 'But there was something you wanted to talk to me about, wasn't there?'

'Yes, Mrs Sayer. Ideally, I'd have liked to chat to you and your husband, but I understand he had to return to London?'

'That's right, he drove back late last night, he's not due home till Friday.' Melanie has seen him since Georgie was admitted but, aside from the odd text message, she and

Gareth haven't spoken directly. Taking it in turns to sit by their daughter's bedside, deliberately avoiding one another.

'The test results have come back.'

'And?' Panicking again, she grips her knees to steady herself.

'They're showing us that Georgie has celiac disease.'

'*Celiac disease*?' Melanie parrots, not understanding. 'That sounds serious. Is it serious?'

'If it goes undetected, yes, extremely,' Mrs Brookes is blunt. 'I understand Georgie's been feeling quite unwell for some time?'

'On and off, yes. Complaining of tummy aches, bloatiness, occasionally vomiting. I noticed a rash on her neck, too, the day before she collapsed and was brought in here. I thought it was a reaction to a new washing powder I was using,' Melanie explains.

'All symptoms of this condition, I'm afraid.'

'But why wasn't it diagnosed before now? We've been to our doctor at the Pencarew surgery loads of times. He ran tests, but they didn't reveal anything.'

The consultant scrunches her lips, looks down at the printouts on her clipboard. 'Your daughter is rather underweight for her age; did you notice she was losing weight?'

'Yes, I told the doctor that too. I told him she'd been a bit wheezy as well. I've been noticing it on our walks to school together,' Melanie adds. 'Our doctor told me it was probably just a cold, but could that be connected too?'

'This condition can often go undetected for a long time,' the paediatrician sidesteps the question. 'But Georgie's been lucky, there's been no obvious damage done to her small intestine, which sometimes, if this goes undiagnosed for too long, can be a problem, especially in children.'

'Is she going to get better?' Melanie, imagining all sorts.

'She's going to be fine, so long as she avoids gluten from now on.'

'So, this is, what? An allergy to gluten.'

'To wheat, rye and barley,' Mrs Brookes confirms.

'But how did she get it? Was it something I did?'

'No, nothing you did. It's something the body can develop, we've no idea why. But, please, don't be alarmed, we can help you with diet sheets, what not to eat, that kind of thing. All the supermarkets sell gluten-free products now.'

'Yes, I'm familiar with that. I've got friends who are intolerant to wheat.'

'This condition is rather more serious than an intolerance, Mrs Sayer. Your daughter cannot eat any gluten at all. If she does, she will very quickly become ill again.' The tone is firm, and Melanie listens to it carefully.

'So, we're talking no cakes or bread or biscuits, that kind of thing?' She is thinking of Delyth, of the countless treats she's brought round and how much Georgie's loved them. In a way, Gareth was right, wasn't he? They were making her ill. But this isn't Delyth's fault, no one knew Georgie had a problem.

'That's right. But you can bake with alternatives, buy alternatives. So long as everything's gluten-free, she'll be safe.' Mrs Brookes eyes her through her pebble glasses. 'You'll be sure to pass this news on to your husband, won't you?'

'Yes,' Melanie says, unsure why she's being asked this.

'It's just that he's been ringing the hospital non-stop, wanting to know how Georgie is and what's happening. You are happy to explain things to him? Because from what he said, it sounded as if the two of you weren't in touch. And with him not being here,' the consultant pauses. 'Things are okay at home, are they, Mrs Sayer?'

Out in the corridor, a leaflet on celiac disease in her hand, Melanie goes off in the direction she's been given to find Georgie.

'Melanie . . . Melanie Sayer?'

Someone calls her name and she turns to a stout, round-faced woman fastened into a tight-fitting coat.

'Are you Melanie?' the woman asks, fiddling with her cuffs.

'I am.' She stares, thinking there is something oddly familiar about her.

'How's your daughter? We heard she was poorly.'

Melanie flutters the leaflet between them and smiles. 'She's doing okay, thank you. Gave us all a bit of a fright, but, yes,' she hesitates, thinks about how different things could have been. 'Yes, she's going to be okay.'

'Oh, that is good. We've been so worried. The two of us.'

'*The two of us?*' Melanie repeats. 'I'm sorry, have we met?'

'Oh, didn't I say, I'm John's sister. Nerys.'

'John,' Melanie's jaw drops open. 'You're his sister?'

'That's right.' The same lopsided smile; she sees the resemblance now. 'He's told me all about you.'

Her insides flip-flop. 'About me?'

'He's been telling me how kind you've been by looking after his dog and bringing him food.'

'Oh, right. Y-yes, that's right. His dog.' She sags with relief.

'Blasted thing, he brought it to live with me. Couldn't stand it, I'm not a dog person, so good on you.'

'Erm,' Melanie hesitates, unsure how to broach what it is she wants to know. 'How did you know about Georgie?'

'The whole town knows.' Nerys gives Melanie a look that says the state of her daughter's health isn't the only detail of their opening night that's doing the rounds. 'It's not gossiping,' Nerys knits her brows together. 'People are worried about Georgie, and about you.'

'About me? I'm not sure I like being the talk of the town.' Melanie scratches her nose. 'So, did you come to the hospital to see me?'

'Oh, no.' A nervous laugh that withers before it's properly formed. 'I'm here to see John. He's in the men's ward, next floor up. I thought I'd take a—'

'John's here? In hospital?' Melanie gasps. 'My God, is he all right? He hasn't tried to hurt himself again, has he?'

'Oh, no. Nothing like that.' Nerys is quick to understand. 'So far as all that goes,' she says, skipping around the edges of her brother's fragility. 'He's been feeling rather a lot brighter about life recently.'

'What's wrong with him, then?' Melanie listens to the fear in her voice, hopes the sister can't identify it.

'He's got pneumonia,' Nerys says, shifting sideways for a nurse pushing a child in a wheelchair. 'Sleeping in that cold, damp room, it is. The daft sod. I don't know why he likes it so much. I've said he can have a room at mine.'

'But pneumonia's serious.' Melanie looks at the floor. 'I thought his cough sounded bad the last time I saw him. I should've made him go to the doctors. But he doesn't like people fussing, does he?'

'No, he doesn't.' The sister's eyes tell a story. 'But it's all right, he's going to be fine. They've caught it in time and he's reacting well to the antibiotics.'

'Can I see him, d'you think?'

Nerys stares at her dumbly. Melanie can tell she's turning something over in her mind. 'Won't your Gareth have something to say about that?' she says, at last, eyes glinting with mischief.

'Gareth?' Melanie's turn to laugh. 'No. And anyway, he's not here to mind, he's in London.'

'What? With your kiddie in hospital.'

'He had to go back to work.'

'If you say so.' Nerys wrinkles her nose. 'Give you that, did he?'

Melanie's hand flies to her brow, to the residue of

bruise and the inch of scar tissue that in her mad dash to get away, she forgot to touch-up with concealer. 'Yes, but,' her excuse fizzles out.

'There's always a but, *cariad*.'

'It's not what it looks like.'

'It never is.' The look is knowing. 'I had a bloke like that once, used to beat me black and blue. Always sorry afterwards, mind.'

Melanie doesn't answer, her fingers sifting the sand and shells in her coat pocket.

'You should go to the police if he hits you, though. He shouldn't be allowed to get away with it. Your Gareth always was a nasty bugger. Used to bully John something terrible. He hasn't hit your daughter, has he?'

'*Georgie*? God no.' Melanie, resolute.

'I'm just saying to watch him. I wouldn't trust him, not that one.' Nerys holds her gaze. 'A lovely looking woman like you,' her voice is tinged with sadness. 'You shouldn't have to put up with that sort of nasty business.'

But a less lovely looking woman would deserve it then, would she? Melanie thinks, but doesn't say, she knows the woman means well enough.

'Which ward is John in?' she asks.

'Fifth floor. He's in a side room. On my way up there now, I am.'

'Tell him I'll come and see him in a while,' Melanie says, then makes her excuses.

FORTY-FOUR

Melanie drifts off to sleep in the armchair beside Georgie's hospital bed. When she eventually opens her eyes, it's a shock to find someone standing over her.

'Delyth.' She jerks upright. Half of her wondering whether she could still be dreaming. 'My God!' She rubs her eyes to clear the way but, no, she's not mistaken. 'What the hell happened to you?'

Delyth looks as if she's been involved in a motor accident. Her left arm, cradled in the other, has been crudely bandaged across her front and the discoloured bruising around her eye makes Melanie grimace. As does the falcate cut on the bridge of her nose that someone's tried to cover with a plaster.

A flashback to the opening night at the Monkstone Arms. Gareth, drunk and wild with rage, threatening to: 'Put a stop to that fucking woman once and for all.'

'Please don't tell me Gareth did that to you?' The horror of Melanie's question oscillates between them.

Delyth doesn't reply. She hangs her head. Her newly-styled hair knotted and dull looking, her eyes wet with tears. And when Delyth undoes her coat a fraction, Melanie notices what looks like dried blood on her top.

'Please, tell me,' she whispers, fearful of waking Georgie.

Melanie hears the click of Delyth's tongue, a dry sound in the over-warm room.

327

'Yes, it was Gareth,' she admits at last. 'He came up to the farm Saturday night. He just lost it with me.'

A nurse comes and busies herself around the sleeping Georgie. Inspecting her monitor, the IV drip, tucking Murray in on the other side of the bed. It's a frustrating few minutes waiting for her to go, but when she does, Melanie pulls the screen around them, wanting the privacy.

'He did that? — to you.' She gulps down her revulsion, waves a feeble hand over Delyth's injuries. 'I can't believe it, I can't,' her voice trembling. 'It's terrible. How could he?'

'Easy. He hates me. He always has.' Comes the meek reply.

Melanie makes an involuntary noise and twists to check on Georgie. The disgust she feels towards her husband, trapped in her throat.

'No,' she says, recalling John's theory about Gareth's problem with this woman. 'I think his abominable behaviour towards you is because he hates himself. You remind him of what a shit he used to be at school.'

'But he did it to you too, and he's supposed to love you.' Delyth, not seeming to have noticed the expletive, adjusts her damaged arm and emits a groan of pain.

'I've married a monster.' Melanie looks up at a woeful Delyth. 'I can't believe anyone would do such a thing to another person; it's disgusting. Honestly, Delyth, I don't know what to say to make it better . . . there's no way for me to make this right. I'm so ashamed. It's terrible. Does your arm hurt dreadfully?' She takes a breath, leans out to offer comfort but Delyth pulls away, screws up her face in agony. 'Have you had someone look at it? It's not broken, is it?'

John's sister's words find Melanie as she focuses on Georgie for a moment. What's to stop him hurting her? Her child is as defenceless as Delyth. Why has she never seen this side of him before? And more importantly, why has it taken this timid, submissive woman to show her what her husband is capable of? Were there no clues in the years they've been together?

'I tried, I tried to stop him. I did.' Up on her feet, Melanie wants to console her friend but again Delyth ducks away, obviously in too much pain to be touched. 'Christ,' she plonks back down in the armchair, raises a hand of apology for swearing. 'I married a monster.'

'None of this is your fault, Melanie. Please don't get upset, you're not to blame. You've been a good friend to me.' Delyth, as compliant as ever, displays no hint of animosity. 'Anyway, more to the point, how's this little one doing?' And she moves to the bottom of Georgie's bed, strokes the primrose-yellow blanket.

'She's going to be okay.' Melanie swings her attention back to her child, to the wires, the IV drip, the beeping monitor, then returns to Delyth. 'But what about you, what are you going to do? Have you reported him?'

'No.'

'Are you going to?'

Delyth shrugs her response and clutches her bad arm.

Melanie, troubled by the small, childlike quality of this woman, tries not to stare at her damaged face. She is as vulnerable as an orphan. The way that old wax coat drowns her narrow frame, it's pitiful. How could anyone, let alone the man she's shared such intimacies with, the father of her child, raise a hand of violence against her? The idea is so distressing, it makes her stomach somersault.

It is a loathsome act.

An unforgivable act.

It is the final straw.

'I hope your decision not to go to the police isn't out of some loyalty to me? Because he shouldn't be allowed to get away with what he's done to you. Listen to me,' she urges gently. 'You've got to talk to them, look what he's done to you . . . if he'd done that to me,' she stops, realises the irony.

Delyth lifts her dark irises but declines to speak; it seems there is no need for words. Melanie touches what remains of the cut on her own temple, traces the inch-long snake of proud flesh she fears she may always have.

'We're over. Me and Gareth,' she announces suddenly, her voice low. 'There's no way back for us now.' Turning to her sleeping child to hide her hot and painful tears. 'He's not even sorry, d'you know that?' she sobs. 'He's not sorry about any of it. He couldn't care less that his actions destroyed your family, that you needed to sacrifice your life to bring up his child. No, I'm sorry to say, but there's no way back for us, we're over. Finished. I can only take so much, I'm not a mug. I'm sorry Delyth, but I can't be like you and turn the other cheek, I've got to protect Georgie.'

Delyth passes her a tissue from the box on the bedside cabinet then, unzipping a new, smart leather bag that is looped over her shoulder, takes out the rolled-up school photo she took without asking. 'You can have this back now,' she says, passing it over.

Melanie raises the flat of her hand. 'No. You keep it, I insist.'

'So, you and Gareth are definitely over?' Delyth puts the photograph away.

'Yes,' Melanie bites her lip, determined not to give way to further tears. 'Yes. I never knew him, did I? Him and me,' she sucks back her breath. 'We were a lie from the start.'

'You told him that?' Delyth asks.

'Not yet, no.' Melanie, wipes her eyes. She wants to say it's the damage he's done to Delyth that has ultimately made her decide but would hate for this woman to feel responsible for the breakdown of her marriage.

'What about the pub? You had such plans for the place.'

'I don't know.' Melanie sighs into the torpid air. 'I

haven't thought that far ahead.'

'But you'll keep in touch with me, won't you? Let me know what you decide.' Delyth fumbles for Melanie with her damaged arm then, appearing to change her mind, pulls it back into position.

'Of course, I will.' Melanie yawns; suddenly overwhelmed with tiredness.

'I'll ring you some time.' Delyth pushes aside the curtain and makes to leave. 'You've been a true friend to me, Melanie,' she turns briefly. 'Thank you for that. And for what it's worth, I'm sorry it's come to this between you and Gareth.'

'Don't be, this was his doing,' Melanie gives a weak smile. 'It had nothing whatever to do with you.'

'Mummy.' Georgie's eyes snap open. They look unnervingly bright in the fluorescent lighting of the ward.

'Hello, sleepyhead,' she yawns again and, absorbed with her sick child, when she does eventually look to where Delyth was standing, she finds she has gone.

FORTY-FIVE

Delyth hobbles out through the children's ward and along the corridor. She takes the lift to the ground floor and disappears into the disabled toilet at the side of the pop-up café. Locks herself inside.

'Convincing, or what?' She whispers into the large, square mirror and admires her injuries. A sly smile creeping over her mouth.

That idea to fix a plaster on the bridge of her nose, so the gory-looking cut beneath was still visible, was pure genius. The wound is realistic enough even to make her cringe, small wonder Melanie reacted the way she did. Granted, it took several goes to get right, but it's been worth the effort. The silly bitch might not have been persuaded to leave her bastard husband if she'd not gone the extra mile.

'Amazing, mind. You really can find anything on Google. Especially easy with my new smartphone.'

It only began as a germ of an idea, not for a minute did Delyth think it would be possible to dupe people this easily. But, as it turned out, there was loads of stuff on the internet, even YouTube videos giving step by step guides on how to apply the right colour make-up to give yourself fake black eyes and facial injuries to shock at Halloween. It was fun experimenting; the thing to remember was not to be too over the top. Lucky, she kept hold of Erin's old make-up. A broader smile. She always knew the brassy rainbow colours her whore of a sister liked to plaster herself in would come in handy one day. And those tips on how to pretend you were in agony were especially useful; to accidentally touch your fake bruises and, in Delyth's case, her left arm, and pretend they hurt. Yes, everything's gone like clockwork, it's been a doddle from start to finish. And the great thing is that the stupid bastard's done it all to himself, she hasn't so much as needed to raise her voice. Apart from showing up now and again to rattle his cage, all she's had to do is keep up the pretence and persist with her timid, hard-done-by act. Quite brilliant to achieve what she set out to do, quietly, without violence or committing any sort of crime — not this time, anyway.

'I'm more brilliant than Google in many ways,' she congratulates herself. 'I doubt there's websites that give instructions on how to destroy a marriage and walk away scot-free like I've done. But I did warn her, I did say a leopard never changes its spots. *But we're happy together — me and Gareth . . .*' Delyth mimics Melanie's voice, embellishing it with an irritating whine and delighting in emphasising her slight East Anglia burr. '*He's the happiest he's ever been.*' She pauses to watch her expression harden. 'Not so fucking happy now, though, are you? I reckon I've done you a favour, you gullible bitch.'

Delyth unravels the bandage from her arm, folds back both sets of sleeves to the elbows to examine the thin red scores that have healed into scars. She will probably always have these, which is a shame, as they're pretty unsightly, but who has she got that's going to notice?

'Bit excessive?' the more rational side of her questions. 'No,' the other voice in her head is vehement. 'Desperate means required desperate measures. Everything I did was totally necessary. How else was I going to get that dopey wife of his on my side? I had to make her feel properly sorry for me.'

Delyth rebandages her arm and returns to her reflection.

'I couldn't believe him moving back here with his

333

lovely wife, his lovely child: a big, fat success story.' She mutters and punches the air. 'Yeah, I was jealous, show me someone who wouldn't have been. But in the end, it was better for me because it was him who had everything to lose.' She presses her fingers firmly against the plaster on her nose to secure it.

'Oh, yes,' she says, happy with it, before moving on to prod the fake bruising around her eye. 'That's pretty damn impressive. You had 'em all fooled. It's lucky for me that people are always eager to hear the worst of others. And men who hit women are the worst kinds of scumbags.' She chuckles, pleased with her cunning.

'I must have looked totally convincing because even them nurses on the desk kept looking at me all concerned. I wish they'd asked me who'd beaten me up, cos I'd prepared my story in advance. I, more than most, know how important it is for lies to be consistent. There's no way I'd have got away with what I've done in the past if I hadn't been good at lying,' she grins at her reflection.

Her grin widens when she thinks about Gareth turning up at the farm pissed out of his skull that night. She can't remember the last time she's needed to wield her father's old Purdey. But what a hoot that was. It's the most fun she's had in years, putting the shits up him, the arrogant fuck. Because Delyth's always been a cracking shot and could have taken him out easily, if she'd wanted to, and in many ways, she wishes she had. Because if you've killed once, it's always easier the second time around. Or so they say.

'I'm a saviour, I am. I saved Melanie from a life that was killing her too. Just like I saved Erin.'

She stops fiddling with her fake injuries, afraid of smudging them. If this trick is going to work, she'll need to keep up the pretence for a good while yet. Although, with a few weeks off work, as planned, it's going to be a doddle to hide away at the farm. She got away with hiding Erin for all those years, didn't she? Aside from the time she escaped and ran away to Swansea, it was easy keeping her prisoner. With a mother either working or too drunk to notice what was going on under her own roof and no one, not even the post van, coming up to the house. The track to the farm, treacherous as it is, has served her well.

'Funny, but it's true, everything does come to those who wait. And no one could say I haven't had to wait to have my revenge. Seventeen-years is a long time. But, in the end, I couldn't have planned it better, even down to their kid getting sick. Talk about playing into my hands. That Gareth was more of an idiot than I ever gave him credit for,' she chatters to herself in a hushed, imperceptible way — fearful someone might be listening at the toilet door, yet unable to quite contain her glee.

'Certain people,' she says, digging out the old school photograph from her new leather bag. 'They just don't deserve things.' She proceeds to shred it into strips, taking special care to rip Erin's face clean in half, before putting the lot in the bin. 'That's why it's a good job I'm here to see that people get what they deserve.' A throaty chuckle. 'Because there's no way Gareth deserved a lovely family, or a woman as beautiful as Melanie . . . or his kid, come to that.'

Delyth reaches inside her top and yanks the chain with its crucifix clean off. She sneers at how the cheap metal has already tarnished, before binding it in a scrap of tissue and dropping it into the toilet bowl with a satisfying plop.

'But then Melanie doesn't deserve Gareth, either,' she prattles on. 'Same as Erin didn't deserve him, the druggy little slut.'

Delyth flushes the toilet and the necklace disappears.

'Because that should've been me with Gareth the night of our end of school party. *ME!*' She snarls at her reflection. 'Erin didn't deserve him any more than she deserved to have his baby. But I did. And I got him. I got my Andrew all to myself in the end, didn't I? I made sure I did.' A blood-curdling grin. 'It didn't take much with her standing with her back to an open window . . . it didn't take much at all. Just one little push to kill her . . . to kill Erin.'

SIX WEEKS LATER

A weak wind blows flakes of snow against the glass patio doors. Melanie hopes it settles; she has a childish fascination with snow. Staring out over the desolate-looking beer garden, at the flutter of house sparrows she has tamed in from the wild to feed from her bird tables, a memory of her, Gareth and the twins finds her. That bright, crisp morning when they woke to a silent world of white and built a snowman on the front lawn of their Bromley home, is so sharp it could have been yesterday. And yet it was a lifetime ago, she thinks sadly, the image gradually furling backwards into her memory. They used to be happy, didn't they? They used to laugh and dance and love one another. Melanie's problem is that so much of her still loves Gareth and life as a single parent is proving difficult to adjust to. Come the weekend, half of her hopes it could all have been a horrible dream and he's going to walk back through the door and be the man he always was.

But here she is, in the last week of January, after a New Year that came in without celebrations, but it's not as if running this place and looking after Georgie doesn't provide plenty to occupy her. Truth is, she's finding it a strain on her own the busier it gets. But she's determined to succeed. John helps when he can, in fact, he's looking after Slinky this afternoon, she's to drop by and pick him up on her way back from collecting Georgie from school. Not that she's going to have John around for much longer. He told her at Christmas, he's decided to leave Pencarew. That he's moving to France to join forces with an ex-squaddie friend who's opened a second-hand bookshop. He says it's because he needs a warmer climate, that his doctors warned that another bout of pneumonia — the way he's heading if he persists with living in that damp, little space — would be the death of him. But Melanie's sure there's more to it than that. Since their kiss, things between them have been awkward and, although they haven't discussed it, she suspects John can tell her heart isn't in it, that she isn't over Gareth.

Weird not to have seen anything of Delyth, though. Melanie's been sending texts, telling her there's a job here if she wants one, but she's not replied. She can hardly blame her. After what Gareth did, Melanie's probably the last person she wants to see. But it's only a matter of time before they bump into one another in town, or at Georgie's school. Melanie isn't concerned.

Cold, she tugs her chunky cardigan around her and buttons it to the throat. Is debating whether to light the wood burner early, when the call of the telephone slices between her indecisions.

'Good morning, Monkstone Arms,' she speaks into the receiver. Bingo, handsome and nearly the fully-grown cat he's going to be, circles her ankles.

'*Erm,* hello. *Er* . . . could I speak to Gareth Sayer, please?' The accent is heavy, it doesn't belong to a voice she recognises.

'I'm sorry, but he isn't here,' she answers. 'What I mean is,' she clears her throat, 'he doesn't live here anymore.' She swaps the receiver to her other ear, pushes it under her hair which is now almost shoulder length. 'But, erm . . .' she dithers, then decides it can't do any harm. 'I can take a message for him, if you like?'

'Well, *er*, yes . . . it's Dai Williams, it is. *Er* . . . it's about this horse of his, see. I've been keeping hold of it for a good few weeks now, as a favour, like. I've sold it to him,

I have, but thing is, I can't be keeping it on my land no more. Lovely gelding, he is. Dutch warmblood, he's got all his papers and that. Bloody brilliant, er . . . I should better check with you though,' the speaker pauses, 'you're not his wife, are you? You're not Gareth's wife?'

'Um,' Melanie hesitates, looks at her hand. No wedding ring. As if she needed the reminder. This man can't be all that local otherwise he'd know. News that she and Gareth split up did the rounds almost before she'd brought Georgie home from hospital. 'Um, no,' she replies eventually. 'I run the pub. He's my-my . . . business partner.'

'Ah, good. Aye, aye. Because all this is meant to be a secret, see?' The voice rumbles on, unperturbed and rising to a near-deafening crescendo. 'He bought the horse for his wife, it is. Surprise present, for Christmas, he said, but I've heard nothing from him for weeks. Bloody smart horse, he is. He had a good buy there . . . and *er*, well, he was good enough to give me cash. I can't be messing with them cheques and stuff.' The man's Welsh accent thickening to a glue inside her ear. 'Anyway, I've been ringing his mobile, but not getting no answer. And the problem is, see, is people taking advantage. I'm needing the grazing and he promised he was going to find new pasture come New Year.' The speaker takes a breather. 'I don't mean to bother you, but er, problem is, see, I've been happy holding on to the horse till now, but it's getting difficult with new foals coming, isn't it?'

'Difficult?' Melanie knits the words together, grasping at: horse . . . surprise present . . . and bites down on her bottom lip. Hard. 'Yes,' she says, barely a whisper. 'Yes, I see.'

'So, there you are,' the man coughs loudly into the handset. 'If you get to speak to him, could you tell him, tell him to ring Dai, soon as possible, like. I can't be keeping the horse for much longer. But, er, Gareth . . . lovely boy, he is . . . give me the full asking price. A full three grand. Yes, lovely boy, Gareth.'

ABOUT THE AUTHOR

Rebecca Griffiths grew up in mid-Wales and went on to gain a first class honours degree in English Literature. After a successful business career in London, Dublin and Scotland, she returned to rural mid-Wales where she now lives with her husband, a prolific artist, four black cats and pet sheep the size of sofas.

Also by Rebecca Griffiths:

The Primrose Path (Sphere 2016)
A Place to Lie (Sphere 2018)
Sweet Sacrifice (Amazon 2020)

Printed in Great Britain
by Amazon